"Elizabeth Forrest's DEATH WATCH is one of the best
paperback originals published this year...a dark and
dazzling suspense novel that does something brand
new with the theme of serial killers, and virtual reality.
Forrest's style is cool, poised, and always ready to
pounce." —*Mystery Scene*

"Ms. Forrest's...talents are taking readers on a voyage
to the cutting edge of a new genre. DEATH WATCH is a
literary landmark blending elements from three very
different genres to create something new, dynamic,
and exceedingly evocative." —*The Paperback Forum*

DARK VISIONS

Brand had far more problems than the average teen, fighting each day to keep at bay the persona of the serial killer implanted in his brain via VR. But Brand's troubles were only beginning, for after having eye surgery to "improve" his vision, he was able to see far too well into the dark places humans were never meant to know. . . .

Sergeant Christiansen was a "by the books" U.S. Marine sergeant. But when duty led him from a covert mission in Haiti to a voodoo-tainted funeral service in New Orleans, Christiansen found himself hunted by both the government and an ancient force of evil that had marked him for its own. . . .

Kamryn felt as if she'd been on the run forever, fleeing a blood-drenched past she could never quite escape. And even if she ran as far and as fast as she could, it might never be far enough to save her. . . .

Brand, Christiansen, and Kamryn, three people with nothing in common, nothing except the need to survive—a need that was about to unite them in a cross-country odyssey of fear. . . .

KILLJOY

ELIZABETH FORREST

DAW BOOKS, INC.

DONALD A. WOLLHEIM, FOUNDER

375 Hudson Street, New York, NY 10014

ELIZABETH R. WOLLHEIM

SHEILA E. GILBERT

PUBLISHERS

First Printing, May 1996
1 2 3 4 5 6 7 8 9

DAW TRADEMARK REGISTERED
U.S. PAT. OFF. AND FOREIGN COUNTRIES
—MARCA REGISTRADA
HECHO EN U.S.A.

PRINTED IN THE U.S.A.

Dedicated to Kathy Lewis,
who left this world too soon,
but who leaves good friends
and memories behind.

ACKNOWLEDGMENTS

Anything I did well, I did with the help of those named below, as well as friends and family. Any mistakes I claim as my own.

Special Acknowledgments to:

Lawrence Weber, Emergency Planner, of the City of New Orleans, for invaluable time and assistance.

Paul Britton, Jr., (CWA) of Valley Christian High School, Cerritos, CA, for tracking Hurricane Opal for me.

Also, Shawn P. Keizer, President of Weather Watchers Online for Compuserve. A special acknowledgment that hurricanes rarely reach the "Y" segment of the alphabet.

USMC, El Toro:

Cpl. Chris Cox, also Lt. Col. Farrell, for information on burial and notification.

Sgt. Todd Keit and wife, Cathy Stone Keit, for further insight on the Marine Corps tradition.

Tom Canfield, pharmacist, for his insight and advice.

Julia C. White, fellow author, for her timely and much needed information on Native Americans.

To the Advanced Eye Care Institute of Newport Beach for answering questions about radial keratomy. And, in particular, to Dennis Hollow and Dr. Sandrowski of the Southern California College of Optometry for their help concerning eye surgery.

With apologies to the lovely city of Brea for rearranging her geography and ignoring her state-of-the-art new police headquarters.

PART ONE

Prologue

Early April

They broke cover at 0530. Wind swept a warm rain across them, boiling dark clouds in a night sky which kept dawn at bay. Equipped in field gear, they moved swiftly across the Haitian foothills, the rotary noises of an idling chopper fading behind them. Jogging in point, William realized what it was he didn't like about the observer they were escorting. He dropped back casually to talk to his sergeant.

"Boss man," he said softly.

"Corporal." Sergeant Christiansen was a smart man, smarter than most, and he answered in the same careful tone of voice which would not carry over the rain.

"That's no UN observer. I don't know what he is, but he ain't what he says he is. I got Nawlins ears, and that's no French accent. Not Canadian French, not Creole, not no Parisian French."

Christiansen looked strange, his white face streaked in commando blackface, and his jaw tightened. "I know, William," he answered shortly. "Just get back and do your job."

"Yessuh." William began to lengthen his stride, but not before he heard Christiansen add gently, "and watch your back."

As he loped back into position, skirting bent grasses and the shrubbery whipping at his legs, Christiansen wondered what else his corporal had noticed. The Gore-Tex boots, maybe, not standard issue, with the haft of a knife barely visible atop the footwear's shaft. Or maybe it was the kevlar armor under the neutral UN vest, definitely not standard issue. There was a ramrod stiffness to the man's back which made Christiansen think that he had a weapon snuggled in the small of it, in addition to the holstered Glock on his hip. Perhaps it was the demeanor of the man himself, running through the countryside like a good coonhound on the scent.

They were just Marines, Christiansen thought, doing their duty. They'd been told to take him in, and bring him out. The chopper should not have been in the air—its crew knew it, and its cargo, a seven-man patrol flown hunkered down on the floor of the craft, knew it. But they had been given a window through which to make this approach and, weather or not, had been told to take it.

They were where they were not supposed to be, about to do that which they were not allowed to do. If he had any qualms at all about his orders, it was over why they were there and not the SEALS. He tried not to think that it might be because they were more expendable.

He wondered who the operative could be, with enough clout that they had been boated in from Puerto Rico, encamped on an uninhabited Caribbean island halfway between Guantanamo and Haiti and then helicoptered out in weather that was damn near unflyable. Christiansen snugged into his field gear. He was not there to question. He was only there to *do*.

And the five-man patrol under him would carry out

their orders as well: two Afro-Americans, William Brown and Short Reynolds, and the two *tejanos* Lopez and Aldemar, and Burrows, wiry, nasty, and balding. William was his patrol leader and Christiansen trusted his judgment almost more than his own. So he stopped beside them, one by one, and repeated his advice to the corporal: *watch your back.* All of which made him feel no easier as dawn finally grayed the landscape and they neared the rendezvous area.

The UN observer had given his name as Stark, distinctly un-French even though he was posing as an officer from French troops. Christiansen watched as he paused by a mahogany tree and put up a hand, signaling them to halt. William made a sharp hand signal, and the patrol scattered silently, then flattened. Christiansen, the last to drop into place, did so with pride in his men.

They advanced by increments, one man at a time, at the patrol leader's instruction. Christiansen took the flank, both to protect the vulnerable side of his patrol, and to keep an eye on the observer.

The Haitian foothills were thinly forested, although they moved under a canopy now. He could smell a fragrant cedar as they brushed past, though most of this area seemed to be scrub brush and broad-leafed trees he did not recognize. A poor country, poorly treated by its inhabitants, whose prospects were not likely to improve greatly in the short term. He had not spent time here in the initial occupation, but he anticipated that sometime in his career as a Marine, he was likely to be called back.

The warm rain made his uniform stick to his body like a leech. Although the sun had barely made its presence known behind the cloud layer, this was the tropics. It was warm now, it would be hot and unbearable later. Christiansen hoped to be aboard the chop-per headed home by then.

His efforts to stay abreast of the observer brought him almost shoulder to shoulder with William Brown as they entered a clearing. Stark pivoted around, looked at them, and motioned them to stay afoot and fanned out. To their credit, his men did nothing until Chris-tiansen seconded the signal.

As bare as the foliage was, it had mostly kept the rain from the dirt and bruised grass clearing. A small pool of water churned at the basin of a waterfall so insignificant as to barely rate the classification. There was only one major river on this side of the peninsula, its flow made up of a multitude of tiny tributaries, and this most definitely was not it. The bush and mango trees grew more thickly here, and there was a crude wooden lean-to set up among their trunks. Beyond, Christiansen saw a chalk drawing on the ground—a design that was geometric and yet not. A huge post was set deep into the middle of it, and at the foot of the post lay a dead goat, its blood already turning black, and flies beginning to gather despite the rain, their angry buzzing growing louder. Brown said under his breath, "Uh-oh."

Christiansen flicked a glance toward the corporal.

Before he could remark, the brush parted and a man came forward, six others following him. He was obvi-ously a man of the island, sandal-footed, dressed in casual khakis, but there was nothing casual about his demeanor. Hatchet-faced, with sharp black eyes that glanced piercingly over all of them, and when they rested on him, Christiansen felt the hackles of his neck go up. He carried himself with authority that belied the wiry strength of his body. His smooth, dark skin looked ageless, but the shadow of years lay in his eyes.

"I am Delacroix." The six men behind him stood as if oblivious to the outside world, their muscular torsos showing through the rags of their simple cotton shirts. They carried machetes in their belted pants. Flies buzzed about them, too, and landed from time to time, crawling across their skin, even their faces, without prompting response. Their eyes were coffee-black, without expression. Dead eyes.

"You are the man," the Haitian said to Stark, his voice deeply accented with island French. He waved a hand over the slain animal. "I have asked for a blessing on our meeting."

Stark only replied, "We haven't much time." His own words were flatly American.

William Brown shuffled in the dirt uneasily and rolled an eye at Christiansen. The sergeant felt the palms of his hands itch and he shifted in his field gear so that his weapon would be easily accessible.

"Give me the powder," Stark added. "I have the money." He fumbled at his waist, undoing a money belt which had been tucked up under the kevlar vest, and which Christiansen hadn't even noticed. He tossed it at Delacroix's feet.

He made no move to pick it up, only hitched the rolled up sleeves of his shirt a little higher. His face tightened, accentuating the sharp cheekbones. "The deal was not for the powder. The powder is not mine, it belongs to—" and he spoke a name which Christiansen could not decipher. William gave a violent shudder.

"The deal's been changed. We want the powder. We'll do the converting ourselves . . . it will take too long to do it otherwise."

Delacroix looked at Christiansen and his patrol a second time, and again an icy feeling knifed across the back of the sergeant's neck. "The deal was that you

would bring me men, and I would give you an army."
He turned on his heel and touched the arm of one of
the islanders flanking him. "Like mine."

The man made little response other than to take a
step forward, aggression in every iota of his body language. The eeriness of his silent power pierced through
Christiansen. What kind of soldier was this?

Stark said, "Have it your way." His hand moved, and
he dropped a percussion grenade. Delacroix shouted
something in French to the man at his side, and fell
back.

Christiansen let out a yell, and his men scattered.
The grenade erupted. The blast drove him to the
ground, ears ringing, and as he rolled, he saw Stark
ripping into the lean-to. He grabbed for his rifle. Stark
emerged from the crude chapel, stuffing leather bags
inside his vest and running face-to-face into one of
Delacroix's men.

The islander made no sound, but grinned widely,
flashing ivory death in his dark face, and reached for
Stark's throat with a massive hand.

Stark dodged to one side, going to his knee, and
came up, his hands filled with the assault weapon he'd
had secreted at his back. "Delacroix! I have what I
came for! Don't make me shoot your man! Take my
men and do what you will with them—take the men
and the money, and the deal is made! Marines, marine
uniforms, and gear—think what you could do with
them!"

"Fuck that," grated nasty, balding Burrows and emptied his rifle at the islanders' feet.

Puffs of dirt and grass blew up. Not a round hit
them. They moved with blinding, agile speed that left
Christiansen gaping. Stark lunged with a shout, out of
range of the bullets and Delacroix's man, rolling when

he hit. He came up spraying the clearing with the assault rifle and Lopez went down, blood fluming from his astonished mouth.

Delacroix stood impassively in the chaos, calling out in French and his men responded single-mindedly, going after Stark. Stark spit out a clip, and one of the men finally went down with a dull grunt, his shirt bloodied and in shreds. He fumbled at the jammed weapon, trying to insert another clip.

"Damnit," Christiansen said. "Save his hide!" he shouted hoarsely and got to his feet. His rifle bucked in his hands almost before he made the conscious decision to fire. He'd been brought in to escort Stark. The patrol's job was to bring him back alive, regardless, no questions asked.

Once back, Stark's ass would hang if Christiansen had anything to do with it.

"Bring him back alive," Christiansen ordered, and began to flank around Delacroix's men.

Delacroix met him, weaponless, with hands like steel cables. Christiansen grappled with him, looking deep into his obsidian eyes. Sweaty and rain-soaked, they clenched and Delacroix drew close. He snapped at Christiansen's neck, and bit, as they wrestled. Sharp teeth sank snakelike into tender flesh, and Christiansen felt the flick of the man's tongue over the wound.

He let out a howl of both pain and surprise and wrenched back. Delacroix grinned at him, blue-black lips stained with his blood. "I have your taste, now, man."

Burrows clubbed Delacroix across the back of the head, sending him reeling into the dust. Christiansen staggered back onto his heels. The first thing he noticed was that Delacroix's supermen had stopped in their tracks almost as one while Delacroix writhed on the ground, shaking off the pain from the blow.

Reynolds got to Stark first and literally cherry-picked him out of reach of a swinging machete blade.

Christiansen reacted. "Pull back! Pull back! Head for the chopper!"

One of the islanders reached for Burrows and picked him up, rifle spurting aimless fire from its barrel. He screamed, legs flailing, and his scream ended abruptly as the islander took him in both hands and snapped his back.

William Brown charged forward, yelling, his deep voice cracking with the strain. He pulled his fallen patrolman out of the hands of the Haitian, slugging him in the face with the butt of his rifle. As the islander went down, toppled like an oak, Brown took a flare from his pack and set it up. He stuffed it inside Burrows' shirt. The sodden uniform caught fire reluctantly, in spits and spurts.

Delacroix lurched to his feet and, with a curt word or two, sent his men packing after Short Reynolds. He traded a look with Christiansen, smiled slowly, licked his lips and then ran after his prey as well.

"Shit." Christiansen looked at what was left of his patrol.

"Corporal! Get out of here!"

Brown looked desperately at Christiansen. "Burn the bodies! We've got to burn the bodies!"

"Come on, get out of here!"

"Sarge, you don't understand!"

He snapped, "I don't have time to understand! Move out, Corporal, and that's an order!"

Face slick with sweat, Brown took a deep breath and then broke into a run, taking Aldemar with him. Christiansen hesitated long enough to pull Lopez into line with Burrows. He tore a plank off the rugged lean-to and threw it over their bodies, while the flare burned brightly. Maybe the old, dry wood would catch. Maybe it wouldn't.

He didn't like leaving Marines behind, but their open, lifeless eyes did not judge him.

Trampled ground left a wide trail. Christiansen could hear the shouts and grunts and muffled gunfire. They slowed. He sent William and Aldemar wide to the right, circling the clearing, and he went left.

The islanders had taken Short Reynolds down and had his gear. He saw Stark take one in the shoulder and drop. Brown and Aldemar charged in, firing. Of Delacroix, there was no sign. The three remaining is-landers took their bullets and kept closing on Stark, as he got to his hands and feet, crawling. Blood and sweat streaked their shirts, glistening on their dark torsos.

"Son of a bitch!" Aldemar sang out. "Nothing stops them." He put in a new clip and kept firing, the spit of his bullets echoing Brown's and Christiansen's.

Christiansen's rifle jammed as the last standing man slowly fell to his knees and then, with the only sound they'd heard him make, grunted and sagged to the ground.

Stark stopped crawling. "Sergeant!"

Christiansen stowed his rifle slowly, closing the ground between them.

"Get me on my feet."

He blinked, looking down at the shoulder and neck wound the kevlar vest had not been able to stop.

"You were going to leave us here."

Stark blinked. "You have your orders."

"You're finished. Whoever you are, you're finished." Christiansen watched the crimson fountain from the other's neck.

"So are you." Stark coughed, and pink foam flew from his lips. He smiled weakly as he put a hand up, wiped his mouth, and saw his fingers.

"Who are you?"

"A representative of the United States government, just like you."

"No. Not like me. Never like me."

"They won't know that. They won't care. Bring the powder back—that's the only chance you've got. You—" He shuddered, making a horrible, guttural sound, a last attempt to breathe, and died.

Christiansen looked down at him. William let out a whistle. "I hear the chopper, boss."

"All right." He leaned over and took the leather bags from inside the other's vest. He stowed them in his gear, unsure of what he intended to do with them, certain he was not about to leave them behind.

Brown and Aldemar got Short Reynolds to his feet, bloodied and dazed. He towered above them. Christiansen taking point, they made their way toward the idling chopper.

Christiansen got his men in. Then he looked around. The toothmarks on his neck throbbed slightly. He put a hand to them as the chopper pilot said, "Get your ass in, or I'm leaving it behind."

He got in, crouched in the open cargo doorway as the chopper revved up and began to lift off the ground. Greenery moved, and suddenly Delacroix was there, sighting down the barrel of a rifle.

William let out a cry and lunged forward, knocking Christiansen off his heels, as the weapon fired once, twice. The corporal let out a cry, falling face forward out of the open door. Christiansen grabbed at his pack as he went by.

The chopper bucked and rose steadily, twisting and

lurching, gravity attempting to pull William out of his hands. Christiansen set his heels and Aldemar crawled on his belly over the floor to anchor him.

Brown twisted in the pack, looking upward, his face creased with pain as his shoulder turned fiery red. "Don't let me go," he pleaded. "Don't leave me here."

Christiansen had no time to answer him. He could feel the cords of his arms stand out as he hauled the corporal's slack weight back into the chopper.

The pilot looked back over his shoulder. "He in?" Without waiting for an answer, he pushed full throttle and took the chopper up and away.

Christiansen looked down as Delacroix lowered the rifle and faded to a smudge on the landscape and then was gone. Brown lay against his legs, and began to shake with the shock of his wound. Christiansen leaned over and took a look. It was clean, not too messy, and already the blood had slowed.

"You'll be fine, Corporal."

William looked at him. "We're dead men," he said. "We're all dead men. You don't know what you're dealing with."

Chapter 1

One April Morning, New Orleans

Heat hung like a curtain over the New Orleans day. Magnolia trees, heavy with fuzzy green buds ripening into creamy petals, framed the sidewalks while neighboring Spanish oaks cracked the cement with determined roots. It was early morning yet, and the only creature stirring in the decaying neighborhood plowed through like a mighty barge traversing the great Mississippi. She walked with no-nonsense, business to be done steps, creating an eddy, a stir of fresh air as she approached the churchyard, her dress swirling about in strong, primary colors that set off the rich brown sheen of her skin. She paused at the churchyard of her destination, but her skirt and hair remained alive, as if she herself were part and parcel of the morning breeze.

Shepherd's Mortuary, old clapboard sides whitewashed like the mausoleum ovens in the cemeteries, gleamed in the sun. Detailed wrought iron, reminiscent of the French Quarter, fenced it in. Gray-green moss trailed from massive oak branches against its chestnut-shingled roof, but the wrought iron cross stood out next to the steeple. The only thing more prominent on the roof was the lightnin' rod.

Mother drew her gaze down from the rooftops and sky.

She could feel the stares of others watching, though if she looked across the street to the cemetery, where the ovens and the worn stone crosses dotted narrow alleyways of grass, Mother knew she would not see who. They weren't looking after her, anyways, not now, not this time. She'd pay them no never mind.

Shepherd's had a front door, but she'd been entering through God's door, the churchyard, for the better part of her adult years. Mother Jubilation put her pink-palmed hand on the gate and stepped onto sacred land.

Pain hit her, sharp as a serpent's tooth, and the sheer force of it drove her to her knees. She bared her teeth and sucked her breath back, stunned by the attack. Anger boiled through her. Who dared to give her attitude on her ground! As Mother tilted her head and opened her eyes wide, she saw darkness boiling about the mortuary like thick molasses syrup. Her nostrils flared as she caught the scent of the evil *loa* casting the shadow, and Mother cried with a fierce joy as she saw into the sorcerer who'd brought it into this world to bedevil her and her children.

But they didn't know who they were tryin' to take a bite out of this time! Mother threw her hands into the air with a laughing shout. She grabbed at the shadows, ready to bring them down, where she would stomp them into holy ground. Mother Jubilation got to her feet, her whole body trembling with the joy of her own power. "You won't beat me that way, child!" she cried.

Darkness thinned. For a moment, she saw the face of the other mambo, sharp-featured, jawbones and cheekbones like pointed blades, deep angry eyes. She saw the rune-worked knife clenched in his hand, and the carcasses of the sacrificed animals laying in the dirt about his feet. She saw and felt the essence of him and would know him instantly if they ever crossed paths again. The sorcerer faded, but the bitter taste of his loa remained, and Mother knew that she had more work to do inside.

She dusted herself off, patted down the apron of many pockets she wore over her dress to make sure her fetishes, amulets, and charms were all still in place, and headed to the chapel door.

The chapel door stuck in its frame as though locked when she put a hand upon it. There was a child inside needed her, for that was why she'd come that morning. She'd been summoned during the night for a sorrowing. If the loa lay over that child, she'd not be turned away. She let out a rich chuckle, spoke a word, or perhaps it was just a coaxing noise, and the latch clicked in response.

The chapel smelled of lemon-polished wood and of bruised, heavy-scented flowers under the faint odor of disinfectant, the perfume of the dead. The teak hardwood floor creaked as she trod upon it, her ample weight making its boards sing. Its burnished surface reminded her of her grandfather's face, worn and proud, as she made her way along the outer edge of the sanctuary. The teak boards accompanied her journey, sounding, the rows of pews creaking as she passed.

The chapel had been empty, as she knew it would be, but its air was still and heavy with sorrowing. Shepherd's was modest, as one of the oldest Negro mortuaries in the state, carpet runners laid down over teak flooring throughout, an office and four visitation rooms clustered about a small parlor. The furniture was clean, French classical, dark burgundy upholstery dignified against the paneled walls. Below, the more clinical workings of the mortician could not be seen or heard.

Slightly worn, slightly outdated, slightly second class, it had all the cachet of a Southern black establishment. Like a treacherous undercurrent in a sleepy river, she could feel the presence of her attacker running deep. She shrugged her purse close to her flank, the family gathered in the corridors beyond as the woman who'd summoned her turned and saw her.

"Mother Jubal!"

They embraced. The black woman who'd called her name was not older than Jubal, but she looked it, with knifelike wrinkles about her mouth and eyes, her hair ironed and coiffed fastidiously, her suit a somber charcoal off the rack from one of New Orlean's better shops. She had long since moved from this neighborhood, but she'd come back to bury her dead. Tears brimmed in her eyes. "I'm so glad you could come." Carla Brown Johnson flushed and touched her handkerchief to her mouth. Through it, muffled, she whispered, "He's in there," and pointed.

Beyond, in the viewing room, Mother could see the casket, the finest the Marine Corps could supply, flag draped over it, and a soldier in uniform standing in the corner guarding it. The room seemed to blend into his navy uniform, the brightness of his buttons and ribbons glittering like stars in a winter sky, echoed by the pallor of his face. The guard looked fine, she thought, real fine. A pity she'd never seen William in his dress blues.

No one sat in the viewing room, though there was a settee and a line of folding chairs which had seen better days. There were two wreaths on stands, and one large urn of flowers, and scattered bouquets. She knew the flowers may or may not have originally been intended for William and that, when the coffin left here for the cemetery, some of them might be passed on to the other viewing rooms, where those less fortunate were mourned. No one at Shepherd's ever had a threadbare funeral.

The soldier's gaze caught hers. He was likely to be the only white boy in Shepherd's that whole long day, and for a moment, she thought they communicated that to one another, and the corner of his solemn mouth pulled just a stitch in wry amusement. He looked fit in his dress uniform, though he had to have been tired, having accompanied the casket throughout its long flight home. She caught the aura on him of the loa, but she could not read it for ill or good, just as a hurricane has no morality. He was no sorcerer, but he might have been the "horse" which the loa rode across the mortal world. She might have trouble with him. It was certain they were going to have a world of trouble from her!

Mother took the grieving mother's elbow. "Now, Carla. It looks like you're doing just fine."

Carla's second husband George, the dead boy's stepfather, stood in the corner, his hands clasped, studying the floor. Gray peppered his thick black hair and mustache. He looked up, as if just sensing Mother's glance.

"Madame Jubal."

She nodded briskly as a child darted behind his trousered legs and refused to come out. This was Carla's last child, William's half sister, young enough to be George Johnson's granddaughter. Normally Mother's heart would have gone out to the gawky girl hiding behind her father's legs, but this was not her business today. Their eyes met. The child retreated behind the safety of her father. She did not need Mother's comfort.

Besides, Jubilation had come to help the dead.

Lord knows, she had tried to help him hard enough when William was just a flint-eyed boy, too quick to take the easy way, too smart to not know the difference. Carla had done her best by William and marrying George had helped, but William was still a long-legged boy, a boy for whom the night had seemed to have a strong call. He had, however, found his own in the Marine Corps. Carla had shared his letters proudly with her on many an occasion, and he had done well, earning promotions all the way to corporal.

Promoted himself all the way into a casket, hanged by his own hand.

"I never thought it could come to this," Carla said. Her voice choked with emotion.

With just a touch of "no-nonsense" in her voice, Mother reminded her, "We all come to this."

"But so young—"

"And if it hadn't been for all your hard work and caring, you and George, it might have been a lot younger." Jubal folded her hands over Carla's chilled fingers. "You have pride in him. There's no shame in this."

Carla put the handkerchief back to her mouth. It was a beautiful lacy square of fine linen, with lavender embroidery about the edges, and her bright lipstick had already stained it more than once that morning. "It was *suicide*, Jubal. That's what they told me. Suicide! How could he? He was coming home, William knew he was coming home—why? Why?"

Jubal reached up and put her capable hand to the back of Carla's neck and stroked it, gently. Muscles knotted in distress under the damp, dewy skin and she smoothed them away. "Now, girl, in't that why you called me? I'll lay that soul to rest, right in the cradle of Jesus' hands."

"Amen," seconded George Johnson, watching them with eyes patient and saggy, wearing the look of a man who'd married a woman young enough to have been his daughter. He knew when to keep his silence and when not to.

Carla kept her handkerchief pressed to her lips and nodded.

"Then let me be about my business." Mother pinned a small fetish to her jacket lapel. George had to lean down so she could reach his. He put the palm of his hand over it, covering it, as he backed away.

"Georgia Ann."

The girl peered out from behind her dad and received another fetish, which was pinned to her starched white dress collar. She picked at it.

"Now you just leave that there. I want you all to go into the chapel and pray for William's soul."

"Mother—" Carla began.

She shook a finger at her. "Do as I tell you now. And don't come out no matter what you might be hearin' or seein'."

"All right." Carla took a deep breath and then, surprisingly, hugged Jubal again. "God bless," she whispered in her ear before letting go. She stepped back hastily into the shelter of George's arm and looked away as if she could not bear to watch.

Mother crossed into the viewing room. What Carla only sensed with her maternal instinct now spoke to Mother Jubal with a hard, chiseled voice, mean and small. She followed its invisible lines about the compact, square room. They swirled about the Marine in dress uniform in his own island of unease. The coffin rested in the eye of the storm, and she could hear the dead, restless, fearful. "Hush, child," she whispered. "I hear you."

Her eyes met the Marine's again. He blinked in slow acknowledgment and said, "Ma'am."

"You look tired," she suggested. "Perhaps you should go and get a cup of coffee and sit."

"No, thank you, ma'am."

This was his duty, she knew. As William's closest friend in the unit, it was his assignment to bring the body home, see to it through the services, fold the flag, and return it to William's mother. He would do it with honor and, if there were tears in him over the death of his comrade, he would shed them some other time, some other place.

"Lieutenant—"

"Sergeant, ma'am. Sergeant Christiansen."

A good name that. Perhaps an omen.

"I have business here," she tried again.

"I have duty here, ma'am," he answered respectfully. "Corporal Brown was my patrol leader. It is both my honor and my obligation to stand for him now."

No one beyond the room could hear them. It was as if a curtain had dropped between the rest of Shepherd's and the viewing room, a veil between the living and the dead. She had work here and there was the thought at the back of her mind that this white boy just might be part of it. The force which she had discerned had subsided, ebbed, as though part of his life's tide. She could not determine whether Christiansen's soul was colored light or dark, and that bothered her.

"Very well," she answered. "Remember what you have called upon yourself." She shook an amulet out of her pocket store of charms, a black-thonged necklace with a twisted piece of silver upon it, blessed silver recovered from the salt water of the gulf. Before the Marine could move, she had dropped the amulet around his neck and undone his top button, slipping the silver under his jacket. She did the button back up with a maternal efficiency. "You wear that," she commanded, her tone no less used to being obeyed than that of a drill instructor.

Mother decided, with a twist of her lips, that he would see what he would see. She dipped a hand into her large purse and brought out a triangle of chalk—it had once been a thick square, but usage had worn its fourth side down to next to nothing—and grasping it firmly, bent over and made a series of signs upon the wooden floor. Not a circle of protection, for she did not know whether she wished to contain or repel, but veves of basic protection.

"Ma'am . . ."

"Hush now and let me think. If you're going to be here, you've got to let Mother Jubilation do her work." She paused, and looked up, salt-tasting sweat beading up on her lip. He had not moved from his sentry position, but he looked down at her with fear in his eyes.

Mother smiled. "You tell your mama the next time you see her that she has a good boy. Stubborn, but good. You keep that amulet on, you just might live to see your mama again." She moved away from him, across the creaking floor. "Now don't you move."

"Yes, ma'am."

Then she stepped briskly to the casket and drew the flag from the end even as Christiansen protested.

"Ma'am! It's been sealed and it needs to stay that way." He started out across the wavery chalk edges, looked down and hesitated.

"Not to me, child." Even as she spoke, running her fingers over the lid, it clicked open to her touch, its weight keeping it lowered. She drew more symbols upon the seal and, for an icy second, gathered her power to open the coffin.

"Do you go to church, son?"

"Yes, ma'am. I'm a Methodist."

"Fine church. Fine, fine people." She looked across at him. "You'll be seein' things here you never saw in no Methodist church. Now you just bite your tongue and remember that I asked you to step out and have a cup of coffee. What you see, what you hear, what you feel, you asked to."

He swallowed. She could barely hear his "Yes, ma'am."

She placed her palm on the edge of the casket. It felt alive to her, like a living animal, lying and waiting for her touch. Then she pushed it up.

Chapter 2

"Think they'll have a jazz band, and black umbrellas, and high steppers?" Binoculars obscured the speaker's voice, but not his enthusiasm, as he watched the mortuary. "Captain."

"They don't do that anymore. Besides, the cemetery is right across the street."

"They could strut down to the corner and back. I always wanted to see that." The high-powered binoculars wavered slightly. "They don't do that anymore?"

"Not unless you're a celebrity. One of the old jazz greats." The voice, slightly honeyed with the accents of the region, sounded bored. "Disappointed, Lieutenant?"

"Well, yes."

"Don't be. This is Intelligence, son, not sociology." The man designated as captain moved forward in the van, looking intently at his monitors, the pocked canyons of his face shadowed like the surface of the moon. His name was Rembrandt, and he might have been called handsome, if not for those varied craters, but they did not mar him extensively. It was the coldness of his eyes and the downward slant of his eyebrows that made people turn away. He knew his acquaintances called him a real work of art, though not often to his face.

"Whoa. She just took a fall. No, no, I guess she's all right. She's inside the churchyard. Look at the build on her." The lieutenant paused. "My dad liked big women."

"Did he?" Rembrandt said, not really listening.

"Sure did. Always told me, more cushion for the pushin'. Told me I would never want a dry twig of a woman under me, just waiting to go snap."

Rembrandt redirected him with just a touch of irritation. "Anybody go in after that civilian?"

"No. Looks like William Brown isn't havin' much of a send-off."

"Services aren't for a couple of hours yet. Just keep your eyes glued to that building. I want to know everybody who comes in and out. And I don't want to lose our subject."

"Where's he gonna go? He doesn't even know we've picked up what's left of his patrol." The watcher let out a dry snicker. "One murder and two suicides don't leave him much of a command."

"Just keep your eyes peeled, Lieutenant. Christiansen isn't going anywhere, talking to anyone, doing anything, without us glued to his ass."

"What'd he do, anyway?"

Rembrandt did not answer. That was on a need to know basis, and he did not feel the lieutenant he'd picked up yesterday to aid him with surveillance in New Orleans as long as he had a use for him had any need. Christiansen would be picked up as soon the man in Washington who had assigned Rembrandt to follow him felt he had been followed sufficiently. Privately, Rembrandt felt that the sergeant would be picked up as soon as the funeral proceedings were over, bringing the Marine back for debriefing.

And, also privately, he wondered what it was that

had happened on that covert mission in Haiti and how Christiansen had lost his patrol, but he knew better than to ask questions.

The small fiber-optic camera among the flowers in the viewing room gave a restricted angle. He could see Christiansen at stiff attention, the black and white tones of the camera making him appear even more fatigued than Rembrandt had seen him look while escorting the coffin off the flight. The black woman had stepped into range, but with her entrance, they lost audio. "Aw, damn."

Rembrandt adjusted knobs, brought up a static blizzard and quickly dampened it, but although he could see they spoke to one another, the mikes were not picking up anything clearly. He tapped his console, muttering, "We've lost the sound."

"Again?" While still peering through the binoculars, the lieutenant dropped a hand down, found a cold cup of coffee and an even colder beignet and stuffed the powdered sugar delicacy into his mouth, following it with a slurp from the coffee cup. "Ever been over to Cafe du Monde? They've got these homemade doughnuts. Taste just like what my mom used to make Saturday mornings for us kids back home. Make 'em like biscuit dough, then just fry 'em up and roll 'em in confectionery sugar." He popped another one in and added, mouth full, "Won't my mother just shit when I tell her she makes what the great chefs of New Orleans make?" He swallowed. "Check the cables?"

"Yes, I checked the frigging cables." Rembrandt shut his jaw tightly. He preferred to look back to his monitor, searching its eerie green screen as if he might find the secret of life in its depths. The video went berserk and then went south, in the direction of the audio. All he had now was the alarm. He slapped the heel of his hand on the console.

Something pinged.

He straightened. "That's the alarm. Someone's putting the lid up. *Damn.*"

"Thought it was sealed."

"It was. Now it's open." He'd anticipated that, actually, which was why the interior had been wired. He stood, gathering himself to go inside, when all hell broke loose.

The sergeant jumped when Jubal ripped out the wiring and tossed it to the floor at his feet. He bent over and gathered it up, stringing it through his fingers. "What the hell. . . . What's going on here?"

She did not have time for him. She ripped the white silk lining from the inside of the lid. The unpolished wood gleamed rusty brown with symbols already painted there. Mother flinched at the sight. She tsked loudly as she sketched over them, scarcely glancing at William's body as she did so. She remembered him well as a lanky teenager. She did not want to see him as a corpse.

But she saw. She could not help but do so. He'd hanged himself, and so the face was bloated slightly, puffy, lips blue-black. His thick, rich black hair had been so severely cut that he was nearly bald, giving his face the look of a chocolate moon. There was no peace or serenity in it. His uniform's neckline was tucked high into his chin, hiding the ligature marks, but not the face or the eyes—

"Good God."

She knew the white sergeant was looking at William, too, at the wide open, staring eyes, eyes which were usually always closed compassionately by the preparers of the body even if they had to be glued shut. His were not, were instead stretched wide open in horror. An opalescent film obscured the orbs. It was as though he'd been put in the coffin strangled, but still alive.

"This boy did not hang himself. He was *murdered*."

"No. No, he couldn't have. We made it back. We stood up for each other. No. He was scared. I tried to talk to him. Nothing I could do helped. He knew it was going to happen. He tried to tell me. Christ, he picked the casket out himself. Drew those signs all over the inside of the lid." He paused. "I don't know who in hell wired it."

"Oh, he may have hanged himself, all right. But something else drove him to do it. That something I got to beat out of him now or he'll never have peace." She narrowed her eyes at Christiansen. "Hush, child. You want to help your friend, you stay out of my way."

An aura rose from the casket, ominously, awakening fully that which she had only barely sensed earlier. The palms of her hands tingled. She worked furiously, but not quickly enough, for the cross-barred table which held the coffin began to shake and rattle. It started with a low, quivering moan as the braces trembled. Its vibrations translated upward until the casket itself, heavy and solid as it was, began to dance as if caught in an earthquake.

"Hold it down!" she ordered the Marine.

There was an astonished pause, as if disbelieving of her command, but Jubal could not pay him heed, for she needed to sketch over the other symbols and the wood itself bucked away from her touch.

She could feel the strength of the curse, the stranglehold it had on William, the blood wishes of it sunk deep into the earth. Under her feet, the floor began to shake and sway. The joints of the room creaked as the

Marine threw himself onto the coffin and embraced it, attempting to keep it from bouncing to the ground. It rattled against his hold and he grunted with effort.

She could hear Carla's stifled shriek and George's mumbled call upon the Lord as all of Shepherd's began to sway and rattle. The vibrations sounded like a freight train bearing down on the mortuary. The building would come down on their heads and worse, what William had brought back with him would be irrevocably loosed. Whatever had murdered him lay inside him, trapped and entwined with William's tortured soul.

Something crashed against the building from outside. The exterior walls BOOMed under the blow. Glass broke, tinkling to a floor. Shepherd's trembled and groaned as if in pain.

"Ma'am—"

"Not now, child!" Jubal flinched despite her concentration as she laid the casket open wider, her drawing moving on its own, chalk dusting her palm as white, as pale as the Marine sergeant's face.

"Damballah! Aido Wedo! Hear me!" The names of the husband and wife of creation filled her mouth, warm and rich. "Listen to my needs!" Under her breath, she added the sacred name of Bon Dieu, the Lord of all Good and all Creation, to aid her.

In a piercing echo through the chapel doors, Carla shrieked, "Dear Jesus, hear us now!"

Leaning over the icy corpse which had once been William and was now a host, she could feel the loa, the evil spirit, rising. It was angry, it had been trapped in the coffin despite its power and it was hungry. So powerful, it had thrown its aura over Shepherd's even when trapped, and struck at her.

She could feel the starvation gnawing at it, rumbling in her own ample stomach, pinching at guts and bow-

els, aching. It would devour her if it could once she
cast it out, that loa would if it could.

Its undervoice hissed like a snake. Mother threw a
glance at the Marine, who desperately wrestled the coffin to still its shudders. If he heard it, he gave no
sign—but then the whole building spoke and shuddered, complaining and threatening so loudly she could
not even hear her own words and her heart beat as
loud as a drum.

Concentration ran down her face in hot streams of
sweat. The armpits of her dress were heavy with wet-
ness. It rose in vengeful heat as though straight from
the pits of hell. Though she fought to cast it out of
William, she feared where it would go. Would the amulet be the white boy's proof against it?

The casket gave a terrible heave.

"Shi-it!" The Marine wrestled to keep it from top-
pling over on them. The movement sent the body inside nearly upright, and then it settled back onto its
silken pillow. Christiansen nearly dropped the wooden
box with a sound that was half-gasp, half-scream.

"Bon Dieu be with me!" Mother cried aloud for the
Good Lord to shield her. Jubal felt the loa go with a
snap that was as loud as the cry of the wooden beams
in the roof over them.

The coffin ceased its motion though the rest of the
building still rattled. She drew her last symbol, fingers
nearly numbed.

Shepherd's clattered down upon its foundation
where it settled to a kind of percolating.

"Sweet Jesus. What was that?" The Marine stood,
panting, eyes locked upon the body of his friend, the
body which the loa had nearly brought to its feet. He
had wrestled the casket to a halt, but his posture sug-

gested that if he eased his hold, it would begin to jump again.

"Vodun." Mother put her hand to her forehead, mopping up the sweat.

"What?"

"Hush, child," she interrupted, casting her senses about them. The loa was not returning to its master or to the city of loas beyond. She could feel it looming over them, searching. Bon Dieu had laid His Hands over hers, now He was gone, and she was alone, spent. The loa seethed. Its hunger tore at her. She sketched upon thin air, her invisible signs repelling it slightly. She was not finished with it yet.

Then it centered upon Christiansen. The loa circled the Marine, as uncertain about his power as she'd been. A hurricane of force, yet he was the eye of it, the neutral calm. The amulet kept the loa at bay, kept it from possessing the white boy who had no idea of what he was, what his potential could be.

She threw her chalk back into her purse and fished around madly, hurriedly, until she found the small vial of sweet water, holy water, purified not by the Catholics but by her own rituals. She uncorked it with a flick of her thumb.

She sprinkled a little of it over William's body. The staring eyes shut.

"That's enough. Oh, God." The Marine dropped the casket and jumped back. She saw his eyes widen, his jaw clench in disbelief. He did not seem to notice the ever-widening pool of calm which spread away from them. He moved inside his uniform as though it guarded against the harm of a world he no longer found sane. Yet he had become a magnet for the curse. She felt it, knew it was so.

She felt the loa drawn toward him. Jubal tossed holy

water over him, sprinkling him from head to toe. Its
temporary protection strengthened that of the amulet.
Startled, faint drops of water trickling down his face
like teardrops, he stared at her. Like a shadow which
he had thrown, the loa withdrew behind him. She
watched it retreat.

"It'll be all right, child," Mother told him.

With a last groan, Shepherd's hunkered onto its
foundation with an almost animal awareness. Mother
Jubal shifted away wearily. She tangled a foot in the
wiring she'd ripped out of the casket. Whatever had
happened here, this was a part of it and yet was not.
Vodun had no hand in this. She stooped and held it
out to the sergeant.

Dazed, he took it from her. "The casket was wired."

"Whatever happened," she told him, "whatever it was
that killed William was of two worlds. I cannot help
you with this one," and she tugged at a cable. "This is
your problem."

He looked stricken as their gazes met. "I don't—I
don't have anything to do with this."

"So you say. Someone else thinks differently." So
pale his face, this white boy.

The front doors burst open with a clatter of footsteps
echoing throughout the mortuary. Voices shouted,
"U.S. Government! Halt!"

He twisted his head to look back at the coffin, where
William's face had now settled into a slumbering expression, eyes shut. The U.S. flag hung canted to the
floor. She knew then he was going to run. She could
not help this wild one now, if he did, but he would
come back.

"I told him, I swore to him, I'd take care of him if
anything happened. He was my patrol leader. My
friend. He took a bullet for me." He looked at her.

"Mayhap. The loa took him. It could have made him take his own life. It don't matter now. William is at peace. What about you?"

"What's happening here?"

"Who thought Marines could fight this voodoo? Who crossed you against this? Where were you? I'll tell you where you were . . . in the heart of the vodun . . . in Haiti."

"You don't know that."

"I know it. And you know it. And whoever wired the coffin knew it, too." Mother pointed at the casket. "Nobody can you trust. No place are you safe. You were sent to die, but you lived. You have one choice left to you." She whispered. "Run."

He blinked. "I'm a Marine."

"They be hunting you. Do you think they don't know you're a Marine?"

Christiansen shook himself. It was like coming out of a bad dream. The loa would be hunting him again. She pressed. "You leave, you straighten yourself out, then you come back to me, you hear? You come back to Mother Jubal."

"Who the hell are you?"

She rapped a knuckle on his brow, where the holy water still glittered like diamonds, not hard, not gentle. "Mind your tongue. Now you listen. This was evil work. I know. I don't know why William died, and I don't know why the fear of it fills you. But you've got to run, boy, because those men out there don't mean you good. I know this in my bones . . . under my skin. I think you know it, too."

"We followed orders . . ."

He was interrupted by shouting from without. "All persons inside the building. The grounds have been secured. Stay calm. Put your hands up as we enter!"

Christiansen turned slightly to the voice booming orders. She could see the tumult within him.

"I can't run—"

"You can't stay."

"They've got the place surrounded—"

"Go through the door of God, child, and no one will be stoppin' you." Mother pointed back through the chapel.

He let out a tortured grunt as if deciding his destiny, then turned and bolted into the chapel, scattering Carla and George and Georgia Ann from the doorway. Beecher, the mortician, had been frightened up his basement stairs and tottered around like a tall, dark grasshopper in his funerary suit.

They turned to her in bewilderment. Mother nodded, counseling, "Let him go."

Government agents and their guns filled the hallway. Carla and George met them in the corridor, hands outstretched and faces grim, innocently blocking their entrance into the mortuary. Their daughter began to cry softly in fear.

Mother Jubal felt the Marine's spirit leap as he reached the sunshine. But the triumph would be fleeting, she knew. He could run, but he couldn't hide forever. She put a hand to her bosom, where the crystal and the cross it was bound to hung on a chain, and clasped her fingers around it.

She could feel the loa, a nasty, oppressive cloud hanging over her, but it would not leave her world. Behind it, she saw the lean, hatchet-faced man, his skin the color of roasted coffee beans, a man whose soul was as black as that of the loa spirit. His vision snapped into hers, and she knew he saw her as well, this counterpart. His lips thinned, purple streaks of dislike. Mother braced herself. The crystal grew hot between her fingers.

She stared into her inner self. She wanted to send the loa flinging back to him, but she no longer had the strength. She could feel her dry lips moving. "Bon Dieu, help yet once again. Help me!"

The breath which formed her words was nearly still-born, her tone so quiet none but Mother could have heard it, but she knew the greatest God did. Before she could blink, a veil dropped between them, and the sharp visage of the other was gone.

Gone but not forgotten.

She opened her eyes.

A white man stared at her, a man with a once hand-some yet pitted face, a man in a uniform with an un-comfortable starched collar, with anger reddening his expression. For a second she was confused, for though he was white, his eyes held the same sharp glare as the black sorcerer's. They might be two sides of the same coin. Mother took a deep breath.

"And who the hell are you, ma'am?" he said wearily, with the air of one used to being obeyed.

Mother drew herself up. "You may call me Madame Jubal, my son," she answered, though he was nearer her age than not.

He looked down at the coils of ripped-out wire on the floor, and the casket which still rested sideways on its stand. The officer held a cell phone in his hand rather than a gun, like the others, and his jaw slid sideways as if he chewed on a fact he did not like. "There was a soldier on guard here. Where is he now?"

"He's gone, Colonel."

"Captain," he corrected absently. "Gone? What do you mean, gone?"

"I mean that he isn't here." His tones were clipped

now, military style, but she could hear the echo of the South in them. She smiled knowingly at him.

His knuckles paled even more as he gripped the cell phone and pulled it close to report. "Sergeant Christiansen has gone AWOL, sir. Yes, sir, I intend to do just that. We'll find him."

The captain pointed through the walls to the beyond which he could not see, but evidently knew quite well. "I want a spiral search, now, report back in sixty minutes' time, bordered by the streets," and he rattled off the local avenues.

Captain Rembrandt looked back at Mother. "Am I going to have any trouble with you, ma'am?"

She smiled wider. "Why, no, Captain. Not just yet."

He spun on his heel and stalked through the mortuary, an aide trotting nervously just behind him. She could feel the loa tasting his aura. It lowered over him, a vast dark stingray of evil, drawn to the captain and yet held at bay by the man's unconscious spirit. Mother could feel its aching, smell its fatigue from its battle with her. It shadowed the captain.

Mother loosed the crystal from her grasp. She coiled her fingers around the vial of blessed water and when the captain brushed by her again, the heels of his shoes staccato on the aged creaking floors of Shepherd's Mortuary, she threw her hand out, droplets cascading over the man.

He halted and pivoted around, complexion reddening with anger, running the palm of his hand over his face. "What the hell was that?"

"A blessing, Captain," Mother said. "Holy water. You should thank me."

He gazed into her face a moment, a hard stare which did not make her blink though it drilled into the very back of her skull. Then he relented and gave her a nod. "Well, then, ma'am, I thank you. Come on, let's get everybody out of here." He brushed a rivulet of water from his chin as he turned away and snapped at the aide to keep up.

Mother relaxed a little as the mortuary cleared of the soldiers who'd invaded it.

What had been unleashed upon the world? What had all of them been up to? "Ah, child," she sighed to the now silent William. "You always was a handful."

* * * *

Rembrandt opened his briefcase. the van seemed too small after what he'd just witnessed and the vehicle occasionally shimmied as though vibrations still ran through it.

He dialed the phone and waited. As a pleasant voice came on the line, he punched in a series of numbers which abruptly rendered the line still. Then, almost reluctantly, the phone rang. Another computerized voice, this time male and brisk, answered. He punched in a second series of numbers and waited.

He was answered immediately.

"Speak."

Rembrandt knew the gravelly voice. He could picture Bayliss sitting behind his huge mahogany desk, knew his fine Cuban cigar, hand rolled upon the thighs of young Cuban girls, would be clenched in his flashing white teeth. "The bird has flown."

"Well, hell, now why aren't I surprised at that?" A dull thunder accompanied Bayliss' response, the high-backed upholstered chair being rolled closer to the desk, its leather complexion so fine-grained that women would weep to have pores so clean and tiny. "He took out Stark. He kept his patrol out of Delacroix's hands. You had him, Rembrandt. You let him go."

"We had no choice, sir. It's Marine Corps tradition. He had to bring the body back or it would have raised flags all over the place. It was dicey enough covering for the covert action. But he's not talking. Not yet, anyway." Rembrandt felt his teeth click into place when he stopped talking. The line was private and secure, but he did not like his name being used on it, all the same. Nor did he like having been caught with his quarry fled.

"And I suppose deserting is just another fine tradition." Bayliss cleared his throat. "I want him found before that crazy, son-of-a-bitching witch doctor does. You hear that?"

"I hear you, sir." Rembrandt flicked a glance out the paneled side, making sure none of the detail approached. "Budget?"

Bayliss rattled off a code, adding, "Get what you need. It won't be traced."

"How long do you want me out?"

"Until one or the other of you finds him. I want our goods, Captain . . . is that clear?"

"Never clearer." Rembrandt had nearly replaced the receiver when Bayliss' voice stopped him. He snatched it back to his ear. "I'm sorry, sir. Would you repeat that?"

"I said, you checked the cadaver, didn't you, Captain? I remember when the body bags coming back from Nam were full of little goodies."

Rembrandt stretched his neck a little at the memory of the black woman's angry stare as they'd gone over the corpse again. "Yes, sir, we checked it. It was clean."

"Then you're to stay out until you find Christiansen and he gives you my shipment. That understood?"

"Understood." This time, Rembrandt did not replace the receiver until he heard the other end go dead. It only stayed silent for a few seconds, then it abruptly clicked onto the previous line, with the dulcet-toned female voice instructing him, "If you wish to return to the menu, please stay on the line. If you wish to speak to customer service, push 2. If you wish—"

Rembrandt severed the link.

He closed up the briefcase and spun the lock out of habit with the ball of his thumb, thinking. Half the detail who'd been in unmarked cars stood outside, talking quietly among themselves, enjoying the game they played in civilian garb, waiting for him to emerge and tell them what to do next.

He would be better at this alone. He fiddled with the corner of his briefcase another moment, then set it down in the middle of the van. He let out a shrill whistle. The lieutenant came running, with the other half of his detail.

"We're pulling back. Transport is waiting for us at the base. We'll debrief in the air."

No one spoke if Rembrandt did not, and he did not feel like initiating conversation en route to the base. His mind worked with the various scenarios of tracking down the deserter. Christiansen might run, but he wouldn't run far. The sergeant had his background in the Pacific Northwest, states that had been booming for the last half decade, a population easy to hide in. Rembrandt would start there. He carried his briefcase with him as they turned in the rental cars. The van was driving onto the tarmac and left, keys in the ignition, the equipment downloaded and clean, all evidence of their surveillance packed into a second briefcase toted by the lieutenant.

A helicopter waited for them, its blades already twirling in warm-up, the rotor sound cutting the silence with a lazy cadence. Rembrandt stood back and watched the detail board. He had the same pilot and navigator he'd used to take the patrol into Haiti, and the sense of it struck him, like killing two birds with one stone. At the last moment, he leaned in and handed his briefcase to the lieutenant.

"You go with them to Lackland, Lieutenant. I want to check something we may have overlooked. Go ahead and start debriefing."

"Yes, sir."

Rembrandt slammed the door shut. He turned and strode briskly away, got in the van, and drove off base. He heard the copter as it took to the airways overhead, and was still driving when the explosion hit, a shattering boom that rivaled any he'd ever heard. He did not look back to see how total the destruction had been for he had a fairly good idea as the shock wave rocked the van and the sky began to rain debris.

Chapter 3

October, Southern California

"What are you staring at?"

"Nothing."

One teenager had dirty blond hair, the other had tousled light-brown waves, his face nearly obscured behind glasses and accented with a dusting of freckles. They shared the gangliness of their fourteen years, but the brown-haired boy also had an air of wisdom, a maturity in the framing of his shoulders which his friend lacked. The earpieces of his glasses were bowed far apart as if he wore frames meant for a much smaller head. Behind them, the noise of an arcade tinkled, pinged, and boomed as they stood framed in its back doorway. Laser fire exploded with blue-white strobe light frequency.

The first one gargled a noise of discovery deep in his throat. "Oh, I see. You're watching *her*. She catches you, she's going to call the geekazoid patrol." He snatched at the glasses. "Let me handle this for you."

The brown-haired boy slapped his hand away. "Leave me alone." He dodged a second time and then turned, frowning for a second, before reaffixing his gaze.

"Uh-oh. It sounds serious for the X-man. Brandon, she doesn't even know you breathe."

Without moving his stare, the watcher said, " 'Man's reach must exceed his grasp, else what's a heaven for?' " He paused. "Or something like that. Do you think she likes poetry, Curtis?"

"Poetry? Oh, God, you've got it bad." Curtis whipped back his dirty blond hair and waved fingers at him. "Whoop, whoop, whoop, geek patrol, geek patrol."

Brand resumed determinedly ignoring him, watching the young woman emptying trash into the bins behind her store. She was, he reflected, the only spot of beauty in this back alleyway, its corridor of dumpsters and stinking trash cans an ugly underbelly of the mall. Her blue-black hair and porcelain skin looked like sculpture against a graffitied and eroded stucco background. Despite the distance and angle of the arcade from the trendy clothing store and espresso bar, he could see the silkiness of her dark hair, the pale glow of her complexion, the slender, long legs set off by her short skirt.

But Curtis was right. She didn't know he existed and why should she? He was Brand X, the stuff nobody wanted. He'd tagged himself proudly, unhappy with the mundane, everydayness of his name, happier to stand alone, aloof. Only, lately, it had begun to matter to him.

Curtis gave up irritating him and settled a shoulder into the doorjamb. "She's never gonna look at you, man."

"She doesn't have to," Brand answered softly.

"She's not so pretty."

"Is too."

"Julia Roberts is prettier."

"Julia Roberts is bowlegged."

"Is not."

Brand flicked a look of disdain at his friend. "She is

so bowlegged they had to use a body double on that scene you like so much from *Pretty Woman* where she puts on those boots."

"No way."

"Yes, way. From her ankles to her thighs."

Curtis grinned. "Then I'll take the body double."

"Figured you would." Brand turned his attention back to the leggy young woman. "She's hot. She's like Uma Thurmond in *Pulp Fiction*."

"Think so?"

"I know so." Brand sighed. He pushed his glasses back onto the bridge of his nose. "But you're right. She'll never look twice at me."

Someone called from inside the arcade and he swung around, dragging his friend with him. It was a relief not to have to look at her in a way, trying to be himself and yet have the shadow of another in his thoughts, coloring everything he saw. Watching her just now, he was two people, his familiar disgusting nerdy self . . . and the other. He feared the other. He closed his eyes, wrestling images, until he was in control again.

"We're up." He kicked the door shut behind them, plunging them into a netherworld of pinball and computer simulated game machinery.

"So many machines, so few quarters," Curtis lamented.

Brand slit his eyes against the inky lighting of the room. Only the neon blue and white glare of the machine's screens, emblazoned with color graphics and pinball orange could be seen. A host of players ranged about the room, their faces illuminated by the machines they played, their otherwise ghostly forms inhaled by the darkness. Graphics burst like bombs against their expressions which never changed, intent upon moving the joysticks or palming the ball controls which ran the machines. Brand moved through the obelisks of machines, the one marked NOVA his destiny, a black and white No Fear sticker on its outside panel.

A rangy seventeen-year-old shoved away from the control panel with a reluctant grunt. "I coulda used more time."

Brand squared himself away in front of the game. "Wouldn't do you any good," he answered. He dropped his quarters in as he ran his left palm over the trackball to bring up the latest list of scores.

On the top twenty, his name stood out no less than sixteen times. A tiny crease of pleasure quirked his lips. Then he frowned sharply. His name no longer rode the number one position. "What the—"

"One of the skaters," Curtis said, reading over his shoulder. "They were in here all day yesterday."

Brand's mouth thinned. He didn't like skateboard jocks, cement surfers, with their saggy clothes and breezed hair. "One game," he countered. "Then I'm back on top."

"You'll never do it, man. We'll be here all night."

"One game."

"I've got English homework."

Brand kicked a backpack stowed at the foot of the game machine. "Then take your shit and go."

Curtis wavered. He shifted from one foot to the other. Brandon could feel his Mild-Dud-smelling breath down the back of his neck. "One game?"

"Yeah. Watch me."

So Curtis did.

They squinted into the bright sunlight, backpacks on their shoulders like cowboys of old carried their tack, and swaggered into the late afternoon. Curtis crowed, "One game, man! High five!"

Brand swung his hand up obligingly and let his friend congratulate him again.

"You're *legend*, man. Legend."

"Nothing to it." He looked across the mall lot. It was late. He had to get home before his working parents did, bury his head in a book, pretend he'd forgotten about unloading the dishwasher, play the game with the dweeb. He took a steadying breath. Then, "Oh, man."

"What?"

He pointed across the asphalt. "She's out there again, breaking boxes down. They've got her doing stock." Curtis followed his line of sight and saw the girl again, wrestling with cartons, at the cardboard recycling bin which the mall required. "So?"

"So . . . so . . . she's gonna get all dirty doing that."

"Then go help."

Brand blinked an eye at his friend. "Think so?"

Curtis grinned. "Dare ya, X."

"Take my backpack."

Curtis did so.

They paused.

"What's keeping you?"

"Nothing," answered Brand. He wiped his hands on the thighs of his jeans.

"Then go on. She's almost done."

He licked his lips. "Okay, all right, all right." He put one foot in front of the other. Before he had knowledge of it, they'd carried him across the parking lot alley. When he'd halted, he stood in the bunkered area and could smell the rankness of the trash bins, where frozen yogurt had melted and gone bad, pizza crusts and paper plates rose in mountains, and animals skittered under the iron bottoms.

She looked up. His throat had gone dry and felt tougher than the cardboard she was attempting to flatten. He couldn't hear anything but the thunder of his own pulse. Her dark hair swung forward onto a cheekbone. She tucked it back behind the shell of her ear with a slender finger. He thought she might have spoken to him, but he wasn't sure he could hear. He thought of asking if she remembered him from buying coffee, then thought better of it. What if she didn't?

"I—ah—saw you. Need some help with that?" His voice went thready in the middle of his words, but it came back strong, and he stood, face warming, hoping to God that his glasses wouldn't steam. Or slide down his nose. He looked at her hands and arms. She'd rolled up the silky sleeves of her blouse and he saw the tattoos, living art, move upon her skin. They were crude and yet evocative, primitive black drawings upon the pale canvas of her flesh.

He looked away quickly, after that first stab of awareness that he'd seen a part of her he'd never seen before.

She did not seem to notice his stare. She pushed her hair from her forehead and almost smiled. "Actually, I'm about done, thanks. And I think your friend's waiting for you." She glanced over his head and behind him.

His hearing had come back with a rush. Now he could hear Curtis calling, no, *bellowing*, for him. What the hell? Brand's ears went hotter. "Just thought I'd . . . you know . . . ask . . ." and turned suddenly before she could laugh in his face.

He saw the wave of flesh inundate and part around Curtis, snagging at the backpacks as they came, skateboard wheels humming.

Behind him, the young woman muttered, "Oh, shit."

It didn't sound dirty coming from her lips. He blinked, trying to think of what he should do, watching Curtis bend down, frantically putting textbooks, note-books and papers back into the various bags. The skat-ers, five of them in a wedge, began to circle Brandon.

"Get out of here," she demanded.

The lead skater, his hair so far down into his face he looked like a greasy shaggy dog, laughed. "She your bodyguard?" he asked Brand. "Or who's watching who?" He howled at his own wit.

"Leave her alone." He stiffened his spine. He could kick a board out from under them easily enough, but he wasn't sure getting them on his footing would be an advantage. He didn't want a fight, he wanted to avoid one. He wanted them away from her.

The leader waved his buds over to the recycling bins, where they began to haul the bails out. Brand turned around slowly to watch, while the young woman got angry.

"Put that stuff back, you little shits."

None of the boys paid any attention to her. She strode forward, grabbed back a bundle and returned it where it belonged.

"You're going to cost me my job. Leave this stuff alone before I call Security."

"What's wrong with four-eyes here? He not good enough for you?"

"She's gonna have to call Se-cur-ity!"

They began to hoot and play-cry and whistle as they circled, passing bundles back and forth like Houston Rockets players in a basketball court's key. A wiry, dirty-faced skater made kissy noises. "Come get it."

She lunged and caught the cardboard away from him as he slalomed past, daring her. Her movements knocked him off-balance and he and the skateboard went sliding sideways before he hit the ground in a nasty skid. He came up with blood and grime pasted across his legs.

"You're going to get it now, bitch."

"Don't you call her that!" Brandon launched at the youth. He didn't feel the first few blows, striking or struck, but he felt it when one of the others hit him in the back with a skateboard, wheels spinning. The violent bone-crack dropped him to his knees where he fought to breathe. He staggered back to his feet.

Her voice came to him shrilly, "You keep your hands off him! Hang on, I'm getting Security!"

And then he was alone, fists hot and scraped, glasses sliding down his nose, breathing hard and furiously, dancing between jostling bodies. Where the hell was Curtis, he wondered, just before sweaty bodies sandwiched him.

He could feel himself being hefted, his glasses gone, the whole scene blurry, thrown through the air and when he landed, the trash bin lid came thudding down after him, sealing him in darkness.

Then the stink began.

Perfect, Brand thought.

They hammered on the sides of the bin like a gong until his ears rang and his head throbbed.

"Come on out, sheep dip! We'll be waiting for you."

He folded his arms and sat. He could hear the spin of their wheels on the asphalt and their war whoops of victory as they left. The reek and dampness around him began to sink into his clothes. He could feel the blood under his nose congeal as his ragged breathing calmed. What had he just proved, anyway? That he wasn't man enough to protect himself or her?

All he wanted to do was get out of there before she

could face him. He put his palms up to the lid, felt the corroded and gritty surface and braced himself.

A door banged.

"Hello? Anybody out here?"

Brandon froze.

"Sweet God. What a mess."

"I'll get somebody to clean it up later." A man's voice, a young man. "You should get your store to cage the recycling bins. Paper's worth a lot now. The mall gets ripped off all the time. You could get hurt by jerks like that."

"It's not me I'm worried about. There was someone else here—"

Her voice, so near the metal, thrummed slightly with the vibration of her tone. Brand held his breath.

"Hello?"

As the sour and rotting odors rose around him, he knew he couldn't face her, not like that. So he made no answer. He folded his arms and sat.

"Look, I'd like to stand out here with you all afternoon, but I can't." Stud muffin sounded slightly impatient.

"Oh. Right. Well . . ."

"He probably split with the rest of them. What say you buy me a cappuccino and we call it even?"

Her voice chilled slightly. "I thought you worked for the mall."

He could hear their steps drawing away. The mall cop was a jerk, too, of a different kind, but that didn't seem to be stopping her from leaving with him. "Actually, that's what I like about this job. There're all kinds of perks."

A fire door banged shut. A moment of stillness before the sudden chirping of birds told him he was alone again. He'd been holding his breath, but now his chest began to tighten and his stomach to clench. He didn't want to be in here, shut in. The confinement closed about him, but he told himself he would be all right. He could get out. He wasn't locked in. Everything would be okay and, shortsighted or not, he fixed his gaze on single beams of light which found their way in under the lid. He waited until he was certain he was alone.

Then he cautiously stood among the plastic bags and the offal and tried to put the lid back up.

It stayed fast.

Brand swallowed hard. *He would not panic.* Could not, even though *she* had done this to him in the psych ward, locked him in metal drum darkness, floating in nothing but his own putrid thoughts. . . . He scratched at the metal, clawing desperately. Flakes of rusting paint rained down on his face. He blinked frantically to keep his eyes clear. His throat tried to close as panic surged through him.

"Oh, God, oh, God, oh, God, let me out, let me out." He tried to scramble up the mountain of garbage, thinking if he could stand taller, he could force the lid open and, bent under it, tried again. It did not budge. He pushed until he could not breathe and halted, crouching. He tried again.

The sweltering heat and rankness of the enclosure rose to greet him.

He was *locked* in. They'd wedged it shut. He'd be in here till someone else came out to the bins or the collector trucks came.

Sweat poured down his face. He'd be dead by then, alone with his thoughts and fears. He grasped for calmness as it was being shattered and blown away, disintegrating like a target in the video arcade, dissolving into brilliant motes that slipped through his fingers.

Yellow Dog. He would concentrate on Yellow Dog, and that would make it all right. He squinted upward, at the lid, at the yellowish light beaming in, making an image. . . .

He didn't know when he first began seeing the Yellow Dog, but it was unmistakable to him that the creature came to guide him. To aid and protect him. It was an unreliable Lassie, he couldn't always summon it, but when it came, Yellow Dog could always bring him back to the edge of sanity.

The psych ward, he'd been told, would help him. It had at first, just being away from home and the screaming fights of his mother and husband number two had helped. And he might have been all right if Dr. Susan Craig hadn't taken a keen interest in him. It did not help now that she was dead and gone, her deeds exposed. She lay in his mind and it was at moments like these, in the dark and alone, when all that she had done gathered itself like a living, breathing beast, and wrestled him for his soul. Yellow Dog sometimes helped him blunt it. Sometimes Brand fought it all alone.

He'd gotten used to it. There was no one he could tell today about the battle for his brain. He knew the buzzwords to give his current therapist, knew how to tell him just enough to be left alone. He trusted no one, least of all his mother and his psychologist. What would they do if they knew there were two of them inside his skull? The scars Susan Craig left behind ensured that he would never have peace.

He'd lived in a metal tank for her, bathed by soothing water, until his mind was as clean and unfolded as a newborn babe's. Then she'd taken him out and put straps and probes about his body, fastening a helmet upon his head, a helmet which beamed its own private theater with its own very private thoughts into him. Yellow Dog, when it came, guided him home. When it did not, Brand would dare the maze himself, always searching for the light, coming out of the dark. . . .

Golden beams dazzled him now. Yellow Dog hunched over him, showing him the way to freedom, if he could just jar the lid. He looked down at Brand, then began to waver and fade.

Brandon swallowed hard. If he stayed inside the bin, Susan Craig would have him for sure. He took a deep breath and began to pound already bruised fists upon the trash bin. Drummed along the lid, the sides, anywhere he could strike, screaming until he grew hoarse.

Suddenly, the lid split open with a creaking groan. Yellow Dog shone fiercely into his eyes like the sun, then began to waver again, change, mutate into a human face, staring down at him with the light at his back. Brandon recoiled, embarrassed and relieved. He blinked and narrowed his eyes as his rescuer peered in.

He knew the face, begrimed and weathered, hair shagged down to his shoulders, hands seamed with everyday dirt as the man leaned in to look at him. Something metal swung forward on his chest and chimed gently as it hit the rim of the bin, metal to metal.

"Shut up," the man said mildly. "I'll get you out of here."

Brand stood passively as the hose played over him, cold water sludging off the worst of the garbage and smell. It ran down his clothes and pooled at his feet.

"Rough crowd," commented the homeless man who aimed the water at him.

Brandon looked up at him, then away. He could only see the man's face clearly when they moved closer together, but neither of them was particularly interested in that at this point. Curtis had taken the backpacks and run, a fact which had eventually drawn his rescuer's curiosity, and the man had backtracked until he found the trouble. Like a firefighter dousing flames, he aimed the water stream expertly up and down Brand's shivering form.

He turned off the hose. "They'll hear the water running," he said matter-of-factly, "and come check it out. I don't like messing with Security."

Brand cleared his throat before answering. "I don't think I'll get much cleaner without soap anyway."

"Probably not."

Brand watched the other coil up the hose neatly and stow it. He and Curtis had often speculated about this man who lived in the shady environs of the mall and its accompanying plazas. He added, rather lamely, "Thanks."

The other looked up quickly, appraisal in his eyes, then nodded. "All right." He stuck out his hand, unafraid to shake Brandon's, even in its current condition. "I'm Mitch."

"Brand X. You know, like the stuff nobody wants. Not new and improved."

Mitch's face creased slightly under a three-, four-day growth of beard. "Somebody wanted your ass."

"Just long enough to can me." Brand sloughed water off his shirt. "I've gotta go."

"You can't get far without your glasses." Mitch handed something out of a patched shirt pocket.

"You found 'em!"

"Something like that. I saw somebody go by me who didn't look like he should be wearing them."

Brand cleaned them up as well as he could and settled them on his face, thinking that this man was the good guy he'd tried to be, and had failed miserably at.

His lenses brought Mitch's face into sharp focus. "Well. Thanks again."

"You're welcome."

It didn't seem enough, but it also seemed like a terrible breach of etiquette to ask his rescuer what had gotten him here, why he had to live the way he did, what Brand could do to help. Maybe he didn't want any help. Maybe he just wanted to be left alone. Brand swallowed his words back. The line of the sun had been lowering on the horizon. It was too late to not get in trouble, but his condition should rate mercy. Brandon took a soggy step toward home.

"Stay out of trouble now," Mitch offered.

"Yeah. Right. You, too." He stopped several paces away. "I owe you one. Cup of coffee and breakfast."

"Sounds good," the man said.

Brand squared his shoulders and walked off. He had the feeling that he'd managed to salvage the day somehow, man to man.

Chapter 4

The young woman skewed the car around a corner and found the house while the streets were still dark, streetlights burning a dim yellow, swirls of dust kicked up by the Santa Ana winds gritty along the sidewalks. Pulse drumming in her throat, she pulled over and let it hug the curb, watching the rearview mirror warily. The gun under the driver's seat slid forward at the rapid braking and tapped her gently in the ankles.

Kamryn gave it a dazed look. It didn't appear real, looking more like a toy that took caps instead of bullets. She wasn't sure if she should leave it where it was or kick it back under. What if she needed it . . . ? Almost without thought, she shoved it back under the seat where it lay out of sight but burned like a hot coal at the back of her mind.

Kamryn stared out the side window at the street. The winds were quiet now. They'd pick up again when the sun warmed a little. The homes were stucco tract homes from the '50s, looking like they'd been cut out of cardboard and set up like dominoes, like every other home she'd ever seen. Chain-link and grape-stake fences sagged. Trash cans, some battered tin, others tattered plastic, tumbled next to garages. Front lawns were only patches between cracked concrete walks and crumbling asphalt driveways.

It was the kind of neighborhood whose corner houses on the fringe of streets with heavier traffic had become businesses. Accountants, a lawyer, an acupuncturist, and across from her, a dermatologist. None of them, from the houses they occupied, extremely successful. Her gaze darted along the streets, watching the traffic to see if she'd been followed. She was chicken, she knew, but she felt better with the gun.

She shut the car off after a few minutes of empty horizon. It dieseled once or twice, then hunkered down. Kamryn kept watch alertly. She would not move from the car until she felt safe.

She left the radio on, heart fluttering wildly inside her chest. She hugged herself tightly to make it stop. No, not stop, to make it *slow*. To keep it regular. She hugged herself so tightly her breasts hurt. The pain made her gasp.

A glimpse of herself in the mirror as she kept a lookout overrode her vision. Sky blue eyes framed by dark lashes, a fringe of dark hair leaving a crescent scar across her brow, skin paler than pale. A comet's tail of gems studded the outer shell of her left ear, a single diamond stud winked in the right. Frowning, she pushed her hair back off her forehead.

The wad of money felt as though it would burn a hole in the pocket of her jeans. She shifted her weight slightly and the hard knot in her pocket dug into her from a different angle. She shouldn't keep the radio on, it would pull the battery down, but Kamryn didn't want to sit there in silence. Her arms itched, as though something small and creepy crawly moved across her skin. She rubbed at them, first one and then the other, but the faint irritation did not fade.

A brilliantly-diamonded orange and black python coiled down her arm, ringed by Old English lettering and swastikas. A skull and crossbones and several variations of knives and roses decorated the other. Her tattoos rippled, undulating, alive as she chafed her skin. She tugged at the hem of her shirt as though she could pull the short sleeves down over them. Across the knuckles of both slim hands, letters stood out: HATE across the right, LOVE across the left. And, around the ring finger, a tattoo which read Darby, a ring tattoo, instead of a wedding band. She curled the fingers of her right hand about it, obliterating it, and sat tensely, looking down the street, watching.

A late model sedan pulled into the tract from the far side of the intersection and cruised slowly toward her. She watched it keenly until she spotted the driver, a middle-aged man, unaware of her scrutiny, pulling into one of the office-converted houses. He got out of the car, hauling a battered and dull black briefcase with him, lab coat thrown over one arm. He looked like the tract houses, dusty and mediocre, as he opened the locked front door.

Kamryn shot one last glance over traffic, which had begun to emerge and pick up, then bent over, reaching for the gun under the car seat. She hesitated, brushing her fingertips over its cold metal surface, then left it. It wouldn't fit well in her purse anyway. The doctor had been spooky enough about meeting her at this hour. She would scare him out of the appointment altogether if she showed up packing. She took a deep breath to steady herself, then shoved the car door open.

The house creaked as she entered it. Its living room

served as the waiting room and its kitchen had been gutted into an office area, file cabinets against the wall, the pass-through bar now a service counter. The doctor swung around, startled, half-shrugged into his lab coat. He was Middle Eastern, and his rich color paled, extravagant dark eyebrows flying up like wild birds. He cleared his throat and settled his arms into the coat and straightened his tie, grooming. *Like a cat*, she thought, *that licks itself to calm down when it's been scared.* He looked as unnerved as she felt.

"Miss Smith? If you'll have a seat. My nurse isn't in yet—"

"No," she answered flatly. "I can't wait. I've got the money. Let's get this over with."

The doctor's nose flared slightly, but he dipped his head. "Exam Room 1. I'll be in shortly."

Kamryn followed the wave of his hand down a short hallway. The commercial carpeting was worn but clean, and the whole office smelled faintly of lemon-scented disinfectant. She stepped into the room, where crisp white paper already lined the exam couch. Panic ticked in her throat and she fought the desire to turn and run. What was she doing here? She could handle this at home, heat a spoon until it glowed molten-hot and jam it against her skin, burn the tattoos away herself, scarring over the ink-stained pigmentation.

Her flesh crawled. It would hurt like hell. Easier, maybe, just to take a knife and skin herself. But here, maybe here, she could find a way to be free.

Kamryn clenched and unclenched her hands, hearing the doctor's footsteps not far behind her. She stepped to the couch and perched on it, one foot outstretched to touch the floor, ready to flee if she had to.

Dr. Amand stepped in, carrying a stainless steel tray. He smiled apologetically. "I am not quite set up yet."

She felt like gritting her teeth. His voice, faintly yet richly accented, bounced around in her head like a pinball. It set off small explosions in her thoughts, thoughts which careened around her skull, hateful things, ethnic slurs, words which she had promised herself she would never say, never *think* again. As hard as one part of her tried to narrow her eyes and stare at this man, stare hatred at him pointed enough that he ought to drop dead, the rest of her scrambled to not stare, not think, not hate.

She had given her promise.

They were all one people, she breathed to herself, forcing the philosophy down her throat and into her chest, where it weighted her like lead. She had to believe it. She had to. To do otherwise would find her down in the cellar again, looking hate and death in the eyes . . . would have her dying again, with no angel and no miracle to rescue her a second time.

Kamryn found herself losing the battle and looked abruptly across the room. Cold liquid splashed onto her arm and she jumped as Dr. Amand took up her wrist. He'd slipped on glasses, wire, round John Lennon glasses, spindly things perching on a strong nose. "Antibiotic wash," he said. He laid a towel across her leg. "Dry yourself." He stepped back and pulled rubber gloves on while she did. When she'd finished, he took up her wrists again. "Boyfriend do these?"

"Something like that."

"Nearly professional. I think perhaps it might take ten, twelve visits to clear them totally. Colored ink is most difficult to remove." He tapped a gloved finger. "The charge will be the same—$60 an inch."

Kamryn swallowed back disappointment. She'd been told six to eight visits over the phone, depending on the tattoo. "I have the money," she repeated. Her vintage

Kawasaki was gone, leaving $8,000 cash in its wake. First the tattoos, then she would decide what to do with the rest of the money. "Will it hurt?"

"Most of my patients do not need medication. Did it hurt getting this?" He stroked the Iron Cross symbol. Without waiting for an answer, he reached toward his machinery, turning it on, and checking the settings. "You could be a pretty girl. You'll be glad you decided to do this."

Kamryn found herself blinking rapidly as he removed a thick, penlike instrument from its holder, coiling cable trailing behind it.

"This is a Yag, a ruby-laser. It burns away the skin, like a sunburn. You'll be tender. I will give you a topical cream, an antibiotic. Use it as per the directions. I have these gauze sleeves, to protect the tender new skin. They are like evening gloves—see? You will feel like Audrey Hepburn in *My Fair Lady*. Buy fresh ones from the pharmacy. Make an appointment for next week whenever you can, although," and Dr. Amand's almond eyes assessed her through his John Lennon glasses, "I would prefer not so early in the morning."

"I had to get away. It's a bitch to—" Kamryn paused. She wanted to tell him she was trying to save his ass, and hers. If Darby or any of the others found out what she was doing, that she was leaving them, that she was already gone, she was dead meat and so was anybody who tried to help her. He seemed to sense it.

"My scheduling nurse will work with you." He appeared to be choosing his words carefully. "I have done tattoos like this before. Sometimes gang members. I know it can be difficult. But it is a new life, is it not? It will be worth it." The machine hummed. "I will start here." The laser tool poised over the lemon python.

"No," Kamryn told him. "Take the ring tattoo off

first. I want it off me." Just in case she couldn't take the burning. She wanted that gone, no matter what. She closed her eyes as her skin burned and tingled and the smell of singed hair filled the air, and the laser crackled over her flesh, doing its best to obliterate the past.

*   *   *   *

"She's dead, man! She's toast. The freaking bitch is dead, man! No one cuts me cold like that. No one!" The speaker paused for air, his white T-shirt stretched so thinly over his heaving chest that it was like a second skin, his tattoos moving like living creatures under it. "She sold the bike!"

His words bounced off the unfinished basement walls and he paused to wipe the spittle from the corner of his mouth, catching sympathetic glances from the broken-down mattresses scattered around the room. Even the bright dawn light could not scour the debris-encrusted atmosphere, though it tried to pierce through ground-level windows where banked dirt from unsuccessful gardens rose like mountains against the glass. Now and then a brindle pit bull put his nose to the window, aggressively leaving slobber and more grime behind as he snuffled at the basement occupants. It was not a basement, really, more of a crawl space, and if the age of the stucco tract home served, it had probably been at one time intended for a bomb shelter. The low ceiling made it far easier to sprawl than to stand, and the young man in the center of the basement had to bow his head slightly. He looked around for a response.

"No one, Darby," echoed a low voice from the corner.

He nodded and ran the palm of his hand over his closely-buzzed skull. "She sold the bike. And no one disses me. No one disses *us*." Having caught his breath, he began again. "She can't drop me because I'm dropping her *first*. First I'm getting my bike back, then I'm dropping *her*. She's going to freakin' *die*."

"How dead do you want her?"

The voice unfurled from the other end of the room, out of the shadows, as its owner stood up. Tattoos rippled up and down his bared torso as he did, like diamondback patterns on reptilian scales. His face and shaved head were as pale as an exposed underbelly in contrast to his arms and torso. Black pants hung tightly on the points of his pelvic bones. Named for his inkings, Snake leaned one hip against a ceiling beam and showed his teeth, waiting for an answer.

Darby looked across, his petulant fury answered and he took in all the ramifications. Snake had been known to kill people. If he said he wanted Kamryn dead, Snake could make her that way. He swallowed, uncertain of what to say next, though his broken heart seemed to pump jaggedly in his chest.

Snake snagged a nail edge between his teeth and dragged it down. He then sucked on the incisor for a moment as if savoring some private pain. His dark-eyed glance flicked about the basement room, and came round to Darby again. " 'Cause it's up to you," he said. "I could kill her just a little, so she'd be like braindead. She could still hang with us, and be like your slave or something, and she'd be good enough for that, except later, you might get tired all the time tellin' her what to do. Or I could just kill her all the way. It's up to you. How dead do you want her?"

There was more than just him at stake here. She knew about the group, about what they'd done, what they planned to do. He couldn't just let her walk, all snarky the way she was. Ever since Oklahoma, the Feds were thick as flies, all over everyone. Sooner or later, she might tell, and then it would all come down on them. He didn't have a choice. He sucked in a deep breath, feeling it in his chest like a stab wound, where she'd betrayed him. "I want her *dead*, man," he said, and there was no mistaking his meaning.

Snake grinned. "Cool."

Chapter 5

Furtive sounds woke his dreaming. They were his own, a panting which echoed that of the guide pulling him out of his nightmares. Yellow Dog faded away abruptly into a shimmering glow which became a window beating into his vision. Brandon reached automatically for his glasses, even before he was awake. A hot sun slanted through the venetian blinds of his room and cast zebra shadows. Morning had come too soon. He turned his head and a massive blob bumped just into view. "Jesus!" Eyes squinted nearly shut, he jammed his glasses on over the bridge of his nose and the blurs jumped into startling focus.

"Rats! Mo—om."

She recoiled from view. "Sorry, Brandon." The close-up memory of gray hairs trying to disappear among frosted highlights in her malt brown hair and thick gouges of worry lines deep in her forehead between her eyes remained. More potent expletives crowded his throat, but he dared not loose them. Not in front of her. She would die, he thought, if she heard the average language in a high school corridor. But then, she still had trouble dealing with the vending machines on campus being fenced off to prevent theft. She would be more comfortable among the Amish.

She frowned. "Bad dreams again?"

If she only knew. "No." He started to shove his covers down, then pinched them tightly at his navel. "Will you quit hoovering over me? How about some privacy here?"

She drew back, half-smiling. "Hovering. If I were hoovering, you'd be getting vacuum cleaned."

"Whatever." His glasses slid down. He put a finger square in the middle of the frames and nailed them in place on the bridge of his nose.

"It's time to get up. Now, remember, no water. No breakfast. Nothing until after the procedure."

His stomach rumbled in protest. "Shit." Brand swung his feet out, covers over his lap, and stared darts at her. "I thought I was going to sleep in today."

Her lips pinched as she consulted her watch. "You did. Everybody else left for school forty-five minutes ago." She stood, the palm of her other hand unconsciously cradling the slight bulge of her stomach, proof he thought, that husband number three, the dweeb, had done her at least once. The thought of his mother and the dweeb engaged in sex made him nauseous. That, on top of other concerns, made him want to get her out of his room as quickly as possible.

"Mo—om." If she ever left, he could get dressed.

"What? Oh, right." She got as far as the doorway, then turned again.

Brand hastily threw his blankets back over his lap. "What? What?"

"Aren't you excited?"

"Yeah. Kind of."

"Only kind of?"

He was scared, too, so that took a lot of the edge off the excitement. He shrugged. His mother and the dweeb were doing this for him, he knew that, although the dweeb hadn't pounded it into him the way husband number two would have. But the RK procedure hadn't been his idea, he'd been lobbying for contacts. None of this would have happened if Curtis had stuck by him at the mall, but it had and now he was in the process of getting what he wanted. Sort of.

They wouldn't be calling him owl eyes anymore, and he'd have a better chance of surviving gym class, so maybe all this noble sacrifice stuff from her would be worth it. She'd dug the money up from somewhere, maybe the psych hospital had finally settled after what had happened—anyway, she'd announced what they'd arranged for him like they'd gotten him a car. He'd spent the better part of an afternoon with his eyes dilated while the doctor looked at him like he was a prime specimen for alien abduction, measuring him for surgery.

Anything to get the Coke bottles off his nose, to not look at himself in the mirror and see a freak grinning back. Although, freak or not, he was usually happy to recognize himself. His dreams were worse, but he'd keep them to himself. Anything was better than going back to the psych ward.

His mother let out a little sigh, and shifted weight. "I'll be glad when it's over," he said finally.

"Well, hurry and get dressed."

He tilted his head and looked at her. "Duh."

She left, shutting the door behind her.

Brand waited a beat or two to make sure she was really gone, before pushing his blankets to the floor and standing up. His penis had finally begun to wilt, and he hated that, he really hated it, waking up hard every morning. He'd told a friend about it, who'd snickered and called him a "throbbing, pulsating love machine" until Brand had gotten sick of both his friend and the label. It was part of life, he guessed, but he didn't need his mother fussing over that, too, making him miserable. She'd probably make the dweeb come in to talk things over with him and he *really* didn't need that.

What he needed was not to be a freak anymore.

Brand peed and then looked at himself in the bathroom mirror. He had the only other room in the house with its own bath, but he supposed that would change when the dweeb's kids, both girls, got older. He'd get shuffled around again, maybe even thrown back in the hospital. It could happen. But only if someone got inside his skull and stirred around in there, like a rabid bat in some attic. Only if someone knew what he thought. What he dreamed. What lay behind his eyelids as surely as darkness lay on the far side of the moon.

He found himself gripping the edges of the porcelain sink so hard his hands had turned chalk-white, like the fixture. He forced himself to let go, shaking.

Brand X, the stuff nobody wants.

And his mom wanted to know if he was excited about having surgical knives pointed at his eyeballs.

"Shit," he said, and spat into the sink. He ran enough water to wash it down, combed his hair, and left.

His mom was a morning person, but she knew that he wasn't, so she said little in the car. She'd found a more or less current music station on the radio and left it playing, though if Brand had had his choices, he'd have brought his Cranberries tape and cranked it up until the car boomed with the bass. He stared out the window at the still somewhat unfamiliar neighborhood. Orange County wasn't L.A., by a long shot. More palms and ficus, less graffiti. The schools, bankrupt or not, had fields for soccer and baseball and swimming pools, outside, with a deck, not upstairs in some prehistoric building.

The neighborhoods had dress codes, for crissakes, God forbid somebody should paint their house blue or something instead of white or puke color. There were rules about the fences, how high and whether they could be out of wood or cinder block or bars, which depended mostly on how ritzy the neighborhood was and whether they would "obscure a view" or not. Cars could not be left parked on the streets, the beaches had curfews, and the principals had cows if anyone wore a shirt with a rock band or beer brand name on it. Brand's stepfather could not afford a home in one of those areas, for which Brand daily thanked whatever passed for a God. If the conservative county got any more rigid, it would go into rigor mortis.

He wondered how good the doctor was. How could he be, with his office tacked onto the Brea Mall? Was a mall any place for an eye surgeon, for crying out loud? With any luck, he could roll right out of there and head to the arcade afterward. He could page Curtis to meet him. Brand rested his forehead against the cool glass of the side window, wondering if his high score was still riding supremo in the arcade.

"Hey! Slow down."

She tensed at the wheel, even as she steered into the lot.

He bumped his forehead against the passenger window. "Mom, slow down." The power window slid away from him and he hung over the door frame.

"Brandon, what are you doing!"

"Looking for the homeless guy." It was early enough that Mitch might be out, before the security cop wanna-bes were out on patrol. "The guy that pulled me out of the dumpster."

His mother's voice came from behind his head, but he knew the expression that went with the tone. "I don't think I want to meet him, even after what he did for you."

"He's a cool guy."

"He doesn't work and he has no home. I don't think so. We talked about this. I told you to stay away from him. It's not just drugs and alcohol—"

Brand thumbed his glasses up the bridge of his nose and twisted around in the car seat. "I wanted you to see him, to see he's an okay guy. All right? And he's got a name. It's Mitch."

"Mitch what? Or should that be, what Mitch?"

He shrugged. "Just Mitch. And you'd like him, really, and not just because he saved my butt."

"There's a hole under your feet and you're the one digging it." Her eyes looked like baked clay.

"Ohhh-kay." He turned back to the window, dropping the Mitch subject of an interesting guy. Brand had already paid him back the breakfast and coffee. Mitch liked McDonald's coffee, scalding hot and pure, not flavored with hazelnuts or amaretto or cinnamon and whipped cream. Curtis was of the opinion that, slipped ten dollars, the guy might even buy them beer or more. He was obviously a Vietnam vet, his friend pointed out, who'd seen better times. Brand pondered the possibilities of playing in cyberspace while blasted. It might add a whole new dimension.

If he played his mother right, he might even get a second get out of school free card to explore the possibilities. He settled back on the car seat. "Glad we're not homeless," he said thoughtfully. "You worked awful hard to keep us that way."

Out of the corner of his eye, he caught the tightening of her lips at his acknowledgment of her sacrifices. Oh, yes, she'd worked hard, and married poorly, too. That was the only reason he could think of for husbands two and three.

Brand turned away again, blinking. His glasses began their usual slide. He pushed them back into place savagely. With his newfound oily skin it was like balancing on a banana peel, forty, fifty times a day.

His mother seemed more nervous than he was when they parked the car. The north end of the mall was dead, he thought, looking around. Parking spaces as far as the eye could see. He looked at the coffee bar next to the ophthalmologist. "How about a cappuccino, Mom? We've got time."

She looked startled as she locked the car, and then fidgeted with her purse. He knew that look. She was trying to remember how much cash she had on her.

Brand finally looked away, knowing the answer before she gave it.

"Not today, Brandon."

"Sure." He tossed her a grin. "Just checkin'. You don't have to go in with me. I could just have them, you know, call when it's time to pick me up."

A grateful look washed over his mother's face, and for a moment, he thought he would have killed to have brought her that peace permanently. The realization felt like a kick in the gut. She shook her head quickly, brushing aside the opportunity. "No, they want me here. Just in case."

"Sure," he repeated. They both knew that was only half the reason. She was also afraid that if she turned her back, Brand would be gone. He felt sorry for her, but not terribly. She'd spent most of his years wrecking her life and his, too. Husband number two had convinced her that Brand was the core of their problems and, eventually, they'd had him hospitalized, putting him into the hands of a monster.

They'd all found out just in time.

Maybe.

He shoved his hands into his jeans pockets and followed her across the parking lot.

He heard rapid footsteps to his flank and turned. He saw the girl hurrying across the parking lot, going into the side entrance of the mall. She probably had work to do before the boutiques were open. He stared at her now, but she did not notice, for she wore evening gloves, it looked like, and she was pulling her sleeves down over them, quick-stepping across the asphalt.

"Hi."

She jumped like a shot rabbit, her startled eyes fixing on him. Then she answered, muffled, "Hi."

He thought his heart might sink, but there was no recognition in her eyes. He cleared his throat. "You work at Hot Flash, right?"

"Right." She looked him over and Brand felt himself shrink a little as she measured him. "Your sister shop there?"

Older sister, she meant. Brand cleared his throat again. "No. Ah—I've seen your tattoos. When you were doin' espressos. Cool."

Her face closed and she said icily, "See you," in a tone which meant she wouldn't be looking for him. She angled away, heading for the steel doors just beyond the fire lane.

He bumped into his mother, who had stopped just ahead of him.

"A little old for you?"

"Yeah. Probably." He felt his face warm and dodged around her, so as not to discuss it. She kept looking for signs of normalcy in him, as though each stage he

reached was a monumental achievement to be cele-
brated. For crissakes, was she worried that he didn't
like girls?

Defensively, he said, "She's nice enough, under all
that. It's just flash, y'know? Inside, she's nice."

His mother reached out, gave him a half-hug.
"You're a good kid, do you know that, Brand? A little
strange, but a good kid."

Her embrace stopped him in his tracks. Instead of
radiating warmth, it iced through him, stabbed through
the bones of his neck and shoulders like a stiletto,
filling him with dread. Because he wasn't a good kid.
He tried, but he wasn't, and if she could see into his
mind, see into his dreams, she would think that Hanni-
bal Lecter was fit to teach kindergarten compared to
him.

Brand shuddered.

His mother let go of him abruptly as if sensing his
rejection.

He closed his eyes tightly for a moment. He wasn't
a good kid, but he could imitate one. If he tried hard
enough. If he walked that tightrope very carefully, no
one would ever know.

He could do it. He had done it, and he could keep
doing it.

"Come on, we're late," his mother said sharply.

His entrance into the ophthalmologist's office
seemed unreal, after that. There was a time where he
sat in one of several chairs arranged in a waiting room
that was supposed to look like somebody's living room,
if that somebody lived with dissections of the human
eyeball hung on the walls, and with golfing magazines
strewn all over the coffee table. There was a hushed
discussion in the corner between his mother and one
of the women who worked behind the counter, about

money he presumed, because she had that defensive look on her face again.

And then, finally, he was being called in. His mother took his glasses and looked as if she wanted to say something or give him another hug. Brand pushed past her before she could take the opportunity. He felt himself moving mechanically, watching himself out of body go through the drill. Given a backless smock to wear, having his hair put in a matching bonnet, being laid down on a surgical table where a special pillow held his head steady. A nurse smiled down at him. "I've got your eyedrops for you."

Brand felt like saying something smart-ass, but his tongue felt like his comforter from his bedroom and stuck to the roof of his mouth besides. He stared up at her, watching her somewhat pretty face through the floating teardrop as it splashed and stung briefly into his eye. She had to hold his left eyelid open.

"Remember what the doctor talked to you about. Keep your eyes focused on that target and don't move. This won't hurt at all, I promise—" Her bleary image crossed her heart over her uniform. "He'll be right in."

Brand knew better. The drops would take about fifteen minutes to be at their optimal. The doc wouldn't be in before that. He watched the target design which had been tacked to the ceiling overhead. He couldn't see the tacks today, without his glasses, but he'd been shown it two weeks ago when he'd been brought in to have his eyes tested and measured. He thought now, as he'd thought then, if the doc was really all that marvelous—how come he still used knives instead of lasers?

So if he felt that way about it, why did he even agree to it? Brand listened to his inner voice and returned a

shrug. *Pull out my fingernails, stick pins in my eyes—
just don't send me to school!*

His thoughts wandered and before he knew it, there
was a noise at the side of his table and the doctor had
come in. The nurse had reappeared with him. She held
something shiny in her hands. "I'm going to secure
your eyelids. The human eye blinks every five seconds.
Even if you tried not to, you probably would, and we
can't have that."

"What is that?" His dry throat squeaked on the last
word, and he felt his face go warm, but they ignored it.

"Lid speculums." The tips of her fingers were incredibly cold as she pulled his upper eyelid into a steely
hold, then positioned the instrument and captured his
lower lid.

Strange, but not unbearable. He felt her repeat the
sequence on his other eye.

Then they dropped the target rings gently onto his
staring eyeball. That, the doctor had warned him
about. It would help pinpoint the direction of the scalpel. Brand closed his jaws very tightly.

Brand desperately wanted to change his mind as the
scalpel descended toward his eye, but he dared not
move. He tried to focus on the target, as the steel-blue
edge dove closer and closer.

The nurse, not the doctor, said, "You're going to feel
a pressure, like someone pushing a finger into your
eye, but it won't hurt. It might even make a small pop,
but don't worry."

He had no choice about not moving, or staring upward. What was he doing here, anyway?

The surgeon stood over him, a white cloud, and the
steely instrument in his hand arced downward like
lightning. Brand could feel his entire body go rigid.

How much, for a moment, the vision looked like Dr.

Susan Craig, standing over him. How much at her mercy he still was. She was dead, wasn't she? Dead, but not gone.

And with her, she brought the other, the hunting man, the killer, looking down at him instead of out through him.

He thought for a moment he'd gone to sleep and was immersed in the dream that continually haunted him, but the face behind the knife was different. Awake or asleep, he knew he was dead if he stirred or showed any fear as the blade dipped near.

"Just hold very still."

A dead man. Dead. Dead.

Chapter 6

"Life sucks and then you die. How do you think I feel?"

Brand felt, rather than saw, his mother recoil from his response to her question. He couldn't see her—he couldn't see a damn thing beyond the end of his nose since they'd left the doctor's office, a disposable pair of solar shields resting across his face like a bad pair of 3-D glasses. The car swerved slightly with his mother's movement. He continued looking out the window even though all he could see were dark clouds rushing past him. He felt like a vampire. As dim as everything looked, the daylight made him flinch. Brand sighed and added brutally, "You had to ask."

"But I didn't have to hear that."

"You want me to lie to you? Look, I'm fourteen. I get trash-canned with regularity, leaned on about my grades, my skin prefers to get pimples just before picture days, I've had two stepfathers—and I can't see shit." His shoulders twitched. He did not add that he could not afford the luxury of moods. She watched him like a hawk and if he so much as sneezed, she thought of throwing him back in the psycho ward. But she'd asked. Why would she ask if she didn't want to hear the answer. "What do you expect? What if this doesn't get any better? At least I could see something before."

He knew what she wanted. She wanted another

round of thanks for the RK, but he didn't feel like giving it to her. If he'd had his way, it would have been more useful for her to take the settlement money and buy a newer car, and he could have nagged that off her in a couple of years. But, no, she had to make a noble sacrifice. And what if she'd ruined him . . . left Brand alone in the dark, with *him?*

"Brand, they told us to expect this. Haziness for the first day—that's one of the reasons they told you to go home and go to bed. Keep pressure off the eye, no bending or stooping, just go home and rest. Sleep if you can."

"I hurt."

"I know, honey. And you're swelled up like—" She paused. "Like when you were first born, and they used the forceps on you." Her voice softened into sentimentality.

"Oh, jeez."

The car stopped for a red light. Her fingers played lightly over his hunched left shoulder like a spider crawling on it. He suppressed a shudder to listen to her.

"It'll get better. He told me he was really pleased with the incisions. As long as you don't get fluid buildup and those light auras, you'll be fine. I've got the Vicodin and the eyedrops. We'll go home, you'll take your pain prescription and go to bed."

"Right. And when I wake up, everything will be wonderful." It never had been before. His face itched. He put a hand up to scratch and bumped the dark glasses off his nose.

"Don't take your glasses off, honey!"

"I wasn't. They just fell." He maneuvered them back into position.

"Well, you don't want any side effects. Burst, or whatever they called it."

Flare, Brand thought but did not say it aloud. She would never get it right anyhow. He didn't know what it was, except that the doctor said it was a common side effect. Brilliant light, sometimes auras, around objects, disrupting the vision although it would eventually go away, if he developed it. He would welcome that if it happened. What he had now, along with the blurriness, were dark smudges, as though someone had clouded everything over with dirty fingerprints, blinding him.

Blind.

He shuddered again, and tasted something bitter at the back of his throat. He made a gagging sound.

The light changed, the car surged forward cautiously. "You just have to be more patient. With the operation, me, your stepfather—"

"Right." Brand cut her off. He didn't want to hear a thousand reasons why he had to be a saint while the dweeb could be a total jerk and get away with it. Although, he had to admit, the dweeb wasn't a jerk. Usually. And even if he was, Brand could deal with him. Brand had experienced worse in his life. Wrestled with it every day.

"Just think positive, all right? Do me that much of a favor."

"All right, Mom." Brand didn't turn around or take his clouded vision off the road. "You want it, you got it, Toyota." Landscape slid by. He wondered how blind he would get. If it didn't get much worse, he might be able to get by with a cane and a dog. Dogs were good. Girls liked dogs. The tattooed girl—

Of course, nobody would look at him twice with these things the doctor gave him hanging off his face.

Brand turned around in the car seat. "Hey, Mom."

"Yes?"

A little cold, but nothing he couldn't handle. "How about hitting the drugstore on the way home? I need some decent shades. I can't wear these things to school tomorrow. Not Ray Bans or anything, maybe just some imitation Quentin Tarantinos or something. If there's enough money left."

He thought he saw her lips tighten slightly. It wasn't as though he asked for much, ever. He waited.

Her jaw loosened. "All right. I think we can do that."

"Thanks." He settled back. Misery could be profitable. Not fun, but profitable.

* * * *

Nicholas Solis smiled into the vanity over their dresser as his wife put her arms about him. Her shapely arms were in sharp contrast to his police uniform and his own, squarish bulky body, crow's-feet etched heavily about his eyes and the whitish square above his left eyebrow where someone in South L.A. had once told him exactly what he'd thought about law enforcement.

He felt no small pleasure that, despite their decade's difference in age, his muscle tone was better than hers. That's the way it should be. He worked at it, to protect her. He concentrated on buttoning his uniform shirt and she seemed intent upon distracting him.

"Freeze," her small, muffled voice declared from behind his shoulder. "I've got you surrounded."

"Covered," he corrected.

"No," she insisted, her head nestled between his shoulder blades. She butted him gently to make her point. "Surrounded." She clasped her hands and

squeezed her arms tightly around him. The firm ro-
tundness of her six-month pregnancy pressed into the
small of his back, and Solis thought he could feel the
baby move in protest.

He laughed. "Hey! Both of you. I'm going to be late
for roll call."

"Tell them it was a hostage situation." Andrea Solis
moved slightly, her heart-shaped face coming into view
in the mirror. Soft hair, like waves of chocolate, broke
from her forehead and lapped about her shoulders. Her
eyes, neither green nor brown, smiled at him with tiny
lines echoing those around her generous mouth.

For just a half-beat, his heart responded to both the
unconscious sexuality of her beauty and the police situation she described, his pulse beginning to race. He
didn't have time for the one, and the likelihood of such
a situation in Brea took care of the other. This was
most definitely not South Central. He reached back
firmly and drew her away from him.

"I've got to go to work."

"I know, I know." Andrea made a fleeting pouty
mouth. "Still, I might have had fun with the SWAT
team."

He placed his palm over her stomach. Their unseen
child swam again under his touch. "You look like you
had fun with somebody."

"You should know." Andrea made a sandwich over
his hand with hers. "I wish you didn't have to go
today."

"I've got a double day off in just three days. We'll
do something then. Dinner, a movie—"

"I know, but I feel good today. No nausea, no back-
ache, my ankles are a normal size. Who knows what
kind of a wreck I'll be then?"

"I guess I'll just have to take my chances." He slid his hand away, picked up his cap.

"You think I'm spoiled."

"Not half as spoiled as I'd like you to be." Nick brushed his lips across her forehead. He would give her anything he could, this tiny, funny miracle who had, literally, saved his life. He had hoped, two years ago, that someone similar might be in his future, but he had never hoped for someone as wonderful as Andrea.

His dad's birthday was coming up the first of November. Nick would have to call and thank him, one more time. Thank him for the advice which made him change his job and think about picking up the pieces of his life instead of opting out. Thank him for taking him out of the line of fire and putting Nick just around the corner from this heart-shaped face with espresso eyes who would rescue him.

Andrea paused and gave him a look, brow crinkling at his sudden silence. "Nicky . . . what's wrong?"

"Nothing." Heedless of putting wrinkles into a crisp uniform shirt, he wrapped his arms around her and drew her as close as he could. "Absolutely nothing."

"You're sure?"

"Very sure." He released her. "Now remember, I'm not off until eleven."

"I won't worry! I promise." Andrea crossed her fingers. "Breakfast with my mom tomorrow?"

A groan escaped him. Andrea's mouth twitched slightly, but the gleam in her eyes danced. "Just to pick out wallpaper for the baby's room. You promised?"

"I know, I know." Actually, Andrea's mom was a good thing. If the rose didn't have a thorn, he might think he was still at the bottom of a bottle, still in the middle of a bad divorce, still asleep in a living nightmare. He could take Andrea's mom easily, when push came to shove. She just wanted what he wanted, the best for Andrea, although she seemed to enjoy butting heads with him to get it. He could manage. He had a pretty damn thick skull, witness the scar over his brow. "Set the alarm, we'll do breakfast. Just don't ask me to eat chorizo."

Sunshine broke on his wife's face.

He crossed the bedroom and reached into the hat shelf in the closet, where he kept his gun belt and shield, and took it down. He wouldn't put it on in the house, her unspoken request and his quiet compliance. When the baby came, they had agreed to put a lock on the closet. There would be no gunfire accident in this household. No tragic scenario. They had their whole future in front of them.

"Wake me," she said softly at the front door. "When you come in." She quirked an eyebrow to punctuate her request.

Nick grinned, bathed in the light of mid-morning, as he walked to his car. The job wasn't glamorous, it was even dull by his old standards, but it brought him home every night and that was a big plus. He had a life.

* * * *

Rembrandt stretched his legs as he got out of the rental car. He rubbed his eyes, then dropped his sunglasses back into place, his forehead smoothing after squinting into the glare off the parking lot. The air was dry and gritty. He could smell the smog, and the sound of the 57 freeway just to the east of the mall roared annoyingly in his ears.

Welcome to the good life in Southern California. He retrieved a folder from the front bucket seat and then shut the door, listening to the electronic locks secure the vehicle. He understood only one thing about why Christiansen could be in the area: the weather. Even at its worst, one hardly faced freezing to death while huddling over a heater grate. No, a derelict here was most likely to be clubbed to death by the state's active skinhead groups or maybe run over by a DUI while trying to cross the street . . . but Mother Nature was not likely to be the killer. Not that it didn't get cold and frosty once in a while. It did. But nothing that would pose a threat to his sergeant.

A Marine wasn't a Marine without a thick skin and good survival skills, and Christiansen had shown himself to be one of the best. Rembrandt had trailed him down the coast for the last few months until losing him completely just over the Oregon border. Once in California, his job was damn near a fool's errand. There was a whole civilization of derelicts on the Gold Coast, an underground if you would, and picking a single man out of it was like isolating a particular grain of sand from their ubiquitous beaches.

Finding him in the beginning had merely been a matter of tracing banking transactions, but then Christiansen's father had died, leaving him a considerable wad, and once that had been cashed, the man was gone. Bayliss had talked Rembrandt into setting up circumstances that made that old man's death look suspicious, just to get even, and that had forced Christiansen out of the area entirely. He couldn't go back unless he was willing to discuss with the authorities just how an ailing man had passed on, and if suffocation had been involved.

Beyond his skills at tracing, a little luck had been involved. Among the vets who worked the Santa Monica parks and beaches, he'd found someone who'd met

Christiansen. Had to have been the sergeant . . . no one else could have spouted a story of voodoo and military treachery and betrayal like his quarry, drunk or not. At that point, he was only two months behind him.

So what Rembrandt was doing now was searching inland, then coastal, zigzagging all the way down toward San Diego and Baja, California. In late October, even the homeless had moved off the cooling sands, to more sheltered parks and freeway underpasses. It rained even in Paradise.

Someone honked behind Rembrandt. He twisted about. A large woman with fashionable silvery hair leaned out of a forest green Jag. "Are you leaving?"

"Leaving?" His train of thought had been momentarily derailed and he was uncertain of her intention.

"Are you leaving the parking space?"

Ah. He shook his head courteously. "No, ma'am, I'm sorry. I just arrived."

Without another word, she pulled her head back in the window and patched out, the speed of her disappearing vehicle expressing her contempt. Rembrandt watched her drive the aisle at a rate of speed which might have qualified for the Indianapolis 500 and then gravely moved toward the bank of stores himself. He had work to do. He would start at the arcade, passing around the most decent photo of Christiansen he could dig up, then show the artist's rendering of what he might look like after months and months of neglect.

Someone might know his face.

*   *   *   *

Snake came back to the car, climbed in through the open passenger window and sat, sweat bubbling up through the pores of his head. He gave a wolfish grin.

"Found her." He licked his fingers before Darby could see what it was that stained them—slick and pinkish, he thought, but he couldn't be sure.

"That easy?"

Snake rubbed his hand dry on his jeans. "Quick, not necessarily easy." He looked out the window back up the weed-choked sidewalk to the small bungalow-style home. Sheets hung sloppily across picture windows. One of them rippled slightly as if the occupant pulled it aside to look out, then hastily draped back into place. "Kamryn tells Lyndall everything. Always."

"That bitch," Darby muttered and ground the gears of the car as it lurched forward. "Where is she?"

"Working. At the mall in Brea. She's got a place up there, too, somewhere. But it'll be easier to find her at the mall. Place called Hot Flash."

Those were more words than he had ever heard out of Snake at one time, but the information they contained held volumes. "I'm bringing her back," Darby said.

Snake writhed into a more comfortable position in the car seat. "Go by the pad first," he responded. "I need my stuff."

"I want to bring her back."

"And if she don't come, I'll need my stuff." Flat-voiced. Snake turned his head, so his eyes could meet Darby's. Flat eyes.

Darby swallowed hard at what he saw in them. "All right." He swung the car toward Costa Mesa. "If she doesn't come home with me, she's toast."

"She's mine," Snake corrected, his attention gone back to the windows and whatever it was he saw out of them.

Chapter 7

"Ma'am, I'd be pleased to stay with you until Animal Control arrives, but I want you to understand there's nothing I can do." He used the reassuring voice he'd learned to adopt on calls, but the agitated woman did not respond. Nick waited patiently before repeating, "Ma'am?"

A handkerchief, rapidly getting sodden and stained with mascara waved in answer. "Oh, I understand, Officer, I do, I really do. But . . ." The plump woman's face collapsed into a moon-round echo of an apple doll. "Tigger wouldn't hurt anyone. Not anyone. How anybody could do something like this . . .?" The handkerchief played over the body—half body—of a beloved cat. Its red-orange furriness lay in extremis on her well-manicured front lawn. There was a tremendous amount of fur, but little blood in what was left of the cat.

Nick squinted down the hillside at the line of brown-and-sand-painted homes which took up territory that had previously only been occupied by the oil company and coyotes. As the foothills had become more urban, the previous occupants had only withdrawn, waiting, as if hoping to reclaim their lands. The oil company had recently announced it was giving up. The coyotes were still there.

"Ma'am, you can't tell a coyote what to eat and what not to eat. We're not allowed to kill or trap and relocate them. We just try to live with them. As I understand it, you let your cat out early this morning and didn't find the, ummm, remains until just now."

She looked at him with eyes bloodhound red and sagging. Her lips thinned. "Officer, I don't need your lectures. Tigger was a longhaired cat, purebred Persian, and he enjoyed the coolness of the morning hours. But I did not shove him out the door. We keep him in the backyard. And I knew he was missing hours before I found this!"

Solis pitched a glare toward the house's backyard. Like all the others on the street, it was restricted to black bar fencing. Small dogs and wily coyotes could easily slip through the railing, although hers did seem to be hedged inside. "Mrs. Davis, ma'am—"

"Oh, for heaven's sake. Do you think I'm an imbecile? Young man, I have my yard fenced from the inside, where the association guard dogs can't see it. I don't want things wandering in and out of my yard all day and night. Come with me."

She pulled up the hem of her violet-flowered muumuu and strode determinedly away, stepping over the body of her late lamented buddy as though he no longer existed, and leading Nick toward the back of her property.

"See? There!"

He followed the pointing finger. Inside pink hawthorn and privet hedges, he could see the cleverly concealed fencing. It should have been, he reflected, effective against even high-jumping coyotes. "Perhaps," he suggested, "a meter reader let your cat out."

"I would be filing a complaint against the company now if I thought that." Mrs. Davis shook her head.

"Officer, Tigger was murdered, tortured, and I expect you to take a report."

He smothered a sigh. Sooner or later, he'd been told, he'd run into one of these. Ladies, mostly, who insisted their property bordered on the edge of a satanic coven, miserable people whose sole joy in life consisted of stealing, torturing, and quartering beloved pets. Stu Randall had told him of one of his calls where the woman actually kept the corpses in her deep freezer, hoping one day to prove her claim against her neighbors.

The county, of course, had looked at every corpse and pointed out the signs of coyote kill, but the woman had not listened. Did not to this day.

And Solis had had the luck to run into one of her disciples.

"Officer." Mrs. Davis stared at him with her gimlet eyes.

"I'm listening," he responded dutifully.

"I hope so. At the end of the street, where it leads out of the tract, there's a dirt road that goes into one of the back canyons. It's a fire lane, but there are squatter homes in there." Her faded lipstick mouth made another hard line. "When the oil company moves out, they'll be cleaned out, too, when the developers go in, but until then, we have to deal with them. The bikers are bad enough with their choppers, but then there're the others."

Solis kept his eyes on his pad as he took notes, smoothing down the expression of his face to a careful neutrality. He did not want trouble here. He did not *need* trouble. It was almost dark, and almost time for his dinner break. He found himself thinking about Andrea's promise to wake for him at the end of the long day. "Tell me about the others." He steeled himself for the satanic cult routine. The religious right slept hand in hand with the political conservatives of the county. They suspected everyone of either being anarchists or devil worshipers or gays, and his shift had already consisted of rousting one poor homeless guy from the environs around Brea Mall just because someone was offended he slept in the bushes. The guy would be back, he knew it and Solis knew it, but in the meantime some fat cat in his Mercedes had gotten his taxpayer's worth of his being displaced. Nick readied himself to listen to the woman's complaints.

"Young man, I know you're being civil, but it's written all over you." Mrs. Davis looked down at Tigger's body and pressed her handkerchief to her face, as if all her resolve had suddenly disappeared. She cleared her throat. "I'm not going to tell you it's witchcraft."

His pencil point stopped on the pad. "You're not?"

"No. I wish to be taken seriously. Have you heard of *Santeria*?"

Only when he'd served in hell. Nick found himself staring quietly at her face while she patiently waited for an answer. He shrugged a shoulder. "I worked in L.A. for a while. It's not unheard of."

"Animal sacrifice. That's what we've got living down in the canyon. I won't say they're evil, but they are opportunists. I think they needed Tigger, so they took him and then they returned what they didn't need. They kept his . . ." she sniffled "head . . . and . . ."

He saw a white panel truck pull up out of the corner of his eye. Solis interrupted. "Ma'am, here's Animal Control now. Let them examine the remains, dispose of them if you want them to—you can't bury him legally up here, but I understand if you want to—"

"You don't believe me."

"No, ma'am, I do." He snapped the cover over on

his notebook and stowed it in his uniform pocket. "Have you got a picture of your cat? An extra one?"

She blinked rapidly, then dipped her hand into the side slit pocket of her muumuu. She brought out a little plastic folder, filled with pictures of grandchildren and several of a magnificent rust-colored cat. She pulled one out.

"If it'll make you feel at ease, ma'am, I'll just drive over. This will help me ID any remains."

"Thank you, Officer. Thank you very much."

Nick nodded and started down the sloping driveway. The female Animal Control officer swapped looks with him, and he just dropped his head in a short salute of acknowledgment. He did not think Mrs. Davis would fare so well with the no-nonsense looking woman, who'd probably had it up to her eyebrows with people who let their adored animals outside to become coyote appetizers.

On the other hand, he did have more than a passing familiarity with Santeria, not devil worship, but a religious ritual which did require sacrifices. Out of all the officers in Brea's police department, he was probably the only one who would have understood. So for that, if nothing else, he owed her a side trip down that dusty road. Dinner would have to wait, even though he had a distinctly empty feeling inside.

The sun lowered behind the scrubby, heat-burned hills, casting the canyon in long, purple shadows. It was that eerie time between dusk and night, and Nick found himself looking forward to the not so distant weekend when Daylight Savings would be repealed. Always around Halloween it seemed nighttime would never come and then the hours changed, and it fell, dropping like a guillotine blade into place with its immense darkness. The changing of the hours was the start of the winter season in Southern California, which only really had two seasons, winter and summer. Darkness and light.

His right front tire hit a rut in the dirt road and the car skewed around for just a second, headlights piercing off the road into eucalyptus and brush, and he saw eyes reflecting back at him, eerily, in the twilight. The hair went up on the back of Nick's neck. He wrestled the car back onto the road. He spotted the goat again, eyes shining, and saw the rope around its neck, tethering it. Beyond, the shanty-sided house.

This had to be the Santeria suspect house. He did not recall that bikers had any particular fondness for goats, while the beast was an almost staple for sacrifice in Santeria. In this country, old goats had little other use as goat meat was not often eaten in the U.S. Some of the immigrants from the south were starting to change that, but it was not a meat, which, barbecued or stewed, had found many converts yet.

So the goat which watched him warily, yellow pupils gleaming like snake eyes from the shadow, probably was not here for its meat which, although it did not prove Mrs. Davis' statement, gave her more immediate credence.

Nick pulled the patrol car into the driveway, noting the mid-80's model Malibu which sat close to the door of the house, its springs broken from the way the frame sagged to one side. He had easy flight blocked with his unit. He pulled up the mike and gave his location. Dispatch didn't respond immediately, then gave him an answer, distracted.

"What's up?"

She gave him the code for a freeway high-speed chase. It meant he wouldn't have backup available, but he didn't really think he needed any. He responded, "Tell 'em good luck."

"I copy that," she said and left again. Nick clicked off, knowing that all attention, including TV network helicopters, would be following the chase drama. Last month some kid had stolen a fire engine and taken it from North County all the way to Laguna Beach, chippies and locals following him all the way. It had been prime time on the news channel for nearly ninety minutes.

He hung up the mike, took his flashlight off his belt, and turned it on. The torch was a substantial weight in his hand, meant to be used as a weapon if necessary. He didn't think it would be. Santerias were, mostly, nonviolent. He did not approve of them, but he knew that if Mrs. Davis' cat had been taken by them, he would have died at their hands rather quickly and cleanly before being harvested for his other organs. Only kosher butchers killed more humanely. He did not expect any trouble.

Then, of course, there were always those times when he was wrong.

Within four feet of the front door, he could smell the sweet coppery reek of blood and hear the panicked bleating of a lamb.

* * * *

It was after midnight in Haiti. Delacroix sat comfortably in the dirt, the small creatures of the night crawling over his bare crossed legs as if as unaware of him as he was of them. Their chirps and hums underscored the sound of his barely audible chanting. The air was thick with evening moisture and warm and redolent with the smell of his last offering and the incense he burned.

Because of the time of year and the phase of the moon, he knew that other people in other places would also be making sacrifices, though they prayed to other gods than he did. It scarcely mattered. He had been given such power that the common tie of spilled blood gave him entrance to their ritual, if he wished. He knew every drop they sprinkled, every twig and ash they burned, every syllable they uttered.

He had little care for their petty and feeble attempts to gain favor. They scarcely understood what they did. They were beneath his contempt. Others would deal with them. Delacroix had no need to be concerned for them.

Tonight, however, something stirred. It was not another mambo, though he knew it was inevitable he would someday spar again with the woman who had fought his loa. No, this was different. It came to him on droplets of crimson, riding the back of another sacrifice, far, far away. It brought to him not only the rich scent of freshly spilled blood and homage, but a touch of the man he searched for. Delacroix's back stiffened as it touched him.

So faint was the trace that he had to withdraw from his other thoughts and focus his trance on this single incidence. The vision came to him through the death-dimmed green-gold eyes of a rusty-haired cat.

The man in question wore a uniform and he was police, and, ah, Delacroix had had much dealing with police. He knew their lust for power was universal, and their cruelty, and their corruption. How different could Haiti be from this other spot in the world? And though this man was not the military man Delacroix sought, he had passed him by recently. Perhaps that day, last week. The resonance was unmistakable. Once the loa was in possession, he could use the policeman to back-track and find the man he sought.

Delacroix began to chant loudly, swaying from side to side, and he fanned his hands out palms up, gesturing to the night and the sacrifices he had made and he felt the loa returning to him, still hungry, still filled with the powerful magic Delacroix had given him. Delacroix felt his body move with the ecstasy of the forces filling him and when it was time, he sent the loa to do his bidding. For a moment, his own spirit soared as well, leaving the empty body to topple over sideways and lie twitching in the dust like a lizard's suddenly detached tail.

They came, like invisible smoke, out of the cat's green-gold eyes, exploding into the eyes and mouth and nose of the policeman as he bent to look, and they took him with no trouble at all. He had been holding the platter with the sacrifice upon it, and dropped it suddenly, stricken, the bleating of the lamb pulsating in time with the pounding of his heart. The loa was well pleased.

Delacroix withdrew before his own heart began a troubled beat and found his flesh cooling like the night, softly, gently, inexorably. He would be stiff in the morning, and perhaps insect bitten, but he would be full of the might of his magic.

He felt his loa take the blood of the lamb and leave the shanty, striding within the body of the policeman. The hunting would be good.

* * * *

Brand lay curled in a fetal position. It seemed to help, although he could count on the fingers of both hands all his ex-wardmates it *hadn't* helped. He lay willing himself to see when he opened his eyes, the blankets of his bed all skirled around him like some gigantic nest. But he wasn't alone.

Bauer lay curled with him. Breathing with his breath, thinking with his thoughts, and all Brand could do was lie very still, terrified, horrified, at what would happen if he were blind, shut into the darkness with Bauer.

Bauer liked slicing. Maiming. Torturing. He lived somewhere deep inside Brand's mind, and he was imprinted there, behind his eyeballs. When there was nothing to be seen, he liked to show Brand *his* visions. Blood-streaked sights. Torn flesh. The cries of innocents.

Dr. Susan Craig had given him Bauer. Wrapped them together like a ball of yarn, rainbow yarn, whose strands changed color as you pulled them free, never quite sure which color would follow what. Brand's grandmother had always liked to knit with yarn dyed like that, until her heart had attacked her and she'd died. He twisted his fingers now in one of the afghans she'd made for his room. Indigo fading into blue fading into green fading into lime fading into indigo. . . .

Brand knew that Bauer was just waiting for Brand to fade away completely, waiting quietly, coiled away in the corners of his mind and thoughts, hiding in the shadows. As long as Brand could see at all, any point of light, he could wrestle Bauer back. This was still his body, his life.

As long as he could see. They wanted him shut away without light, warned him against it, but they did not understand it was more necessary than air to him.

Brand opened his eyes. As he looked across the room, the door jumped into sharp relief and then blurred abruptly. His heart leaped too. He'd never been able to see the door well without his glasses before. He sat up in bed, his chest thumping with apprehension, as a smudgy cloud lowered itself over everything he tried to view.

"Oh, God." He put his fingers up to his eyes, thinking to claw the veil away, unable to do more than just touch his flesh, unable to save himself, afraid of doing more damage than had already been done. Nothing he could do erased the smudges.

His heart felt as though it dropped away, right through the bottom of him, sinking like a lead anchor, through the bed, through the second-story flooring, the first floor, the house's foundation, the bedrock below it, and on into the center of the world, plunging downward.

Right into hell.

His chest immediately caved in on the vacuum. He couldn't breathe. His throat clenched. He was blind and locked in with Bauer. He was the scum of the Earth. He was *evil* beyond imagining.

He was alone.

Brand hugged himself, doubled over. He panted, and his ears dully told him that he whimpered, over and over, "Yellow Dog, Yellow Dog," like it was some kind of mantra which would save him. His face grew damp. His heart returned to thump like a painful drum inside his body, making his pulse roar. He thought it would explode.

His mother knocked on the door.

"Brandon? Brandon, are you all right?"

He stuffed his fist into his mouth, as Bauer fought to answer, something incredibly crude and cruel. He chewed on his knuckles. He couldn't let her know. He found his tongue, forced a voice out.

"What?"

His mother peeked in. "Were you sleeping?" The hallway light was faint, a parchment yellow, but he found himself blinking painfully at it.

"Yeah."

She smiled weakly. "That's good, isn't it?"

If a living nightmare isn't in residence, waiting for night to fall. . . . He heard the relief in her voice. She walked the same tightrope he did, he thought suddenly, and she no more wanted him to unbalance her than vice versa. And part of that delicate act was not to be too involved. What he wanted, he thought, was a hug, but he would not get it from her. She feared he would shatter. And he feared she would refuse if he asked. So he did not.

"Yeah."

"How do your eyes feel?"

"Sore."

One of his sibs poked her head in. "Brandon, your eyes are all swollen! You look like a Mike Tyson fight victim."

"I wish." He grinned feebly. "Think of all that money."

She beamed even as their mother gently nudged her out the door, saying, "His doctor said bed rest today. Now leave him alone."

"But we're hungry."

"I want to make sure Brandon's all right."

He didn't need her hovering over him. He wanted company, but not theirs. He wanted to walk with people who knew him well enough to thump his shoulder but didn't ask him if he was sleeping well. If he was still sane. If he was going to be all right.

Phil appeared in the doorway, too, his bland face a pleasant blur. "Awake, sport?"

He really, really wanted all of them to leave. "Not much. Why don't you take the gang out somewhere? I'll be okay."

"What are you going to eat?"

"I'm not hungry."

"Well. . . ."

He could see a tiny movement of hesitation. Sweat beaded his upper lip. He was going to have another anxiety attack, he could feel his chest closing, like a vise of ice was gripping it, and he did not, DID NOT, want any witnesses. "Order me a pizza."

"I could do that."

Phil added, "I'll leave the money on the sofa table by the door, okay?"

A long pause. His mother repeated. "Okay, honey?"

He balled his hands back into fists. "Right. Gotcha." His voice sounded strained to himself, but they backed slowly away from his door.

"Don't forget to take your medicine," his mother called out faintly, and then she was gone.

He found himself holding his breath, looking at the closed door, as though she would come back, would invade again.

He had to get into the light. Nothing blazed brighter than the mall.

But he couldn't go like this. Brandon pushed himself out of bed. His eyes focused, then lost it again, but he knew his room well enough to get to his bureau. Once within hand-reach of it, even his damaged eyes could see it well enough.

He tore through the clouds and found the drawer he wanted and pulled it up. At the back, stuffed behind clothes which had been thrown in every which way, he found his stash. He took the bandanna out and opened it carefully.

Even to his dimmed sight, he could see the reds and yellows and blues, the black and whites, capsules and tablets. Hands shaking, he picked out what he needed. Horseshoe-shaped, with a hole in the center. Haldol. One made him mellow, dealt with anxieties and depression. Psychoactive. They'd taken him off it when the doctors had decided he wasn't schizophrenic, but they hadn't taken the prescription away, and he'd hidden his remaining tablets, for they had shielded him against Bauer. Today, he decided he needed help to keep Bauer at the gates. Two should do it. He shoved aside the bentyls and the Prozac. Not strong enough. He looked up, saw the vial of Vicodin the ophthalmologist had given him for pain. They had worked admirably so far that day. Again, two. "Better living through chemistry," he muttered and choked them down, following it with half a glass of tepid water left on the nightstand.

He crawled back into his nest and hugged his grandmother's afghan to his body. He kept his eyes wide open until the first of the drugs overwhelmed him, and then the wave hit, an onslaught which quelled even Bauer, and Brand fell back onto the bed.

He was not used to the Vicodin, he thought. The codeine was giving him hallucinations. He thought he could hear a muttering, a snuffling, a dragging, like something from the graveyard coming after him. He could feel a cold touch sweep over him, blindly searching. He opened his raw eyes wide.

He saw it then, not Bauer, not Yellow Dog, but a thing . . . a thing like an elongated human shadow, a hungry thing, with a sucking mouth, traveling through his house, across his ceiling, searching, questing. He thought to touch it, and then recoiled.

Whatever it was, it was not human. Unlike Bauer, had never been.

And was far, far worse.

It responded to his touch, shadow-thing and dove down at him.

Brand screamed until his throat went raw and flailed to leap out of bed, knocking his curtains aside, letting the last of the afternoon sun flood in. . . .

Yellow Dog leaped out of the sunlight, barking, snarling, after the shadow-thing, driving it away.

Brandon snatched up his sunglasses, both grateful and alarmed, and lay still on his bed until the pharmaceuticals began to buzz in his bloodstream. He did not remember Yellow Dog leaving or falling asleep.

He was awake, without remembering he'd awakened, the room smelling of pizza and cheese stringing from his fingers. He looked at himself in the mirror, image sharpening as he leaned toward the glass. "What a buzz! You answered the door and don't even remember it!" The Vicodin and Haldol surged through his bloodstream, an overwhelming sense of well-being and even, hey, how about this, happiness.

There were times when his mother approached all right, catching a glimpse of himself, dark hair and all, like a protegé Quentin Tarantino. The shades were awesome, even if he did have to stand almost chin close to see himself. His pupils looked huge, staring out of puffy lids. Brand giggled slightly, then cleared his throat and sobered. "I had eye surgery today," he told himself. "Keep your shades on."

The house was quiet. This feeling was too good to contain stowed away in his bedroom, with the lights on low, extra cheese and pepperoni dripping over the crust, munching and wondering what to do.

He wanted to be hip, not good.

He wanted bright lights and action. Even if it hurt. Because nothing could touch him now.

Brand sighed.

The phone rang. He wiped grease-glistening fingers on his jeans and picked it up on the second ring. "Speaking."

"Hey, X-man. Feeling better? Your mom wouldn't let me talk to you earlier. Told me not to call on your line."

"No surprise. You're not exactly her favorite person after letting me get canned."

Curtis made a rude noise and said, "Your mom eats it."

"Hey, don't rag on her, all right. She tries, sometimes."

"No kidding? She must have done something right, huh, for you to care. So tell me."

"I've got Tarantino shades."

"Oh, shit. Really? How do they look?"

Brand sat straight up in his bed. The pizza box slid off his lap and landed sloppily on the floor, but it was still cool, it landed pizza side up. "They look great."

"Wear 'em to school tomorrow."

"Can't."

"Why not?"

"Don't think I'm going."

"Still feel bad?"

"No. I feel stoned. I need to make the mall. Okay?"

"Cool." Curtis hung up.

Brand stood up quickly and felt the answering throb in his eyeballs, reminding him. "Whoa—head rush." He put a hand to his brow as if he could check the sensation. He grinned at himself as he climbed out the bedroom window.

Chapter 8

It wasn't dark yet, but nearly, and the concrete peaks of the mall threw long, dark purple shadows across the canyons of the parking lot as Kamryn pulled in and scanned the employee lot over the steering wheel. On the unpopular side of the mall were the freight ramps where, descending into the lower level of the older mall, there were all sorts of nooks and crannies that she hesitated to walk by. The security cameras tended to focus on the front two-thirds of the oval shopping center, protecting the customer rather than the worker. Weather had been no factor in designing the center—what weather?—and so the parking lots swooped around the shops like a Grand Prix street circuit, flat and open to anyone and everyone.

Only the new, upscale stores had garage structures. Built on graded acreage, the mall was single story at the south end and rose three stories toward the grander shops at the northern end.

At the upper level, the new end, the parking garage which twinned Nordstrom's glared with light, except she saw, the third level, which lay plunged in darkness. Someone must have gone through and broken the bulbs again. Probably the skaters, intent on vandalism. It would take a day or two for maintenance to get in there and replace the fixtures. Meanwhile, there was no protection for her at all except alertness. Leaning over, she thumped all the door locks into place, as though that could make some sort of safe house or fortress out of the vehicle. The irony of her actions did not escape her.

She gathered her wallet and climbed out the driver's door, looking across the lot. It wasn't too crowded, which might give her something of a break as it was her night to work the coffee bar, something she normally did not mind, but she did not feel right about tonight. An odd sensation had been crawling over her skin all day, a sensation she would not place and did not like. She had tried several times to call Lyndall to talk things over with her—her friend had a natural psychic sense about things, but the ringing phone had never been answered.

She chafed her fingers lightly over her long sleeves, trying to soothe the healing skin underneath. Maybe it was just her nerves reacting to the laser work. She felt raw, every nerve exposed. Or maybe she just didn't feel like going to work. Sometimes she wondered how other people did it, by rote. Not that Darby had ever worked to take care of her. Darby was only a temporary port in a storm, shelter she'd taken out of desperation, and now that she could think clearly, she was well rid of him.

Kamryn slowed as she approached the concrete stairwell which descended into the back wing of the mall. The store didn't want employees coming in the back door anymore. Hot Flash had posted a new policy that entrances must be made into the mall itself, and then into the store by the front. She hesitated at the top step, looking down into a hole that already lay pooled in darkness, thinking that she was probably the only one who minded.

Her feet refused to make the descent. Kamryn swallowed tightly. For a moment, she thought she could feel the steely hand upon her neck, gripping her, the hard barrel of a gun digging into her flesh just below her opposite ear.

Come on, sis. Come down into the basement with me. I've got a surprise for you.

Her joints locked. She could not move, could not take that first step. It wasn't the basement of her old Pennsylvania home, she knew that. But she couldn't help staring down into the black pool of shadows, and she couldn't help the tremors of fear that began to ripple through her body.

Come on, sis. I've got a surprise for you.

Now, as she had then, she began to pray. *God, get me through this, and I'll change. I swear I will. Just get me through this.*

Those stairs were not these stairs. As she told herself that, her knees bent and she went down a step. Kamryn fought to take a steadying breath. Was this like claustrophobia? Did it have a name, this choking tightness in her chest, this panic that made her ears deaf and her heart explode into her throat and her bowels clench?

Stair-o-phobia.

The thought loosened a squeaky laugh. She put a hand out to catch herself, and jammed a thumb into the hard wall of the stairwell. That brought a curse, hoarse and barely audible, but the sound of her own voice echoed. It pierced the numbness that gripped her. She cleared her throat, stuffing down the air, trying to relax.

There's nothing down here but a turn at the bottom and a door into a universe of shoppers. That's it. That's all.

Kamryn managed another step. She could feel the

leading edge of coolness where the shadows lay. It was like plunging into a swimming pool, she told herself. Brisk. Cold. Frightening, but without reason. There was nothing to be afraid of here. She had run from Pennsylvania and even though Darby was not the haven, the guardian, she'd wanted him to be, still she was not living the nightmare any longer.

She plunged down the last four steps, stilt-legged, at breakneck speed, but that was the only way she was going to get down them, at this rate, and she dropped her wallet on the last step and kicked it, skidding, around the corner toward the entrance door. It disappeared in the darkness. Anger replaced the phobia.

"Oh, shit." Kamryn bent over to retrieve it.

"I've got it."

Her choked lungs kept her from screaming. She bolted backward, fetching up against the wall, trapped, caught, nowhere to run. She felt her eyes bulge, her throat paralyzed. Grime-encrusted hands came out of the enveloping darkness, groping toward her, fingers wrapped about the wallet.

"Don't scream. I didn't mean to scare you."

He took a step toward the mall door and the faint illumination cast from it. She saw the disheveled hair, the worn and somewhat dirty clothes, but it took a moment longer to place the face. She knew this man, a transient who'd been hanging about the mall almost as long as she'd been working there.

Kamryn didn't feel much better about touching him. She stared at her wallet.

"I'm sorry. Really. I didn't mean to scare you," he repeated. "Don't yell or anything. Please."

"I'm lucky I can breathe." Kamryn took her wallet back gingerly. "What are you doing down here?"

"Other than scaring people?"

"This is an employee entrance. I *know* you're not working here."

"No," he said dryly. "I'm not working here." He looked behind her, to where the sunlight gleamed across the top of the stairs, as if deciding on something. "I'm trying to avoid somebody."

"What did you do?"

"Nothing."

"Someone's looking for you?"

"I think so."

"Police?"

He hesitated, then shook his head.

"You must have done something."

"Sometimes," he answered slowly, "all you have to do is exist."

She wasn't all that certain that what he was doing was even on that level.

She steeled herself against her gut reaction, answering, "I won't tell anyone you're here, but if you're hiding, this is not the place to do it. Hot Flash has everyone coming in here now."

"Thanks for the tip." He started upward, then turned. "You won't tell anyone—"

"You scared the hell out of me? No." She felt her lips twist in a lopsided smile. "Besides, somebody's already done that to me."

He gave her a saluting nod and continued to the parking lot. She watched him disappear. The panic had ebbed, leaving behind a raw chill. She decided she needed a good, strong cup of coffee and she knew exactly where to get it. Kamryn pressed through the door into the mall, gathering enough wits to think, *Thank God it wasn't Darby.* The thought sent her hurrying down the marble corridor.

* * * *

"Watch out for Brewster's Rottweiler," Curtis warned as they skirted the corner.

"She loose again?"

"Mom says she's going to call Animal Control. Says the dog's gonna kill somebody someday."

Brand took his friend's opinion in silence. He personally liked Rottweilers, but like many of the bigger guard dog breeds, they'd been spoiled by bad owners. He was of the opinion no dog was born bad. As they rounded the yard where the dog was kept, he looked through the chain-link. The wind, threatening all day to pick up into Santa Anas, rattled the fencing and the dog came charging from behind the stucco house, barking loudly. To his surprise, he could see her quite well.

Curtis jumped, but Brand halted. She was a beautiful dog, even frothing in anger at their intrusion as she was, heavily muscled, black and tan, with eyes a cinnamon brown. He looked at her, wondering what she saw in him, gawky teenager in cool shades, and something dark and splintery crossed his eyes. *Damnit*.

The dog's barking beat at his senses. He waited to see if the splinters would leave, but they didn't. He clenched his jaw in irritation. Curtis tugged at his arm, indicating they should beat it, but Brand shook his head. His eyes watered a little and he blinked furiously to clear his vision. The dog lunged against the chain-link, spittle flying, ivory teeth clashing. With every bark, a cloud of hatred seemed to be emerging, a thin, smoky substance which enveloped the animal. Brand stood in wonderment.

"What is that?"

"That is one angry dog-bitch. Now let's get out of

here," Curtis shouted over the Rottweiler's incessant barking.

Froth from her lips splattered the knee of his jeans. She snapped at the air and more spittle went flying.

"Oh, man," Curtis groaned. He wiped his face with the back of his hand. "This is too gross. Come on!"

Brand stayed, rocked back on his heels, transfixed. "You don't see anything else?"

"I see a fence between us, and a house that's gonna spit out some angry broad in about two seconds. Brand-on, please."

Brand put the tip of his forefinger at the edges of his glasses frame and, very carefully, edged them up, just a little, so he could look at the dog. He could see the charcoal smoke had not really dissipated; but had settled about the animal like a cloak, like a big, dark Darth Vader cloak.

"Brand!"

"All right, all right, I'm coming." He let Curtis haul him down the street until the dog's baritone barking faded to nearly nothing. He looked back over his shoulder. The Rottweiler stood in the full blast of the last of the setting sun, and she looked like a thunderhead. The clarity with which he'd first seen her fled. Brand stood a moment, dealing with the uncertainty of his life and vision.

"I can't deal with this if you're going to weird out on me," Curtis said.

He didn't know if he could deal with it either. He didn't have that many drugs. The irony of it tugged at the corner of his mouth before he answered.

"I like dogs."

"Not that one. I swear she's a killer."

"Only because she's been taught that way."

"Mom says it's the backyard breeders. You know,

cross one bad temperament with another. Anything for money. You end up with mean pups, or scared ones that'll go mean. Anyway, she doesn't trust that one."

"Don't blame her."

Curtis looked him full in the face. "Thought you liked her."

"I do, but—" Brand shrugged. "There was something about her. You know?"

Curtis tried a demented laugh, finishing, "The Shadow knows what evil lurks in the hearts of men. And dogs."

Brand smiled thinly. "Something like that, I guess." They crossed the last intersection approaching the mall and its lesser plazas. "That must be where Nova got Captain Evel from."

"The Shadow?"

"Sure. He can see the alien possessed, right?"

"Yeah, but—"

"They stole him. Plain as anything. I wonder if they can sue."

"Who?"

"The Shadow people. Wonder if there's anybody alive who owns the rights."

"Like I care."

"Your dad's a lawyer. You should." Brand gave Curtis an affectionate shove.

"My dad," said Curtis in a mix of admiration and disgust, "can sue anything that walks." He added, "Anyway, Nova's a cool game."

"It doesn't exactly suck," Brand agreed.

"So, if you could do it, would you?"

"Do what?"

Curtis twisted his face. "See evil."

"If it were possible."

"Let's say it was. Let's say you went to see the Dalai

Lama or somebody like that, and they took a sacred crystal and they implanted it in your forehead, right between your eyes, like a third eyeball or something, only nobody else could see it. And whenever you looked through it, you could see all evil."

"You're really into this."

Curtis bumped him. "Just answer me. Would you?"

He didn't want to answer, but he knew Curtis would bug him all the way to the arcade if he didn't. "Hell, no."

"No?"

"No. Everybody's got their dark side—we've all done something. Stomped ants or something. Forget it, Curtis." His voice changed slightly, uncomfortably. "And don't tell me you would. You'd rather have X-ray vision and see through people's clothes."

"You wouldn't do?"

"Absolutely not."

"But you play Captain Evel."

"That's different. I like stomping aliens." They completed their walk arguing over finessing the finer strategies of the game.

Approaching the arcade, Curtis ground to a halt. "Whoop, whoop. Old dude at the doorway."

Brand looked. He saw a tall, dark-haired man in a suit half-blocking the doorway, with papers in his hands. He wore a tie, but had unbuttoned the collar of his shirt and loosened the knot. His skin had been pitted horribly and Brand let his stare slide away.

"Evenin' boys," the man said and let his white, even teeth show in a half-smile.

They stopped warily.

"I'm looking for somebody. Think you might help?" He had a slight accent, just enough to tell Brand

that he wasn't from around Southern California, and
his tone was a little too casual. He didn't look like a
casual person. His spine was ramrod stiff.

"Aren't you a little old to be hanging around ar-
cades?" Curt answered.

The man flushed slightly, but Brand sensed it was
not with embarrassment. The man's hands twitched.
He held up the pages. "Maybe you can tell me if you've
seen him around anywhere?"

"You a cop?"

"No, no. Nothing like that. I'm an attorney. He's
inherited some money and the family wants me to find
him. You could help him out. He might even be real
grateful you did."

Curt bypassed Brand and kicked him lightly in the
foot as he went, and disappeared into the arcade. The
man stayed, head slightly atilt, eyes locked on Brand.

This was no attorney. Curt had let him know that
as he went by. But Brand didn't think he was a cop
either. So the curiosity of what he was, and what he
wanted, held him. His gaze flickered to the pictures,
one a copy of a photo, and the other a drawing. He
looked at them briefly through his Quentin Tarantino
shades.

Then he shook his head. "Haven't seen him."

The inquirer shook the papers. "You're sure?"

"Listen, like I pay attention to people like that. I've
got better things to do." Brand shrugged. "Try a milk
carton."

He turned sideways and shifted past into the arcade.
Curtis was waiting for him. He snaked his hand out
and collared Brand, dragging him into the twilight
safety.

"What'd you say to him?"

"Nothing much. Did that look like Mitch to you?"

"No. What do you think?"

"Maybe," Brand said slowly. "Maybe not. What do you think he wants him for?"

"Nothing good," retorted Curtis mournfully. "Nothing good."

Brand looked back over his shoulders where the propped open door showed no one lurking. The man had gone. He straightened his shirt where his friend had collared him. "Did he look funny to you?"

"He looked scary."

Brand was not sure he had repaid his debt to Mitch. He pulled aside, to the pay phone, and placed a call to the Brea police department. He cleared his throat, waiting for the desk to pick up. The faint *beep* which told him the call was being recorded sounded almost before the desk sergeant's voice.

"Brea Police."

"Hi. Um, I'm calling from the mall." Brand let his voice go high and breathy, trying to recapture the tones of his immature self. "There's a guy hanging around here—an old guy—and well, he doesn't seem normal, if you know what I mean."

"Has he been bothering anyone?"

"Well . . . not yet. But he has this picture he keeps showing around, someone he says he wants to find, and he wants one of us to go with him to look."

Curtis twitched a lip at him as their eyes met, and he gave a thumbs up. "We shouldn't go with him, should we? I mean, my mom always said—"

"We'll send somebody over to talk to him," the desk sergeant said. "Can you give me a description?"

Brand repeated the most accurate description of the stranger he could remember. He added, "Uh-oh," and hung up, cutting off the desk sergeant in mid-sentence.

*   *   *

The desk sergeant listened to dead air, and then the dial tone. He thought for a moment, when a faint *beep* reminded him that the call had been monitored. If it had been legitimate, and not a prank, there would be a record. And if it had been some kid fooling with his mind, there was a record of that, too. It was a win-win situation from where he was sitting.

He took a look at the duty board. Nicholas Solis was cruising the afternoon shift, one of the few who hadn't been involved in the high-speed chase and wasn't up to his knees in paperwork. Nick was amiable and streetwise. He put out a call, sending him to check up on things at the gaming center at the mall.

"That ought to take care of him."

Brand pushed his sunglasses into place. "I think so."

Curtis turned away, his interest already riveted on the machines. "Got any more quarters?"

Brand slipped one from his pocket, rolled it through his fingers and produced it, sleight of hand, in midair. His friend snatched it away. Despite the wave he rode, of being stoned, events were eating away at his edge. He did not know sleight of hand—Bauer did.

Oh, my, Grandmother, what quick fingers you have.

The better to slice you with, my dear. And, instead of the silvery coin, he could see a knife blade gripped in his hand.

He would not scream. Or sweat. Or faint. He just simply would *be*, and in that being, Bauer still could not gain the foreground. As long as there was light, as long as he could see, as long as he was not left alone with the dark. Brand did not move for another long minute, staring at the beam of sunlight through the doorway, weak and diluted as it was as the sun set. When he finally turned away, it was fighting the instinct to rub his eyes, as though he could clear them of the smudges. The doctor had warned him of flare, but this was not a flash of light or bright aura. The blurring had begun to sharpen, replaced by this strange phenomenon he could not name.

This was something dark and dreadful.

Nick found himself sitting at the light, coming down out of the Brea hills, waiting for the signal to change. He stank of blood. His driver's side window was down, as if he'd needed to gulp in fresh air. He looked at his hands and found them, still pink and sticky, fingers wrapped tightly about the steering wheel.

"Oh, Jesus." He pried his hands away, the skin burning, as though the dried blood had stuck him like glue to the wheel. He leaned over to the glove box, where he kept those packets of cleansing towels and as he did, he saw what rode in the passenger seat.

"Shit!"

The cat's head seemed to eye him with fogged green orbs, the rusty hairs of his neck serrated and matted even more rusty with dried blood and ganglia. Without conscious thought, he scooped up the object and threw it out his window, then sat sweating by the open portal.

"Dear God in heaven." How had he gotten it—and why?

Nick tore the towelette open and rubbed his hands clean, scrubbing them over and over and over. When he'd finished, he found himself thinking of retrieving the head, bringing it back to the woman who'd owned and loved that cat, but he couldn't bring himself to touch it. Not again. His mouth felt dry as cotton, and his hands shook as he put the window back up.

This was stupid. But he'd gone into that arroyo and done something he couldn't remember, and come back with an object so horrible that it gave him the heaves just to think of it—

Get a grip, Nicky. You've seen worse in South Central.

Yeah, which is why I'm riding *here* tonight.

Nick took a steadying breath.

There was nobody at the light but him, and so he sat through two complete cycles, shaking, trying to remember what had happened. Nothing came to mind. When the dispatcher came over the radio, sending him to the mall, it sounded like a good idea. Bright lights and people, mindless yuppies, shining auras of streetlights over the parking lots.

Nothing like the dark canyon where he seemed to have temporarily lost his mind.

Nick gave a last shudder and when the light turned green, he let the patrol car surge forward in answer.

Chapter 9

Sandy had purple-red hair, finger-waved about her head, large hazel eyes, and a sprinkling of cinnamon freckles over her nose. She also had a navel ring, set off by the trendy crop-top blouse she wore and a short suede leather skirt. She met Kamryn at the espresso bar, her full lips set into a pout.

"Cam-er-on," she greeted. "The freakin' espresso machine is not working a-*gain*. I can't do anything."

Kamryn stifled a sigh as she pulled the hot pink and yellow chef's apron on over her head. "Did you close the valves, Sandy? Did you check them?"

Sandy put a hand on her hip, the Hot Flash bar where one of the front display windows would normally have been, and studied the monster espresso machine that took up half the back counter. "The whole flippin' machine is nothin' but valves. How would I know?"

Kamryn approached the machine, assuming an air of calm. If she said anything to Sandy, she would get a mouth full of attitude back, and sulkiness all evening. Espresso bar duty was hellish enough without having to run it by herself—and Sandy in a sulk was less than nothing. She checked the settings and valves swiftly, found that two had been left open, closed them, and then ran through the last of the check. "Got it. Why don't you weigh the grind, make sure we've got enough for tonight?"

Sandy stepped in and busied herself.

Kamryn opened the refrigerator doors to double-check the milk, whipping cream, and other perishables. "Looks like we're in business."

"I don't know," Sandy said slowly, her voice muffled as she looked into the various coffee grind containers, "why I just can't seem to get the espresso machine to work."

"It's just temperamental. And it's not that you can't get it to work. You just have trouble getting it started. It's working now," Kamryn said pointedly.

"True. You're just cool with things like that. And, like with the gloves you wear and all." She cast an envious hazel eye on the lacy half-gloves Kamryn wore. They hid the rough pink patches from the laser work. She'd cut the fingers off halfway, like some of the winter mitten styles, and Sandy was one of the girls from Hot Flash who'd commented on them. Sandy measured out some Java Gold beans and poured them into the grinder. "They've got the transfer aps out."

"Oh?" Kamryn had been waiting for the forms. "Where to?"

"Seattle and Palo Alto. I don't know." Sandy shrugged. "The Bay area is all right, but I wouldn't want to go to Seattle. For one thing, it rains all the time, and for the other—half of everybody there is already from California."

"Sounds all right to me."

"Yeah, but—" Sandy gave her a sideways glance from under a swinging purple tress. "Don't you have a boyfriend or something?"

"Had. The farther away I get, the better."

"Oh." The girl punctuated her understanding with a

burst from the grinder. "It won't get busy for another half hour or so, when the theater lets out. I'll watch it if you want to pick up some applications. You have to ask for them ... 'opportunities are limited,' " she added, mocking the cold tones of the store manager. She poured the freshly ground coffee into the container. "And if you're looking for a new boyfriend, you could always pick up the one from the arcade." She laughed, a high, whining sound.

"The arcade?" Kamryn was halfway around the counter, and stopped.

"You know the one. He's about shoulder high—got a crush on you, girl. In fact, he's watching you now."

Kamryn got an icy feeling up the back of her neck and turned her head slightly, trying to see into the dark mouth of the arcade, several door fronts away. She could see only milling forms, and then one stood out, his pale face accented by sunglasses, ridiculous to see in the gaming den's twilight. She let her breath out.

Sandy added her opinion. "He'll be cute when he grows up."

Kamryn twisted her lips into a smile. "If it's a male, you think it's cute," she returned.

"Hey." The girl shrugged. "Aren't they?" She corrected herself. "I guess not if you're leaving one behind."

Kamryn didn't feel like talking about it. "I'll be right back," she answered, and pushed her way into the clothing store.

"Pull in over there," Snake told Darby. He lay half-coiled in the back seat, one shod foot firmly planted on the back passenger window, the other tucked away under his leg. The parking garage had corners full of dark possibility, and the level they drove on had few cars—no one wanted to walk if they had to, and so the lower levels were packed. Snake took his foot down and straightened in the car seat. He stuck his hand out over the seat.

"Gimme the piece."

Darby opened his mouth as if to protest, then shut his lips firmly. He handed over the .32. Snake closed his fingers around the heavy chrome piece and said, admiringly, "This is going to make some fuckin' noise when it goes off."

Darby looked at it, thinking of Kamryn. Thinking that he had made his choice, and the bitch deserved everything that was coming to her, but even so. . . .

"I promised you, didn't I," said Snake smoothly, as if reading his mind.

"You did."

"The bitch earned it. You took her in when she was in trouble, protecting her, protecting her brother, and now she's turning her back on us. On the Brotherhood." Snake's eyes were avid on the gun. He held it to his lips and his tongue flicked out in a quick caress, tasting the cold metal. "I ought to put it in her mouth and make her suck it off, just like it was a cock, my cock, and then—BAM! Brains all over the place."

"Snake—"

"Shut up." His languor fled, his attention to the exterior, to the parking garage. "Somebody's out there."

"What do you mean—"

Snake threw himself into the front seat of the car. "What the fuck do you think I mean?" He tucked the gun under his thigh. "Get out and go find him."

"He couldn't have heard anything."

"Doesn't matter." Snake showed his teeth, yellow, crooked, too sharp. "If someone else is up here, sneaking around, I want to know about it. Now go get him."

Darby slid out of the car reluctantly. He could see nothing, but he heard the sound as the vehicle *ponged* faintly to remind him that he'd left his keys in the ignition. The scurrying noise could be rats or it could be someone else hugging the shadows. He walked casually toward the garage elevator as if he had heard nothing, had nothing else to do but take the elevator down and enter the mall, all the while listening behind him and to his flank, where shadows pooled the darkest behind cement columns.

Another scrape. Darby whirled, took three leaping steps and came upon the man. As the quarry straightened, Darby swung about, kicking high, and took him in the chest, hard. He could feel it all the way through the heavy lug nut soles of his shoes.

The other fell back with a gasping grunt, collapsing onto the balcony edge of the garage. His face caught the scant illumination from a nearby lamppost.

White scum. Worse than black or brown or yellow scum, because he was white. He could have been somebody.

Darby inhaled tightly and stood over the man, taking in the worn clothing, the long hair, the clean but sundarkened face. "Homeless scum," he said, and spat, out of the way of the approaching Snake.

"Good job," Snake told him, as he came into the small beacon of light himself, and his tattoos glowed. The butt of the gun showed from his waist where he had tucked it in.

The scum saw it, too, a quick look, and Darby tensed.

"I've got nothing."

"You've got a white skin. That counts for something, don't it, Darby."

Don't use my name, Darby thought, too late. He sniffed. "He's a disgrace."

"Maybe. Maybe not." Snake walked one way and then the other, sizing up their prey. "Maybe he's just tired of all of them little brown faces and black faces getting what he ought to. Maybe it was all just enough for a fella to quit, instead of fighting back."

Their prey straightened up a little. Darby watched him catch his breath, knowing he could be dangerous now, if he wanted to be. But he wouldn't be. This type survived on being anonymous, like a piece of litter on the beach.

The captive held up his hands. "I haven't done anything, and you haven't done anything. Let's call it square, and I'll be on my way."

Snake dropped a palm onto the handle of the .32. "I don't think so. I think we need your help."

"What kind of help?"

"Directions. You probably know this area pretty well. Darby and me, we don't. We're lookin' for a place called the Hot Flash."

Darby shifted his weight uneasily. He didn't like Snake's tossing around of his name, nor could he see the sense of getting someone else involved. As he rocked from one foot to another, Snake uncannily looked at him, and straight into his eyes, and smiled. As if he was reading his thoughts again.

"I could probably help you with that," the scum replied. "Unless you're planning to rob it."

"Smart man. You're talking about this," and Snake rubbed the butt of the revolver again. "This is just for protection. We're not too far from La Habra, y'know, and there's a lot of gangs in La Habra. Some of them have no reason to like us." Snake's eyes glittered. "No, my bud got a girl works here. We're here to give her a ride home. We're like, her bodyguards."

Darby thought, *Who's he fooling?* but the white scum flexed his shoulders and said, "I can live with that."

"Good. Let's go see if we can find her."

The scumbag looked across the floor of the parking garage, hesitating. Then, "What's in it for me?"

"I don't need a gun," Snake answered, "to do a lot of damage. You're like a scab on the face of the community. I don't think anybody would mind if we picked you off."

Their captive made up his mind quickly. "I get you inside the door, and I'm gone."

Snake showed his teeth slightly. The tattoos on his skull rippled. "Oh," he agreed. "You're gone, all right."

Jon Fleming looked at himself inside the Brea security office, catching his reflection on a monitor as his Casio went off, beep-beep, beep-beep. He punched it silent and rechecked the time. Yup, it was just about time for break and to mosey down to the Hot Flash espresso bar. That dark-haired girl should be there, the one who was older, wiser, and prettier than most of the high school bimbos who worked down there selling to the trendies. She liked him, he sensed it instinctively. He'd known it the first time they'd swapped gazes. Now he wanted to be swapping spit with her. No time like the present to go down and make his intentions known.

He smoothed down his collar and hiked his belt. He liked the mall security uniform, it was almost as good as the county's sheriff uniform, although his time in that one had been very short before he'd washed out. He liked the center's winter outfit best. The summer outfit came with a pair of tailored bermuda shorts that, frankly, made Jon look like a mailman. He preferred the power image of the full suit. The mall was the best of both worlds, he'd decided long ago. It had the prestige, the community service, with little of the stress. Not that ugly things couldn't happen in here, like the year some woman was killed in the parking lot by her estranged husband, but that didn't happen on his watch, by God. Not on his watch.

As he approached the door to the tiny cubicle of the security post, it began to swing open with a fraction of a squeak. A man leaned in, nicely suited, though his shirt had been opened at the collar for comfort, a man who was both handsome and ravaged looking at the same time.

Jon instinctively reacted to protect his territory. "Excuse me, sir, but this area is not open to the public—"

"Officer Fleming? I was hoping to have a word with you." He flashed a badge that Jon barely caught a glimpse of, save perhaps the image of the spread eagle. ATF? Had it said ATF on it?

Embarrassed at his failure to recognize the emblem, Jon retreated. "Is there a problem?" His chair hit the back of his knees, and Fleming sat abruptly.

"No, sir, not at all. I was hoping that you could be of assistance to me in locating a suspect."

His help was needed. Jon put his chin out. "I could certainly try."

"Good. Good. I thought you might. But I was hoping to review the perimeter security videos over the last, say, forty-eight hours."

"Review the tapes?"

The agent smiled. "That's the idea, son. Now, I don't want to get anybody in trouble here, this isn't being done officially. Yet."

"You don't have to worry about that. I have the authority. Have a seat." Jon pointed a finger at the extra chair and swung his about, reaching for the tape library. The bank of monitors showed him his profile, lean, decisive. There would be time later to go down and make a good impression at the Hot Flash. He had business here and now.

"This will take a while," he said. "Even skimming it."

"That's all right." The agent unbuckled his jacket and sat back in the chair. "I have time."

* * * *

The October night had grown chilly, dry and cold, and the few leaves which had fallen skittered outside over the mall parking lot like scurrying animals. Kamryn caught a hint of the wind and night every time the main entrance to the wing opened, and new customers hurried in. The line at the espresso counter went knee-deep. She found herself barking at Sandy to keep up.

She mopped her forehead once, and found her lacy mittens were almost more damp than her skin. She wanted to strip the gloves off and cool down, but the healing scabs from the lasering made her hands look like pink, scaly freaks. She topped off another cappuccino with steamed milk and smiled at the customer. "Cinnamon sprinkles or chocolate or both?"

"Both, young lady, if you don't mind," said the gentleman. He had gray feathering the wings of his hair, and the woman he was ordering for smiled indulgently as if aware her escort was flirting with Kamryn.

She smothered a sigh and bent her head over the drinks.

"I think it's time for a break," Brand said. The back of his neck itched, and he could feel sweat trickling down his pits inside his shirt. Sweating off the drugs. Not too fast, not too soon, he prayed. He hitched up a shoulder to relax muscles grown tense at the video game. It was too hot inside the arcade, overcompensating for the briskness of the night outside.

"Something cold and wet," Curtis agreed. He stepped away from the main floor of the arcade, and followed the direction Brand stared in. He groaned. "Coffee was not what I had in mind."

"Jerk," returned Brand. "They've got cold drinks, too."

"If you don't mind me saying so, caffeine is the last high you need."

"I mind." Brand repositioned his shades. "I'm wired for sound and I'd like to stay that way." He stepped outside the main arcade entrance and maneuvered his way into the line at the espresso bar which the girl was serving. He could see her name tag from five deep in the line, and read it. Kamryn. He tried it out silently, tasting it, and liked it. She stood, half-shadowed by the espresso bar sign, or maybe it was his sight again, for she was neither wholly in the light nor smudged completely. He lifted his glasses and rubbed gently at his right eye. It felt as though smog was eating away at it. He dropped his shades back into place and waited.

A blast of wind skirled down the marble corridor and he turned to face it. He could not only smell and feel the air, he could see it, thin blue-gray, like the exhaust from a car or the last puff from a smoldering fire. Like some kind of toxic fog, it wafted toward him and he stepped backward instinctively, bumping into Curtis.

Curt shoved him gently aside. "Watch it."

"I am," Brand answered absently. He found himself blinking rapidly, but the smudge through his eyesight stubbornly remained. "Shit."

"What is it? You weirding out on me, X-man?"

"I'm not doing shit," Brand fired back, "and if you don't like it, you can just shove off."

"Hey." Curt lifted his palms in surrender. "Chill out, okay?"

Brand did not respond. He stared down the mall floor, toward the source of the breeze, and saw three people crossing the marble expanse. His newfound vision sharpened for a moment, then blurred again, but not before he'd recognized Mitch through dark fractals splintering his view. Mitch shone silvery, as though he attracted what light his vision could pick up. The other two he did not know and he paused, waiting for them to draw closer.

"That's Mitch, isn't it?"

"Think so."

"Who's that with him?"

Curtis grabbed his elbow and started to pull him away from the coffee stand, saying, "I don't think those guys like us."

Brand identified their shaven skulls. "Skinheads," he muttered. What was Mitch doing with skinheads? They wore jackboots, and their progress was anything but quiet. It discomfited him to see Mitch elbow to elbow with them.

Curt let out a low, breathy whistle. "Can you see that, Brand? Can you see the tattoos on that guy?"

He could, for a cystalline, if dark, moment. The guy wore his shirt open and short-sleeved, and the skin artwork moved over him as if it were alive. Brand brought a hand up to rub his eyes and rid them of the stain. The inkwork reminded him of something, but he could not quite grasp it, except to stand and stare in thought.

The low, gentle murmurs of customers waiting in

line were shattered by the fall of a coffee mug to the marble below. Brand whirled around and saw Kamryn, face as pale as ice, staring. She pushed behind her assistant as if she thought to flee the stand. One of the skinheads moved out, flanking her.

"Where do you think you're going, Kamryn."

She stood her ground, one hand tugging absently at her apron. "Don't bother me."

"Oh. I get it. Don't freaking bother *you*." The young one, the one with dull brown hair, what there was of it, let his lip curl. "You stole my bike and sold it."

"You gave it to me. I needed the money." Her voice shook a little, but her face, her stance, stayed dead calm.

Brand felt his knees wobble slightly in sympathy. People, muttering, moved away. Kamryn watched them go and called out, "Someone call Security. Please."

The tattooed one flexed his biceps. "Now the bitch says please."

Her eyes shut for a long second. "Darby," she said. "I won't go with you."

"That hog was a classic."

"I know." Something like a smile flickered briefly over her mouth. "I got good money for it." She tugged the apron off over her head. The ruffled edges of it caught on her mittens and one of them came off as well, exposing pinkish, raw skin.

Darby stared.

Her hand fluttered away as though it had a life of its own, hid in the wrappings of the apron.

"Where's my name, Kamryn? What happened to our ring tattoo?"

"Gone. Just like me. And I'm not coming back. I don't know how you found me . . . Lyndall, I suppose. But I'll just go farther next time. Now why don't you

leave before Snake talks you into doing something
stupid?"

Darby protested, "Snake don't tell me what to do,"
but it was punctuated by Snake's hissing laughter.

Brand thought it was funny. Before he could stifle
the impulse, he laughed, too. Aloud. Loud enough that
Mitch looked at him. Looked sharply at them and then
down at Snake's belt buckle. Brand followed the
glance, saw that the belt buckle looked bulky and
warped somehow . . . the butt of a gun.

The sucker had a gun tucked inside the front of his
jeans. He stopped laughing abruptly.

"Come on!" Darby started forward, grabbing at her.
She twisted away and kicked him, trying for his balls
and missing, catching him in the long, lean thigh muscles. He let out a blistering curse and doubled anyway.

Brand lurched forward to help Kamryn. Curt caught
at his elbow, bumping him, and his glasses came off.
They hit the floor with an explosion of plastic, and it
seemed that time came to a halt, everyone moving with
slow, exaggerated gestures.

The tattooed skinhead reached for his gun. Mitch
moved then, striking at the pistol, and Brand realized
why he had been standing there, why he had stayed
with them, why he now lunged for the weapon, lightning moving among the stormy clouds of darkness in
Brand's vision. They grappled and the pistol fell. It slid
across the marble as if across ice. It came to a rest at
Darby's boots. He scooped it up.

Brand unfroze his own feet and shook off Curt. He
threw himself through the thickening air, forever it
took, forever and a day, through fog and blazing sunlight, through the dappling of light and shadow, the
figures etched crystal clear and then blurred almost
beyond recognition.

He hit the skinhead's wrist as Darby leveled the pistol, saying, "I'm not taking no for an answer, bitch."

The gun fired. Kamryn jerked with a scream and went to her knees, scrambling across the tiles. Brand could hear other screams of panic, and the glass behind the espresso's neon sign shattered into a thousand diamonds, cascading downward.

Brand tottered off balance and went down on his hip point. He could see Kamryn scrambling, knew she hadn't been hit, she was moving too well.

The gun shouted again. Someone screamed sharply and went down, the other girl at the counter with the waved purple hair, her eyes opened and glazed, staring nowhere. Brand looked into her face. He thought he saw . . . but how could he . . . he thought he saw a fine white steam coming out of her half-open mouth, and her nostrils, and even—Jesus, even her eyes. He shrank back.

Real time came back with a thundering in his ears. Someone grabbed him by the ankles and yanked him away from Darby and the line of fire, flipped him onto his feet. Mitch stared down at him.

"Run," he said. "Get in the arcade." He left Brand standing and started for Darby, and Snake tackled him.

"Holy shit," Curtis said, and they hugged each other and ran like they'd been tied together for a three-legged race for the safety of the arcade, which had gone abruptly dark, the store lights turned off, only the machine faces gleaming like obscene stars. He stepped on someone already hugging the floor.

Curtis couldn't stop talking. "What did you do that for? What did you think you were doing? Did you make him shoot that girl? Was she dead? You looked at her, Brand, right in the face . . . was she dead? He could have killed all of us, he could have—"

"Shut up!" Brand shouted in his face, and his friend went still. Mitch fought with both men, and he watched for a moment, appraising the action. Mitch looked like he could handle himself.

He went down on one knee, yanking Curtis down with him. Where was Kamryn? What was she doing? He peered around the base of the arcade machine.

She came toward him.

"Kamryn!" He held his hand out.

On her hands and knees, she looked up, ebony hair wispy about her face, eyes wide with desperation. The struggle of the three men behind her framed her. She saw him and reached for him.

Like the snake for which he was inked, and named, the skinhead wrapped himself around Mitch, bearing him down. Darby lunged free of the tangle, pistol still in his hand, barrel waving about wildly.

Brand sucked in his breath, took her hand, and pulled her into the cloak of the arcade room. Curtis bolted to his feet.

"What are you doing—"

His voice cracked, breaking off high and sharp. As Brand turned to look at him, he realized the pistol had spoken at the same time.

Simultaneously.

Exploding high and sharp.

Curtis toppled over.

He flopped against the base of the arcade machine like a rag doll. "Brandon," he exhaled fearfully, voice bubbling out, weak and thin, white with foggy condensation like that girl's had been. A crimson flower blossomed down the front of his shirt.

Brand let out a tiny sound. It might have been a sob. It might have been a gasp. The girl moved against his knees, and they both looked up, toward the doorway, where Darby stood, pistol in hand.

* * * *

Nick wheeled into the south end of the mall as the dispatcher's voice crackled urgently, "All units, we have a report of shots fired at the Brea Mall. All units, shots fired at the Brea Mall."

His pulse quickened.

He reached for the mike. "I'm already here, send backup."

"Roger that, Solis. Unit 5 is already on the scene, backup requested."

He could see people running from the southwest entrance and guided the patrol car down onto the lower level of the center. He could feel the adrenaline begin to surge, a fire in the blood, and his senses leaped to embrace it with a fervor that surprised even him. Nick got out of the car, ran his hand down his left hip to make sure his nightstick was in place, his holster thumping heavily on his right as he shut the car door.

Someone screamed, "Officer, at the arcade, bullets everywhere—"

A teen put his face in Nick's, blotchy with acne, sheet-pale between the eruptions. "Some guy shot up the espresso bar at the Hot Flash. There's a chick with blood all over her . . . now he's in the video room."

He could smell the blood and fear on them. His nostrils flared, and something primitive reared in him. He was like a wolf, a goddamn wolf, his senses were so keen, and he knew what he wanted, what he hunted for lay within—*what he hunted?* The realization frightened him.

And a second self, shunted aside, the police self thought, *Dear God, in the arcade, the kids, like shooting fish in a barrel, who went insane here, what am I up against, will I get home again if I go in there—don't go in alone.*

He'd never been afraid like this. Not of himself or what he would face. Not in the South Central riots where the very sky seemed to burn, not when the hoods were calling in and ambushing policemen, not when he'd been caught and earned the scars on his face. Never had he been terrified to do his job, to work alone.

But he was not alone. There was something that rode with him, coiled inside him, and it took over now, propelling him toward the disaster.

Rembrandt felt something icy lance through him, and he straightened in his chair, alerted. He knew the feeling, though it took him a moment to place it. He had been touched by the uninvited, the dead, a frosty assessment—he knew the feeling from something that had happened at the funeral home months ago. New Orleans, that black woman who'd stared him in the face and flung holy water over him—and something else.

Something cold and unforgiving and hungry.

It passed him now like a bullet ricocheting by. It left a chill behind. Stunned, he leaned toward the live monitors, thinking that he had let the tapes lull him while something was taking place in real time. He saw shapes struggling.

"What was that?"

The security man stopped the tape. "Ah, nothing, I guess. I mean . . . I don't see anything." He never resembled Kato Kaelin in stumbling confusion more than he did at this point.

Rembrandt stood up, leaning over the console, pointing at the live monitors. "What the hell is going on there?"

The phone began to ring sharply in the security office, despite the blockout Fleming had put on it. Someone was using the emergency code. He grabbed it up and his face immediately grayed under his tan.

"Oh, hell." He kicked his chair out from under him. "Shots fired."

It looked more to Rembrandt like a fight, but then he saw a man separate himself out, and he was carrying a weapon as he headed down the mall. He let the wanna-be sprint out the door ahead of him and followed, the Glock in his shoulder holster a comforting bulge.

Beyond the young man Kamryn had called Darby, who stood disheveled and wild-faced, Brandon could see Mitch was in a fight for his life, and losing. But his predicament seemed that much more urgent. Curtis lay collapsed at his side, either already dead or bleeding to death. Kamryn hugged his knees, trying to disappear into the pooled shadows. And this skinhead guy, this freak with a gun, stared at both of them, trying to decide which one to shoot first.

And then there was this business of his eyesight which had finally begun to focus normally, but was hampered by what he could only call the lava lamp syndrome . . . great blobs of darkness which blotted out and then revealed whatever he looked at. It made him want to puke that the first thing he could see clearly, really clearly, was the barrel of that freaking gun.

"Trying to make a decision?" he asked, getting to his

feet, feeling Kamryn's hand first tighten, then give up and go slack, releasing him. He stepped into a pool of illumination from the mall. "Which one of us to shoot first? Why waste bullets, I say. Take us both out with one shot."

"Get—get away, kid. I got no quarrel with you. I just want the bitch."

"Well, you're not getting her. Because you just took out another kid, and he's probably the best friend I have in the whole world. He means more to me than anything I have waiting at home, and if he's gone, I might as well go, too. So long as you're running around pulling triggers, you better get me, too." He felt calm inside, dead calm, and maybe it was the pills talking, and maybe it wasn't. There was a limit, he thought. A limit to the shit which he was willing to take, and he'd just passed it.

Kamryn murmured softly, "Get out of his way."

He did not answer her, but waved his fingers at her, signaling. *Stay cool, stay down.*

"I wasn't supposed to do it," the skinhead muttered. Darby ran his free hand over his sweating head, and flung drops all over when he shook his palm. "He was suppose to do it."

Mitch landed with a heavy grunt, punctuating Darby's words, and Snake kicked him in the ribs with his jackbooted feet, once, twice, hard, to make sure he was going to stay down this time. Brand could see that Mitch breathed, and that was about all. He wet lips gone inexplicably dry.

Snake ordered, "Gimme the gun."

Darby narrowed his eyes at him. "No."

"C'mon, we've got to do it and get the hell out of here."

Darby hesitated.

* * *

Nick kept his back in the shadows, out of sight, watching the punk with the gun. He didn't know how to use one, wasn't comfortable holding it, wasn't blasting at anything that moved. He could probably be talked out of it once he saw Nick in position. His policeman's gut told him that, but it was a tiny voice compared to the other inside of him who wanted— what? Blood awash on the white marble flooring, a tidal wave of crimson, copper-tanged and warm, powerful. . . .

Nick shook his head, trying to clear it.

He watched the two fighters grapple, and the shaggy man go down, and stay down. The compulsion to get him, the true quarry, flooded him. This was the one he'd come for.

Nick knew he'd never seen the man before in his life.

His job was to get the others out of harm's way. *To serve and to protect.* He inched closer.

No, he'd come for the downed man. The fallen warrior. He must be brought back, to be tortured and die slowly. . . .

Nick swallowed hard. What was he doing there, arguing with himself like a, like a man possessed? His heart felt as though it had swollen and filled his entire chest cavity, throbbing with every beat, heavy as an anchor, he could not breathe for the pressure his heart exerted on his chest, his lungs. He fought to keep thinking, and realized that, the longer he waited, the closer he came to losing a final battle.

He moved closer to the scene when a kid stepped out of the arcade, and moved into the line of fire between them. Nick tried to inhale, to shove enough air into his lungs to call out.

He listened to the exchange as the tattooed perp moved in, and wanted his piece back.

He could wait no longer. He stepped forward.

"Put the gun down. This is Brea police."

Brand was beyond fear, but he whirled about, startled, and saw the uniform, the man's stern face above the police-issue gun and collar, and an immense cloud of soot hanging over him, about him, smothering him. More than sight, it was sound, dry mutterings in a language he could not understand, even if he were to hear it distinctly; it was touch, icy cold and beslimed, like carrion. It was feeling, ravenous, empty hunger and, even more, it was *evil*.

It would gladly slaughter him and anyone else standing before it.

Brand saw all that crystal clear, and it sank to the core of him, to that center which even drugs could not protect, and he felt a sudden urge to scream and pee his pants, the realization scared him so badly. This thing, like a funnel cloud of destruction, was going to suck him up, all of them, and it would be a worse thing than dying. Involuntarily, even though he knew the skinhead stood behind him with a gun, he took a rapid step backward.

"Don't move, son."

It looked human. Brand squinted slightly, he could see the white knuckles of the fingers the cop wrapped about the gun, see the struggle of the man holding it. He *was* human. He stood in the vortex of all that awfulness, and he fought to stay human.

Brand swallowed.

Suddenly the gun barrel swung, the cop fired, marble shattered, Mitch twitched as the shards showered about him, and the cop shouted, "I said, don't move!"

His voice bellowed like thunder. "Put your gun down, and the three of you move over there."

He motioned to Mitch, Darby, and Snake where to put themselves.

Brand did not dare even look to see what Mitch was doing. But he could see the cop cared, cared intensely, his white-rimmed eyes kept flickering to where Mitch probably lay.

Snake muttered, "Fuck *this*."

Brand heard him and dropped like a ton of bricks. His knee joints just went, like water, and he fell.

A calm, collected voice, unheard before, but familiar to Brand, rang out.

"Officer, I have them in a crossfire. You have backup."

Brand looked up as Darby let out a howl of pain and disappointment. The gun flash exploded near his eyes as he screamed, "This is for you, Kamryn, you bitch," bullet whistling into the arcade. Kids screamed. Brand could hear them shift and tumble, and he could not tell if she had been hit.

"Son of a bitch!" cried Brand. Darby swung wildly in response, and the gun roared a second time. The policeman went down.

Snake hit the deck by Brandon, slid past on the marble, momentum taking him to the open door of a storefront which stood abandoned. He kicked a hard boot, the glass front shattered, and with its shattering, another pistol shot, and Darby collapsed. His face slammed into the marble a hand's width away from Brand who watched as his tongue slammed forward in a rush of bloody vomit. Brand turned away.

He did not want to see what he had done, what he had caused, but it was either look one way or the other. The policeman lay, panting, his leg a bloodied mess, his face gray and sweating. His eyes rolled wildly and he tried to gesture, tried to get up. Coming down the stairs from the second story, Brand saw the man who'd fired the shot that got Darby.

It was the suited man with the ruined face who'd been asking after Mitch in the arcade. He stood beyond Hot Flash, where the wings of the mall intersected, in an FBI shooting stance, and as the building quieted, he took his supporting hand down and lowered the gun.

He walked up to where Snake crouched by the abandoned building and kicked him in the jaw. Snake's head snapped back and he lolled unconscious on the glass-covered tiles. Brand heard someone sob. It sounded womanish. He thought it might be Kamryn. How had Darby missed at such close range?

He scooted away from Darby, who must surely be dead, from the tide of blood and vomit which rose about his slack body, and got shakily to his feet. He looked for Mitch and saw—nothing. No one lay there.

He turned back to the cop as the security man and the suited man came up. What could he say? What could he do? Something sour burned at the back of his throat. *What, smart-ass, cat finally got your tongue?*

"Oh, God, I'm sorry."

"Not . . . your . . . fault. Protect . . . and serve." The wounded man gasped for breath.

Brand wanted to touch him, to hold his hand tightly, to take the pain away, but he couldn't. He watched in horror as every gasping mouthful released flames of soot. He jumped back, lest they touch him. The vortex about the cop grew more and more vast until it reached the immense ceiling above them.

As the policeman bled to death, this *thing* had a life. Brand stood frozen, holding his breath, afraid he might breathe it in.

The cop reached for Brand and caught him by the ankle, dragging him close. Brand recoiled. The policemen stared into his eyes.

"My name . . . is Nicholas Solis. I have a wife. Tell her—" He gasped again.

The ruined man, who had been trotting the perimeter, came up. He got to one knee. "It's a thigh wound, and it's deep, Officer, but you should be all right." He ripped at the torn uniform trouser, tearing a strip off, and tied a pressure bandage on, quickly, efficiently. Brand thought, *Whoever he is, he's done this kind of thing before.* The ruined face glared at Security, who stood absolutely dumbfounded, tousled blond hair and tanned face slack. "Get paramedics down here, Fleming."

"No good," protested Solis weakly. He arched his back. The cords of his neck stood out. "Pain." He managed to put a hand on his chest.

"That's just adrenaline pumping. You get a hold of yourself, son, and you'll be fine."

The ruined man laid a hand over the pale other one. He frowned. "I think he's having a heart attack." He leaned over, as if thinking of CPR.

"Don't touch him!" Brand blurted. He could feel the shadowy cyclone, whirling, casting, searching. It pulsed, as if throbbing with the struggling heartbeat of Nicholas Solis. It raced, then ebbed, slower, slower. It drew near the ruined man, even as it abandoned the police officer. "Can't you see it?"

They locked eyes.

"See what, son? This man needs CPR."

"Can't you see— Can't you—can't you tell?"

The dark thing spread out like ebony wings over the ruined man.

"Why don't you tell me, son? This man is dying."

Brand looked at Nicholas Solis. The policeman looked back at him, a sudden calm expression on his face. He knew. Maybe he even understood. Brand swallowed down a tight, dry throat. "There's nothing you can do. He's hollow inside. There's nothing there but that black stuff—"

"What black stuff?" The voice of the suited man had been soothing. Now it coarsened with impatience.

Solis put his head back, kicked once, and stopped breathing. Every orifice of his body gouted black flame. It spumed out of him and Brand put his arm up to keep it from striking his face, inhaling the last of it himself.

The ruined man got up without concern. Leaning over the body, he said, "Why don't you tell me where your friend went? What did he have to do with all this?"

"He's not my friend!"

"You recognized his picture, didn't you? And you protected him. That's something you do for a friend. What was he doing with these two?"

"He didn't do anything! And I don't know where he went." Brand kicked loose as the fingers holding his ankle convulsed.

Nicholas Solis, whoever he was, whatever had happened to him, whatever had possessed him, was dead, and had died trying to tell Brand that he loved someone.

It didn't matter. Curtis, dead. The skinhead dead. The policeman, dead. The funny, harmless little bimbo from the coffee stand, dead.

And it wasn't enough for what hung over them. It rumbled over them as though life itself offended it, the joy of life and warmth to be destroyed. The KillJoy.

The ruined man gestured. "I think maybe you'd better come with me. I have questions to ask."

Brand shrugged. "I don't have any answers to give." He could feel the hunger watching them, tasting them. It drew close to the ruined man. It wafted across Snake's quiet form, circled, then brushed it again. Hunting for a new home.

"Now I know you didn't mean to get that policeman shot, boy, but you've got some explaining to do."

Snake twitched and writhed on the floor. Brand could see that thing injecting itself into him, sucked in through the tattoos, inhaled through the eyes, ears, nose and mouth. Snake coiled and recoiled, like a reptile constrictor seeking a victim.

That broke Brand's nerve.

Brand bolted, and he could hear the ruined man cuss behind him, then say, "Let him go." He bulled through the arcade where a dozen teenage boys jostled him, and hid him, and let him bolt out the back door into the night.

He ran all the way home. Nothing was darker than that which clouded his vision and awaited an opening to come in, that hunger which he had only left behind momentarily.

Chapter 10

"Phil, it wasn't his fault."

The dweeb and his mother arguing, muted by the distance of a bedroom between them and him, still distinct because of the anger in their voices. He lay in bed, cold, very cold, in pain, his ears still ringing from the shouting. He was grounded, of course, but that hardly mattered. They'd been home, waiting, when he came running in, and the shouting had barely begun when the police called, to ID him, and to request an interview in the morning.

He had not even had a chance to tell them about the worst thing, about Curtis. Not that either of them had been in a mood to listen. No. It was blaming time and until that was settled, there would be no listening, no discussion.

"It was his fault he was at the arcade. He had no business leaving. He's playing you for a fool, Lucille. He got us out of the house and as soon as we were gone, boom—he was at the arcade. Every time he ditches school, he's at that arcade. While you try to decide between being a mother and being his best friend, he's running around, doing everything he wants. He's a bad example for all the kids—"

"For God's sake. He had surgery. He was in pain. I should never have left him alone."

"The boy's fourteen. He's old enough to stay home alone while the rest of us have a life, too. You shouldn't have to worry about him."

"That's not fair. You don't know what he's been through."

Phil's tone rumbled, a thunderhead voicing an ominous future. "I know what he's put you through."

"I've got a call in for the therapist. God knows what this will do to him—"

"Lucy, you've got to stop handling him with kid gloves. He's responsible for his actions!"

"He was in a shooting!"

"Yes. He saw a shooting. And the police want to see him in the morning."

"No police. You heard him, he won't talk to them, no matter what. Maybe the therapist could interview him . . ." her voice dwindled.

A pause. Then Phil's baritone. "I'm taking him down there tomorrow morning. He's not a child, Lucy, and you've got to let him face the consequences of his action."

"His action? So he's responsible for some—idiot—who went in and shot up the mall because of his ex-girlfriend? I don't think so! And I don't think you're trying to understand what's happening here."

Brand rolled over. He was clammy, and his pajama bottoms stuck to his legs. He kicked free of his twisted sheets and tried to fasten his pillows to the sides of his head to muffle the argument. He would never, never sleep at this rate, and he had to sleep, had to, because sleep would sometimes shut Bauer out of his mind, until that last, inevitable nightmare. His thoughts rattled around in his skull like a desperate, starving creature in a cage. He had to stop thinking and only sleep would bring that. He thought of hitting his stash again. Three Haldol would put him out for a day or so. Blessed numbness. Only, he wouldn't be in control then, and he had to be. Had to keep beating Bauer down.

His phone rang sharply, two, three, four times. Only Curtis ever called. He stared at it, with no intention of answering it ever again. It rang two more times, then stopped.

Then his mother's bedroom phone rang, trilled softly twice before it was picked up.

"Hello? June, how are you? Yes, he's here—how is Curtis? Oh, God. Oh my God. In shock, I don't think Brand even knew, he didn't say anything. Is there anything I can do? In the morning. Yes. June, I . . . there aren't words . . . I'm so very, very sorry. Call me if you need anything. Day or night. Tomorrow. Yes."

Voices paused.

"God, Phil. That was Curtis' mother. He was killed in the cross fire! Brandon didn't even . . . he didn't even say anything. Do you think he knows? How could he not tell me?"

"He and Curtis have been joined at the elbow for the last year. How could he not know? You're taking too much bullshit from him. He's probably waiting to tell you, to pull some ultimate sympathy card! You've got to stop letting him slide through life."

"Phil!"

Phil's baritone mumbled something which Brand could not hear through the pillows. Then his mother's high, clear voice again.

"I don't . . . I don't want to put him through it, but you're right. Curtis' death makes a difference. Surely he'll want to help find who did it. He must have seen something. I have to work tomorrow—"

"I said I'd take him down."

"Yes, I know, but . . . the therapist says I need to be there at times like this. He says that Brand doesn't trust me, but I can't do this. I can't. Phil . . ."

"That's why you married me." The deep voice softened. "To help you through the tough stuff."

"What am I going to do?"

"That's what we have to figure out, together."

Their voices lost their clarity, dropping into a comfortable, lulling murmur. They were still discussing him, he knew it, but the edge had come off his thoughts, finally, and he no longer cared.

He heard little more, his eyes drooped, but never quite closed, seeing Curtis in his mind's eyes. The dead skinhead. The cop.

And the nothingness, the void, the awful thing which had shadowed all of them. The hunger of the KillJoy. The evil. He'd seen it in the cop. What had it been?

He knew what it wasn't. It wasn't good. It wasn't benevolent. It wasn't anything he ever wanted to see again. As he began to fall into sleep, he wondered what the difference was between it, and the void between his thoughts and his dreams.

Had he seen Death itself?

And as the paralysis of sleep claimed his body, twisted and unhappy, sheets wrapped about him like pythons, Brand fled the mall again, his throat stretched in a scream which he could not let out, loss he could not howl, and the thing followed him.

He tried, but could not wake, could not forestall the fatigue he fell into. The blanket of drugs were now wiped out of his system by the adrenaline rush of all the fear, all the terror he'd been through, leaving him almost comatose. The rest he'd prayed for was now his prison.

Bauer had been prowling through his thoughts,

drawn by the blood and carnage earlier, disgusting Brand with his reaction to the events, and now the thing which pursued Brand attracted him strongly. Behind the flickering of his eyelids, played against the theater of his sleeping mind, Bauer hunted as much for the phenomenon as it searched for Brand.

He had to keep them apart. They were separate evils, but they called to one another, power to power, and if they joined—he had no chance. He would be overwhelmed. He did not want to see evil, hear it, taste it, smell it, but he would do all that and more, as long as it did not possess him. As long as the KillJoy did not creep within and take up residence as Bauer had. Anything that gave him some chance of remaining himself, wrestling with demons.

And in his dreams he was, as he usually was, alone, hoping for Yellow Dog to appear and guide him, to keep him away from both Bauer and the thing that devoured. He raced fleet-footed down the slipstreams of his mind, calling for Yellow Dog in the dark corridors, searching for that beam of gold.

He saw a glimmer. Brand altered his course. Around a corner it was, sharp and slippery, like a knife it would cut if he did not make the turn, but he saw the yellow dog, lips curled in a doggish grin, feathery tail waving.

It was a golden retriever he dreamed of, a heroic dog, and he did not know where he'd gotten the image from, for they'd never owned a dog, but he'd seen his like in commercials and on dog food packages, and so he knew what it was.

Yellow Dog tossed his head, brown eyes gleaming, soft golden-red ear flaps moving, the ruff at his throat swelling as he barked his doggy greeting. Brand put his hand down. He touched—he could swear he touched—the silky softness of his fur, the warmth of life coursing through the canine body, so real, so very real, this dream ghost dog. Yellow Dog bent his body, bringing his chops around so he could lick at Brand's wrist, wet but still warm, alive, happy dog pup.

The moment of joyous reunion was replaced as Brand could sense the snuffling of the hungry thing hunting him.

"Take me away," he said to Yellow Dog. "Hide me. Please."

The retriever let out a low woof, and bounded away, his tail flagging behind him, urging Brand to follow. He sprinted after. He would not be able to catch up to Yellow Dog again, he never did in his dreams, but the guide would take him on until morning, chasing safety. The dog knew the turns of his mind better than he did.

Then Brand stumbled. He saw the dog's hindquarters bunch, launching him into the air—over something—what? Brand's heart thumped in panic as he slid across the darkened corridor of his dream, slid across slick icy marble, hit a fault and fell.

His body jolted to a stop. Brand lay, gasping for a moment, looking upward, waiting for Yellow Dog to come back and get him out of the pit, how, he didn't know, but somehow—

A hazy golden aura lit the edge of the pit, something looked down at him. Brand got to his feet, extended his hand, breathing gratitude.

But it was not Yellow Dog who looked at him. It was Mitch, and for a mumbling second, Brand thought— I'm in the dumpster again, trapped, and Mitch is helping me out. There was even the faint metallic click as something Mitch wore around his neck swung forward, hitting the rim of the trash bin.

Brand accidentally touched it as it did so. A shock

zapped through his fingertips and he snatched his hand back, but not before reaching the awareness that he had touched something else, awakened something else.

* * * *

Two in the morning in New Orleans. Mother Jubal had told her client to come when the tide changed, and so she had, seeking her love potion and her reading, murmuring, "Madame Jubal, I pray this works," and she making polite, soothing noises back, looking into her crystal after stoppering up the potion she'd cooked and wrapping it in a clean cloth to give to the woman.

Outside her shop on the back side of Pirates' Alley, a cab sat waiting, its lights on, engine idling. The white woman sitting on the edge of her chair opposite Jubal had tiny lights about her eyes and her mouth, knife-edge lines of unhappiness. The white woman was not one of Mother's congregation, and so she did not do what she would have done for one of her many children, but instead she worked by means more acceptable to her client. She put her palm over the crystal, feeling its coolness against her warmth. Unseasonably warm still, for Narlins, and the touch of the crystal felt as good as the perpetually blowing air conditioner at the back of the candy counter beyond the curtains.

She could see the blurred image of her client reversed in the crystal, and concentrated, bringing up new images and sights. The woman sat so tensely on the edge of her chair that her butt might be made of porcelain, but she began to relax as Jubilation spoke, and the corners of her mouth slowly crept into a half-smile. She tucked the handkerchief-wrapped perfume bottle into her purse, and hesitated for a moment, then brought out her wallet.

Mother shook her head. "Now don't you be doing that. You've already paid me."

"But it's so little—"

"Little enough to see you smile. Now you run on. You've got fine things waiting to happen to you." Jubal reached for the midnight blue swatch of velvet she used to cover her crystal.

The white woman stood, a pale splinter in the dimness of the room, and the crystal reflected that splinter, then suddenly, the image shattered into a spidery picture of darkness and light.

Jubal hastily covered the crystal, walked the woman to the door of the candy shop, the store smelling of brown sugar pralines, and let her out to the waiting cab. She watched behind the door, looking out through the grille to make sure her client entered the vehicle safely, then bolted the door.

The cloth, so hastily spread over the ball, had slipped and fallen to the tabletop as if some unseen force had pushed it aside.

Mother sat down firmly to draw the crystal toward her. Arrayed in its depths rested a silver amulet, fingers grasping it.

"So this is the way it is," she told herself, and looked closer.

She did not see what she expected—a boy pushing his way into manhood, sable brown hair waved across his forehead, a sprinkling of freckles across his nose and cheekbones, eyes bloodshot with worrying (or sorrowing, perhaps, she thought), and shadowed by dark purple bruising beneath. The fringes of his hair were plastered wetly to his light forehead. Had he been running? And if he had, from what?

Mother had barely asked herself the question, when she felt the answer, the fear, the terror welling up in this child as if he were a newly dug spring. Dark water geysered upward from below, swamping him near to drowning.

She wrapped her hands firmly about the crystal ball.

"You come here to Mother Jubal," she instructed the man-child. "You come here and I'll help you. I know the loa, and it knows me. You come to me. I know what to do."

She exuded more confidence than she felt, but she knew she was the only hope.

The boy's face looked out at hers, and his eyes widened, as if he both saw and heard her. "You see," she said, and threw her power at the loa following him.

She surprised the spirit and it withdrew abruptly, and Mother Jubal laughed at her triumph, small though it be. Next time would be harder, and the time after that, harder still.

But she took her joy where she found it, and let it fill the room.

The astonished boy met her glance for a second longer, and then power recoiled spitefully, a last bitter blow from the loa. A sharp sound cracked through the air, and the crystal split into three shards between her palms.

"You remember," Mother coaxed the now empty crystal. "You remember me, child."

She let go, and the seeing glass fell hollowly upon the tabletop.

Chapter 11

"How the hell did you get caught in the middle of that?"

Rembrandt sat back in the rental car seat, looking at the stars through the sunroof, his laptop resting on the passenger bucket seat, his phone connected through the system, and listened. It was early morning on the East Coast and Bayliss was up—did the man ever sleep? Up and angry. Idly, he tracked a star which was not a star, but a satellite, visible even through the L.A. Basin's murky night sky, and wondered if it was the com satellite he had hacked into to make his call. He listened to Bayliss thunder about making preparations, ordering supplies, finding a wilderness camp, building a voting bloc, laying a foundation, the need for secrecy intensifying . . .

Rembrandt interrupted mildly, "I found our man."

"Found. Not have." Bayliss stopped rambling, became instantly alert.

"Not yet. I will. First, I have to make sure that things here are tied up."

"Were you identified as a shooter?"

"No. I managed to convince the security man that I was undercover and wished to remain so. He was more than eager to take whatever credit he could."

"Those malls are up to their knees in monitors—"

"It's been handled."

"Witnesses."

"They'll be taken care of." Rembrandt watched as an owl flew overhead, low, silent, a shadow coasting by.

"What does our man have to do with it?"

"He was there. I'm unsure of his role yet, but he was in the thick of it."

"Damn. Local yokels spot him?"

"He bailed."

"Anyone deal with you?"

"Just Security." *And the kid*, Rembrandt thought, but he would have a handle on that shortly, too. As far as Security was concerned, he would have an accident soon, but not too soon, nothing spectacular, just a run of the mill traffic fatality. "Everything's been arranged."

"Good. I can't brook much further delay. I need my shipment, Rembrandt."

"Yes, sir," Rembrandt answered, and heard the line go dead. He reached over to his keyboard, typed in a string, entered it, got a response, entered a series of codes, then backed out.

He hung up his phone. Initiating action and taking responsibility for the reaction, that's what his job consisted of.

He did it well.

He ran his tongue over his teeth, probing for an uneven spot, thinking. What to do with the kid? It might be best to proceed slowly there . . . the kid might help him find Christiansen. Also, there would be family involved. Best to avoid additional entanglements. He could handle the kid alone, and he would be solitary now, his friend had died in the incident.

Perhaps suicide might be appropriate after Rembrandt had learned what he wanted to know. It afforded a solution which, although painful for the family, would not involve a great deal more of tidying up. Yes, suicide was a definite option. He must not forget that. Sometimes he did, in the fervor of the moment.

He had been accused occasionally of enjoying his work.

He secured the laptop under the car seat, deciding where he would begin picking up the threads of finding the boy, without disturbing people who might ask questions later. After a long moment, he withdrew the laptop again, opened it, activated the modem, and began to search for the local school district's private records. After hacking into the Defense Department systems, the effort was surprisingly simple.

He would begin checking absenteeism records, and he had the name of the other victim. A correlation would soon come up, Rembrandt was certain. They had been friends, those two, and undoubtedly shared the same vices beyond the arcade. Truancy, detention, sooner or later, he would have a record with possibilities.

He would find the boy.

* * * *

She was hyperventilating, she knew she was hyperventilating, and it was all she could do to stay conscious. Maybe passing out would be better. Kamryn leaned over the steering wheel of her car, feeling her heart thump through her chest like some kind of weird machine. She looked out over the small city park, the Brea plunge, a great empty swimming pool until next summer, the streets of bungalows, built in the '30s, the city traffic humming sporadically down Brea Boulevard, and tried to catch her breath. She had bolted

from the mall and just driven, then she'd found herself
here, and the park was quiet, slumbering. She knew
the police department was a shout away and for now,
the park was safe. She was alive, and it was awful, and
it was a relief, and it was frightening. So much blood.
Poor Sandy. And the kid in the arcade. And the cop.
She wanted to feel sorry for Darby, too, poor, unhappy,
stupid Darby, but couldn't.

Someone was singing an off-key song, a litany really,
a chant: "Oh, God, oh, God, oh, God."

Kamryn took a deep breath and realized that someone was herself.

She pushed her bangs from her face, found it sop-
ping wet with tears, and twisting the rearview mirror,
took a look at herself.

"Oh, God," she said one last time.

She looked awful. Some women looked radiant when
they cried. Not her. Her eyes swelled until they were
beady, piggy little eyes, and her face went blotchy, and
her nose ballooned up until she resembled a clown.

The mirror in her hands gave a tiny ping and something metallic fell out of it, hit the car mats, and rolled
out of sight. The mirror instantly lost all firmness in
her hand and when she let go, it dangled weakly from
its post, completely vertical.

"Oh, shit."

She leaned over and felt the car mats for the screw,
brushed her fingertips over the nap of the fabric, forward, backward, as elusive as finding a fallen contact
lens. On her side, scrunched over and awkward, under
the car seat, she bumped the hardness of her gun, and
paused. If she had had the gun with her, perhaps none
of this would have happened. It was not enough to
carry it in the car. She should have had it in her purse,
under the counter, something, anything—

Who would have thought Darby could have killed her?

Kamryn sat up, and leaned her chin against the steering wheel again. She let out a shuddery, hiccuping sigh.

Come on, Sis. I've got something to show you downstairs.

Tears began to cascade down her face again.

"Dear sweet God. Mom, Dad, I'm so sorry. I'm so sorry. I let you down, I let you all down. I just thought—" Kamryn swallowed tightly. "I just thought, one step at a time. Just get away, get clean—" She scrubbed at her arms despite the pain of the raw skin. Even in the dark, she could see the faint outlines. Almost gone, but not quite. And now she was afraid to go back.

Darby was dead, but Snake, who had worshiped Darby for some peculiar reason, would be looking for her. Kamryn dried her face against her sleeve. It had been Darby who'd done the shooting, so Snake would probably be questioned and then freed. He would not rest until he had her. There were secrets to protect, and then he would be getting even for what had happened to Darby.

There would be questions she did not want to answer. They might find the gun and take it from her. They were sure to turn up the false Social Security number she'd given to work at Hot Flash. They might even discover her name was not her name. They would be all over her about the shooting, and Darby, and Darby's background. There would be press, too. Cameras in her face. Stupid questions.

She couldn't go back. She could only go forward. Somehow.

But she had to find a starting place. How? Where?

She couldn't sit in the park all night. The police patrol would notice her eventually, stop, check out the car, ask other questions.

Her nose began to run. Kamryn searched through her small purse until she found a worn tissue, not used, but carried around in the purse until it had gotten dirty and wrinkled. Mommie Kleenex, she'd called it when she was young. Mom.

She began to cry again. She blew her nose hastily, then found a corner and blotted at her eyes.

She had to stop this. Toughen up. Do what had to be done. She closed her eyes. There was no going back.

Someone rapped sharply on the driver's side glass. Kamryn stifled a scream and looked into the face peering down at her.

* * * *

Snake sat in the chair, admiring his tattoos as he flexed his forearm and made the patterns ripple. He kept his mind clean and clear of anything except the skin art, so that he would not forget the objective he had picked up that night.

He would hunt Kamryn down and kill her for betraying Darby, and before she could betray the Brotherhood. It was his sole reason for breathing, his destiny. In that way, he would keep himself and the organization pure. He had always been very careful to keep everything simple, uncomplicated, direct. He had no record because of it and he knew, that even though they were talking to him about that night's happenings, they were running his prints looking for a clue as to his past. The weapon wasn't traceable and neither was he, not without eyewitnesses.

A voice intruded on his meditation and Snake lifted his chin to stare at the speaker.

". . . I said, we had a cop killed here tonight. Does that make any difference to you?"

The cop had a lot of red to his brown hair, under the station lights, and Snake wondered if he'd been a potato-digging Irishman. He wondered if the burrito cop and he had known each other. He closed his eyes and opened them again slowly.

"I had a friend who got shot. I don't see the bitch in here anywhere. Why aren't you asking her questions?"

"What makes you think we aren't?"

Snake tilted his head to one side and looked at the cop.

The lieutenant cleared his throat and adjusted his nameplate slightly. Graham, it read. Lt. Peter Graham. Snake let the name roll down his gullet, held it inside like he was doing a toke, let it live inside of him, and didn't let it go. Then, slowly, he exhaled. He wouldn't forget Lt. Peter Graham.

"Let's talk about the gun."

"We already talked about the gun."

"You told me it was Darby's."

"Yeah. I had taken it from him, but he took it back inside the mall." Snake inhaled deeply again. "And the rest is history." He looked at his hands. "You tested me. I'm clean."

"You didn't pull the trigger," Graham returned. "That doesn't make you clean."

Snake wrapped his ankle about the chair leg. "I have a suit," he answered. "In Costa Mesa. Do I need one at this point?"

"You agreed to talk to us, to give a statement."

"Which you got. So. Now, do I need my lawyer?"

Graham's ruddy complexion began to darken again,

when a fellow officer came out of the adjoining wing
and approached from the rear, leaning over him. Snake
half-closed his eyes and watched the other's mouth,
knowing they were talking about him.

The computer hadn't pulled anything up. He stood.

Graham watched him, his mouth tightening as the
other policeman finished informing him.

"You're free to go. But I advise you to stay close in
case we have any more questions."

"Cool," said Snake and turned to leave.

*   *   *   *

Brand awoke, suddenly, sharply, crusty with dried
sweat and as stiff as if he'd been pounded on. He lay
in the night and blinked once or twice, then reached
quickly, out of habit, for his glasses. They weren't
there, of course. His hand brushed the touch-sensitive
lamp on the nightstand and it glowed.

Brand didn't know what woke him, but the readout
on the clock told him it was 4:30 a.m. He rubbed his
eyes carefully. Shadows were cast in sharp relief on
the far wall. His heart did a doubled-up beat that hurt
in his chest, then steadied. God, he could see! He
could see!

But what was he seeing? Were they shadows, or the
KillJoy looming over him, waiting, even though Yellow
Dog and the other, that black woman, had chased him
off? Had it filled Snake and then had enough left over
to come looking for him? Because it had been looking
for him, sifting through his dreams. That hadn't just
been a memory of the massacre. That had been real.
As real as anything which had been happening to
him lately.

He shifted in his bed and tried to make a nest in

the crumpled covers, punched his pillow with his head and lay back down, balled up, wary.

Something tap-tapped on his bedroom window. Brand sprang upright in his bed, eyes wide, throat tight. His head froze to his shoulders, it wouldn't turn to let him look to his right at the second-story window. Slowly, aching inch by inch, he cranked his head about on his neck. His muscles grew tighter and tighter until he thought his head was simply going to shatter at the neckbones and fall off. Fall off rather than let him look at the windowpane to see who or what tapped for him there. *Don't look. Whatever you do, don't look.* It could be the KillJoy coming for him. Or the ghost of Curtis. Or the ruined man.

Brand looked.

Chapter 12

Light from the nightstand caught it full in the face, reflecting a silvery moon back at Brand, a moon fractured by an ink-dark splinter down the center. The disk looked like nothing human. Now he wished that he could not see, that his vision had not sharpened, returned, giving him the ability to see it. Eyes widened, he stared at the creature and it stared back at him. A tiny slit opened near the bottom of the silvery reflection and mouthed at him. A hoarse, whispery voice it had.

"Brand. Let me in."

The shock that the thing knew his name kept Brand from taking a breath. He sat, his head twisted at an angle to his body, aching, turning blue for the lack of air, unable to move. He would die like this, he thought. Frightened to death. Had Bauer somehow gotten outside as well, to attack him from both within and without? It did not look like his mind's image of Bauer, the computer-generated photo of a serial killer which Susan Craig had shown him over and over and over again.

But who said his attacker had to play by the rules and show himself as he really was? Who knew what forms the KillJoy could take?

The thing moved, a shadowy limb became recognizable as an arm, a hand, and it rapped gently on the windowpane.

"Brand X, let me in."

No! He managed a tiny squeak of protest. It was like sticking a pin in a balloon ... suddenly, the blockage in his throat leaked out, explosively and he began to gasp for much-needed air.

The onslaught of air unfroze his thoughts, his jaw, his lungs. He blinked rapidly and the moonish face at the window suddenly took on proportions. Longish hair and trimmed beard framed it—it was human, looking in at him, someone human, despite the chasm down the center of its face and it was—

"Mitch!" His voice hissed out of him.

"That's right, buddy. Let me in." Mitch leaned on the window, voice pitched low, no one could hear him but Brand.

Brand, who'd made the trip in and out that window more times than he could count, knew it took someone fairly athletic to be kneeling on the eaves. Thought, which had been frozen, thawed at the speed of light. Was it really Mitch? How had he gotten here? What did he want? Why had he been with those two skinheads, and *Why had he let Curtis get killed?*

As if he could read his thoughts, Mitch said, "I let you down, I know that. I thought I could take them before they did anything. I'm in trouble and I've got nowhere to go but here. Let me in."

There were questions now. There would be tons more of them if the man were found in his room. It might even bring the ruined man, and Brand instinctively wanted nothing to do with him. And just who had Mitch been, anyway, that he thought he could handle two men with a gun?

Suddenly furious, Brand leaned forward. "No way."

"I need your help."

Brand rubbed at his sleep-ridden eyes. The silvery illumination which shone around Mitch lessened slightly, as did the chasm which cleaved Mitch's face almost in two. *I'm seeing things again*, thought Brandon. Not Mitch, he's here, but the way he looks. . . .

Maybe he was going crazy again, and Mitch was just part of it. He shook his head emphatically. "Mitch doesn't know where I live."

"I tracked you home weeks ago, making sure you didn't get trash-canned again. Brand, I've got nowhere else to go."

He couldn't stand the begging tone of the other, but was he even real? Brand leaned so close his breath steamed the glass pane. "You're in trouble, I'm in trouble. And if I get caught with you here, I'm in worse trouble. You're on your own."

"Just for the rest of the night, and the day. I'll hit the road when it gets dark again. Hell, if there's room, I'll sleep in your closet."

"What do you mean, if there's room?"

As urgent as his expression had been, Mitch grinned. "I was a kid once."

Brand said wryly, "You'd die in there."

"I know what old socks smell like." Mitch put his palm against the windowpane. "I need your help."

He couldn't stand crouched outside the window much longer. Brand decided that the scream of a falling man would attract more attention than letting him in. He moved to the window to unlock it.

Mitch came in swiftly and silently. He helped Brand tug the screen back into place before locking the window back down.

He tracked a broken fingernail down the screen's

framework, looking at the wear. "You ought to put a door in."

"Then think of the visitors I'd get." Brand sat down on his bed Indian-style. "There's cold pizza in the box," and he pointed at his bureau where he'd tossed the remains of dinner. The meal seemed so long ago, it was ancient history, because of everything that had happened since, but he knew the slices would still be good, and that Mitch was probably hungry.

"Don't mind if I do." His guest grabbed up the box, sat down, and began to eat. He held the slice by the crust and devoured each slice in two or three bites. Once inside, with full lighting on him, he looked near normal. The shining aura had retreated to a slight glare, or haze, and the chasm looked more like an irritating interruption. Brand watched him eat, thinking of the darkness of the hungry thing, the KillJoy. His eyes blurred suddenly, aching, throbbing, and he shut them tightly in fear.

Suddenly, he was glad he'd let Mitch in. He didn't want to be alone in the night, blinded, vulnerable. He found himself sitting with his arms folded tightly about his rib cage, hugging himself. He waited until Mitch was finished before telling him the bad news.

"You can stay here until morning, but the dweeb's going to take me down to police headquarters after that."

Mitch, who had been busy chowing down, grew suddenly alert. "Why?"

"Because they want to talk to me. About . . . Curtis . . . and everything."

"About me."

"Probably. The ruined man was hanging around, showing pictures, and asking questions."

"Pictures?"

"Yeah." Brand tilted his head. "Was that you in uniform?"

"Don't know. Didn't see the picture. And," Mitch looked at him steadily, "it's better you don't know, either."

"Who was he, anyway?"

"Who?"

"The ruined man."

Mitch found a half-filled glass of soda and drank it down, made a grimace as if it were horrible tasting, which it probably was, warm and gone flat. "Don't know," he repeated. "Haven't seen him."

"He knows you. He shot the skinhead. I think he's probably FBI or something."

"Think so?"

"Yeah. Anyway, even if you don't know who he is, you probably know someone's looking for you."

"What I do and don't know is not open to discussion." Mitch looked around the room. "Could you tell if someone's gone through your things?"

"Of course I could!"

"And?"

"Everything's right where I dropped it."

"All right. I'm good for the rest of the night. What about later?"

Brand thought. "There's a studio over the garage. A loft. The dweeb was going to make it into a studio, but he's never done it. I have a key."

"What are the chances anyone would go in there?"

"Practically none. Only the dweeb would ever go in there, and he's going to be busy with me."

"But you have a key."

Brand shrugged. "Never leave home without one."

"Then I should probably go in while it's still dark."

Brand tried not to let his disappointment show. He

slid a hand under the top mattress and fished around until he found a key. He tossed it. "Here."

Mitch caught it in midair, a silvery object disappearing into his hand. Without looking at Brand again, he said, "It's been a long night. I think I'll just bunk down in here anyway, if you don't mind."

Relieved, Brand threw him a blanket, too, and added, "Just lie down anywhere."

Mitch found the comforter Brand had kicked off and straightened it, then folded it. He lay down and pulled the blanket over himself, then looked up to meet Brand's amused look. "I'm old," he said. "I need more padding than you do."

Brand reached out. "I'll get the light."

*   *   *   *

The glaring white light in Kamryn's eyes flicked away, and she could almost see the policeman as he leaned close. "Are you all right, miss?"

Middle of the night, and she'd been crying, and she was hiding out in the city park. Kamryn smiled. "Of course. I was just . . . my mirror broke." She pointed. "I was at my boyfriend's, and we had an argument, and I was driving home and the damn screw broke, or something."

"Would you open the car door for me, ma'am?"

Hesitantly, after another look at him to make sure he wore a patrol uniform, Kamryn unlocked the door and swung it open. Flashlight in hand, the man leaned inside and aimed it at the mirror which now hung limply in the middle of the front windshield.

"Shouldn't drive around with it like that," he commented as he straightened back up.

"I know, I know. But it just happened. I thought if I found the screw. . . ." Her voice trailed off.

"You're headed home, then?"

"Yes, sir."

He had no expression on his face. Did he know she was lying? Did he care? Would he be looking for her because of the shooting?

He reached for his pocket. "I'd like to see your registration and license, please."

Her heart sank. A ticket! She couldn't believe it. She fished her registration out of the glove box, then pulled her purse onto her lap and rummaged around until she found her wallet. As she shifted her weight, the back of her heel struck the butt of the gun.

Shit! Could he see it from where he stood? They'd haul her in for that. Carefully, she nudged the gun further back under her seat, as she pulled out her license. The address was no good, but she didn't care about that. By the time they backtracked it, she'd be gone. She passed everything over.

He balanced it on the citation pad as he began to write. "This is what we call a "fix-it" ticket. You have thirty days to get the mirror replaced before we actually issue a citation. Just bring the car in to the station so we can see everything's in order."

"That's all?"

He smiled briefly. "That's all. Just bring it in, let anyone look at the mirror, and we tear the ticket up. Okay?"

"All right. Thank you."

He handed her the citation and her license and registration back. "I wouldn't hang around here too long. It's pretty late, and there's been some gang activity in the area. And don't you let that boyfriend of yours bother you, okay? You shouldn't even be driving if you're too upset."

Kamryn tried a brave smile, let it fade from her trembling lips. "I won't. And, thank you."

He stepped back so she could close and lock her car door. With him watching, she pulled out of the little park's lot, and headed for the streets. If only she had somewhere to go.

*   *   *   *

An hour after dawn began to lighten the streets of the Quarter, Mother packed up to leave the candy shop. Her sister and her sister's daughters were already busy in the candy kitchen, cooking up bubbling pots of brown sugar syrup to make pralines and chopping pecans on marble cutting boards to add to the candy just before it set. They sang as they worked, and their voices and the rich smell of the brown sugar filled the air. They nodded at Mother as she walked through, past the glass candy counters and gondolas. Her youngest niece was cleaning the interiors, whisking them out quickly and efficiently, getting ready to restock them with fresh dipped chocolates and turtles and pralines.

Though the sign of the door was marked both Candy Kettle and Madame Jubal, there was no sign of her place at the back of the sweet shop. Only those who knew her, knew how to find her, or had been directed to her, looked for Madame Jubal. She liked it that way.

Her sister, putting the cash drawer into the register at the front, looked up. Geneva was too young to remember their mother well, but she was the spitting image of her, Mother thought. Just the spitting image.

She smiled, but there was a little worry frown between her eyebrows. "Mornin', Mother. Late night?"

"Sure was, Geneva. I've shut down the shop for the mornin'. Just let the answerin' machine catch my messages, all right?"

"All right. Trouble brewin'?"

Mother paused by the front door. She could not put a finger on what it was about the boy which bothered her, or why she had seen him through the amulet, or why the crystal ball had shattered. Stranger things had happened to her. But perhaps her sister had put a finger on it. Trouble brewing. She smiled widely. "Always brewin', Geneva, always. Just like the candy syrup in the pot. The Good Lord above is always workin' on something for us. I'll see you later."

Despite the earliness of the hour, despite the relative coolness of the day, the sun smote her like a hammer as she stepped out into it. Mother paused on the sidewalk and cast her eyes down from the glare. There was a breeze in the day, a goodly one, and as she looked down, she caught sight of a crow's feather. The wind caught it up, set it down on its quill end, and it revolved in a flurry, trapped. Mother watched the feather spin, knowing Aido Wedo had sent her a message, a sign, but one which she was not sure she could read.

Then she looked around, and leaves and debris from the night swept about her in a bigger, wider circle, faster, more furiously, so that the island of calm in which she and the feather stood was like standing in the eye of a hurricane.

Hurricane. Mother took a deep breath and stared down the alley-street, past the wrought-iron balconies and toward Jackson Square. Chalk artists were already out, sketching their livelihood onto the walkway. October neared the end of the hurricane season and few reached any strength this late. Hugo had, though, up the Atlantic coast. Any 'cane getting a start this late might well stay in the gulf waters, swinging toward Louisiana or Texas. Might. Might not.

The wind flurry died as quickly as it had come up. Mother hugged her purse under her elbow. She would have to do some thinking about the sign when she came back, after a short nap.

The sign and the boy. She had to work on bringing him to her, him and the wearer of the amulet. They would need her before they were through.

As for the 'cane, that would be a work of nature, and it would do what it would do, uncaring of the good or evil of its destruction. That was the way of the wide world, and why men prayed to gods. Mother took another deep breath, smelled the sea and the morning, and started the day's journey.

Chapter 13

"You're sure you're not too upset over this?" the dweeb asked, for about the fourth time, over cereal.

Brand looked at him. The dweeb had carefully blown-dry, caramel-colored hair, with wings of graying blond at the temples, glasses, and a clean-shaven face with a sincere expression. He looked like a banker (which he was) and someone who could say, "Thank you for banking with us" while he foreclosed on the mortgage (which he had also done). There was not a visible shred in him of the frustrated artist, although that was supposedly why they had a loft/studio over the garage. Brand had not known the dweeb to visit it since they bought the house and moved in. The loft had originally been advertised as a "maid's apartment" or "granny room" as it had a half bath and a very small kitchenette, although the kitchenette was not currently hooked up. Why run gas to a stove top never used? Why call it an artist's loft if there was no visible artist?

As for being asked if it upset him, he'd already been told he had no choice. Short of going into a coma (and he'd already done that, thank you very much, Dr. Susan Craig, and didn't particularly want to do it again), he knew he was going. He didn't want to, but he had not yet figured out an escape route.

Brand put his spoon in his mouth carefully before

answering, "No. Another day off school is what every kid wants." The house had cleared of the other children, only they three sat at the breakfast table.

"Don't talk with your mouth full," his mother said, without looking at him.

Brand grinned. Milk slid out of the corner of his mouth and he grabbed up a wadded paper napkin. If he were younger, he'd consider barfing in the dweeb's car on the way to the station. He could pass it off as nerves. But, as he wasn't younger, there was a line of irritation he could walk, and it was a fine one.

In despair, his mother said, "Brand, don't do that. You look like a drooling idiot."

"Lucy."

"Honestly, what am I going to do?"

"You don't believe me."

"Brandon, honey, how can I? What do you expect? They told you what could happen. You wouldn't wear the solar shields they sent with you, you went to the arcade, you're telling me you see things, you're lying . . . it's just like it's happening all over again—"

"Lucy," the dweeb repeated again in a low warning.

Flushed, she looked away, then down at her wrist. "I'm going to be late. You'll take him to the therapist later?"

"I've got the whole day off work."

She stood, brushed a kiss across the dweeb's receding forehead, and left without glancing back.

That left the two of them staring across the table at each other. Brand lowered his gaze and paid serious attention to finishing his cereal and wondering how he could shake loose.

"You look like that surgery's really taken hold. No glasses?"

"Yeah." That, at least, had been a relief. But his

failure to explain the side effects to his mother left him isolated. Even as he thought about it, a charcoal-gray smudge drifted cloudlike across the dweeb's banker countenance and floated away.

"I'd like to try RK sometime," the dweeb mused, as he scraped his cereal bowl clean. "I've worn glasses since I was a kid. It gets tiresome. Someday I'd like to buy myself a pair of those Italian wraparound sunglasses. . . ." His voice trailed off.

Brand pitied his mother. It looked like the dweeb was about to enter the "driving a convertible, bald-headed with groovy sunglasses" phase. He decided not to aggravate his stepfather overly much. "Sounds cool."

The dweeb blinked as if bringing Brand back into focus. He checked his watch. "Your therapist should be in now. Want to give him a call before we go see the police or after?"

Oh, please, Br'er Dweeb, don't throw me in the Brea police department patch. Brand sighed. He thought of Mitch hiding in the loft. A talk with down-to-earth, understanding Mitch would do him far more good than his twitchy psychotherapist who, Brand was fairly sure, got into psychology with the hopes of analyzing himself. Although Brand had to admit, he had not yet told Mitch of what he'd seen happen, there was an adult who might be inclined to listen and judge later.

Brand pushed his bowl away, resigned. "Let's just do it."

His stepfather made no move to stand. He did, however, carefully dab at the corners of his thin-lipped mouth with his napkin. "There's something else we have to discuss. Your mother is having almost as much difficulty with this as you are, so I agreed to tell you. But I don't want you to think she's avoiding this."

Oh, no, not Mom. Brand pushed back in his chair. "What is it?"

"They're holding the funeral for Curtis tomorrow morning. I'll be taking you there."

His stomach did a flipflop, and the milk and cereal went sour immediately. "I don't want to go."

"I know it's not pleasant, but you were his best friend. His family would feel better seeing you there."

He didn't want to see Curtis laid out, whiter than marble, eyes closed, sleeping the sleep of the dead. "I don't care. I'm not going."

"Brand, we don't ask much of you. Taking out the trash now and then, your turn with the dishes, good grades in school—and now this. Death is something we all have to deal with." The dweeb smiled slightly. "After all, none of us are getting out alive."

"Well, Curtis got out a hell of a lot sooner than he expected!" Brand threw his napkin on the table, felt like he was going to lose his breakfast as well. "You can't force me."

"Actually, we can. You need to function within certain limits of normalcy, Brandon, or your mother is obligated to hospitalize you again so that you receive help. That's part of the agreement with the social services department and the hospital after the fiasco with Susan Craig. Your mental well-being is being monitored. As of right now, your behavior is borderline."

"So that's it. Go or you'll send me back to the loony bin."

"That's the general idea. Stay in school, try to be a member of this family and normal society, or we'll see you get additional help adjusting."

"Since when is being a member of this family being normal?"

"Don't push it."

Brand stood up. "I'm not pushing, I'm shoving. Mom keeps trying to marry a solution to her problems, you married a pair of nice boobs and a great pair of legs fifteen years younger than you are—and the rest of us bounce around like we're in a Pachinko machine. I'll go, but I'll tell you this—this game can be played both ways. Forcing me to go just might push me over the brink, and you two will be responsible."

"Don't threaten me." Now Phil stood, to his full adult height.

"That's not a threat, it's a promise." His mouth tasted sour. Brand swallowed it down. "I want to talk to the police now."

The Brea Police Department was not at all like Los Angeles. He remembered Parker Center in all its glory. For a few days there, he had an entourage close to that of O.J. Simpson during the trial days: his mother, his then-stepfather, two or three social workers, the attorneys and their team, the hospital representative and their attorneys and someone who had been related to Susan Craig and represented her estate, and then, of course, there had been the media. His face had been hidden whenever it was shown on television, but the cameras had been there, right in his face, every time they went to be interviewed at the police center or at court. The then-husband had caved under the pressure, partly because he had wanted to sell Brand's story to the tabloids and to trash TV.

His mother had been by his side then, fighting like a wounded female bear over her cub. He thought now, as they pulled into the parking lot, that it was probably only because such interviews and appearances would have ruined their settlement against the hospital and Craig's estate. He didn't know how much it was, but it came in regular increments, and after the first one which had bought their current home, he saw little difference in their lifestyle except that she met the current dweeb while setting up bank arrangements. As far as his mother was concerned, it was over, done with, finished. Gone with the wind and the second husband. It might never have happened except that she had a new home, a new husband, and had to take her son to regular therapy appointments. The exceptions were a little like speed bumps in her road of destiny, he thought. He was more like a Botts dot, one of those hard and round lane markers that let people know when they veered on the highway. A minor, sometimes helpful, inconvenience.

His life, of course, had never been the same. The therapist was good only to vent to about the inconveniences of what the shrink called a "blended family." Brand privately thought that if he ever shared what really went on in his head, let Bauer get hold of the shrink and show him just how blended things could get, the man would probably pee his pants just before turning him in to the psych ward.

Phil leaned back into the car. "Are you coming?"

Brand realized that they had been stopped for some time. He felt his face grow warm having been caught daydreaming. "Can't wait."

He had resorted to wearing the eye gear the surgeon had given him, his new shades lost. Even as he looked at the humble Brea police building, hacienda style as so much of the area was, it swam in and out of focus. He wondered what normalcy would be for him and when, if, he would reach it. Brand tilted his head back and looked up. Dark, smoky clouds drifted over the building, gathering, building like a massive storm front. Behind it was a typical late October day: dry, wind

swept, slight smoggish tint to the air, not a wisp of a
cloud in sight. Even the sky looked faded. But not
where he directed his gaze. The sight made him stumble on the walkway.

Phil said impatiently, "Thought you couldn't wait
for this."

Brand tightened his lips, then realized he might look
like the dweeb when *he* did that, and instead twisted
the corner of his mouth. If he had anything to do with
it, anything at all, no one was going to be happy with
the outcome of this interview.

They gave him a private room and it was clean,
cheerful, and laid back. Brand let himself slouch down
into a chair across from two suited policemen, while a
uniformed cop stood in the background, near the window. The older man placed a tape recorder on the table
and his partner a file of papers and a notebook. Phil
took the other chair, straight-backed, with a flip of his
suit jacket coat.

"Our understanding is that this is just to ask a few
questions."

One of the plainclothesmen smiled at the dweeb
while the second took a pair of folded sunglasses out
of his pocket and slid them across the interview table
toward Brand. "I think these belong to you."

Being nice to the kid. Brand looked at the glasses.
"Maybe," he said. "They look like a pair that I lost."

Phil sat up even straighter. "How could you lose
them so soon? Your mother just bought them for you
yesterday."

Brand reached out and curled his fingers around the
glasses. If the police had tried to take prints from them,
they'd all been cleaned off. There was a scratch across
the top of the right lens, high, and crooked, like a

lightning bolt. "It happens," he answered, before picking up the glasses and dropping them in his lap. He looked at the officer across from him. "If he keeps interrupting, this is going to take twice as long."

A stir ran through the room. The two suited cops sort of leaned toward one another as if in silent communication, and the uniform by the window twitched a little.

Then the policeman opposite Brand looked at Phil and said, "If you don't mind, sir, I'll ask you to be quiet. We'd like to get this statement in the boy's own words, as much as possible. If you have any objection, we understand, and the questioning can be stopped. Then we'll have to get a court order and do this officially."

"There's no need for that! We said we'd cooperate."

"Sir."

Phil stopped talking with a familiar grind of his teeth, and his thin mouth stretched out like an unhappy rubber band.

The policeman opposite Brand was the oldest person in the room, and he wore a dark blue suit with a blue and white striped shirt and a dark blue tie with a Snoopy Joe Cool policeman on it. He was tanned, and crow's-feet webbed out from his eyes all the way to the bottom of his cheekbones. He wore a wedding ring that had been put on when he was a lot younger and thinner. It looked almost embedded in his finger. But he was not a heavy guy, and Brand got the impression that this man might have been a soccer coach or maybe even Pop Warner football . . . something wholesome, to be by his kids.

The other guy was Hispanic, cool olive skin and luxurious dark hair, and warm brown eyes. He'd lost one earlobe somehow, and he was the one taking notes, and occasionally his hand would sneak up and tug on that ear. Maybe he'd pulled it off during a particularly difficult case.

The older man said, "I'm Officer Leopold and this is Officer Ramos. That's Patrolman Katz."

The uniform gave a curt nod.

Brand thought of Nicholas Solis in his uniform. "Anyone tell the wife his last words?"

Another ripple ran through the room.

"What last words?" repeated Leopold.

"I told the guys who showed up last night. It was like he knew he was dying, only it was just his leg that was trashed. Anyway, he told me his name and said, 'Tell my wife I love her.' Didn't anybody get that?"

Katz said hoarsely, "I'll tell her."

Ramos shifted in his chair. He slid a piece of paper out from under his notebook, marked something on it, and quietly slid it back.

The report, Brand thought. That's the report from last night. And somebody is going to get their ass chewed.

"Thank you, Brandon, for letting us know."

"Brand," he corrected. "I like to be called Brand."

"Okay. Why don't you tell us what happened, as far as you know."

"These guys came in, skinheads. I was in the arcade with Curtis and—"

"Curtis. The boy who was killed."

"Yeah. My ex-friend. Anyway, we were going to head over to the espresso bar at the Hot Flash when these guys came in the mall entrance."

"Know any of them? Ever seen the skinheads before? Can you describe them?"

"I didn't know them, I never saw them before, and the dead one wore blue jeans, Doc Martens, suspenders over his T-shirt, and real short hair. He was kind of blond, I guess. Didn't see his eyes until he was dead. They were blue then. The other guy, he wore heavy boots, too, and jeans, and his shirt was opened all the way, and his sleeves were rolled way high, to show off his tattoos. His head was shaved."

"Anyone else?"

He meant Mitch. Brand did not want to name him, but knew there were probably others who had seen him. "Yeah. They were flanking this homeless guy who scrounges around the mall. I don't think he was with them, exactly."

"Can you describe him?"

"Scruffy. Long hair. Beard. I don't know. I was watching the skinhead with the tattoos."

"What makes you think," Leopold prompted, "that the third man was not 'with' them?"

"He just didn't act like it. And when stuff started happening, he tackled one of them."

"What stuff?"

"When the young one . . . the one called Darby . . . grabbed the gun from the other guy's pants."

"The one with the tattoo had the gun?"

"Yes." Brand stared at Leopold. "Does he have a name?"

"Snake."

Brand did not attempt to hide his shudder. "And the scruffy guy tried to stop it, but he couldn't, and Curtis and I were like caught in the middle, because Darby wanted the girl at the espresso bar, and the gun went off and Curtis—he sort of turned around and fell back into the arcade and then the cop came."

He let his voice go high and trembly, and jumbled his words together. "And I was still out there in between and then Darby started shooting, and the cop went down, and Darby got shot, and he fell and he was holding onto me, and all this blood and vomit came out of his mouth   "

He halted.

Leopold looked at Ramos and Ramos returned the look.

Leopold reached forward and pushed a button on the tape recorder. "I think we have all we need."

"But that's not all that happened—"

"Our concern here is identifying Darby as the shooter. You've done that. We have witnesses from the dress shop who saw most of the incident."

"That's . . . that's all?"

"Yes. For now."

"Aren't you going to arrest me for leaving Curtis?"

"No, son. I don't think you meant to leave him, and even if you hadn't, there was nothing you could have done."

Brand looked at the dweeb and breathed heavily. "He told me—"

"I did what?" Phil half came out of his chair.

Brand looked back at Leopold. "He told me I could be arrested. That I had to come in today. I couldn't sleep all night. He got shot, and I couldn't do anything about it—" He let his voice rise high, and break.

Leopold stared at Phil. "I think you need to take the boy home and get him settled. He's been through a lot, and he needs help to deal with it."

Phil had gone pale. "His mother and I—"

"I'm sure you have, sir," Ramos answered smoothly. He stood and offered his hand. "Thank you for coming down today."

Phil did not say another word as they left and walked down the rows of cars in the lot. Brand took a last look. There were officers walking in and out of the building, and none of them seemed to notice the cloud boiling overhead, or the strings that reached down and touched them from time to time, strings that wrapped around and around their uniforms, their souls.

Death touched them all.

Brand shuddered. He no more trusted the police than he did Snake. If they had wanted the truth from him, they would not have let him go. If they had been interested. If they had not been shadow eaten.

Chapter 14

Black and white TV. Cary Grant wooing Myrna Loy
with patter about the man who has the power. What
power? The power of voodoo. Who do? He does, the
man who has the power. What power? Kamryn blinked,
focusing slowly on the classic movie, having fallen
asleep to a late evening infomercial and now waking
up to Grant and Loy at their most witty and hand-
somest. She looked at the program guide. *The Bachelor
and the Bobby-Soxer*. Shirley Temple had the sidekick
role as younger sister. The movie was older than her
mother.

Kamryn rubbed her eyes. A cheap hotel bedspread
with a waffle weave seemed imprinted permanently in
her cheek. She yawned.

If anyone here had been interested in the shooting,
she hadn't noticed it. She'd checked in, paid cash, and
crashed in the room sometime after Tony Little ranted
and raved about washboard abdomens for the one hun-
dredth time. She'd paid for two nights, not knowing
if she was going to sleep at all, or if she'd sleep the
day through.

Kamryn levered herself up, reaching for her duffel
bag and rummaging through it for some decent clothes.
She always carried the bag, and as luck would have it,
there was also a basketful of dirty laundry in the car's

trunk because she had thought about going to the laundromat after work. The thought of chores and a regular day rattled her. How could anything go back to normal? After a shooting. After a murder.

She showered and changed, and left the room long enough to go to the news racks at the front of the hotel office and buy a local paper. The shooting had made front-page news, along with the latest international blowup. She went back to the room and read the story without looking at the pictures. Some of the detail was the way she remembered it, most was logical conjecture, and there was a good deal left out.

She paused when a teen's half-awful, half-sincere school ID picture interrupted the column despite her efforts not to look at any of the victims. This was not her boy, it was his constant companion, although she did not know how her boy, as she thought of him, had not gotten killed as well. He had tried to save her, putting himself in the line of fire. It had been his best friend, instead, who'd caught the bullet.

Too upset to finish the story, Kamryn shoved the paper aside. She dropped her face into her hands and dug her fingers into her hair. She had a long list of amends to make, and now this added to the weighty length of it. How was she ever going to make up for all of this?

It made no difference. She had promised, had bartered her life for it. If it cost her her life doing it, then she could only hope it was better than costing her soul. God, maybe it would have been easier if You had just let me go in that basement along with Mom and Dad.

She opened her eyes and pulled the paper toward her again, unable to think of anything else. Before she had descended into that bloody basement in her Pennsylvania home, she had fallen into a pit of hatred and

violence. Perhaps her mother and father had deserved
to die. Perhaps none of this would have happened if
she had taken just one step differently, long ago. It
wasn't just the steps she'd taken, but those her parents
and her brother had. Was she responsible for all of
them? Logic told her no. Hope told her that she was
no longer responsible even for those she had taken in
the past. Just the new path, the new road.

She ran her fingertip along the newspaper fold. She
would have to leave. Snake would be looking for her,
to finish what Darby had begun, knowing instinctively
that she had not only turned her back on Darby, but
on the entire movement. She knew too much, she was
dangerous to all of them. She could not stay.

But she could delay a day or two to say good-bye.
She creased the paper where it told of the funeral arrangements for the dead. She owed the boys this much.

* * * *

Rembrandt stayed at the Ritz Carlton. He sat on his
balcony, drinking a glass of fresh squeezed orange
juice, into which he had sprinkled, but not emptied,
vodka from the room's minibar. He liked his juice relatively pure and natural. The day was crisp and a little
overcast, but the marine layer would burn off before
noon. He sat back, a copy of the county's conservative
newspaper across his lap, and watched the tide on the
beach below. Its teal phosphorescence boiled pleasantly onto beige sand, and the tiered walkways from
the rear of the elegant resort hotel led people down
to walk romantically entwined along the water's edge.
Brilliantly red bougainvillea bloomed extravagantly
along the atria and pathways and stone walls of the
hotel, edged by iceplant and grass upon the grounds.

The view refreshed his eyes as much as the juice did his throat.

Sucking orange pulp from between his teeth, he finally scooted himself closer to the glass-topped table and looked at his laptop screen, scrolling through the files it displayed. "Let's see what I can find, boy."

He had managed to cull a list of five names from school district records. He had had more, but had tossed most of the Latino surnames, though in this county he knew he stood a chance of being wrong, as the intermarriages and cultural interlacings of the population were myriad. Orange County had long ago lost its staid white only face and now wore the melting pot mask that the entire nation was famed for. He knew he might have to backtrack if he were wrong on the surname of the boy he sought.

He looked from the screen to the paper one last time. "Gotcha." With a brilliant red felt tip, he encircled the notice in the paper. Curtis Reynolds, fourteen, memorial services the day following at Brea Evergreen United Methodist, eleven o'clock. The picture was not good, but he recognized the companion to the one he sought. The boy ought to be there as well, belonging to one of the four names left on the screen, staring him in the face.

"You just hang out, son. I'll find you. You don't have to have a name. I just need to get my hands on you. And I will."

Rembrandt could find him sooner, if he wished, driving from southern Orange County and the pleasant atmosphere of the beach, crisscrossing north to Brea at the other end of the county, but then there was still the matter of isolating him from his family and whatever police surveillance might be upon him. The funeral, however, posed opportunities. Vast opportunities. There would be plainclothesmen there, as well, but he could deal with that. Like riding a good cutting horse, he could separate the calf from the herd.

Rembrandt closed his files and shut down his laptop, and sat back once more in his chair. He poured another glass of iced juice from his carafe, saluted the surf, and proceeded to enjoy his day of leisure. There would not be many more of them once the base camps were set up and basic training had begun. There would be logistics and intelligence to work out, but the program would not be fully operational until Christiansen was located. First the boy, then the Marine sergeant. Tomorrow the hunt began in earnest.

*   *   *   *

He looked and felt ridiculous. They had dressed him in black jeans, one of Phil's old navy sweaters, and a dark banker's tie, too long, its length buttoned away inside his shirt where it tickled him around the navel. All of this could have been done in the relatively private confines of the home, but no, they were doing it here in the church parking lot. The dweeb solemnly tied the knot and then tugged it into perfection, murmuring, "You ought to learn how to do this someday."

"Why? So I can be like you?" *More than half dead less than halfway through life?* Brand stared into Phil's eyes.

His stepfather's mouth thinned again, but he said nothing, merely took him by the shoulders and spun him around so his mother could look at him. She pressed a handkerchief to her lips.

"Don't make a scene, Mom."

She put her back to the car and looked around at the multitude of other vehicles. "I have no intention of doing so." She scanned with the practiced eye of one used to dodging the media and commented, almost disappointed, "No one's here."

"There's a hostage situation in a mini-mart in Stanton," Phil told her. "And there's a baby getting a heart and lung transplant at Loma Linda."

And Curtis' death was obviously old news. Brand took a deep breath. The church was nestled deep between housing and a golf course. He looked at the groomed fairways of the course, wondering if it used to be a cemetery at one time, so suspiciously close to the sanctuary. The trees which edged the course and made a natural hazard also framed the back and side of the church. Watered by the golf course, they were a deep, dark green despite the fact that the rainy season had yet to hit the area. Their soothing color attracted him.

"Brandon, I want you to take your glasses off the minute you get inside."

He pushed his shades into better position on his nose. The lightning bolt etch mark floated just above the vision of his right eye, sort of like a pointer. He shrugged inside the stiff collar of the new dress shirt and felt the tie uncomfortably hug his neck.

"Brandon, did you hear what I said?"

"Yeah."

Her eyes narrowed, but she turned away. Phil said, "We'll be right behind you."

Cutting off escape, Brand thought. He took another deep breath and crossed the parking lot to the big, wooden double doors which had been flung open to the crisp October day. He passed through, noticing their surfaces, carved with the symbols of Christianity and the promised afterlife.

He could hear bagpipes playing "Amazing Grace"

and it struck him funny. Fartbags, Curt had always called them. Scottish sphincters. He used to play his armpit and drone in imitation. Brand did not think Curtis would have been happy to have bagpipes played at his funeral, but it was not something they'd ever discussed.

Nobody his age ever discussed funerals. Kids weren't supposed to die. He remembered the rash of car accidents last summer, when 16- and 17-year-olds were flying out of smashed cars at an incredible rate, by the dozens it seemed. It had been shocking, but it was something everyone knew wouldn't happen to them. Till the next time somebody went cruising and missed a tight turn at, oh, say, eighty miles an hour, aluminum beer cans soaring clear just ahead of bodies. Just another hazard of the California lifestyle.

But here they were, freshmen in high school, confined to campus during hours, when the drivers, the juniors and seniors, cruised away for decent food, screeching back seconds before the final tardy bells. They had counted the hours until Curtis would get his learner's permit. He would have turned fifteen and a half first, barely a year away.

A year to freedom. The first rites de passage. A year that would make their miserable existence gain hope, become bearable even. A year closer to manhood.

They'd never thought about ducking bullets.

He'd barely set foot inside the chapel when Mrs. Reynolds descended on him. She wore a black jacket dress, with a thin white pinstripe, and it was new, because she preferred jeans. He didn't think he'd ever seen Curt's mom in a dress before. He could see why. Her legs didn't look like they were meant for the public to view. Her face was puffy and her eyes bloodshot from crying, and his father stood in the corner, gray around the mouth, his dark eyes sunk in his face, saying nothing.

Curt had been the only boy.

Before he could duck, Mrs. Reynolds wrapped her chubby arms around him. "Oh, Brandon," she whispered hoarsely as she hugged him tightly. "You must go see him. He looks so . . . natural. We decided to leave the coffin lid open so everyone could say goodbye."

She knocked his glasses nearly off his face, and he stared down the row of double pews at the white and gold coffin at the front, where the alter was, and smelled the heavy perfume of the flowers.

Half the school was here, it seemed, and their heads all turned and a whisper started through the chapel that he could almost hear. Bzzz, bzzz, bzzz . . . the shooting . . . bzzz, bzzz.

He shrugged out of June Reynolds' death grip. He retrieved his shades and tucked them inside his shirt pocket, as promised. The inside of the chapel seemed to glow in matching whites and golds, like candlelight, and he stood for a moment, bedazzled. The sharpness of his newly created vision wavered, then darkened, then lightened. He fished around for courage to step down the aisle toward the coffin and found himself empty inside.

He had spent most of the night talking with Mitch. That had kept the darkness and Bauer away for a while, but Mitch wasn't here, and he did not like taking drugs, so he hadn't hit his stash again. He hadn't induced a chemical calm, he had no pharmaceutical well from which to draw safe emotions. How do you manufacture something out of nothing? Where could he find the backbone to go say good-bye to Curtis?

Mrs. Reynolds seemed to sense how difficult it was. She reached for his hand. "I'll walk down with you."

"No! I mean, that's all right." Brand cleared his throat. He put a hand up to the tie knot and tugged at it, trying to loosen it a bit. He could hear his mother and Mrs. Reynolds hugging and talking in a muted tone.

The coffin beckoned him. He slid a foot forward and started toward it.

His face felt chilled and clammy, and his hands began to sweat. He turned suddenly, looked back through the tiny lobby of the chapel, and saw signs for restrooms. Just in time. He pushed hurriedly past Phil and his mother. She made a sound of protest, but Phil said, "Let him go. He looks pretty pale."

He made it to the tiny bathroom and threw up in the stall toilet, until he was dry heaving, his throat burning. He flushed, then went to the sink and washed his face. The water felt tepid and smelled stagnant, like old pond water. He wondered where they pumped it up from. He stood there over the sink a long time, running water now and then, splashing it on his face.

"It's not a good thing to see, is it, son?"

Brand froze. He raised his eyes, caught only a corner of the speaker's visage in the mirror. A vertical fraction of a face, sharply contoured, skin ravaged by old scars, eyes coal dark. The ruined man.

"They're waiting for you now. Any minute now, someone's going to come in after you. So you better get yourself straight."

Brand stared at the splinter of the man's face. So soft-spoken, so hard behind the words. "What do you want?"

"Why, I want to get the men who got Curtis killed. Don't you?"

"I don't know what you mean. The skinhead's dead."

"Ah. But there's more to the story than that, isn't there, son? You know it, and I know it. I should think you'd want to tell me . . . to get justice for Curtis. Someday you'll be crossing over, too, and he's going to look you in the face. He's going to wonder why you didn't stand up for him. He's going to wonder why being your friend got him killed. You know, he was still dying when you ran. The paramedics tried working on him, but it was too late."

"You shut up! He was dead! I know he was. I saw it in his eyes—" Just like Darby. It wasn't like the eyes stopped glistening or anything, they just stopped . . . reacting to life. There was nothing, no one, no soul, to see.

"You ran, and I don't blame you. You saw a terrible thing happen. But you should have heard the machine. A high-pitched whine, and then the paramedics would yell 'Clear' and then his body would flop when it got all those volts. They did it again and again. Once they thought they got his ticker jump-started. But it didn't keep. No, sir, they worked real hard on him, but there was nothing they could do."

"My being there wouldn't have made a difference."

"Wouldn't it now? Well, that's something you'll never know."

"Leave me alone," Brand said softly, but it was as if the ruined man couldn't hear him.

"You and I need to talk, son. Or else the guilt is going to eat you up inside."

Brand wiped his hands dry. "You stay away from me."

The ruined man held up a hand. "I'm ready when you're ready. But don't you forget we've got things to talk about."

Brand started to turn around and confront him.

The bathroom went dark. "Shit!" Brand stood, his heart in his throat, thinking he'd gone blind. The bathroom door opened and he saw the silhouette of the ruined man slipping out.

Brand grabbed the door before it eased shut and slapped his palm against the wall and found the light switch. He turned it on before leaning out. The lobby was empty except for Phil and his mother standing in the chapel doorway. She turned, as if alerted by his very presence, and waved.

"They're waiting for you," she mouthed, and took him by the elbow.

He took her hand off his arm. Her fingers were chill, and she gave him a look that, just for a moment, he imagined hurt lay in. Brand turned toward the coffin and began to drift toward it.

Drift, because he could not feel his feet touch the carpet runner. Drift, because there seemed to be no time, no heartbeat, no sound. The church had swelled to overflowing, people crowded the side aisles along the wings, but he could not hear them breathe, they might as well be the dead themselves who waited to welcome Curtis into their ranks. He thought he recognized faces from his school as he floated closer toward the coffin, teachers, counselors, students, past and present. Where had they all been when he and Curtis were being taunted, snubbed, trash-canned?

A handful of people were still making their way past the casket as he drew near. They parted to let him close.

If he couldn't hear their voices, their breathing, their steps, it was because his pulse thundered in his ears. Every breath he took sounded as though some immense bellows must be sucking in the air and releasing it. With each inch he came closer to the coffin and seeing over its gilt-edged rim, his body reminded him that it was he who lived and Curtis who did not. Every part of his body except for his guts, which had disappeared, leaving an ice cold cavern in their absence.

He put out a trembling hand and touched the rim. Like a ship docking and throwing out an anchor line, it steadied him and he pulled himself closer. Curtis' face became visible, no longer eclipsed by the coffin's side.

Brand held his breath. It was and was not his friend. Curt had never worn suits, never intended to, but they had him laid out in navy blue. His hair was freshly washed and someone must have lightened it, because it was a true blond now, not the dirty blond he remembered so well. And he'd never known Curtis to be without a pimple or two, smooth peach makeup hid the red blotches. Now his face looked serene, both older and younger than the friend Brand had known, childlike, peacefully asleep in the coffin, but with a newfound maturity in the suit and the solemn expression of his face.

But it wasn't Curtis. Not the one he knew. Curtis was always laughing, talking, or eating, his expression in constant motion, his hair uncombed, his skin outraged by an excess of hormones, his eyes open and defiant. Curt, the coward, the brave fool, the scholar, the delinquent, the kidder, the loyal best friend, Curt . . . *the dead*.

Brand found himself wondering where the bullet holes were and how much damage they'd done.

"It's good luck if you kiss them good-bye," a girlish whisper said in his ear.

He flinched, caught a glimpse of Curt's mother in the corner of his vision, and bit his tongue on his reply.

As he shied away from the edge of the coffin, he looked up and saw darkness dripping from the rotunda ceiling overhead. It flowed down the back of the altar and geysered up from the pulpits, charcoal fog, and it was hungry and cold. It fell, like rain, with a plink and plunk, onto the casket.

It did not pool like water, but gathered, like smoke or fog and as Brand stared in absolute horror, the coffin filled with it. The KillJoy snaked along the white satin lining and smothered Curtis' torso.

"Shit," Brand murmured. He hoped he had imagined it, stoned as he'd been, afraid as he'd been. He hoped that perhaps Bauer had thrown him a curve and that nothing was what he'd seen, what he'd imagined.

The darkness inundated the chapel. The large crucifix hanging on the wall deterred it not at all, and as Brand stared aghast, Jesus disappeared from sight altogether.

Mrs. Reynolds' grief-pale face bobbed through the dark air toward him, like a hot air balloon. "Brandon, are you all right?"

"No." His knees went like water and the only thing holding him on his feet was that he leaned on the corner of the casket, gripping it tightly with both hands. "You need to get out of here, Mrs. Reynolds. Now. You need to get everybody out." He could feel its overpowering appetite. He knew that if he turned and looked, he would see it tasting the people sitting unaware in the pews, licking at their faces, nibbling at their eyes. But he would not, could not, turn and look. He watched as the KillJoy enveloped Curt's body altogether, until nothing was left but his ghostly, powdered face.

It was real. He could see it. Any hope that it had come out of the codeine and Haldol vanished. He'd been stoned, but he had seen a true thing. It had existence, and he was aware of it, and he didn't know what to do. He had a margin of safety, that he did know. Although it had chased him through his dreams, Brand thought it could be nothing personal. It hungered as a shark hungered. If he stayed out of its waters, he would be safe. He stared at Curt's placid face.

And then the eyes popped open. They were opaque and filmed, gummy and still, and they looked right into his. The jaw cracked open, issuing misty dark words.

"I know you," the corpse said. "Brandon, Brand, Brand X, the X-man. I come for you, too."

Brand let out a yell that tore through the hushed quiet of the church. He pelted through the side door.

Chapter 15

Kamryn found a quiet corner of the chapel near the exit doors and waited. She observed as the building filled, watched the faces of the young so shocked and curious to be there, and the old, so tired, so worried. She found herself humming lightly to the music being piped in. She thought of her aunt who, in the last decade of her long life, had refused to go to any funeral, even of her best friend, even of her husband, as if fearing a preview of her future.

She would like to have told her aunt not to worry, but she couldn't have then and even now was not entirely sure. Simply being in the church almost overwhelmed her. She had never seen God, but she was not certain that she hadn't felt His Presence, or at least that of one of his Angels. It left her feeling tremulous as she stood in the sanctuary, tremulous and on the verge of some vast emotional experience she could not quite understand.

She saw the boy start to enter the chapel, then push back and hurriedly leave. Kamryn thought of going after him but held back, thinking his parents surely would, but they did not either. After many long minutes, after several more hymns during which the crowd grew so thick she thought of leaving rather than be trapped in the multitude, the boy came back. He went

down the center aisle so quickly that Kamryn had
barely a glance at his sheet-white face. The music had
changed to "Morning has broken, like the first
day. . . ."

She wished that she had not stayed in the back, but
had gone to the front so she could join him, that he
didn't have to make the walk alone. The dead boy's
mother hurried to catch up, but he seemed oblivious.
The few mourners already at the casket moved aside
to give him clearance.

Kamryn folded her hands tightly, trying to send him
courage in her thoughts, understanding what he must
be feeling. There had always been for her, as young
as she was, at her great-aunt's services, and then her
grandfather's, and then her parents', a sense of unrec-
ognition. It was as if, when she faced the living, that
whatever it was in the other person that she greeted,
that she recognized, was intangible and left when life
departed. It was more than warmth and animation . . .
it was . . . oh, she couldn't explain it . . . but she knew
as the boy stood over the open coffin and looked down,
that he would be searching for the familiar in his
friend, that which had always leaped out to greet him,
and was now missing.

The dead boy's mother moved up and said something. The boy reacted as if shocked, and then stood
and looked around the room wildly. Kamryn felt a chill
touch her. Despite her long-sleeved dress, despite the
warm-winded October day outside, with the sunlight
streaming in the open doors, an icy feeling permeated
the chapel. The faint tattoo scars prickled in her skin.
She hugged herself, her purse with its gun-hard bulge
digging into her rib cage.

She decided to leave and quietly ducked out, and
had her key in the car door when she heard the agoniz-

ing cry. It was primal and drove the very hairs up on the back of her neck, a primitive wail of loss and fear, a raw file of sound against her nerves. Emotions cascaded over her and gooseflesh raised on her arms. *Come on, Sis. Come down into the basement. I've got a surprise for you.* Her throat closed slightly and she could feel her pulse ticking wildly in the hollow of her neck. Death and grief. Before the echo of the boy's cry faded, she had turned back as if she could do something. Then she saw the man waiting in the grove where the golf course met the churchyard, waiting as if he knew someone would come his way.

At first, she thought it might be a driver for the mortuary, but he wasn't dressed right, and he had an attitude to his body posture. Kamryn slid quickly into her car and fought the desire to hide further, watching, as the side doors flew open and the boy bolted out, head down, running for his life.

He barged right into the waiting man. There was a brief struggle, and then the man picked up the boy, right off his feet, Kamryn's boy, and hauled him toward the grove where a car waited. He threw his captive into the car, got in, and started up, heading down a service road to the back of the church, into the golf course.

Kamryn's jaw dropped as she tried to decide what she'd just seen, when people boiled out of the building, and began to fill the parking lot. A woman in a blue-dotted swiss suit cried, "Brandon! Brand! Come back here!"

A tall man joined her and added his shout to hers. "Brandon! Come right back here, young man!"

Brandon. Her boy. She should tell them what she'd seen, but she'd also watched their strained, cold faces in the church. Whatever fate Brandon had awaiting him was not much different back here.

Kamryn started her car and backed out slowly, until she hit the gravel service road the first car had taken. No one paid any attention to her.

* * * *

Brand sat in the front seat, nursing a sore wrist, shoulder up against the door panel so he could be as far away from the ruined man as possible. He watched the groomed fairways pass by and become undeveloped land, eucalyptus and pepper trees brushing the car window as he drove through, toward the foothills, toward the canyons.

"Well, now," said the ruined man in that faintly accented drawl of his. "I didn't think it would be this easy."

"Congratulations."

The ruined man smiled broadly. "Sounds like you had some of the sauce knocked out of you, son."

"I'm not your son."

"Well, let's trade names then. I'm Rembrandt and you're . . ."

"Brand," he answered reluctantly. He did not want to look at the man, but he did. His eyes were smudged again, and he blinked several times to clear them, but nothing helped. He finally closed them in frustration.

"If I were you," Rembrandt said, and the road swerved away from them, shifting Brand into a door handle, "I'd want to stay awake and alert. My life might depend on it."

Brand opened his eyes to stare out the front window. They were on a firebreak road now, and the tires sent puffs of dirt out behind them like smoke signals. He said wearily, "If you think I'm scared, I'm not. You just want to ask me some questions."

Rembrandt's smile disappeared as if it had never been, and he jerked the steering wheel to a hard right, bringing the car to a stop, headed into a small copse of pepper and oak trees. The car filled with the smell of dirt and freshly-bruised grass.

"You're not as smart as you think you are, son. Because I do intend to ask you questions, and I intend on killing you if I don't get some answers."

Brand snapped his head around. "What the hell are you talking about?"

Rembrandt shoved the car door open, fishing something out of its pocket. "Your quarter's finished. Game time over. I get some answers or you're as dead as your little buddy back there, and I'll tell you something else. The way he died will be easy compared to the way you're going to die."

Words dried up in Brand's throat as he watched Rembrandt get out of the car carrying a rope. Massaging it through his hands, the ruined man went to several trees before finding one he liked, and throwing the end of the rope over a convenient tree limb. At the realization, Brand kicked his feet over the center console, ready to bail out the driver's door, but Rembrandt moved amazingly fast. He snatched the door open and buried his fist in Brand's collar, lifting Brand out of the seat. He manhandled Brand across the ground until his back hit the rough bark of the tree, and the limb and rope shadowed his face as he looked at the ruined man.

"Don't mistake me, son."

"Who are you?"

"You don't really want to know that, because right now you have a choice. If I told you, you wouldn't." Rembrandt removed his hand from Brand's collar, giving him breathing room, and quickly fashioned a slip noose.

"We don't know each other very well, you and I, but I know you've got a quick tongue. So I'm going to save you some valuable time." He pulled the noose over Brand's head. "I want to know what you know about Mitch Christiansen. Where's his crib, how long has he been hanging out at the mall, and who else might know anything about him."

Brand felt the stiff bristles of the rope cut into his throat as it settled into place. "I—I don't—"

Rembrandt jerked the noose tight. "I said I was going to save you some valuable time." He tied the rope around the tree and left, coming back with weathered wooden crates in his hands, bee boxes. He stacked them on top of each other, next to Brandon. He pointed at them. "I'll ask you one more time, and then I'll make you stand up there, and then I'll make you jump. You'll hang the way they did a couple hundred years ago, before the hangman's knot was invented. Do you know how the knot works? It breaks your neck when your weight hits the rope. Takes only minutes to strangle and die that way. This way could take hours. But you'll still be dead before anybody finds you."

Brand tried to gather his thoughts as Bauer barged in, thinking of the time he hog-tied one of his victims around the neck and every time the child grew weary and dropped his legs, the noose got tighter and tighter. Bauer appreciated the image. The remembrance made Brand sick. Sweat popped out on his forehead as he fought for composure.

Rembrandt let out a sigh. "You're tough to convince. Well, son, I've been doing some research. I pulled up your school records. I know you've been in and out of psychiatric care. This is going to look like suicide. Isn't anybody going to come looking for me. I've got nothing to lose here, and you've got everything."

"Just a minute!" The rope cut into his neck. "I met him a couple of weeks ago. He's been hanging around the mall and plaza for a couple of months, though. He doesn't make friends. I don't think anybody else knows him. And I don't really know him. Just Mitch, that's all he told me." His voice sounded strange to his own ears. "That's all I know. Everything."

"Everything?"

"I swear!"

"Get up on those boxes."

His vision swam. Perspiration cascaded down his face and the wind dried it, but he could taste the salt of his fear on his lips. "What?"

"You heard me. Get up on those boxes."

Brand climbed onto the wooden crates. They creaked under his weight. They were empty, abandoned, and the thought lanced through him that at least they were empty of bees. He balanced gingerly on his feet.

"He never took you to his crib."

Brand wet his mouth again. "We just used to say hi around the parking lot."

"Where?"

"Behind the arcade, in the storage areas outside Hot Flash and the other stores."

Rembrandt ran his fingers across the rope. "Who'd he talk to besides you?"

"No . . . nobody. He kept to himself. The mall cops ran him off a couple of times. If he stayed anywhere, it was probably behind the plaza across the street."

"But you don't know that."

"No." Brand tried to swallow again and found his mouth dry of spit. He could stand here until doomsday and not work up a drop. He wondered if Rembrandt could tell that he was lying.

Rembrandt wrapped his hand in the rope. "Thank you, son," and began to take up the slack.

Brand felt the noose tighten. The air whooshed out of him, leaving him without protest. He clawed at the noose. He was being hanged anyway! The air grew dim in front of his face.

"Stop it! Hold it right there!"

Rembrandt turned, and behind his lanky form, Brand could make out a blurred figure with a determined feminine voice. And she was pointing a gun.

"I mean it!" Kamryn called. She twitched the gun aside, fired twice, puncturing both rear tires of Rembrandt's car. "Brand, quit fooling around. Get yourself free and get over here."

He tore a nail to a bloody quick getting the slipknot to budge, then pulled his head out of the loop and jumped toward Kamryn, shying away from Rembrandt.

"Get in my car." She pointed an elbow toward the firebreak.

"Wh-where?" His breath choked up in his throat.

"Back there, behind the curve." She eyed Rembrandt over the barrel of her gun. "Hurry up!" She started to walk backward.

Rembrandt had been holding his hands out at his sides and moved, ever so slightly, dusting off his suit jacket. "I did not think about you, ma'am. I see now I should have given you more consideration."

"Forget me. It's the gun you're giving credit." She stumbled over a knot of grass, but Brand was there, reaching for an arm, steering her. She looked briefly at him. "I told you to run."

"I'm not leaving you alone with him." Still white-faced, still determined.

"Okay. Can you drive?"

"I'm only fourteen."

"Screw that. Can you drive?"

"Sure. As long as I don't have to parallel park."

They were bracketed together like a three-legged race at a picnic. Rembrandt was slowly walking toward them, cautiously, a step to every three or four of theirs.

Kamryn took a deep breath. "Run," she ordered and shook him off. Rembrandt let out a bellow and charged. She fired into the ground, and he plunged to a halt in astonishment.

She turned and took to her heels after Brand. He already had the car in gear as she grabbed the open passenger door and jumped in.

* * * *

They'd switched drivers and reached the open road before she spoke. "I was at the church. I heard you scream."

Brand was looking out the rolled-down window, his sable hair tousled and swept back from his forehead. He made a wry face. "The whole world heard me scream."

"Why?"

"Just did. It gave me the creeps, seeing Curtis like that, y'know." He shut his mouth firmly, looking back out the window.

If he didn't want to talk, she couldn't force him. But she had things she wanted to say. "I want you to know that I know what you did."

Sharply, "When?"

"At the mall. I know you tried to protect me."

"I guess you didn't need all that much protection."

"Maybe. But I'm sorry for your friend, Brandon."

"He wasn't trying to protect you."

"I know. He was just . . . there."

"In the way." Brand rubbed his nose briskly. "I suppose you're taking me to the police."

Kamryn shifted weight. She had the gun secured under her thigh. "No, I don't think so. Maybe that's a decision you should go home and make."

"I don't have a home," he said bleakly.

"You have to go somewhere."

"Yeah." He chafed at his throat lightly, where the rope had bitten into tender flesh. "I have to go away from here."

"Brand, you have family. You can't just run like that."

"They'll put me back in the psycho ward. You were listening to Rembrandt. You heard him. I have a rep." He looked at her, hazel eyes reflecting his misery. "You don't know. I can't stay here. I can't tell you everything, but It knows me, knows my name—I can't stay."

The desperation in his voice struck a chord in her. She knew what it was like, and she knew she couldn't stay, either. "You won't get far on foot."

"I don't know where to go either. Mitch would know. And I've got to tell him about Rembrandt."

"Mitch," Kamryn repeated with a faint smile. "And you wouldn't know where he is."

"He's in the loft above my garage, but we can't get in there until after dark. If I know my mom and the dweeb, they're talking to the police right about now, shifting the responsibility for finding me. Then they'll round up my siblings and head out to dinner. We'll park around the block and come in through the backyard."

"I'm going with you."

"You volunteered, didn't you?"

Kamryn guessed she had.

Chapter 16

Rembrandt watched the bumper of the car disappear in a cloud of dust and dried grass, as it pulled around the curve of the road. He waited a moment to be sure that the young woman hadn't changed her mind and decided to come back with her firepower, but the air cleared of the engine's drone.

He turned and surveyed the damage to the car's tires. He had only one standard spare in the trunk, but she'd known that. He wasn't going anywhere unless he wished to ruin the tire rims. It wasn't his car. He got in and fired up the vehicle, then pulled back down the road. By the time he reached a main street and a filling station, he had Bayliss on the cell phone.

"I want two agents."

"Street ready?"

"I want the best we've got."

Bayliss did not ask why. He said only, "We don't have expendables at this point."

Because of the systems they had routed the calls through, and because of the scrambling, there was a slight delay between each phrasing. It made it difficult to read the nuances of Bayliss' voice, but Rembrandt caught that last.

"Christiansen's made me."

"That is not good news."

"No. But I'm close enough to be breathing down his neck. I need our best."

"I'll have them sent out by jet. Where to?"

"John Wayne Airport. Page me with their ETA. And, sir—"

"Yes?"

"I apologize for the difficulty."

A long pause. Then, "You're the best man I've got. There is no one more loyal, more serving. Not even that voodoo priest could give me a better right hand."

"Thank you, sir."

"Just find Christiansen. My timetable is losing flexibility."

"I understand."

Rembrandt hung up. A spark burned in his chest, as it always did, when he thought of what they were trying to accomplish, just as it did whenever he saw the flag being raised or heard the anthem being played. This was a time of trials and bold decisions. Judgment would come later, generations later.

He was prepared.

He stowed the cell phone in his briefcase as the sound of air wrenches filled the air, making normal conversation nearly impossible. He had paid the attendants well, but not too well, for new tires and a quick transfer. He had his own personal timetable now. The quarry would be running again, and easier to track.

This time he would have the woman and the boy with him. He did not know if Military Intelligence was also still tracking Christiansen or if the local police would be looking for him, but he knew what they did not. Christiansen would take them along, for the camouflage they offered. He would be right behind.

* * * *

"No," said Mitch flatly. "It wouldn't be right."

"I have the car," returned Kamryn. She sat cross-legged on the dusty floor, showing a good deal of leg, unaware of it, flexing chopsticks in her hand. The loft smelled of lo mein and pork fried rice. "And we all have to leave."

"Brand doesn't have to."

She flipped a look toward Brand, her dark hair feathering about her face as she did so, wings of ebony accenting her movement. "Rembrandt tried to kill him."

"If I move on, Rembrandt will come after me. I can guarantee that." Having a name, at last, for the shadowy adversary helped. It made his flight and fight more concrete instead of abstract.

Brand whispered hoarsely, "I have to leave more than either of you." He had not eaten much and now pushed his lo mein noodles aimlessly about his paper plate. She wondered if his throat hurt, or if the rope burns had only chafed his skin. It did not matter. He had been close enough to hanging. She would not feel much like eating either, but her last good meal had been yesterday.

"You have family."

"They won't protect me. They never have. If you won't take me, I'll hitchhike out. As far as I can get. I can't stay!"

"Brand, I can't take anybody with me. You've met Rembrandt. This is the first time I've known his name, but he's been on my heels for months, and he doesn't take prisoners. I don't know how much longer I can stay two jumps ahead of him, and if and when he catches up, I can't keep either of you safe."

"I didn't ask you to," Kamryn said brusquely. "I can take care of myself. You're not taking my car and leaving without me."

They studied each other. To Brand's surprise, these two seemed to know each other almost as well as he knew Mitch. When told who they were going to meet, Kamryn had stopped at a mini-mart as well as for Chinese take-out, and bought razors and scissors. She had insisted on cutting his hair and making him shave before they ate, and she'd worked quickly, paring him down to a civilized look. His skin showed one or two small cuts where the razors had bitten lightly.

"The shooting's over," he commented. "You're not even front page news."

"Snake will come after me and probably others. They won't let it go until I'm as dead as Darby." Kamryn put down her plate and chopsticks. She hesitated a moment, then rolled up her sleeves. Like the lower half of Mitch's face, her skin was too tender, too pink . . . and the tattoos imprinted up and down her arms were faded, but still visible. "I've been having them lasered. It takes about ten treatments, but that's only skin-deep. I won't tell you why I did it in the first place, but I'm not that person anymore."

Brand stirred. He reached forward tentatively, then pulled his hand away. "It must hurt."

"It hurts worse having them." She shuddered slightly and let her sleeves fall back into place.

Mitch's gaze stayed on her face. "You know too much."

"About what?" Brand looked back and forth.

"About the skinheads."

Brand curled a lip. "They're thugs."

"That, and more. They're organized. They have cash sources of money, weapons and publications, paper printed and electronic. Hatred is an easy culture to spread." Mitch raised his eyes and rocked back on his hips, forgetting the plate of Chinese food in his lap. "You're right. You can't stay here."

"And it *is* my car."

"We might have to exchange the car."

"I've got some money." She put her chin forward defiantly. The color of her eyes deepened.

"I'm thinking of backtracking up toward Seattle. Rembrandt's already been up there. It might throw him off."

"No," interrupted Brand. "That's the wrong way."

"You're not going," Mitch responded, without looking at him. "You've got family and it's time you took the responsibility for getting along with them. It's not a one-way street."

"You don't understand—"

"No, you don't understand. I can't take you with me."

Brand mumbled something. Both Mitch and Kamryn said, with irritation, "What?"

"Nothing." He folded his plate up and squashed it until the food ran out of it in dribbles before shoving it into a trash sack. "You can't leave here until I do or the police will be all over you."

"In about two hours, most of the West Coast will be sound asleep."

Brand hunched down and folded his arms. "I'll wait."

Kamryn asked, "What will you need?"

"I have most of my things in a duffel. No ID. Very little money. What about you?"

"I have," she said firmly, "clothes, my car, money. And my gun. I've got everything I need."

"ID?"

"Several."

Mitch's eyes widened slightly, but he did not comment on that. "We should take the 5 up to Sacramento and on up. There's a lot of agricultural traffic, nobody will notice us one way or the other."

"We won't get out of the area before dawn if we try to exchange the car here."

"No. We'd better wait until we hit Sacramento. You've got ownership, registration?"

"All the papers."

"Okay."

Brand tried to listen, but his throat hurt and the little food he had gotten down hit his stomach like a nice, warm ball, and lulled him. He lay down on one of the blankets he'd given Mitch to use and curled up, puppy style. They were just like his parents, they wouldn't listen, and he didn't want to tell them everything or they'd be the first to drop him off at the lunatic ward. He had plans of his own to develop, to either go with them or get out as well. He still had a set of Curtis' keys. Maybe Mrs. Reynolds' spare car key was on it. He could drive, as long as it was in forward. He didn't have much practice backing up. He had forty bucks for gas. He could get maybe all the way to Phoenix on that. . . .

He sleepily asked himself, *Why Phoenix?* Because that was the way he had to go. And because it sounded great. Mystical. Anything was possible in Phoenix. He fell deeper. Sleep cushioned him.

Yellow Dog came to greet him, tail waving enthusiastically, chops grinning. He pricked his ears forward alertly and Brandon checked behind him to see if he'd brought anybody with him. Could Yellow Dog sense Mitch and Kamryn?

But he stood alone in that netherworld, an ambiguous landscape around him, nothing distinct but himself

and the dog, young dog, old pup. Brand chucked him
behind the ears, and the dog pressed his ribs against
his knee. The dog was always so real, warm and silky, his
nose damp and cold, and Yellow Dog slobbered at his
hand as if to prove the point. What had happened to
him, Brand wondered, that the dog had been exiled to
the realm of dreams and nothingness?

Why didn't you go to dog heaven, huh, boy?

Yellow Dog looked upward with eager brown eyes.
He shook himself all over and bounded a step away.
He hunkered down on his forelegs, haunches up in the
air, canine language for, "Let's romp!"

Brand stepped after him. Yellow Dog let out a tenor
bark and trotted off, stopping now and then to make
sure he was being followed. Brand told him all that
had happened, Yellow Dog bumping into his legs now
and then in that herding way dogs have, listening with
his doggish sensibility to every word Brand said. It was
strange and delightful to be with the creature without
the threat of Bauer or the other. They trotted side by
side down an unknown road, toward an unknowable
destiny, as if they were making their way down to the
park or the beach for a session with a frisbee.

Brand slipped on something wet and slick, and went
to one knee. He put a hand in it as he braced himself
to get back to his feet. It glistened blackly in the sepia
lighting, but he could smell it: warm blood. Yellow Dog
pivoted on one paw and whined anxiously.

Brand put out the hand to show him, "Look, blood,"
and stopped, aghast.

The dog's throat gaped open at the golden ruff, and
the blood dripped steadily, quickly, from the wound.
Yellow Dog shook his head as if worried and hurt.

Brand stumbled up to his feet. He tried to pull a
length off his shirt, but the fabric wouldn't tear, and

it had to; he had to bind the wound or the dog would bleed to death. Yellow Dog danced away from him when he reached and tried to seal the lips of the gash together, to stop the flow.

"No!" cried Brand. He lunged at the dog, trying to catch him, slipped and fell again in a slick, warm coppery-smelling puddle.

The dog trotted off a length, and turned. He let out a low woof as if to urge him upward and onward.

Brand felt his face grow warm and his eyes sting. "No, come back, come back!"

He got up again and ran after the golden retriever. Yellow Dog stopped once, and Brand could see the bitter slashes on his face. They appeared as if someone invisible sliced at him: down his muzzle, one ear in rags, on his flank. Blood everywhere. Brand whirled, looking for the assailant. He kicked at thin air and screamed at the dog.

"Run! Run!" but the animal took the assault as if it were an expected, inevitable act.

"Jesus," Brand pled. "He's killing you! Run."

The dog seemed weary. His eyes lost their gleam. He panted heavily, as animals in pain and fear do. For a second he leaned against Brand's kneecap, and he could feel the shuddering, the awful agony in the dog's body.

He barked again and trotted wobbily away, drawing Brand after him. Brand wiped his face on his sleeve, sobbing like a baby. All that blood. Even Curtis hadn't bled like that. He staggered after, barely seeing Yellow Dog, being led farther and farther. . . .

The dog toppled. Brand caught up and knelt down next to him. He stripped his shirt off and tried to bind the pup's throat and chest, but there was little he could do. The feathery tail thumped several times as if acknowledging what Brand attempted.

"Is this what happened? Who would do something like this? Oh, God . . . God, make it stop bleeding. . . ."

"Sssshust, boy."

Brand looked up. The black woman leaned over him. She had come out of nowhere, exuding the same kind of goodness that Yellow Dog had, like standing in the basking warmth of the sun on an Indian summer day. "You can't help him now. Not yet. But he feels your love, he does, child. He feels it."

"He's in pain! You've got to do something."

"He feels your pain. Let him go, if you can. Just let him go."

Yellow Dog grew insubstantial between his hands as Brand tried to hold pressure on the wounds, his flesh disappearing, until there was nothing left but a congealing pool of blood and slickness on his fingers.

Brand's nose ran. He sniffed sharply. "Is he dead? Is he gone?"

"No, child. He'll be back when you need him. He has a job to do. He has to bring you to me. When that's done, when that's over, he'll be free."

"It's not fair. He's just a dog. He's never done anything to anybody."

"He's a thread in the cloth, child, just like you and me."

"What do you know?" He swallowed back his tears.

"I tol' you to remember."

"Mother," answered Brand.

"Mother Jubilation," she repeated firmly. "In New Orleans. I know a lot o' what you need to know. You look for me in the Quarter, do you hear? And come quick. And you bring your friends with you. I can't help you if you're scattered all over the face of creation."

"In New Orleans," Brand repeated. "In the Quarter." He suddenly added, "Why do you smell like incense and candy?"

She laughed, flashing good strong white teeth, her bosom heaving. "You know when you get here! Come quick, child. It's your only hope."

"You know about the KillJoy, don't you?"

"That's what you named it, did you? You're a clever one. Don't out-clever yourself, now. Naming something gives it power. Calls it."

"They won't bring me."

"Then you bring them. You tell the white boy, the soldier, I gave him his charm." The black woman began to fade, her handsome face and snapping black eyes all he could see of her now. "Mother Jubilation," she repeated one last time. "Now wake up."

He was left with nothing but a shirt dripping with the brave dog's blood. Brand hugged it to his chest and let himself cry, alone, not knowing how to go ahead or back without his guide.

"Wake up, Brand."

His face felt wet and chill. Someone stroked it. He sobbed in his waking, still crying. He blinked his eyes. A blurred Kamryn reached out and wiped his cheeks again. He shook the tears from his face and dug at his eyes. The clarity came back, but he could not depend on it. The fear of that chilled him further.

"Brand, it's all right. Wake up."

His nose throbbed and he wiped it on the cuff of his shirt.

"You were dreaming."

Her face looked unhappy, as if she shared with him.

He took the napkin from her and scrubbed at his face, hard, ashamed that Mitch had seen him like that, embarrassed that she had. "Leave me alone."

Mitch passed him a dry napkin, emblazoned with a red Chinese dragon. "Here."

He took it because he had to, and blew nosily. Kamryn's mouth twitched, and he stared away from her.

She put her hand on his shoulder. "It's good to get it all out. I cried like a baby about ... about Darby, in spite of everything."

"I don't cry," he said stubbornly. And he didn't, not usually. He could not afford to. Even through sorrow-swollen eyes, he could see that Mitch and Kamryn had cleaned up, and Mitch's duffel waited by the loft doorway. They were ready to go. He did not know how long he had slept, and wondered if they were going to leave without waking him. He could not let them.

"Rembrandt had my school records. He knows where I live. He won't let me go again."

"You tell Rembrandt I've gone south, to Baja. He'll follow," Mitch explained patiently. He tied the strap on his duffel.

"You can't leave without me. I have to—we have to—go to New Orleans."

Mitch's head snapped up.

"Why New Orleans?" Kamryn offered him the damp towel to wipe his face.

"We have to, that's all." He cleansed his face in desperation. Mitch was shining all silvery again, except for that shard of ink which seemed to cleave him in two, and even Kamryn had smudges floating across her, like storm clouds, and he knew he was going to lose his sight and be left behind, alone. Alone with Bauer and the KillJoy. "I saw it," he started, and stopped. They would think he was raving. He put his face in his hands. "You won't believe me."

"Does this have anything to do with what Rembrandt

was talking about? Your . . . record?" asked Kamryn gently. She sat down next to him, knees touching.

"Record?" repeated Mitch.

"Psychiatric record," Brand told them bitterly. "I'm certifiable, okay? You leave me, and my dear mom will just have me stowed away again. But what I'm seeing is there, it has to be, it's just that nobody else can see it—"

"See what?"

Brand turned desperately to Mitch. "You've got to believe me."

"I have to understand you first. What are you seeing?"

"It's usually in my dreams. I have bad dreams, really bad dreams. I was diagnosed as having fragmented sleep patterns and depression and a couple of other psycho babble disorders. You need regular REM sleep for your brain to process everything okay, only I don't. Didn't. I've been hospitalized for it a couple of times. They wired me, gave me drugs . . ."

"Everyone has nightmares."

"Yeah, right." Brand thought of telling her about Susan Craig and the permanent houseguest she'd imprinted into him, and changed his mind. She would never understand that. "Only now I'm having them awake."

"Schizophrenia."

"Thanks," Brand said dryly. "I need all the help I can get. No, not schizo. At least, not yet. They tell me that's an organic brain dysfunction and usually appears in the teen years. Look what I've got to look forward to."

Mitch cleared his throat. "You're carrying a heavy load."

"I don't want pity. I deal with it. I see a therapist and

I take melatonin to help me sleep, and I can handle it. I just don't want to have to go back to a ward. But this is different. This is something I can see, and no one else can, and it creates death. It's like a . . . a black hole or something, and it's hungry and that's the only thing that can feed it. I saw it at the mall. And it came to the church today—"

"Brandon," soothed Kamryn.

He swung on her. "It knows my name. It's real, only I don't know what it is or how to fight it or why it wants me. And the black woman, she said to come to New Orleans—"

Sharply, from Mitch. "Black woman? What black woman?"

He looked over. "She says her name is Mother Jubilation. I dreamed about her. Look I know this is crazy—"

"You saw her in your dream?"

"She knows what the dark thing is."

Mitch straightened. He picked up his duffel. "It's getting late."

Kamryn stared over her shoulder. "You're not going to leave him like this."

"You think I'm crazy."

"No. But I can't take you with me."

Brand stood up. His legs felt like pins and needles, half-numb, half-pain. He stared at Mitch, at the open throat of his shirt, at the black cord lying against his tanned neck. "She gave you that charm. Mother said to 'tell the white boy I gave him his charm.' "

"You know what he's talking about?"

Mitch shifted his duffel from one hand to the next, reaching for the threshold, but Brand had already seen it in his eyes. Realization, and denial.

"Tell her!"

Mitch shrugged, turning to Kamryn. "He's seen me wearing it around."

"Did she give it to you? Do you know what he's talking about?"

"We can't go to New Orleans," he told her flatly. "No way."

Brand closed his eyes. Giving it a name gave it strength. Calling the name would call it near. He took a breath. "KillJoy."

Kamryn bore down on Mitch. "I won't leave him behind if they're going to put him in an institution—"

"Maybe that's where he belongs. Maybe that's the only place they can help him—"

"KillJoy."

The loft grew cold. The wind began whistling in along the cracks in the unfinished walls, skirling along the bare floors. He could feel the chilling as the temperature began to drop rapidly.

Kamryn and Mitch stopped arguing.

"What are you doing?"

"Seeing," said Brand tightly, "is believing." He took the doorknob from Mitch's hand and flung the portal open. "And maybe I'm the only one who can see it, but you've got to feel it! You've got to! It's like being in a cemetery or a morgue. It's cold and empty and hungry. It makes you feel like you want to kill somebody to stomp out the warmth."

A blast of air drove him back, almost into Kamryn's arms, and it was a raw October wind, a Santa Ana, but this had come from no desert. It smelled faintly of carrion and embalming fluid, and Brand knew he had called it from its temporary resting place within Curtis. It rushed into the loft as if filling a vacuum and Kamryn let out a faint cry as it grazed over her with its shadowy touch.

"Holy Christ," Mitch said. He put a hand to his charm, still tucked inside his shirt, and balled his fist around it.

Brand did not wait for an invitation. He bolted down the garage stairs, and he could hear Mitch and Kamryn clattering down behind him.

Mitch passed him on the back lawn and threw his duffel over the fence, then cupped his hands for Brand. "Go, go," he said.

He tossed Brand over the block wall fence as if he were a rag doll. Kamryn came scrambling over the top on his heels and Mitch thumped down last.

"How fast can it move?" he asked.

"I don't know. I've never had it chasing me before. I think it . . . I think we might be able to outrun it."

Kamryn had her car keys out and loped away from them. Mitch found his duffel in a rosebush, bit out a curse as a thorn pricked him, and grabbed Brand by the elbow.

"I'm coming."

"Damn straight you are. At least until I find out what's going on here."

Kamryn hit the Porters' garage cans and vaulted over their gate. Not silent, but not incredibly noisy either. Mitch boosted him up and pushed the duffel into his hands.

Their eyes met in the moonlight.

"You know the black lady, too."

"Maybe."

"Why?"

Mitch's jaw flexed. "It's better not to know."

"All right." Brand threw his legs over and hit the ground lightly. Kamryn already had the car started.

They all squeezed into the front seat. Mitch bucked

shoulders with Brand, said, "To hell with it," picked him up and threw him into the back.

Brand dusted himself off with dignity. "Okay. You can ride shotgun."

Kamryn pulled away. She watched in the rearview mirror as if expecting to see what Brand had told her she couldn't. "How long before it follows?"

"I don't know!" Brand swiveled around on the car seat. A vortex of incredible, icy darkness filled his vision, his eyes feeling as well as seeing the terror. Even as they retreated, it sensed him, drawn toward him. It would follow. God, what had he done? Let it leave his family alone, half-dead though he thought they were. Nobody deserved this. Nobody. Brand buried his face in his hands, unable to watch.

PART TWO

PART TWO

Chapter 17

Rembrandt was on the phone before he had fully entered the darkened recess of his suite, cradling his laptop in one arm, the card key to the room in his other hand. He hooked a foot around a chair leg and dragged it to him as he sat down, waiting for the various satellite connections to be made and redirected, tapping in strings of commands whenever necessary. Only the computer screen's glow illuminated the room, an eerie greenish flickering. It steadied when the final connection went through.

Bayliss answered, deeper-voiced than usual, but crisp and curt. "Speak to me."

"The crib is clean," Rembrandt told him.

"Shit. You searched the entire area?"

"Every nook and cranny. There's no place he could have secured your goods."

"Then he has to have stashed it somewhere."

"He's never abandoned the crib before." Rembrandt paused. "I found a box with his medals and service ribbons."

"You surprised him, then. It *has* to be stashed," Bayliss repeated, "unless he carries it on his person."

"I agree with you, sir."

"What are your plans now?"

"I can go back to the boy, but that might entail some cleaning up later."

"You're the best at what you do, but the more cleaning up you do, the more risk you run."

"Yes, sir." Rembrandt had plans, but he could tell that Bayliss was also thinking, and he wanted to let his boss play it out. After his failures, he needed to know where he stood with Bayliss, and what, if any, reservations had now arisen about his service. He needed to draw the other man out. Something stirred in the room, a current, like fingers caressing the nape of his neck. It smelled briskly of the ocean—and something else. Something feral, something human, richly-scented sweat. Rembrandt said, "I'm open to suggestions," and turned very quietly in the chair, eyes now adjusted to the dark, searching his room.

"Option one is that I pull you, and bring you back to base camp, where I need you badly right about now. We have SALUTE reports coming in which you need to review." Bayliss cleared his throat, as if admitting need bothered him emotionally. SALUTE reports came from intelligence, referring to the operations of clandestine groups: size/number, activity, location, unit, time, and equipment. They had groups to keep track of, and ensure that their own newly burgeoning operations had not yet been detected.

"I can make the next flight out," Rembrandt answered. He saw nothing in the room, though the corners pooled inky-dense and revealed nothing. Then, he found the source of the current.

The heavy, brocade drapes at the balcony were slightly open, edges of the gauze sheer behind them rippling with the night sea breeze. The balcony glass door showed the barest of cracks where it should have been securely sealed and locked.

His safe place was safe no longer. Security had been seriously breached. His invader might still be here, trapped on the balcony overlooking cliffs that sheared away to the sand below.

Rembrandt instantly ceased to listen to the nuances in what Bayliss said. He stood up, interrupting. "Sir, I've been on the road all evening. You keep talking, but I'm taking the phone into the bathroom. I've got to take a leak."

Bayliss stopped cold as if offended by Rembrandt's unusual lack of courtesy and by his crudeness, both extremely out of character. Then he said, "Are we being tapped? Is this still a secure connection?"

"No, sir, not exactly, but along those lines." Rembrandt smiled, in spite of his tension, admiring the quickness of the other's mind. Bayliss was sharp. It was one of the first things which had drawn Rembrandt to his employment. Rembrandt tolerated no fools, either under him or over him. He rose from his chair and crossed the carpeting.

"Call me back," ordered Bayliss, and disconnected.

Rembrandt continued to talk smoothly. "I think you need to cancel those flights into John Wayne. I'm going to grab some sleep, get a decent meal, and then drop in on the local police, see what I can find out." He threw open the bathroom door, placing the cell phone on the sink. "I'm putting you on speaker phone, sir. I need both hands to handle this." He stripped off his jacket and snugged his shoulder holster tightly, readying for an assault.

He snapped on the switches. White light flared like a beacon, cutting through the room, dazzling light he kept at his back as he wedged himself through the balcony doors.

The October night was filled with the scent of salt

and sweat. He lost the element of surprise with his charge onto the balcony; it scarcely mattered. He knew after the first blow that the two had come, not to spy on him, but to kill him. Rembrandt caught glimpses of ebon skin, moon-white teeth in a rictus smile, open-throated island shirts and fists like hammers. He ducked and rolled and fought back, slamming into the balcony glass-topped table which skidded with a screech across the decking.

He regretted not having pulled his gun first. Their numbers and their intensity surprised him. He took a blow to the gut and doubled over, breathing through his mouth roughly. He did not try to straighten as his assailant approached confidently. He charged headfirst, driving into the assassin's torso. His opponent fell back with a grunt and then windmilled, the small of his back against the balcony's edge. Rembrandt thrust his right arm straight out, slamming the heel of his hand into the young man's dark chin. His head snapped back and he went over the balcony wall, silently, arms and legs flailing. Rembrandt watched him slam into the rocks and sand a hundred feet below. High tide would take his body out.

His partner flinched, then looked back at Rembrandt. He, too, was a young man, rock-hard muscles showing in the biceps revealed by his short-sleeved shirt. He had already taken one solid hit from Rembrandt, blood that looked purple in the pale moonlight trickled from one nostril.

Rembrandt did not know how much time he had before the scuffling on the balcony alerted someone. The suites on either side were empty, but there were people above and below. The evening was late, the sky pitch-dark, the moon a pale, pale sliver. He readied to defend himself, curling his hands into position.

They were not American. They did not dress American, smell American, or fight American. If he had to guess, he would say Haitian, but he did not want to have to guess.

"You can go back to Delacroix," he said softly. "If you leave now."

His assailant's eyes widened in recognition, but he did not answer. He took several breaths, preparing to move in.

Rembrandt shifted his weight, giving himself the reach and experience advantage. His opponent moved nearly imperceptibly also; still Rembrandt did not expect what happened next.

He kicked up, his foot thudding harshly into Rembrandt's chest and then into his neck. He staggered back, shaking his head, reeling out of range, ears ringing, his breath stuffed in his throat. The assailant made a sound of pleasure and closed in.

Rembrandt grabbed a patio chair and slid it between them, fighting to get his breath back, eyes blurred. He coughed once or twice, then got a deep swallow of air. He threw up an arm to block the next kick, grabbed the leg and tossed the fighter onto his back. He followed up with a punishing blow of his own. He only had time for one, then his opponent was up on his feet again, circling warily.

Adrenaline surged through Rembrandt. Adrenaline and the knowledge that he could die this time, he had met his match. Not in cleverness perhaps, but in speed and decisiveness. They closed, knees, hands, and elbows flying, trading vicious blows that could break ribs and sever carotids if landed properly. Rembrandt pulled himself back, breathing harshly, night air ripping through his bruised throat.

His opponent fought like a soldier, a well-trained

and conditioned soldier, one who knew no fear, who
would never hesitate to fight, for whom retreat and
detente were not an option, one whose body was a
finely-tuned weapon which knew no pain. He felt a
grudging admiration for the assassin. Rembrandt put
the table between them momentarily, watching the
whites of the other's eyes, gauging the strength he had
left. He had heard bone crack when they'd closed. It
could have been him, but he thought it was the other.
The pumping rush of adrenaline masked pain; he might
not know until later, much later.

If he lived.

"How did Delacroix find me?"

His opponent flexed, broad muscles rippling under
his tropical shirt. "You were kissed," he said, "by the
loa. Delacroix knows where you are."

Rembrandt hunched uneasily. Little of what the
other said made sense, but he thought warily of voodoo, and then shook it off. He was not superstitious,
he had no time for the spiritual, he placed his trust in
research and planning. If they were trailing Christiansen, then they would have crossed paths with him also.
He had thought his unknown shadow to be MI, trailing
the AWOL Marine. Perhaps it had been this pair
from Delacroix.

He sucked in a painful breath. Decision time. He
knew that, in all likelihood, he would get no more information than that which he had guessed. If he had
time, he might be able to torture more answers, but
he did not have time.

Rembrandt took a step back, felt the balcony ledge
grind into his pelvis. In the wan light, his assailant saw
also and smiled widely, white teeth cutting across his
face. "You are mine, now." He moved close for the kill.

Rembrandt pulled his gun as his assailant drove into

him. They met, body to body, and he pulled the trigger three times in quick succession, feeling the other jerk with every muffled report.

"Think again," he said, and twisted to one side, his free hand wrapped in the other's collar. He levered him over the balcony and let him drop.

Again, there was no sound, no scream. But this time it was because the man was dead before he left his feet.

Rembrandt wiped the gun clean on his shirttail and tossed it as well, leaving the tide to obscure the rest of the details of what had happened.

He went back into his room, packed his bags, cleaned the sliding glass door, shower, and sink, and whatever else he might have touched. He returned to the balcony a last time, cleaned the chairs and the table quickly, then withdrew.

He made a last sweep to see if he'd left anything of gravity in the room. There would be hairs, fibers, but he doubted if anyone would do that thorough a sweep. It might be days before anyone locally connected the bodies below with a balcony above. By then, the maids would have changed linens and vacuumed several times over.

Rembrandt decided to delay a while longer calling Bayliss. He used the express checkout after first opening and then altering the electronic clock which stamped the paperwork fed into it. He took the back way out, through the gardens and pathways and into the underground garage.

As he pulled the rental car out of its space, he tried to gauge what Bayliss' reaction would be to the attack. There would be some surprise. There might be enough concern to curtail plans which had been months coming to fruition. Rembrandt decided that Bayliss could wait an hour or so while he determined his options.

He decided to make that determination outside the boy's house.

The freeways were relatively clear on a cooling fall evening. He found the housing tract, upper middle class and newer, but old enough to have mature pepper trees and eucalyptus shading its boulevards, not far from the Brea Mall. It fit the boy's pattern. The high school was farther north, up the 57 freeway, but not so far he could not hitchhike back down to the arcade whenever he wished. Rembrandt did not know if the environs had caused Brandon's trouble or if Brandon had already been a troubled kid, and the environs drew him naturally, but the pattern had been laid out.

When he took the boy this time, no one would question his disappearance or his ultimate fate. Rembrandt parked his car, carefully away from the corner, watching the house on a slant, knowing that the boy must come home eventually. He had nowhere else to go.

Rembrandt watched as a Brea Squad car slowly slid past the house on its frontal street, not stopping, but observing. The parents must have put out a report on the missing child. The cops were checking the neighborhood, as he was, reading the same human behavior he did.

He checked his watch. It was later than he thought. He knew Bayliss would begin to edge toward unhappiness by now. Rembrandt pursed his lips, debating with himself over his final course of action, when the evening breeze grew chill, very chill, and he looked out the car windshield in surprise.

Tree leaves shivered and danced in frenzy, their edges growing frost-rimed, and blackening. Rembrandt lowered his car window to look closer, as his breath had suddenly fogged up the inside, so much warmer than outside. He leaned his head out, and saw the tiny snowflake pattern of jackfrost across the asphalt, over the boulevards, leading straight to the boy's house.

Or, more accurately, to the built-over garage in back. Rembrandt rubbed his eyes as the cold wind dried them, rubbed his eyes and wondered if he had slept, if he had been unaware of some happening, as a finely-iced wave rolled toward and then over the garage.

He saw nothing else, but sat next to his rolled-down window and shivered. He had not been this cold since his survival training days when, stripped down to the bare essentials and a compass, he had been told to find his way back through an unforgiving wilderness. He'd done it, though three of his companions had died of hypothermia that night.

He breathed in deeply, and immediately coughed, for the autumn wind bearing the frost also carried a scent, foul and fetid. He coughed harshly several times, put a hand to his rib cage, just now finding out that it was his own bone he'd heard crack hours ago, and tried not to cough anymore, though his lungs fought that smell with all their might. It coated the back of his throat and Rembrandt finally spat outside the car, trying to rid himself of the nastiness.

It was then he saw the three sprinting down the back of the garage staircase, running like gazelles ahead of the hunt, across the backyard and fence. Rembrandt hurriedly started his car and backed it up, cautiously, quietly, along the block, until he could see the adjacent street, on a diagonal.

A silvery Honda pulled away, the girl driving, and it shot away toward the freeway. Rembrandt watched it for a second or two, patiently, then followed after.

Once on the freeway, he stayed as far behind as he could and still keep it in sight. Down the 57 to the 91 toward Riverside, San Bernardino and the east. Traffic

in Southern California was always there on the high-
ways, though sparse in the dead of night, so he found
it not too difficult to keep three or four cars between
them. He drove with his left hand pressed to his left
rib cage, feeling the bone grate, wondering when he
could get a corset, though that was old-fashioned now.
Ribs were left to heal on their own, but he could not
leave that to chance, he was too active. He drove with
one eye on the economy Honda, watching the girl skill-
fully negotiate the traffic lanes, and the other eye on
any other cars which looked as if they might be
following.

When the 91 ended, the Honda unerringly went to
the 10, just outside Riverside, the 10 freeway to Palm
Springs and beyond, across the desert. Rembrandt kept
an eye on his gas gauge. He would lose them when he
stopped for a fill-up and he would have to stop soon.
His full-sized rental car did not have the economy ca-
pacity of the Honda.

He wondered where they headed. Not west, to the
ocean, or south to Baja, or north, but east. To Phoenix—or beyond.

Then Rembrandt smiled, peeling his lips back from
his teeth, remembering what had brought the police to
the boy's house, what had brought him to the boy's
home. The fugitive invariably traveled in circles.

Christiansen was headed back to New Orleans.
Whether he knew it or not, consciously yet, that was
his inevitable destination.

He had to have stashed the goods there, perhaps
even before he had delivered his corporal's body to
the funeral home. And, if Christiansen was the Marine
Rembrandt thought he was, he had to realize that only
by recovering the powder could he possibly hope to
negotiate for his life, for the girl's, for the boy's.

He was wrong, of course, but that did not matter. Whether the decision had already been made or would be made in Phoenix or Tucson or Denver or in New Mexico, the course would be charted.

Rembrandt could pick them off any time he wanted. His grin widened.

"Gotcha," he said.

Chapter 18

DAY ONE

NWS 0630 AM EST
BULLETIN
National Hurricane Center

A SYSTEM APPROACHING THE LESSER ANTIL-
LES HAS ORGANIZED ENOUGH TO QUALIFY AS
A TROPICAL STORM, NAMED TS YOLANDA. AS
LATE IN THE SEASON AS IT IS, THIS DISTUR-
BANCE IS GATHERING STRENGTH AS IT
LEAVES THE COAST OF AFRICA, PROCEEDING
IN A WESTERLY/NORTH WESTERLY DIRECTION.
SUSTAINED WINDS OF 55 MPH HAVE BEEN
MEASURED. THE STORM IS EXPECTED TO PICK
UP STRENGTH AS IT PASSES INTO CARIBBEAN
WATERS.
PLEASE CONTINUE TO MONITOR THESE
CHANNELS AS WE UPDATE THE STORM'S
PROGRESS.

Rembrandt read his laptop screen, then tapped a few
keys to take him out of the weather news and into the
stock market and headlines, far more current than
those on the newspapers lying about him. Airport noise

hummed busily, but he had not yet been paged and his flight to Albuquerque would not be called for another hour. He reached for the paper cup of coffee and sipped it as he pulled up the headlines.

THE DOW DROPS STEADILY AS INDICATORS THE FED IS CONSIDERING AN INTEREST RATE HIKE AFFECTS TRADING.

A fairly decent brew of domestic coffee blends eased down his throat, fulfilling an intense need for the taste and caffeine. He continued to scan the immediate online news.

SEN. HANOVER BAYLISS URGES A NO VOTE ON THE $400 MILLION RENEWAL OF THE 1995 DISARMAMENT PACKAGE, STATING THAT SENDING MORE MONEY TO THE FORMER SOVIET UNION REPUBLICS WHERE CORRUPTION IS RIFE IS UTTER FOOLISHNESS. SENATOR BAYLISS, MEMBER OF THE ARMS COMMITTEE AND THE BANKING COMMISSION AMONG SEVERAL OTHER IMPORTANT POSITIONS, CALLS FOR SENSIBILITY. MONIES BEING FUNNELED TO THE UKRAINE AND OTHER AREAS TO DISMANTLE REMAINING MISSILES, ARMAMENTS, AND MISSILE SITES IS A BURDEN THE AMERICAN PUBLIC SHOULD NO LONGER CARRY. BAYLISS STATES THAT FISCAL RESPONSIBILITY FOR PROGRAMS AT HOME IS MORE IMPORTANT. FURTHERMORE, THE SENATOR VOWS THAT THE NATION CANNOT WAIT FOR THE NEXT ELECTION FOR CONGRESS AND THE PRESIDENT TO COME TO THEIR SENSES, THAT PAR-

TISAN POLITICS IS DESTROYING THE FABRIC OF THE COUNTRY.

The computer screen filled with a three-quarter profile of Bayliss, his leonine hair curled back from his dynamic, square-jawed face, his hand gesturing. The computer-generated image was nothing less than compelling.

Rembrandt's mouth curled. Bayliss was giving them hell again. The senator would be heard.

One way or another.

The airport paging system came on. "Flight 213 from Albuquerque now arriving Gate 5B."

Rembrandt checked his watch. Twenty minutes early. Good. It would give him time to debrief the recruits before their turnaround flight. They had work to do.

Chapter 19

The International Terminal at Acapulco had been given a new wash of bright white paint, disguising the old-ness of its stucco walls. Its large, cavernlike terminal reflected more of a whitewashed warehouse than it did a jet-set airport, guarded by Federales, some not old enough to shave as they cradled their rifles slung over their shoulders. It was old under its new coat, old and not extremely well built, unlike the Haitian airport which, although old, had been built by the French. Only the X-ray machines, their plastic arches and con-veyor belts were relatively new, as embarking passen-gers waited in staggered lines to pass through them.

Customs, on the other side of the terminal, seemed lax. A stream of passengers heading for cruise lines chatted and passed through in endless streams until the crowd finally thinned out. A tired woman, her uni-form creased with the tropical heat that permeated Acapulco even at that time of the year, opened a pass-port and readied her stamp.

She paused, glancing at the two passengers. "Profes-sor Delacroix?"

"Of Haiti," the gentleman said quietly, in English, though it was liltingly accented.

She thumbed through the passport until she came to the visa, folded over and stapled to the inside back cover. The tension in her shoulders relaxed abruptly. "You are here," she noted, also in accented English, though hers was Latino in origin rather than Franco, "to study our Day of the Dead."

"Yes. This has long been my wish, despite political difficulties. I am here at last!" He smiled, giving warmth to his sharp, lean features, his brown skin glowing with the heat of the building despite the fans moving raggedly in alcoves overhead. "And this is my assistant from the United States, Alexander Stark." He shrugged a shoulder to let the unmoving man at his back be seen more clearly.

She fingered the second passport, also with a stapled visa, then briskly stamped them both. "Do you have anything to declare?"

The professor shook his head, but laughed and said, "When I leave, I may have a suitcase full of your masks and dolls. Is there a duty on them?"

"Read these papers. It depends on the value, and if they are antiques or not." Rather impatiently now, she shoved brochures into the passports, her eyes already moving on to the next passengers in line, having dismissed these two.

The man designated as Stark moved to pick up the two suitcases, lifting them as if their weight was inconsequential. Delacroix said, "Follow me," and walked through the terminal toward the signs marked AUTOBUS. He did not wait to see if he were followed, as if it were unthinkable for Stark to do anything else.

Outside, in the warm, moist air, jitneys and buses of various worn-out facades waited for incoming passengers. They sat at the edge of broken tarmac lanes, pastureland edged with bananas and other palms lying fallow beyond the modest lanes heading into Acapulco proper. Delacroix removed his panama hat and wiped his forehead. Stark made no movement of comfort, whether to ease the burden of the suitcases or to dry his brow.

"Put the suitcases down," Delacroix said mildly. "We have a moment."

Stark did as he was bid. Delacroix appraised him, looking for signs of infirmity from his mortal wounding, but he saw none. The man had healed well, exceptionally well, and his skills were proving invaluable. Stark would take Delacroix into the States, and guided by the loa, he would track the men who had betrayed him and desecrated his powers, and take his revenge. It would be all the sweeter knowing he was turning their own weapon against them. Surely the legba who was the gateway for all things spiritual had blessed him with this man, just as Delacroix had been blessed with the loa of his vengeance. It was fitting that his visa gave him permission to study the festivals known as the Days of the Dead.

Calmly, to Stark, Delacroix noted. "I have done as you told me. Does this mean all arrangements will be followed? A boat will be waiting to take us to Baja and then into the States?"

Stark looked at him, flat, expressionless eyes like those of a shark in the water, calmly seeking its destiny of being a killing, feeding machine. He nodded.

"Good," answered Delacroix. He spotted a bus pulling up, in a little better condition than the others, its routing card reading "Acapulco Princess." There was some slight hope of comfort in that the windows remained closed. It must have air-conditioning that functioned. He motioned to his bags. "Here is our transport."

Stark silently picked up the suitcases and followed to the bus.

*   *   *   *

Junior, called because he wasn't, rode alone because he liked it that way. He worked weekdays in a lock factory in Anaheim and weekends he rebuilt classic hogs in his old lady's living room, because the garage was full of bodies and fenders and tires and he didn't like working in the driveway because the old bikes he built were worth somethin' and he didn't want the neighbors to know. Octobers called him to the mountains in Big Bear, where the mostly German founding fathers threw one helluva Oktoberfest shindig, although Junior had to admit it wasn't like in the old days. In the old days, one hundred, two hundred bikers came up the mountain and drank their beer and owned the roads, because the San Berdu police couldn't get up the hill in time to stop them. Now, the policia maintained a presence in the resort community and bikers were tolerated, but their meets just weren't the same.

But it got Junior out from under the glare of his bike bitch and above the smog line, and the beer was still just as good as it always had been, and so the ride down the road was just as sweet even though he had to wear a helmet now. His long hair fuzzed under the helmet, and his kinky beard caught bugs in the wind, and he didn't mind it. Hell, this was living.

But he'd overstayed his welcome in Big Bear. He'd found a woman and forgot about the weekend and now it was mid-week, and word was his old lady had been calling for him, and maybe he'd even lost his job for not showing up. Unlike the old days, Junior now had rent to worry about, and bills, and he'd woken up from a five-day drug and beer binge with his skull caving in and his buddies pounding on his cabin door.

Junior wasn't stupid, and now he was headed down

Highway 38, the back way, through Redlands and San Berdu, in the middle of the night, and he realized he might not be welcome at home when he got there. So he peeled his hog off toward Beaumont, naked and alone on Highway 10, a slight detour toward the east, and he found a gas station with a lone attendant. He parked his bike by the garage bay, which didn't look like it had been used by a real mechanic in some time, and approached the attendant cautiously, looking for surveillance cameras. There was one, but its eye was still, and the swivel base was broken, and Junior determined it was a fake.

He dismounted and sauntered over to the booth, pulling on his leather vest to straighten it over his paunchy stomach, a well-earned beergut, he reflected, and smiled at the attendant.

"I wonder if you could help me."

The attendant, a thin, wiry man who was not American, and probably was Indian or Pakistani or one of those funny-lookin' foreigners, eyed him nervously. "Yes, please? All pumps are open."

"Naw, naw, I don't need gas." Junior put a finger to the corner of his eyelid and dragged it down. "I got somethin' in my eye. It feels pretty sharp. Think I got some glass in it, blew up from the road. Take a look, will ya, and see what you can see? I don't want to mess with it, if it is glass. I'll just call 911."

The attendant squinted out through the barred window. "Please, I see nothing."

"Naw, you gotta look closer. Lissen, this is real painful, y'know? I don't want to go blind or nothing. See, it's right . . . here."

The attendant danced on one foot and then the other, then came out of his booth to lean closer. "I still don't see anything."

Junior's finger had pretty well made the eye blood-shot and tearing, and he smiled. "Maybe this will help." He took his helmet off.

The attendant peered very close again, and Junior head-butted him with all his power.

The man dropped like a wet sack of cement. His head made the sound of a ripe melon as it hit the drive.

Junior shook himself. "You still got it." He reached down, grabbed the foreigner by his twiglike ankles, and dragged him back inside the booth. The cash drawer was crammed full. It looked like someone had not made the day deposit.

"Jackpot. Just like Vegas." Junior gave a sigh of contentment and began to roll the bills into a wad, taking care not to touch anything metal or plastic. He used his leather vest like a potholder, opening and closing bins.

A car pulled in before Junior had finished. He watched it circle the pumps, then back into the one it wanted, a Honda, a Jap car, ruining American economy, and Junior sucked at a tooth. He looked at the switches inside the booth. He could shut down the pumps if he wanted, denying the car fuel. Or he could just wait it out.

A guy got out of the passenger side, walked across the way, slid a twenty in the cash window, said, "Pump seven," and left without a second look.

Junior took the twenty and added it to his wad. Like taking candy from a baby. The attendant at his feet groaned. Junior gave him a tap in the temple from his Doc Martens, and silence rewarded him.

He leaned his elbows on the counter, watching the man fill the gas tank, and the woman who drove got out. She was a looker, though a trifle thin for his liking, the more cushion for the pushin' was his motto, but she looked familiar. She had an attitude. The guy didn't want to check the water, but he could hear her voice clearly in the booth.

"If I'm driving to Phoenix, I want the water checked. We're here, let's do it." No nonsense, all attitude, but the other finally did what she wanted.

A small portable TV on the booth counter caught his attention. The color picture wavered every now and then as the local news portion of Headline News came on.

"In Brea today, (*Yesterday*, thought Junior, *don't these freaks know it's the middle of the night?*,) police from all over the county and even Los Angeles came to the funeral of Brea police officer Nick Solis. Solis, who had transferred to the Orange County city department only a few years ago, was shot Tuesday while answering the call for a domestic violence situation at the Brea Mall. An estranged boyfriend pulled a gun and shot two innocent bystanders while terrorizing his ex-girlfriend. Officer Solis was then himself shot when he attempted to intervene. However, local authorities credit Solis with shielding public areas with his own body, preventing further deaths. A commendation will be issued posthumously. Solis is survived by a widow who is expecting their first child. This channel would like viewers to know that donations for the welfare of Mrs. Solis and her unborn child can be sent to a trust fund at Brea Bank of America—"

Junior looked away. Policemen rode their motorcycles like they had broomsticks up their asses. The scene of the funeral no longer interested him. The man and woman were discussing something he could not hear, until her voice rose. She looked aside, saw him watching, ducked her chin down, and he could no longer hear them.

Junior sighed. The newscaster added, "In news which is related, one of the bystanders who fled his best friend's funeral, is reported missing tonight. The parents of young Brandon Dennis ask for your help in locating their son. Fourteen-year-old Brandon was on the site when the gunman accidentally shot and killed Curtis. At his funeral, also held on Thursday, Brandon bolted out of services and disappeared. His mother pleads for anyone who knows of his whereabouts to contact her through the Brea police. Brandon has a history of depression requiring medical and psychiatric attention. Again, anyone with any information as to Brandon's whereabouts is asked to contact the Brea Police Department. Locally, temperatures drop a bit lower tonight, weatherwise and there is a chance of—"

Junior blinked as the slender bitch turned and came to the booth.

"Change, please."

He looked at her. He'd emptied the cash drawer. "Isn't any."

"He gave you a twenty. That car doesn't hold more than fourteen gallons of gas. Now I know I have change coming."

He looked at the board, where the readout told him the gallons and the total. She had $3.20 coming back. She flipped her head, dark hair winging around her face and neck, short, not the way he liked it, but there was something about the broad.

He dug in his jeans and pulled out three bills and then fingered two dimes out of the rear of the cash drawer. He dropped it into the cash window. She scooped it out.

"Thank you," she said with sarcasm and walked back toward the car.

"Come again," Junior called. He had her placed in

his mind now, all legs and cool expression. He watched them pack the car back up and pull out. He dug some more change out of the drawer, wiped it as clean as he could, then went to the pay phone.

He had to feed in nearly two dollars to get the number he dialed. He watched in the dark fall evening as the car's rear lights faded, heading toward the 10 eastbound.

"Yeah."

"It's me, Junior. Tell Darby I just saw that biker bitch of his, and she wasn't with him." Junior chewed on a strand of his kinky beard, and listened as the other end of the phone told him the sad story of Darby's death. "Shit, man, you're kidding! I just saw a tape of the cop's funeral on HNN. God's nuts, I've been out of it this week. I didn't know. That's too damn bad about Darby. Well, she's headed toward Phoenix, driving an '86 Honda, silver, with a guy in the passenger seat. She gave me a mouth fulla bad attitude. Thought Darby should know what she's up to. Guess he's too gone to care now. Well, I gotta get the hell out of here before my old lady comes gunning for me." Junior hung up, feeling good. Buddies had done him a favor, waking him up to his situation on the mountain, and now he'd returned it, down the line. Too bad about Darby. If he'd known that, he'd a hit on the bitch, even though she wasn't his type.

He hesitated at the side of his bike. That little TV wasn't such a bad piece of shit. He oughta take it home, too. He walked back to the booth. To his surprise, the foreign dude was on his feet, back to the counter, shaking.

Too bad, because that meant Junior would have to finish him off. A second look at his ugly mug was one look too many. He put his hands up, palms out. "Just give me the set, man, and I'm gone."

"No. You rob me, I lose the money, my job. No. This too much." The gas station attendant pulled out a black automatic, his hand wavering from the weight of the gun.

"Whoa, now. I think we can settle this. Just put the gun down, and let me walk back to my bike, and leave. Or," and Junior smiled crookedly. "I'll have to tell somebody it was your idea to be robbed and we was gonna split the money."

"No!" The gun barrel waggled furiously. "No, I'm a good man. Good. You're the bad man."

Junior eased a step closer. "You sure about that, little buddy? You've seen enough real cops on TV. They're going to ask a lot of questions, a lot. By the time they're finished, you won't have a job, anyway. Ever seen the inside of a jail? They'll eat you up for lunch."

He took another step. "Besides, you haven't got the balls to shoot me. Now, give me the TV, and I'll be out of here. If you like, I'll even tie you up, loose like, so it'll look good."

"You no take anything more!"

Junior was close enough to grab the man by the neck. His hand and arm shot out, like a cobra striking, lightning fast.

The gunfire was faster. It reverberated through the tiny booth. Junior felt his chest grow hot and fiery and damp. He looked down in astonishment, then slowly went to his knees on the pavement.

"I am American citizen," the man said, his voice growing thin and high. "I know my rights! You a bad man."

Junior heard sucking and bubbling when he tried to breathe. His vision narrowed, and he had the sensation of racing his bike, hell-bent for leather, down the side of a mountain.

"You not take anything anymore."

He was gone.

Snake hung up as the line flattened to a dial tone. He put a palm to his bald head, where he could feel the heat of his tattoos, as though he wore a living, breathing, snakeskin. He had been restless all day, with the need to get out, to be moving, searching . . . something inside driving him. Now he knew why. Now he knew where.

He knew where she was headed.

Chapter 20

Mitch caught her yawning just outside Indio. It was one of those endless yawns that seemed to go on forever as if she were trying to swallow the moon, and tears came to the corners of her eyes.

He waited until she had finished, then mildly said, "Pull over and let me drive."

Kamryn sniffed and blinked several times, shaking off the yawn. "In a minute. I've got somewhere to go first." She aimed the Honda for an off-ramp.

"We don't need gas."

"No. Darby and I biked out here sometimes. We need to pick something up, and this is probably the best place to get it in this direction." She took a hand off the wheel and dabbed at her eyes. The sky had begun to lighten ever so slightly. Dawn must be about a half hour away. Traffic was light, but it would be getting heavier as early morning workers started their commute.

"If this trip is long enough, you'll have to explain to me about that."

Kamryn looked at him. He had dozed for a while, head against the passenger side window, which had left a tiny mark on his temple and a shadowy crease down toward his jawline, like a sexy scar, as if he'd been a sword fighter sometime in his past. "Explain what?"

"About you and Darby."

"Mmmm. I'm not sure I know you well enough for that."

Mitch smiled crookedly, as though the creased side of his face were still asleep. "There is that."

She turned down a side street. A car delivering the morning papers crept in front of them, its headlights a yellowy streak. The houses were seedy, sidewalkless, fenceless, in most cases even garageless. She watched as the newspaper deliverer made a sporadic throw or two before pulling away.

"I guess not too many people out here are interested in the news."

"I guess not too many people out here even know how to read," she said shortly. She found the house she wanted, with a perpetual YARD SALE hand-lettered sign, faded and tattered, nailed to the front tree. Junk was piled all over the front lawn. It looked as though the inhabitants had either been thrown out, or that the yard sale was never picked over and cleaned up.

She stopped the car. Mitch frowned.

"The kid needs clothes," she said. "He looks like a junior Perry Como in that outfit. Besides, he needs to be comfortable."

He looked in the back seat, where Brand was sprawled, snoring lightly, his eyes twitching under faintly blue-veined lids. "Think you can find anything?"

"Sure." She swung the car door open and paused. "I had a brother once, know my sizes pretty well. How about you?" She looked him up and down, amused as faint color came to clean-shaven cheeks that had formerly been hidden behind his beard. "32-32?"

"32-34," he corrected. "Levis. If you can get longs."

"Never know until I look." She leaned back in and

pulled her revolver halfway out. "Use this if there's trouble."

Mitch looked down at it. "Jesus," he said. "I thought you said a gun. That thing's a cannon."

"The intimidation factor is almost better than the ammo." Kamryn grinned. "Be right back."

It took her about ten minutes to find the boy two pairs of jeans, one flannel shirt and one T-shirt, with Earthworm Jim in his mighty spacesuit emblazoned across the front. She also found briefs which were still in their package, and a single pair of Levis, well worn, in Mitch's size. She stuffed a ten in the coffee can sitting at the base of the pepper tree and hurried across the lawn, as waking householders and their dogs began to prepare for morning.

She went to the passenger door as Mitch scooted over, got in, and buckled her seat belt.

"Back to the highway?"

"Take two rights here, and straight on till morning." She yawned again as she folded the clothes into a neat stack on her lap.

He guided the car through the residential streets and back toward the highway. As if refusing to be impressed, he asked, "What about shoes, socks, toothbrushes?"

Kamryn gave him a look. "We'll find swap meets. The great cash society of the U.S. Even if I had found a toothbrush back there, *I* wouldn't have wanted to use it."

"No argument there." Mitch twisted his head, waiting for a signal change. "Coffee and doughnuts?"

She was hungry. She also wanted to use a restroom, but she shook her head. "Not yet. We've got another three, four hours to Phoenix. Let's get closer to the border."

"You've been this way once or twice."

Noncommittal observance, but she knew that whatever she answered, he would file away, a piece of the puzzle he had made of her, a puzzle which he would try to put together. That gave her a funny feeling, that someone cared enough to wonder about her, and worried her because she did not want to let her personal life jeopardize their flight. "Once or twice," she agreed. "Skinheads are big in Arizona. Our—their—printing plant is outside Phoenix."

Flatly. "Hate literature."

She looked down the highway, crossing gently rolling desert, as the road moved away from irrigated, agricultural Indio. "Hate literature," she repeated. "Always a big business." She rubbed her arms gently, as if she could brush away the remnants of her tattoos. "Always." A third yawn caught her up.

Amused, Mitch told her to grab some sleep. She put her head back on the car seat and tried.

She had had a brother. Lanky and wiry, dark-haired and hazel-eyed, who had liked jeans best when they were soft and faded and had straight legs. Blue jeans and plaid shirts, rolled up at the elbow . . . covered in blood.

Come down to the basement, Sis. I've got a surprise for you.

Kamryn caught her breath and held it, trying not to see what she saw behind the darkness of her closed eyes. Held her breath until it went away. But she could not sleep, so she feigned it, listening to the sound of the car tires on the asphalt, catching pebbles and the grooving meant to keep desert rains from flooding the road.

Somehow, she fell asleep anyway.

*   *   *

Brand woke, with a crook in his neck from being jammed up against the car door, and an urgent fullness in his bladder. Mitch had a hand over the front seat and shook his knee again. "Rest stop," he said. "And breakfast."

Brand sat up, wedged his body upright against the other door, trying to fully wake. The car was streaming with light, brilliant, clean, painfully so, and he slipped a hand inside his shirt pocket. He still had his shades. He put them on, but not before seeing Mitch, aglow as if he were radioactive, except for that chasm down the center of his being, and Kamryn, asleep in her bucket seat, curled up like a kitten, dark smudges drifting across her like clouds of woe.

Fear and sunlight struck him like a physical blow, and something in the pit of his stomach churned. Would his sight never be normal again? Had it gotten better? The focus had, no doubt of that, he would never need glasses again—but if all the world were reduced to brilliant flares and despairing pitch, what would it matter?

Or could it be worse, far worse? Did the inky veils mean that the KillJoy had touched her, marked her for its own . . . was he seeing the aura of death to come? Had Mitch been so marked and then escaped it in the mall? Was that why he sparkled except for that fractal of darkness? Death delayed, all but defeated . . . death retreating to its normal mortality?

If that were it, if that was what he saw, then at least he'd been forewarned. Kamryn was in terrible, crucial danger.

He would have to do anything he could to protect her.

Mitch looked at him closely. "You awake?"

"Pretty much." His mouth felt like glue. His breath

carried the scent of Chinese spices and garlic. He didn't want to breathe and smell himself.

Mitch handed him a stack of clothes. "Why don't you go in first, and change. Some of these places even have showers."

Faintly surprised, Brand took the clothing. He doubted the showers, but headed for the concrete block building anyway, knowing that if anyone knew, Mitch would. They were in the desert, and off to the side of the sparsely landscaped rest stop, several Indians sat at the edge of spread-out blankets, goods for sale catching the glint of the sun. Beyond, the highway rolled with traffic. An arrowhead of bikers drew close, riding bikes with the long forks, their seats slanted for long-distance comfort, the man in front wearing one of those Nazi helms instead of a proper motorcycle helmet. They were moving at a near blur, like a hundred miles an hour. As if sensing his stare, the biker glanced over as he sped by, his face a pale streak clouded with darkness.

Light mirrored off the riders, cold light. It struck his eyes like an icicle spear, with the feeling of the KillJoy. Brand stepped hastily behind the corner of the building, and watched. He shuddered in his tracks as the phalanx passed and the glare washed over him. For a moment he stood dazzled, blinking despite his glasses. Someone honked, and he stirred. The feeling had gone. He put up a shaky hand to make sure his shades still rested on his nose, that his head still sat on his shoulders. The car horn sounded again, a musical blast, and the crowded rest stop bustled with activity.

Inside the parking lot, a catering truck was doing a brisk business with a lineup of trucks and tractor-trailer rigs. He could smell the hot coffee and frying eggs.

His body reminded him of essentials and he broke into a jog.

No shower, but he washed at the sink. Someone had left behind a mini-tube of toothpaste and he'd scrubbed his mouth with his finger. All in all, in jeans which fit pretty decently, and an Earthworm Jim shirt that was nothing less than cool, he felt a lot better when he left the restroom. He'd wanted to trash his other clothes, but instead rolled them into a tight bundle and brought them out with him.

Mitch was carrying a cardboard food box away from the catering truck as Brand fell into step. He dropped the toothpaste tube into the corner of the box. "Goodies," he said.

Mitch canted an eyebrow. "We could all use that." He nodded. "Fried egg sandwich on toast, coffee, cream, and sugar."

Brand laughed as he looked into the container. "And tea and yogurt for Kamryn."

"She told me she's on a diet."

"Aren't they all?" Brand dipped a hand and brought up the slightly greasy, waxed paper bundle. He unfolded a corner and began to wolf down the sandwich. It was fresh, sizzling, the egg cooked in real butter—he'd developed tastebuds for that a long time ago and could never understand how people couldn't tell the difference—and had his breakfast half-eaten before they were back to the car.

Kamryn sat on the fender. She'd changed, too, into cords and a denim shirt. She smiled as she lifted the yogurt cup. "Pineapple and coconut. My favorite."

"Good. Check the expiration date." Mitch sat the box down, popped the lid on his coffee, and chugged it.

"That's the beauty of yogurt," she answered. "You can hardly tell the difference." She found a plastic spoon and began to eat, delicately, like a cat lapping at cream.

His sandwich had fogged up his shades before he finished the last corner. He looked at the empty waxed paper wrapper, then back at the catering truck. "Seconds?"

Mitch wiped a bit of yolk from his lips. He looked at Kamryn, and she shrugged. "Better hurry. He's pulling out in about ten minutes."

Brand put his hand out and Mitch slapped a five into it. As soon as the bill touched his palm, he sprinted to the truck.

He came back with a thick, chunky bundle, and two and a half dollars change. He gave it to Mitch who solemnly passed it to Kamryn.

"What is that?"

"A chorizo and bean burrito. This ought to stick to my ribs." Brand stretched his mouth for the first bite. The glorious, hot Mexican sausage exploded warmth and spices into his mouth, cooled by sour cream and refried beans.

Kamryn looked away, but her shoulders shook a little. Mitch said to her, "He's a growing boy."

"He's going to be an exploding boy, at this rate," she answered.

Brand would have complained, but the burrito took his attention. Mitch finished his breakfast and strolled over to the bathrooms. The catering truck pulled out with a "La Cucaracha" playing horn, and most of the other truckers left as well.

The air was tight, tight and dry in his nostrils and his chest. As he looked around the barrel of his burrito, he spotted the glint of Indian jewelry and trinkets again. He swallowed and pointed. "Can I go look?"

"Sure." Kamryn had a small jar in her hand, and she

appeared to be rubbing cream into her skin. Brand walked away, wondering how much of what he thought was beautiful about her was natural and how much applied. He fought the instinct to tell her that it wouldn't matter, that if what he'd seen were true, she wouldn't live long enough to wrinkle.

He choked back the mean-spirited thought and strolled along the rest stop. Bauer had awakened, for that had been his style. "You're a shit, Bauer," he muttered under his breath. "A real shit."

He finished his coffee and tossed it in the trash can. A third of the burrito was left. He wrapped it carefully in its paper and foil, intent on saving it.

Instead, he gave it to the hollow-faced Indian boy perched at the edge of his mother's blanket. Then, hands free, he shoved them into his jeans pockets and looked over her goods. For the most part, the jewelry and dolls and hats were disappointing, no different from anything he could see at a swap meet or in the stores, although the prices were a little cheaper. He smiled at the woman who leaned forward, gently hawking her goods.

He came to a dead halt as her waving hand flowed over a line of charms and amulets, all on black cord, their silvery facets cut and molded in a variety of ways. One was damn near a dead ringer to the amulet he'd seen Mitch wearing. He squatted down to look closer at it. His ever-present sunglasses cut down on the glare of silver metal, and the crooked etch in the lens echoed a bolt carved in the amulet.

"You like?" she said softly. "Ten dollars, please."

He shook his head. "I haven't got any money. These are nice, though. Do you know what that one means?"

"No, no. I don't make those. Those are made by the tribal shaman. I make these others."

He stabbed a finger at the twin to Mitch's amulet. "And you don't know anything about this one? I mean, like if it's good luck or to chase away bad spirits, or anything?"

"No, I'm sorry. They are good magic, that is all I know. You like? Seven-fifty. You were nice to my son."

Brand straightened. "No, I can't, this time. Good luck to you, though." He backed away. As he left, the boy was sharing his breakfast with his mother.

Mitch and Kamryn were waiting in the car. He got in the back. "Hey, Mitch. She's got an amulet just like the one you wear."

Kamryn's head turned. "You wear jewelry. I never would have figured."

"It's just something someone gave me." He stared at Brand. "Couldn't be the same."

"It is, I swear it. Take it out and show Kamryn."

"I don't think so. Listen, you ready to hit the road again? No stops between here and Phoenix."

"Yeah, I'm ready." He rolled the window down to let the fresh morning air into the car. The Honda moved forward across the parking lot, slowed behind a line of semis getting back onto the highway. The car crept along.

Someone pounded on the back window. Brand turned, and saw the Indian boy, something clutched in his fist. As soon as the boy saw him looking, he dashed around the car and ran to the window.

He shoved his fist in and dropped the object in Brand's lap. "For kindness," he said. "My mother sends." He sprinted away across the parking lot, laughing as semis honked at his impudent path.

Brand looked and saw, through the tangle of wrapped black cord, the twin to Mitch's talisman.

"What is it?"

"Nothing," he told Kamryn, and poked the item deep into his pocket. "A dolphin on a string."

"We sell those in our shop," she mused. "They cost us next to nothing, but they're popular. We always sell out."

Mitch said nothing, but Brand looked at the rearview mirror and saw Mitch watching him, a slight frown between his eyes. He bit his cheek and moved away, to the corner of the seat, where he could not see Mitch's eyes. He might tell Mitch what he had later, but now was not the time. All he had to do was figure out how to get Kamryn to wear it. If it helped Mitch, perhaps it might save her.

Chapter 21

The Bell Ranger lifted him over the sparsely-treed mountains and dropped into the foothills, where drought-tolerant pines and a few aspens lined the edge of the valley and the growing encampment. The northern mountains of New Mexico's landscape found rain scarce, but greenery did hold the range up to the timberline and then broke into what was best described as high desert foliage. Rembrandt stirred impatiently, leaning out of his seat, straining against the harness, looking at what had only been planned a few short years ago. Excitement flooded away the fatigue of a few short hours' sleep and the flight to Albuquerque and the subsequent copter tour here. He had not seen the camp yet, and his first glimpse was exceedingly promising.

Camp Second Hope, it had been named, hidden behind a maze of corporate blinds that he doubted anyone without inside knowledge could ever pierce, even with the aid of computer tracking. Ostensibly, it was a nonprofit religious institution, a wilderness survival camp designated for juveniles in trouble. Because it was religious, it could be hidden fairly benevolently for several years before it would attract attention. By then, it would be too late. This was the second of the camps to go on-line. There was one in eastern Oregon, a third in Michigan, and a fourth in West Virginia, not too far in striking distance from Quantico, Virginia.

Secure measures had been taken against satellite surveillance, the spies in the sky, sweeps through camouflage by nature and by intent. Rembrandt found himself picking out huts, training ranges, and ammo dumps only after intense scrutiny, as the helicopter drew nearer to the landing field. As good as the cameras in the sky were, as intent in focus as the lenses shot, he did not think the true scope of the grounds could be discerned. It would take an on-site visit to determine the exact nature of the camp. He knew bureaucracy. If they kept their noses clean, if they had handpicked their troops as well as they thought they had, by the time anyone thought to investigate them, it would not matter.

He had the other camps to visit, but if they were set up as well as this one, the future held only great expectations.

The pilot tapped him on the shoulder. "I'm taking you down, sir."

The corner of Rembrandt's mouth twitched at the statement of the obvious, but he said nothing, counting it to courtesy. The two men sitting in the back of the chopper had not spoken a word since leaving Phoenix, and that was as it should be. They had been in the air nearly thirty-six hours, sent out and brought back on his command. They had no questions or, more likely, if they did, they did not voice them. If they were disappointed at the abort of their mission, they did not show it.

Rembrandt spotted a welcoming committee at the edge of the pad. The chopper settled down, and he cracked the hatch, and was out and hurrying before the pilot could finish his warning about the blades. He knew choppers. Damn, he'd nearly cut his teeth on the aircraft. He could remember the days when they'd been called whirlybirds. Rembrandt straightened up, the current from the blades still whipping around him, and felt his thinning hair stand nearly on end.

Josey Meales strode up to meet him, snapping off a salute which Rembrandt returned. Josey took his suitcase, but not the laptop computer. A man's computer was his lifeline and coded to him and him alone.

Josey was in his early forties, and looked as if he had once been a military man, despite his shortness in height. He wore khaki with his pants tucked into his jackboots. The boots shone, but they also looked comfortable, well-broken in. Gray hair was sprinkled liberally at his temples and there was a palm-sized balding spot at the back of his head, but there probably wasn't a man in camp who was fitter or faster.

"Pleased to see you again."

Not many, reflected Rembrandt, could or would say that to him. He nodded brusquely. "Same here, Josey. I need to get up to speed on happenings as soon as possible, and then you and I need to reestablish my mission."

"Right this way." Josey indicated a path off the landing field with the suitcase, despite its weight, as if it were no more than an empty briefcase. "I wonder if I might ask a favor of you, sir."

Rembrandt looked at him. Josey did not often offer more than was required of him. "What is it?"

"It's noon, sir. The trainees are gathering at the mess hall. I wonder if you might say a few words to them. They know you're arriving and although you won't be here long, I think it would be important to them. They've been working hard and making a lot of progress. I'd like to think we could reward them with about five minutes of your time."

If the request had come from anybody other than Josey Meales, Rembrandt would have suspected brown-nosing, but this man did not curry favors by words, but by deeds, hard work in the field. He'd been hired by that ethic as well as ideology. Rembrandt checked his watch. It would take more than five minutes to handle the request, but he had time.

"Josey, I'd be pleased."

The commander smiled. "Thank you, sir. Let me show you to your quarters where you can freshen up and secure your equipment, and then I'll inform the mess sergeant."

Rembrandt followed, stretching his long legs to keep up with Josey's brisk march. The trainees he'd seen at the field's edge were given no time to watch him, they were already engaged in tenting camouflage nets over the Bell Ranger and staking them down against the ever-present wind. The two men he'd brought back with him fell out at Josey's orders and dog-trotted back to their barracks.

Josey had more than comfortable quarters set up for him. There was a hot meal platter waiting, its savory smells filling the suite. Meales had also laid out fresh clothes and an encrypted bulletin from Bayliss. Rembrandt closed the door behind him with gratitude, but also with a slight bit of worry. Josey was this camp's commandant. He did not need to be acting as Rembrandt's aide-de-camp. He would have to remind Josey that his efforts were better turned elsewhere and that he could, for the time being, take care of himself.

He took a stinging hot shower for two minutes to awaken himself, then sat down and ate. Steak with bernaise, fresh asparagus spears, orange slices with

Spanish onion salad, and a cup of sorbet, along with a carafe of newly brewed coffee. He doubted the trainees in the mess were having much less of a meal. These people had been culled as the premium of troopers, they deserved and got nothing less than the best.

He'd barely set down his fork when a tap came at the door.

"Enter."

The door opened. A young woman saluted and informed him, "I've come to escort you to mess. The lunch hour is over, but you're expected." She wore a minimum of makeup, but needed none to accent her high cheekbones and rich, full mouth. Her glossy dark hair was bound back in a French braid, and she looked at him without looking at him, respectfully.

Rembrandt caressed his lips with the fine linen napkin and stood. "Lead the way and I'll follow."

"Ten-*hut!*"

Chairs scraped as fifty recruits sprang to their feet. They wore cammies, only their faces distinguishing them above their collars. Rembrandt scanned the room, seeing an egalitarian reflection of race and gender in the young faces looking back at him. His escort peeled off and joined an end table.

Josey had a modest podium and speaker set next to him at the head table. Rembrandt saluted back and told them they were at ease. He did not sit at the podium until they had settled, the chairs noisy in the confines of the mess hall. The cooks and cooks' helpers leaned out over the kitchen, listening, wiping their hands on their white aprons.

"Commander Meales has asked me to say a few words to you. First of all, let me tell you that I feel privileged to be here today. Although my stay here is scheduled to be very short this visit, and I have not been able to take a tour of the camp, I have already seen results of your hard work. All of us enlisted in this effort would be proud. I am proud of all of you.

"We have come together because we felt that, if an opportunity to save our country was to come, we would have to make it ourselves. We have evolved from a fiercely independent, self-ruling country to a land of sheep led by media and image, style not substance. Results of the recent election left us no choice but to join together in an effort to save what remains of our nation's original principles.

Rembrandt paused, to gauge the effect of his words. Faces rapt with attention watched him. "We can no longer afford to leave our material, spiritual, physical, and ecological rescue in the hands of those committed to lining their wallets, to being guided by pork barrel politics and shiny images on television. The partisan mind of our governing branches is hell-bent on destruction. We cannot afford to make war on ourselves, while supporting foreign nations which despise and cheat us. It is painfully apparent we have to take action ourselves. We have to pull ourselves up by our own bootstraps, before it is too late.

"All of you chosen here are training for elite jobs of position, to be in readiness for what must come. You have months of difficult training yet ahead, but you must not falter. Some of you will go out in the field, as Seals, ATF, FBI, Department of the Treasury, the Pentagon, wherever you will be needed. Others will stay behind, forming task forces for covert operations. No one of us is more valuable than the others; we are all in this together. We are of a common mind to do what needs to be done. We will turn this tide and though it seems a thankless job now, future generations will remember our names as we remember those of Jefferson, Adams, Washington. Welcome, ladies and gentlemen, to the next American Revolution." Rembrandt paused and then saluted the trainees.

The mess hall vibrated with the sound of their applause. He met their enthusiasm with a solemn face, looking over the crowd, knowing that, in the weeks ahead, there would be defectors from these ranks. And, in all likelihood, despite careful screening, there would be agents, gathering information, already debating what to tell their Intelligence operations about just what this group had planned. That was the way of these things. It was inevitable.

Which was why he could afford to stand here and bask in their approval. The sooner he had recovered the chemical compounds Christiansen had stolen, the sooner this front would become impenetrable, defectionless, undefeatable. The voodoo priest had promised Bayliss soldiers without pain, without doubt, without betrayal. What the superstitious world had once called zombies had nothing to do with the raising of the dead to do one's bidding. Delacroix had discovered a chemical compound which was even more powerful than legend. What Rembrandt had nearly had his hands on was a powerful psychoactive drug which channeled free will into one will, tireless, loyal until death.

The chain of conspiracy was only as strong as its weakest link. The drug promised by Delacroix would eliminate any weakness. If Rembrandt had to go to hell and back to retrieve the drug from Christiansen, to ensure the success of this endeavor, he would.

Meales, who had a sense of timing, bellowed, "*Dismissed!*"

* * * *

Geneva came in quietly, not intending to disturb Mother, but although she said nothing, she brought a freshly dipped turtle with her, and the smell of a newly-minted piece of candy filled the air as she entered the back room. Mother sat back in her chair with a sigh, then looked around with a grateful smile at her sister.

"Sometimes," she noted, "the smell of a good chocolate and caramel turtle is a heap better than incense."

Geneva handed over the patty, still cooling on a hand-sized sheet of waxed paper. "You're working too hard, Mother."

"I have to. I haven't much time. You, Geneva, need to shut the shop and pack up the girls." Mother pinched off a bit, pecans and caramel and milk chocolate, and savored it.

"Why?"

"Things are stirrin'."

"You've never had any trouble taking care of matters before."

"You know, girl, there are two sides to every coin. I fear that this man is the other side of me."

Geneva wiped her hands carefully on her bakery apron. "D'you think so?"

"It appears like it to me. I can take care of myself, but you and the girls need to be gone."

"The shop—"

"Can be shut a week or two."

"And what will you be doin'?"

"They have to come here." Mother stretched her neck and straightened her necklaces around her throat. The lemon boa around her wrist raised its delicate head, then settled again when she stroked and murmured to it. "Do all white children have such thick skulls?"

"Mmmm-hmmm." Geneva began to clear the round

table in front of Mother. She pinched out candle flames, renewed incense sticks in their holders, set out new herbs, her hands efficiently whisking through the religious objects Mother studied. "But you won't give up on 'em, girl. I know you."

"Do you know?"

"A-course I do. You raised me when Mama took sick, and Papa left. You took me under your wing like a mother hen, and I've never seen you let a chick go by without takin' it in, just the same."

"Do you think Mama had the power?"

Geneva paused, put one hand on her hip as she tilted her head to the side to think. "She must have. How could she have named us so—you Madre and me Geneva? You always mothering everythin' and me always the peacemaker, always trying to settle the troubles you couldn't. But you should know that."

"Sometimes I think I know nothin' anymore." Mother rubbed the deep crease between her eyes. "I remember Granma better than you, child. Oh, if she didn't have the true power, then she had the meanness to scare the bejesus out of you!"

Geneva laughed sharply. "Didn't that woman! No wonder Papa left." She paused. "Do you ever look for him?"

"I looked, but Damballah does not let me see. Maybe it's because I'm not mambo enough—because I have a foot in this world and a foot in the other. I don't practice one religion or t'other, but both. Is that right of me?"

Geneva patted Mother on the shoulder. "Whether it's right or not, it's *you*. I don't see you ever being any different than you are." She headed back to the candy kitchen and shop front, pausing at the door. "We'll go.

Tomorrow. But. . . . if you needed help, Mother, would you ask me?"

"I would, Geneva."

Her sister nodded, then stepped through.

Mother waited until the door shut firmly, finishing, "If I thought it would do any good." She stroked the ivory-and-lemon-yellow-patterned reptile. "If it would be any help at all." She stared down at the corn-grain drawing she had done on the tabletop, and lit the new candles her sister had laid out for her. She did not know if the boy was coming her way or not, bringing the others, but she could see that trouble was on their heels, very close. If they were not moving, they would soon be swallowed up.

And she had sensed the moment Delacroix had stepped onto North American soil, like a trembling deep in her soul.

She had no answers, but she had a heap of questions, including wondering what that mambo was doing. Why was he sendin' a curse after the others? How could she shelter them from it?

She had never regretted the path she'd taken, not the one her mother would have chosen for her, not the one her granma had chosen and trained her for . . . but a middle road, her own. She had chosen the Christian church, as well as the chants and charms and superstitions, the gri-gri bags to be tied to the thigh to bring a lover home, the cursing and uncursing. She was neither deacon nor mambo, but both, and she prayed in both voices, and saw miracles with two sets of eyes, and had become convinced in her lifetime that the great God above all, the Bon Dieu, was all one and the same.

She had never doubted her ability to face down anything the dark side might raise. She was a force of her own, and she had felt the goodness of Bon Dieu, and knew it was right.

Until now.

Now a mambo came who had been trained in the discipline of true vodun. She had already tasted his power, and it was considerable. Had she made a fatal mistake which she no longer had the time to rectify? Would she be strong enough to vanquish this foe?

As she stared into the drawing, she could feel the power emanating outward, the aura, but all it would do was knit closer to itself and spin, a hard, brilliant knot of energy. Spinning and spinning and spinning.

Chapter 22

The desert outside Phoenix was not a desert. It rippled in carpets of green, grain and vegetable and fruit, piped in through irrigation networks which lay at the edges of the field, doling out water like the precious commodity it was. Brand watched the scenery in vague disappointment, not knowing what he'd expected, not seeing anything he had. Crossing the last of California had been flat and uninteresting—the painted rocks and sands only meant a reddish tinge instead of dirt-color beyond the fields, and to watch any of it was like sticking his face in an oven. His eyes rejected the reflected heat and light, flinched from the ribbony highway, until he finally sat back in the car seat and watched nothing. The backs of Mitch's and Kamryn's heads. The dashboard. Anything he could to ignore the sun and light.

He'd been excited at first when Kamryn pointed out the fields, knowing they were close to Phoenix, and seeing them had been like looking at the Emerald City of Oz—much better farther away—and now he laid his temple against the car's glass, bored by row after row of broccoli despite the skyscrapers on the horizon. Even the greenery did nothing to soothe the assault of the daylight on his pupils. He felt like one of *The Lost Boys*, that near-classic movie, morphing into a vampire almost without his knowledge or consent.

He put a hand into his jeans pocket and wrapped his fingers around the amulet. Cool to his touch, the metal warmed only slightly as he held it, counterpoint to the pain of his eyes. He wondered if he still looked slightly like a racoon, or if the puffiness around his eyes had finally gone down. He thought of his mother, lying on her bed after a rough day at work, with brewed tea bags, chilled in the refrigerator, over her closed eyelids. It always looked weird, especially when she used the square bags with the paper tags, but she swore by it. He wondered if he should try that. He'd left his eyedrops behind and hoped it wouldn't be a big mistake. He needed the light. He craved it. The thought of shunning it indefinitely rode him uneasily.

Day-o, day-o. Daylight come and me wanna go home—

Shut up, Bauer, Brand said voicelessly. Bauer, of course, preferred the dark for what he liked to call his wet work. Daylight for stalking, nighttime for pleasure. Bauer went silent, but Brand would feel him, watching Kamryn through his eyes. Bauer tolerated daylight because it was better to see the victim by, but he also hated it because it exposed him and his activity, putting him at greater risk. He'd been caught in the daylight, caught and sentenced to death. He'd escaped later.

Brand sighed and closed his eyes, putting him toe to toe with Bauer, shutting the other off from watching his friends. As long as he could feel the sunlight streaming in through the car windows, as long as he could somehow even *sense* it, Brand could bask in its protection, like a cat in a window-focused ray. Bauer wasn't happy. He wanted to watch Kamryn. He liked her long, slim, angular looks, boyish in a way. He liked boys, young boys, young girls . . . liked them best when torturing them, vise grips on tiny, raised nipples, their torsos slick with blood, his ears filled with childish cries of anguish. Wet work. Brand pushed back, hard, shoving Bauer aside in his thoughts, images, thinking of sunlight streaming in, fiery, yellow-white light burning out his soul, his mind's eye, cleansing it. Bauer retreated, but Brand knew it was only temporary. He felt sick to his stomach.

Please, God, don't leave me blind and alone with him, he prayed silently, unaware his lips moved slightly and his breath made tiny whispery noises.

Kamryn moved her head. "Asleep again," she reported to Mitch. "I thought he said he had problems sleeping."

"He has bad dreams. He's probably exhausted, though, after the last couple of days. Don't blame him. The view's putting me to sleep, too." He checked the rearview mirror, put his hand to it, trying to adjust it.

"Don't touch that! It's hanging on by a stripped screw and a bobby pin."

Mitch grinned as he looked at her. "Did you buy this as is or was it a fixer upper?"

"Laugh, but it's paid for." Kamryn crossed her legs and looked out over the farmlands. "And it's taking you where you want to go."

"We'll be in Phoenix in another forty-five minutes. What did you have in mind?"

"Swapping this baby over as soon as I can. My California plate is like a spotlight, even though there will be a lot of them over here. I have . . . friends . . . who might be able to help. Then I thought we'd get a room. He's had plenty of rest, but I feel as bad as you look. I thought we'd drive down to Tucson after dark, then get as far as we can into New Mexico."

His hand flexed on the steering wheel. He drove with

his left arm on the door's rest, his hand free. "Texas is going to be a two-day drive. Taking the 10 across is cutting through the heart."

"I know," Kamryn answered. "No place else to go."

"Enough money in that belt of yours to buy air fare?"

Reflexively, her hand went to the flat of her stomach and the canvas money belt. "You know, I told Brand I'd help him get to New Orleans, but this money is for the future. I won't have one without it. I don't intend to bankroll this with my last cent."

"You don't."

"No."

"How'd you meet Brand, anyway? Get roped into this?"

"I never met him, really. He was just this geeky teenager down at the mall . . . staring at me. He tried to help me out once, a steak of the Lone Ranger, I guess. Then, when Darby came—well, you saw him . . . he would have taken a bullet for me. For me," she repeated softly, in wonderment. "What makes a kid like that? Willing to sacrifice his life for a stranger?"

Mitch's hands tightened on the wheel again. White knuckles, then loosened. "What makes a kid the other way?"

"That's easy, I suppose. Hatred. Self-hatred. Bad role models. Low self-esteem. Then something comes along, a thought, something that strikes a note, a Pied Piper, something that looks better, at least an escape, maybe. Only it's not. It sucks you in before you notice it's a trap of its own. Then it builds."

Mitch was watching her, she felt, but she did not want him to see her face. She had talked too much, too long, but to stop now would tip him off.

"Is that what drew you in?"

"Sort of, and not exactly."

"I don't see you doing it just for a boyfriend."

"No," she answered softly. "It was in the family. The boyfriends came later. And I'm not a skinhead. Not anymore."

"No," he agreed. "Now you're an avenging angel, dashing in to rescue Brand."

"What about you? Why do you have somebody like Rembrandt asking about you?"

"It's personal."

"It's more than personal, it's deadly. Forget what Brand saw, or thinks he saw, or made us think we saw. He could be psychotic or it could be a flashback from the drugs. Rembrandt is flesh and blood, and he's a killer."

"You're better off not knowing."

"You can't fight what you don't know about."

"I don't know what he is." Mitch licked his lips as if they'd gone dry. "At first, I thought military police."

"He acts like government. Military intelligence?"

"Maybe."

"And why you?"

"I'm AWOL."

"Really? From what?"

"The USMC."

"Well, semper fi." Kamryn looked at him appraisingly. "I can't see you as a jarhead."

"I wasn't a jarhead." He shut his mouth, the lines across his jaw tightened, worked. "I was a Marine."

"Still are, is my guess. You must have done something big. Get the base commander's daughter pregnant?"

He looked across the desert, north, to where lowlying mountains just edged the horizon. Dusty, duncolored mountains. Somewhere beyond them lay the fantastic canyons and gorges of the Grand Canyon. He felt about to tumble into its depths. He did not want to answer any more questions. "You don't need to know any more."

"Yeah, well, I don't need to know any less either." Kamryn let out a short laugh. "I never would have guessed. Only The Shadow knows the secrets which lie in the hearts of men. Or something like that."

He caught sight of the road sign, and said, with a touch of relief in his tone, "Sixteen miles and we're in."

The fields were broken now by squares of commerce, scattered, dusty gas stations and abandoned homesteads, and an occasional bar. She stared at one as they passed, motorcycles lined up outside, haughty, road-faring bikes, monsters of the road. A group of jacketed riders lounged around the doorway of the concrete block building, cold beers in their hands, watching her pass by even as she watched them being left behind, raising uneasy thoughts in her, but as she twisted back to look, the bar was too far from the road and too far behind to tell. She shook it off.

"Ever been to Phoenix?" she asked of Mitch.

"No."

"Well, 10 goes through the southern quarter. Just follow it on in. We'll stay in Tempe, just outside the major part of the city. It's cheaper there. No one should notice us."

"What about Brand?"

Kamryn looked back. "What do you mean?"

"Any chance they'll be looking for him out here?"

"Possibly. L.A. has a pretty wide sphere. We'll have to catch the evening news on that, and do whatever we have to."

"Meaning?"

She gave a half smile. "Meaning we have to get a

more expensive motel, with TV. And at least one of us might have to get a haircut and a dye job."

He ran his hand through his hair. "I don't have much more to lose."

"We all," she contradicted gently, "have a lot to lose if they catch us now."

* * * *

The same recruit who'd escorted him to the mess came to Rembrandt's room several hours later, interrupting his review of the SALUTE reports while he was confirming his feeling that intelligence operations by the Aryan Nations and other groups had been stepped up, equaling only the recent surge in the latter part of 1994 through 1995. They were watching each other, they were, circling warily, looking for that terrorist strike or demonstration which could be capitalized upon. There was, gratifyingly, no mention of his own operations, however. Their build-up had yet to be noticed, as they had planned, giving them a definite advantage. Rembrandt looked up, prepared to be annoyed at the disturbance, but the truth was that she was easy on the eyes, a lot easier than the damned reports, and he ended up scowling to hide her effect on him.

"Recruit Reynolds."

She saluted smartly. "Commander Meales sent me, with a request that you come to the computer room. He says you might be interested in a report he's running for you."

That would be on the Honda's license plate, tracking the girl down. He folded his reading glasses quickly. "Ah. Thank you." He stood and took a few minutes to return the report to the desk safe in his room, then joined the trainee at the door. "After you."

Crossing the squad between buildings, her alarm watch went off. Without hesitation, she reached out, took his wrist and said, "Come with me, sir."

She ducked in under the extended eaves of one of the buildings and waited, motionless, until her watch pealed again. He noticed that all activity between the buildings did the same, and out on the field. He could only think of one thing that would precipitate the actions.

She counted to ten before stepping out from the sheltering eave and apologized.

"Quite all right, Reynolds. We avoiding a sweep?"

"Yes, sir. We appear to be on the northern edge of a rather broad look-see. The commander thinks the main objective is Los Alamos and Roswell."

"Ours?"

"We don't know yet." She smiled grimly. "But we will."

Rembrandt followed after first looking upward, though he could not possibly see the spy satellite which was taking camera surveillance of the area, not with his bare eye, and not in the daytime. He had been in his quarters all afternoon and had not noticed, but calculated that every seventeen minutes or so, or whatever the orbit of the cameras might be, all activity would halt, the personnel of the camp either taking shelter or hitting the ground in their cammies to avoid being identified by the photo reconn. If they were on the fringe of the sweep, such evasive action could be successful for months.

If he were a betting man, he would gamble that Bayliss had not yet heard of this minor complication. Meales would know that the base had been located where it had because of such logistics. The commander might even lose his command and be transferred to another camp, and New Hope abandoned. Josey had worked hard for this promotion, it would not sit well with him to be moved.

It would not sit well with Bayliss to know that they might have been detected. It mattered little if it were domestic or foreign, at this point. Later, perhaps.

Not that he needed to have Meales indebted to him, but it would not hurt to pull Josey's bacon out of the fire. It was possible he could trace the computer connect to the satellite and reroute the camera angles. It would take some time, time he did not have until Christiansen was brought in, but Rembrandt thought he could do it. Meales might even have hackers working who had already traced part of the signal. They should have the facilities to do it.

Even though he had helped to design the communications and computer areas, he was still awed to see the design at work. Reynolds led him into the building, its interior a good fifteen degrees cooler than outside, to keep the equipment at its optimum. Inside, he noticed personnel wearing their long-sleeved uniforms against the chill. The recruit motioned him into a lab, where activity seemed constant yet constrained. Everyone he saw wore headsets, free-roaming, and one or two carried computer notepads, etching as they talked. A phone rang in the corner cubicle, and a fax immediately started to pick up the signal.

The cubicles were set apart, each area a pod of activity, sometimes working on a clear plexiglass board. He recognized a map of Washington, D.C., on one of them as he passed it by, a recruit busily sketching in information as his headset fed it to him. Rembrandt's head turned slightly as he passed it, keeping it in view. The vice president, he decided. They were charting the movements of the vice president. The president was in Canada for the weekend, at a minor summit.

Even more importantly, he could see the recruits, as a second joined the first, charting the movement of the Secret Service detail escorting the vice president. They did not notice as Rembrandt passed, engrossed in their work.

"This is Recruit Trinh, sir. He's been assigned to your request."

"Thank you, Reynolds."

"A pleasure, sir." She smiled fully, her sensuous mouth curving into a bow. "Just send for me when you want to return to quarters."

He was not to move about unescorted. That surprised Rembrandt briefly, but he nodded acquiescence.

Trinh sat in a cubicle dominated by three computers and several external modem hookups in addition to the internal modems of the computer models. His area was messy in a familiar way. The recruit made ready to stand, but Rembrandt pulled up a chair and sat down, saying, "At ease, son. What have you got?"

Trinh reached for a stack of paper with a fine-boned hand. He was Vietnamese, unless Rembrandt missed his guess, probably brought into Camp Pendleton with thousands of others in the mid-1970s and relocated from there. "I checked out California DMV on the license plate you gave me. I've been working all afternoon on it."

This was nothing Rembrandt couldn't have done himself, but he had not had the time. Regardless, getting into the motor vehicle records should not have taken the bulk of the afternoon. "Recruit, I don't know the particulars of your background, but this was not a project requiring the effort—"

"Sir." Trinh looked at him intently, dark eyes narrowing. "Meaning no disrespect, sir, but she left a paper trail I've been several hours following."

"I see." Rembrandt sat back. "Let me see what you've pulled up."

"First, I have the latest registration records. There is a change of address about eight weeks ago. The current address is a dummy, but the state doesn't know that yet."

"But we do."

Trinh nodded with satisfaction. "Yes, sir, we do. The prior registration is an address in Costa Mesa, Orange County, but it, too, was fairly recent. It shows the car was bought and registered there about ten months ago. The car was used and I checked out the former owners, but I don't see anything too interesting about them." He passed over several sheets of paper, printouts of previous registration information.

"What about her?"

"Kamryn Talent? Well, that's the thing. First of all, there is a city police inquiry on the record of the dummy address, but no follow-up."

Rembrandt scanned the hard copy. "Brea P.D. That's possible. She was witness to a shooting several days ago." So now the police department was also aware the address had been a fake. He was glad he'd listened to his instincts and let the girl and kid go. He could strike in Arizona or New Mexico and dispose of the bodies where they would never be found. If he'd done the job in Orange County, the alert would have gone up instantly. He did not like attracting attention.

"Okay." Trinh shuffled more paper from the stack at his elbow. "But there is also a state inquiry, plus two Orange County sheriffs' flags on the authentic Costa Mesa address."

"Really?" Rembrandt checked the printouts as Trinh

fed them over. If she had lived with the boyfriend previously, then the skinhead had drawn attention he probably wasn't even aware that he'd drawn. They'd been watched, and didn't even know it. Interesting, and logical, but not particularly illuminating. But it was obvious Trinh had done more.

"What else can you tell me?"

"First, I checked out the residential address. The primary occupant, male, is deceased—" Trinh paused. "The shooting, right?"

"Right."

"Okay. Well, he has—had—local skinhead connections, but nothing too significant. So I went back to the girl since she was the object of the original search." Trinh paused. "I'm right, aren't I, sir? It wasn't the car."

"No, it wasn't the car."

"Good." Trinh smiled briefly, a fleeting expression that passed quickly over his Asian features. "I decided to check on the driver's license, since I'd already been into DMV. It was fairly new, too, predating the car purchase by only a few weeks."

"Totally new, or from out of state?"

"Totally new. Although," and Trinh paused, looking at his own hard copies, "I don't find any notation that she turned in an out of state license. I find that unusual. She's twenty-three. She should have been driving for at least six or seven years."

It was unusual. Trinh had the same instincts Rembrandt had. "Go on."

"So, I checked birth records as given on the driver's license and in the taxation records. I couldn't find a Kamryn Talent in California for birth, although there have been state disability fund installments for about six months or so from employment checks, in addition to state withholding."

"And you did a national search on the birth?"

"Yes, sir. I used our own databases which seem to be fairly complete and then I tapped into the IRS briefly—that was a quick connect, sir and I had to get out faster than I wanted to, unable to locate an adult record—but I did locate Kamryn Talent in Oregon."

"Oregon." He wouldn't have thought that. She had an inflection to her voice which he had not placed, but she had not struck him as Oregonian.

"But that's the end of it, sir. The skinhead association bothered me, so I kept checking. Death records, this time." Trinh's face blazed with triumph. "There is no Kamryn Talent alive in the United States at this time, sir. She died in 1974 after a very short infancy."

"The birth certificate is fake."

"As far as I can trace."

Trinh passed him the remainder of the hard copy.

"Let me commend you on an excellent job." Rembrandt looked down, reading what he'd already been told.

His question had been answered, but a more vital one raised. There was no Kamryn Talent. The thorn in his side should not exist, but she did. And, for some reason, she had false papers. An identity which had been well-provided, and one which he could assume had come courtesy of the Aryan Brotherhood.

But why? Who in the hell was she?

"What do you suggest, sir?"

"Run a scan on news articles, give me an eighteen-month parameter, with anyone matching her gender, age, and general physical description. Let's see what comes up."

Trinh frowned in concentration. "All right. Anything else?"

This was an unusual trio. He had not been able to understand what brought them together, or what, if any, bonds would hold them together. He thought he knew Christiansen. Now he had to learn what he could about potential allies.

He leaned forward intently. "Let's see what you can help me pull up on the boy. I have some indication of psychiatric problems. I want anything you can pull up."

Chapter 23

Delacroix took a room in a hotel which would not have existed except for the sport fishing in the area, and although he surmised it was not luxurious by American standards from the complaints he heard as he passed through the lobby, it was far grander than almost any establishment he had ever seen in Haiti. Perhaps Port-au-Prince or the President's palace might have more elegant buildings. Perhaps. He had never been to the city or to the capital. Yet. He felt in his heart that there would come a day when he would be summoned. Yes. Summoned and dined and asked his opinion, and offered respect due his position. That day was coming.

But first, he had to pass through this day and night, and the others immediately before him. He would rest in the afternoon and, in the early evening, they could cross the territory overland, and into Arizona. He did not expect trouble. The border guards would have no reason to look for him, no expectation to deny him. He was, after all, traveling in the guise of a professor, a man simply after knowledge and learning.

And didn't Americans think that they had an obligation to educate the rest of the world? Their own arrogance would be their downfall.

He sat down in a comfortable, cushioned wicker

chair by a veranda which looked down on the Bay of Cortez with its bluer than blue waters, and opened a chilled bottle of fruit juice which he had purchased on the way to the room.

Stark brought in the bags and set them down.

Delacroix turned around at his entrance. He pulled a second bottle of juice from the pocket of his jacket and tossed it onto the twin bed nearest Stark.

"Drink," he said. "You must be thirsty."

Stark stared at the glass bottle for a moment as if not recognizing it, then picked it up, twisted the cap off, and drained the bottle in three long gulps.

Delacroix smiled. "Yes. I thought you might be." He swung around in the chair, looking at the ocean again. "My assistants will be here shortly. You might as well rest while you can. We have a long night ahead of us."

Stark took off his safari jacket. His skin showed a faint pinkness from being in the sun at the helm of the boat. He laid the jacket out carefully, stretched out next to it, and closed his eyes.

In a moment, perhaps two, his breathing had deepened into a catlike purr, and he was asleep.

Like the American arrogance that they had much to show the rest of the world, Delacroix would turn this, too, back on them. Stark was his, wholly, despite the years of training and, in fact, the training was what made him an invaluable tool. He knew more than weaponry. Without him, Delacroix might have wasted months and gutted his precious financial resources obtaining the correct paperwork and transportation. His loa rode a man who had found the trail he sought, but it made little difference if Delacroix could not follow after. The loa might capture, might kill, but it would not retrieve the sacred powders. For that, Delacroix trusted only himself. It was Stark who paved the way, like Judas himself, showing the priest the soft under- belly of the American system.

He had never doubted that he could bend Stark to his will, but there had been a time when he was not certain if Stark's body would heal, if it would allow him to follow the new set of his mind and spirit. The man had been abandoned for dead, on the threshold, and it had taken much from Delacroix to keep him from passing. There had been severe bleeding, and in- fection and fever. Weeks of weakness and listlessness had culminated in a body which was only a shadow of what it had been. He did not know if he had a tool he could use or not until the day Stark had risen from his cot in the hut, and come to the altar where Delacroix sat meditating and said, "I must run."

Delacroix had heard him approach in the silence and, without turning, answered, "You cannot leave without my willing it."

"I do not wish to leave. I must run."

And so Delacroix had given in to the strange request and let the stranger run. Stark did so, gone for hours, staggering back pale and deluged with sweat, falling into his cot, unmoving for hours until that day when he did not fall upon returning.

Then he came to Delacroix and said, "I must lift weights."

Delacroix had laughed at that. "Work in the fields. Carry the sheep and goats and pigs. Carry the bails if you wish to lift weight."

And so Stark had done that, all summer, in the fields of the two or three villages which huddled close to the hills where Delacroix tended his church and shrines. He grew tanned and strong and returned to Delacroix at sundown every day, where he said little, but listened to Delacroix as he talked of and to his gods.

As was fitting of Delacroix's position, he explained to Stark the importance of vodun, how it had strengthened the slaves of Haiti, how it had given them the power to rise up and make of themselves an independent nation, though troubled, and how it would aid them yet again. How the United Nations and the Protestant churches were trying to bury voodoo, but how it would triumph. How even the President's palace sat on ground which had been hallowed by its rituals, and although forgotten, would be brought down again and rise again in vodun pride.

How he, Delacroix, and even he, Stark, might have a part in this. All of this, and more, he spoke of in the evenings, in his soft, lilting island French patois, and Stark not only understood, but absorbed every word until it came time to plan these days, and then Stark had begun speaking back to him, in American, but they two understood each other perfectly. Stark, then, as now, confined his speech to only what was absolutely necessary. Then, as now, he had a complete and deep comprehension of what it was Delacroix hoped to achieve.

This, Delacroix told himself, this was what could be achieved with the powers given to himself. Without the touch of the god, the powders were little, without the understanding of the spiritual, the binding of the physical to a purpose was a binding which was brittle, which could not be trusted or would not last. The consecration of flesh to body to will to god was all.

A soft knock sounded on his door. Delacroix dropped his feet to the rug and crossed the room. Stark did not stir in his sleep, but his breathing lightened a little, and the priest knew he was listening on some level, as a soldier would, determining if there were peril.

Genet stood outside, his cocoa face rippling with sweat from the heat of the fishing village. At his heel waited Covarubia. Both men inclined their heads in respect.

"Only two of you," Delacroix noted, as he let them in.

"We are sorry," Genet pleaded. "The others did not return from California. We have not heard from them."

"I am sorry as well. Come in, sit. Rest in the breeze. We will talk about our plans this evening, but keep your voices low. Stark is resting.

Genet flashed the sleeping man a suspicious look, one which Delacroix caught with some surprise. He did not show it, however. He would remedy matters later, for Genet could not be allowed to ruin his plans with petty jealousies. Genet would be reminded that he did as he did not for Delacroix the man, but for Delacroix the high priest, the mambo, and for the dark face of Damballah and for other gods whose names when mentioned would make Genet tremble.

"We must assume they are dead. We will proceed without them."

"My brother!" Genet protested. "Take Covarubia with you, but let me go to California to find him. Anything could have happened. He needs me."

"If he is alive, he will return home. If not, the legba has swallowed him . . . he has passed through the spirit gate, he is no longer someone you can help. Only I can help him now."

Genet's face paled beneath its rich coloring. "He is my brother," he repeated, and his large hands moved restlessly. "I can't leave him behind."

"He is already gone, or already safe. Those were his

instructions if he could not make it here. He understood this . . . now you must understand it also."

Covarubia sat cross-legged on the second bed. He commented, "Rich men must sleep here."

"Rich men or soft men," Delacroix agreed. "Do you have trouble with this?" he added, looking into Genet's eyes, brown eyes flecked richly with green, the features of his face reflecting his heritage of mixed blood.

Genet's mouth twisted, but he said nothing else, giving a brusque nod.

"Good. You two may rest if you wish, or leave to find food and drinks. I must do what I must do." Delacroix slipped off his jacket and his shoes, opened the veranda door, and pushed the small table and chair aside. He sat down, facing the serene view of the sea.

Genet left. Covarubia's snoring twinned that of Stark. Delacroix closed his eyes, seeking commune with the loa he had sent into the world so many months ago seeking his vengeance. It was not his own loa, or he would not have survived its passage for that length of time, but it drew on him and he could feel the tug on himself grow threadier and threadier. This loa had been summoned from its place in the world beyond, and it wished to return, thirsty and eager to do its work so that it could.

It grasped him, cool and unearthly. It sensed the beginning of the end of its hunt. It told him of the chase and where its horse, the possessed human which carried it, had brought it, and Delacroix was well pleased. He urged it to feed, to keep its strength, and informed it of his coming.

It promised to eat.

* * * *

"We should have followed her."

"Shut up, butt-munch," Snake said, and drained the last of his beer from his mug. The dust in his throat stayed there, raspy and harsh. He had not been able to swallow well for days. It did not matter what he did. "If she'd seen us, she would have taken off."

His companion snickered. "Butt-munch. Mutt-munch, that's more like it!"

The object of the derision straightened, his young face reddening roughly. "It's Mott. Not mutt, not butt."

"Might as well be, for all the thinking you do," Snake muttered. "Go get me another beer."

Mott's chin jutted out belligerently, but he grabbed the glass mug from Snake and left, his Doc Marten boots clomping loudly. He pushed his slim, hipless body through the growing crowd in the bar, disappearing into interior darkness, until even his white T-shirt could not be seen.

Snake turned back to Fleer. "Got any questions?"

Fleer shrugged. He had trimmed his blond surfer hair until all that was left was an inch-long fuzz on his crown, and the iron eagle tattoo on his left forearm blazed with the newness of fresh, black ink, its edges still a little pink-red from the needles. "Mott's an idiot."

"So are you," Snake said.

"But a smart idiot." Fleer looked at him with his Southern California baby blue eyes, so innocent, so deceptive. He'd personally helped Snake stomp some homos into the sand at Dana Point not two months ago. "I'm cool if you're cool."

"Right." Snake drew his lips back. "That's the way it should be."

He had wanted to follow the bitch right into Phoenix, but having come this far, he thought he knew where she was headed. She might have left Darby, but

she had not run to the police. The news dudes had
been speculating for days about her noncooperation
with the police investigation and her disappearance.
Snake had found the information vaguely surprising,
but useful. She had drifted into the Costa Mesa community of skinheads via Arizona. It seemed logical that,
in trouble, she would go back.

New papers, new identity. That meant Snake knew
exactly where she was headed.

She'd had passengers in the car, so she would have
to stow them somewhere while she did her business.
When she was alone, when she was in the midst of
the print shop operation, he would do her. He did not
anticipate much reaction to the deed. Better a dead
mistake than a live one.

Mott came back out and shoved his beer in his hand.
Snake took it, blew off the foam, and downed it. He'd
drunk enough that his bladder gave him urgent signals,
but he did not feel as if he'd had enough. The road
dust clotted his throat, knotting there, like something
living.

He coughed. Thrust the glass back again. "Get me
another."

Mott had not yet chilled out, but he took it, and
disappeared.

Fleer said, "Snake."

"What?"

"Don't ride him too much. His dad has a lot of bucks
in the movement."

Striking like a cobra, Snake had Fleer by the suspenders and back up against the wall of the building.
"Don't tell me what to do. Ever."

"Right."

"Don't tell me anything about the brothers. I *know*.

While you guys were still crawling on your surfboards and skateboards, I was kicking in skulls."

"Right."

"When you guys were just sittin' up in your high chairs, realizing that the blacks and the browns were giving you the shaft, I was running 'em down in the street."

"Right."

"When you busted your first cherry, I was papering high school lockers, spreading the truth."

"Right."

"Don't forget it." Snake let him go. Fleer did not move.

He had only decided to flex his shoulders when Mott came back a second time. He traded glances with Mott but said nothing.

Snake drained the glass, then said, "I'm going to the head. Then we're leaving."

"Right," said Fleer again.

Snake marched through them, but he could feel their eyes on him as he went into the cool, inky darkness of the bar. He found the head as much by its smell as by the flaking signs on the eaves.

What light it had came in from a high overhead window. The fixture bulb had either burned out or been broken. One of the urinals leaked through a cracked basin. Snake unzipped and took a stance.

He was uneasy, for reasons that escaped him, and he did not like it. He knew part of it came from Darby's woman. She needed to be taken care of, and that would cause problems among the brothers. For reasons he had been told he did not need to know, she had been taken in and passed along, given papers and money. She knew people and things he did not know, and she had importance to someone in the hierarchy.

But he'd already decided his course with her. She would die, and he would explain later. He did not expect to have to face any consequences. She had left the Brotherhood, she had inside information, she was dangerous. It was all that simple. It should not bother him, and it didn't actually, although it was like an itch somewhere he couldn't quite scratch—and he sure as hell couldn't ask anyone else to scratch it for him.

But there was another uncomfortable feeling sliding around on its belly inside of him, one that almost seemed like it was not part of him, but was. He knew it was there, although it seemed every time he tried to focus his attention on it, it would slip and slither away. He could imagine its track in his mind, like silvery snail snot, and it rubbed him wrong wherever it touched.

And it was an itchy itch. It crawled around his throat, knotting it, like he'd swallowed some kind of hair ball, choking him. Then there were the feelers it sent into his skull, aching, throbbing, creepy shots that iced through and he would have scratched them away, if he could have, if he could have reached them.

But Snake knew they lay more than skin-deep, under bone and muscle and maybe even thought, like a spiderweb which had grown in him, and something skittered along the strands, itching and twanging at him. He did not like it, and the more he thought on it, the stronger he could feel it.

He could feel it growing now, and the warm bleary feeling of the beer coursing through him began to chill. The itchy thing began to uncoil, growing larger and larger, pushing his own thoughts of himself out of the way. The stream of urine he pissed into the broken porcelain basin felt cold as ice water. He felt his eyes roll back into his skull, and found himself looking at his brain from the inside out.

And then he felt nothing.

Delacroix opened his eyes, looking upon the Sea of Cortez. It was very blue, darkening as the sky darkened, as though it drew night into its very depths. He gave a pleased smile.

"Hey, buddy. You tryin' something or what?"

Snake felt himself come awake, as if he'd been standing unconscious, blinking, his eyes narrowing in the dim confines of the bathroom. He stood with his feet spread, his dick in his hands, and did not know how long he'd been standing there. He tucked himself in and zipped up. "Shut up, asswipe," he said, and brushed by the other biker as he went out the door.

Mott and Fleer had edged inside and had their elbows on the counter. Both hurriedly finished their drinks and slid a couple of dollars over the counter as they saw him emerge.

Mott opened his mouth as if to say something, then shut it, twisting thin lips. Fleer merely stared at him with icy blue eyes. Snake wiped the back of his mouth on his bare arm. "Let's get out of here."

Somewhere near the door, a battered brown cowboy boot jutted out insolently from a crowded table. Snake tripped, stumbling violently into the door jamb, where he caught himself. Raucous laughter followed him. He swung around. He could feel sweat springing up through the pores of his naked head.

"Somethin' funny?"

The owner of the cowboy boot dragged his feet back in under his chair. "Yeah. You. Tattooed man."

Snake knew the bar. Knew the drinkers. Knew the type who was welcome and who was not.

And whether Cowboy knew it or not, he didn't care. He stared down. "Listen, beaner. You're in the wrong place at the right time."

Cowboy straightened in his chair, his brown face weathered by the harshness of the Arizona sun. He maybe even had a touch of Navajo in his broad cheekbones. "Shove it up your ass, freak."

Snake could feel the rush. He flexed his biceps. This, *this*, was what would scratch the itch which had been driving him crazy. He knew what he wanted, and it wasn't an apology. "Come on, cucaracha. Let's talk about it outside."

Cowboy leaped to his feet, his sudden movement scraping his chair across the floor. One of his buddies grabbed for his arm, muttering, "It's not worth it, man."

Cowboy shook him off. "You and me, skinhead."

Snake, grinning, followed him out into the blazing afternoon sun. He did not care if Cowboy's friends followed them out or not. He did not care if Cowboy carried a knife or a gun. He beckoned to Mott and Fleer.

"Get your butts on the bikes."

They did as they were told. Bodies crowded the doorway and Snake could hear the noise of their voices, like bees buzzing in his ears. He cupped his hand. He waved to burrito boy. "Come a little closer."

Cowboy made a move to a hip pocket. Snake could hear chain being drawn out, its links clinking. He struck cobra fast. So fast that Cowboy never had a chance to pull his weapon free.

A stomp, a knee, and he drove his fingertips into the base of the throat. Cowboy dropped to his knees, choking, spitting out blood. Crimson gushed from his nose and his lips. He toppled into the dirt.

Over that quickly. Snake grinned downward.

"Don't mess with the big boys. You ain't good enough."

He got on his bike and the three of them pulled away. Damn, but it felt *good*.

Chapter 24

NWS BULLETIN
National Hurricane Center 0600 am EDT TS Yolanda

TS YOLANDA IS CONTINUING IN A WEST, NORTH WESTERLY DIRECTION, GAINING STRENGTH AND BECOMING ORGANIZED. ABOUT TEN AM EDT, TS YOLANDA WILL POSSIBLY BE UPGRADED TO A FORCE 1 OR 2 HURRICANE IF WINDS CONTINUE TO BUILD. STORM WARNINGS ARE ISSUED TO THE OUTLYING ISLANDS OF THE CHAIN. WIND GUSTS OF UP TO 70 MPH HAVE BEEN MEASURED. ANTICIPATED RAINFALL 4–6 INCHES.

PLEASE CONTINUE TO MONITOR THIS CHANNEL FOR UPDATES ON TS YOLANDA.

Kamryn woke, flashes of light playing fiercely upon her face and the cracked ceiling of the motel room, and thought of St. Elmo's fire. It wasn't, of course. It took her another second or two to realize it came from the TV, and Brand sat cross-legged in front of it, an inky silhouette lit by the TV in the dark of the room. She could not tell what time it was, though it must have been early. She had slept in one of the two sagging king-sized beds, Mitch and Brand in the other.

Blackout drapes hung solidly across the motel window, shutting out the world, but Brand sat watching the weather channel.

She rubbed at the corner of her eyelid and sat up, drawing the sheet around her. She watched him for a second, engrossed in reading the storm warning as it scrolled across the screen, a fine classical music piece playing in muted accompaniment. Then it cut to scenes of recent hurricanes and typhoon destruction. A young man with a distinctive New England accent stood in front of a weather map and began to speak, oddly muffled, until she realized he had the sound down incredibly low.

Kamryn swung her feet out. He heard her and swiveled about on his hips, bringing his fingers up to his mouth. He pointed at the mound of tousled blankets that was Mitch on the other bed. She nodded and came over, sitting quietly next to him. One of her kneecaps popped, the one that always did, and it sounded like a champagne cork going off.

Startled, Brand kept his frand over his mouth to catch his laugh. She shook her head.

"How long have you been up?"

"Early. I slept too much yesterday. And," and he tilted his head slightly, the eerie reflection from the TV screen intensifying the dusting of freckles across his face, "I'm hungry."

"So what else is new?"

He shrugged. Mitch snored rhythmically and the two of them listened to it in companionable silence for a moment. Then Kamryn realized she was smiling, like a fool, when Brand asked, "What is it?"

She shook her head. "He sounds like an old dog we had. A big old farm dog."

"Memories, huh."

"Sure." She paused. "You ever have a dog?"

"No." He looked back at the TV as if fascinated by the scenarios of destruction. "Not exactly."

"Well, you should. They're great. I wouldn't be without one, yard duty and all. Every boy should have a dog."

"I guess they thought I was already busy with my psychosis."

"You seem pretty normal to me."

"Other than seeing things."

"Even that."

He looked back and forth. "You didn't like me watching you at the mall."

"Well, you gotta admit, that got a little creepy." She watched his face. So young. So unmarked. No sun lines, no tattoos. No lies.

"I didn't mean it to. I just thought you were, well, pretty."

"Thanks."

"And you thought I was, well, you know, creepy."

She grinned. "Something like that."

"But you're here now."

"You're worth it."

He was silent.

She nudged him. "Come on, Brand. You're worth it, aren't you?"

"Maybe not."

"After what you've been through? You're saner than most of the adults I know."

"It's not that. Do you cook?"

She had, once. Memories of a big kitchen which served as family room, birthday hall, diner, flooded her. "I grew up helping my mom."

"I peel potatoes and stuff. Ever peel a perfectly good

spud and then you get to the inside, all brown and rotten?"

She nodded.

"Well, maybe that's how I am, but you don't know it. Only you kind of do, because you thought I was a jerk."

What could he have done? Ditched school? Borrowed ahead on his allowance and squandered it? God, didn't he realize there were kids his age shooting other kids for their jackets, their shoes? What could he have done compared to what she'd been through? "Brand." She laid a hand on his shoulder, felt the muscles flinch under her touch. "I know we're all leaning on you, some of us harder than others. I know what it's like. But you're tougher than you think you are. You're not going to cave in."

"Did you?"

She could feel her face change. "You know I did. I'd like to think it was only skin-deep, but . . ." She took her hand from Brand's shoulder. "I'm not you. And I'm here to tell you, there's a second chance. If you fall from grace, there's a second chance."

She took a deep breath. Kamryn got back to her feet. "Shower?"

"Already." His subdued voice sounded a little relieved.

"Okay. I'll be out in a couple of minutes if Mitch wakes up. There's a Denny's a couple of miles up—they'll be open."

"Okay." He shoved his hand in one pocket and opened his mouth as if he thought of saying something, then he blushed slightly and looked down at his feet, back to the TV set, anywhere but at her.

Kamryn looked down and saw that her sheet had slipped, revealing one satiny bra cup and cleavage. She drew it back up, pretending she hadn't seen him blushing.

He reared back. In a coarse and cunning voice, he began to recite. "Bitch. Juice box, cunt, hairy clit—" He broke off, choking, stammering, his face crimson, mortified. "That wasn't me. God. That wasn't me."

If it wasn't him, then who was it? Her own face had warmed with shock. She swallowed. "It's all right, Brand. I have a second cousin who had Tourette's— do you know what that is? He'd get tics and twitches. Sometimes he'd rattle off until the air turned blue. It wasn't anything he meant to do. And I've been called worse."

And called others worse, far worse. Brand mumbled again, ducked his face down, unable to look at her.

She gathered up the rest of her sheet like the train of a bridal gown. "If that's all the rotten you get, I guess I can take it." He stood, she reminded herself, over that terrible abyss which separated boy from man. He wouldn't answer back.

By the time she was done showering and had dressed, Brand had found CNN. Flickering light from the screen bounced and reflected off his sunglasses. Odd, to see him wearing them in the darkness of the room. She wondered if he used them to hide behind, still embarrassed.

"Your eyes still bothering you?"

"A little." He took his glasses off and rubbed gently at them. The puffiness had nearly disappeared. "They feel kind of dry and scratchy."

"We'll pick up some eyedrops today if we can. Nothing medicated—the kind contact wearers use. They should help."

"Okay."

"Any news?" Kamryn chewed on her lower lip.

"Yeah, but we were just a blip. 'Two witnesses to L.A. area shooting disappear—boy feared to be suicidal, ex-girlfriend involved said to be avoiding police and media attention.' "

"Any photos?"

"Me. My junior high ID picture. It sucks." His voice had began to loosen up. He sounded like the old Brand.

She smiled in spite of her own tension. "Anyone able to recognize you off that?"

"Not even my mom."

"That bad, huh."

"Worse." He settled his glasses back on his face. "They're not talking about Mitch at all."

"Probably don't have him ID'd. He left the scene before I did." Kamryn let out a soft sigh. "Seems unreal, like it never happened."

Brand tilted his head back a little to look at her more fully. "There's a hurricane coming up the gulf. Forecasters say it's headed toward Louisiana."

Hairs raised on her arms and the back of her neck. "How bad?"

"It's building. Do you think it's going to bother us?"

She shrugged. "Those things sometimes just fall apart. How many hurricanes hit that area? One every two or three years? What are our odds? I'm more worried about people."

"Rembrandt."

"Our number one priority. Come on, why don't you see if you can get Mitch up? I'm going out for a paper."

She came back to some sort of argument between the two that stopped the moment she opened the room door. She could hear the muffled percussion of their voices out in the parking lot, so she knew something had been going on, and she looked at the two who stood close-lipped.

"What's going on?"

Brand, sulky. "Nothin'."

Mitch, only a little less, "It's handled."

"If it's handled, what is all the fuss about?"

"No fuss," Mitch said, and opened the door. "After you."

She scanned the room. "Got everything? We're not coming back."

Mitch said, "All the suitcases are packed and my tux is in the car."

She ignored the sarcasm, turned around, and went to the Honda. Brand climbed in without a word and sat stonily, his nose to the glass. Mitch got in the driver's side.

"Where we headed?"

"38th and Indian School. There's a Denny's on the corner." She folded the local news and tucked it under her leg.

"Anything?"

"No. As Brand put it earlier, we're just a blip. The world is onto much more important things."

"Good." He put the car into reverse out of the parking lot, then into forward and headed out.

She wondered if they'd been arguing about Brand's burst of obscenity. She decided not to mention it, that Brand would be better off if she just let it go. The sun was just rising above the cityscape, still very early in the day. "We should make it into New Mexico today."

"If we ever get on the road."

"Bellies come first. Then I want to see about getting another car."

"Right."

The atmosphere fell into silence as Mitch headed the five miles north and located the restaurant. They found a table and sat. The mild, accented voice of the cook as he talked to the waitresses carried through the nearly empty room. She watched him work, thinning dark hair combed back, dark mustache over a sensitive mouth, and a shy manner even though he talked to the girls as if he'd known them for years. He had a southern courtly charm and gentleness. She wondered how he'd come to Arizona.

She ordered an omelette and listened as Mitch and Brand both ordered the combo special for the day which included everything but the kitchen sink. She ordered cranberry juice, Brand milk, and Mitch got seconds on coffee before the waitress said, "Anything else?"

Kamryn tucked a wing of dark hair behind her ear. "Where's the cook from? I haven't heard an accent like that in a long time."

"Parkersburg, West Virginia." The waitress scratched her chin with the eraser end of her pencil. "He's a doll, isn't he? Ron only works here weekends. That do it for you?"

They nodded and she left to turn in their order.

West Virginia. She thought she'd recognized it, just down the Ohio River from Pennsylvania. A neighbor's voice. A wave of homesickness tinged through her.

No one said anything else until the breakfasts came, and Brand tucked into his as if he hadn't seen food in weeks. Mitch watched him for a moment, then smiled to himself and began eating as well.

Kamryn did not like the silence. She took a forkful of the well-stuffed omelette before asking, "What's going on?"

Mitch put down his fork with a sigh. He glared

a second at Brand, then looked back at her. "You said you had friends who would help with the car problem."

"I do. South of here, along the highway to Tucson."

"I don't think we need to avail ourselves of their services, if they're the friends I think they are."

She considered him. "And if they are?"

"I repeat. We don't need them."

"I'm not asking you to approve or disapprove of them, Mitch. I'm just there to use them."

He shoved hash browns around a bit, staining their edges with golden yolks. "There could be problems because of the Darby situation."

"Not likely. As Brand would say, he was just a blip on the screen. Their concern will be with me, and if there's one thing I don't mind doing, it's using them. That's all they're good for." She stabbed her omelette viciously.

Unasked for, Bran added, "We need a four-by."

That startled Kamryn. "Whatever for?"

He looked at her. He'd taken off his shades and his eyes had cleared, staring at her with innocence. "To get into New Orleans."

"The last I heard," Mitch commented, "Lousiana had roads like everyone else."

"Hurricane's coming." Brand swallowed half a pancake, chased it with a gulp of milk, and finished, under a white mustache, "That part of the state will be washed out."

"This true?"

Kamryn shrugged at Mitch. "Possibly. It's five, six days away. We should make New Orleans in four. Maybe even three if we can get a tradeoff this morning."

"You're insisting on this?"

"Yes. I am. Rembrandt knows the car is an older Honda Accord. If he was quick enough, he even got the license number. I don't know who *your* friends are, but I don't want to take the chance they can track us."

Brand leveled his fork at Mitch. "She's got a point there."

Kamryn turned her attention back to the omelette. "I think the point is, we've all got lousy friends, present company excepted."

Mitch did not answer, but the lines by the sides of his mouth deepened as he ate. The waitress sailed by and Kamryn snagged another milk for Brand.

"He's a growing boy."

The waitress smiled, and Brand changed color again.

South and east of Phoenix, along the 10, the desert was far more intrusive. Brand grew quiet and Kamryn got the impression that he hid behind his shades. The eyedrops they'd bought seemed to have helped only temporarily. Mitch had grabbed up a summer T-shirt on sale, proclaiming Pete's Wicked Ale with roguish lettering, and changed into it. Traffic had been crowded and thinned as they went south.

About a half hour out of Phoenix, she took him off the highway and into a developing industrial neighborhood. Homes were sparse. She pointed at a warehouse type building, set off by itself, worn and uninteresting. Four or five cars sat outside it, parked with careless abandon.

"In there."

Mitch headed the Honda in by the side, where aluminum garage doors were closed. "What's in there? Body shop?"

"Print shop," Kamryn waited until they got out of

the car. Midday sun rippled down on them, at least in the 80's, maybe better. "You won't like what you read. I suggest you keep your eyes, hands and opinions to yourself."

Mitch nodded. Brand started to ask, "What—" but Mitch wagged a finger at him.

Brand shut his mouth. Defensively, he shoved his glasses firmly onto his face.

She went around to the front office doors, where the windows were shuttered off, and knocked. Someone came to the intercom and scratchily asked, "Who is it?"

"Kamryn Talent. I need to speak to Viktor."

The intercom snapped off. She crossed her arms across her chest, waiting. She wore long sleeves again, cotton shirt unbuttoned at the cuffs, but it felt to her as if her tattoos had begun to crawl under the fabric. She rubbed one forearm.

The door opened. Viktor stood there, wiry, nerdy, heavy black glasses, his thin and continually disapproving mouth drawn to one side, dirty blond hair combed from deep on the side of his head to the other, hiding near baldness. "Kamryn! How are you?"

"I need your help again."

His pale blue gaze darted to one side of her and then the other, taking in Brand and Mitch.

"They're friends."

He drew the door open. "Of course they are."

As they entered the office, the sounds of printing presses and the hum of computers and other office equipment could be heard. Viktor smiled, but on him the expression was more one of contempt than humor. "Did you hear about last week? We got an entire printing into Crackerjack boxes."

"No. Not yet. You're clever, Viktor."

He wagged his head humbly. "We try." He beckoned her into the warehouse plant. "Come with me and we'll talk."

She strode after, weaving her way through stacks of printing supplies and bundles of pamphlets and flyers, already printed, getting ready to be sent out. An occasional loose sheet, smeared or crumbled, floated along the cement flooring. Behind her, she thought she heard Brand stumble and then his muffled, "What kind of crap is *this*?" and she could only hope that Viktor, several strides in front of her and next to the presses, had not heard as well.

She heard what it was he'd seen. A single sheet flyer, crudely drawn, hand-lettered "Mexican bitches born pregnant, carry dozens of fertile eggs to make brown babies to steal your tax money!" It got worse. She'd seen it many times. High schools and junior highs got papered with this sort of propaganda several times a year. Childish images purported to show a pregnant Mexican teenager, her belly bulging with child, and then went into biology that was racially inflammatory and physiologically impossible. Cockroaches, maybe, humans, never.

She hadn't thought that once. Kamryn licked her lips as if sensing something distasteful and followed Viktor into rear offices beyond the printing area. Unlike the clutter of the vast warehouse, his office was impeccably clean and straight.

"Sit. Tell me." Viktor made a steeple of pencil thin fingers.

"You know about Darby." Mitch and Brand filed in behind her, but there were no chairs for them. She heard them flank her chair.

"A little. You are a heartbreaker, eh?"

"I didn't intend to be. He was a baby, Viktor. A

mean, abusive baby. He jeopardized the movement by coming after me publicly." Kamryn paused, trying to gauge the effect of her words on Viktor's pale, emotionless face. "I left rather than talk to the police."

"Under the circumstances, I don't see how you could have done anything else. What do you need from me?"

Either he was satisfied or well aware of his ranking in the organization. "A trade on my car. It's in good condition, but the California plates and registration—" she spread her hands.

"Could be a problem. I understand."

"I'd like something with offroad capabilities. A Jeep or Suburban—"

"A BMW, eh? I'll have to see what I can do."

Brand, blurting out, "BMW!"

Viktor looked across her shoulder. "BMW—Big Mormon Wagon. It's a joke in Arizona." His attention returned to Kamryn. "How soon do you need it?"

"Today. Now."

"You challenge me, Kamryn. I might be able to handle it. It won't be new, of course."

"As long as it's in excellent working condition."

"Naturally. You're headed—?"

"North," she answered. "Wyoming or Montana."

"Ah. Give me a minute." He stood and retreated to an inner office, shutting the door behind him.

She knew the inner office was soundproof. She craned her neck and mouthed to Brand, "Shut up."

He pinched his lips together and gave an embarrassed shrug.

They said nothing to each other in the five minutes or so that Viktor was gone. He came back, his spare mouth stretched wide.

"Jeep Cherokee, four years old, 23,000 miles. It's a gas guzzler, but comfortable."

"Hard or soft top?"

"Hard. Winters are harsh in Wyoming."

"What do I owe you?"

"Nothing. I'll take the paperwork and keys to the Honda." He did not sit, but beckoned. "Come sit. The driver will bring the vehicle in, we'll make the exchange, and you'll be on your way."

Mitch traded a look with her as if disbelieving how easy it was. Kamryn got to her feet to follow after Viktor.

The lounge was in one of the garages to the side, not as insulated or cool as the warehouse, two tables with benches, and several broken-down sofas. The door to the bathroom stood open and she could hear the toilet running. Viktor stayed in the doorway as they filed past.

Brand immediately went to a decrepit-looking TV. Mitch stopped at a lunch table, where a deck of cards had been folded in mid-hand. Kamryn hesitated, then said, "Thank you, Viktor."

He blinked. "Later." He shoved her into the room, then shut the heavy fire door. She heard the lock click, and then a bolt being thrown. Mitch leaped to his feet.

"Son of a bitch!"

Kamryn jogged the door handle frantically. "We're locked in."

Mitch scanned the garage. "No way from here. Unless—" He glanced straight up at the revolving ceiling fan. "Unless you're mincemeat."

Kamryn sagged. "I knew it seemed too easy."

"Nice friends."

"Thanks."

Brand said, "Now will someone explain to me all the crap on that flyer?"

From Mitch, "Lies. Twisted lies."

"A touch of truth, with a lot of lies."

Mitch looked at Kamryn. "How can you say that?"

"The only thing that's true is that a woman is born with a hundred or so ovum. A kernel of truth with layers and layers of inflammatory lies." Kamryn sat down. "This might not be as bad as it looks. He could just want to keep us secure."

"He locked us up for our own good?" Mitch had been pacing, studying the converted garage. He stopped to glare at her.

"There's a lot of stuff being printed out there that is important and secret to the organization. He might trust me, but not the two of you."

Brand said, as if still a little dazed, "I used to find crap like that stuffed into my locker. I couldn't wait to throw it away."

"But it still got there. And even if it only got hammered into one or two of your classmates . . ." Kamryn stopped. She did not want to think of it anymore. She sat down and put her face in her hands.

"How long are we going to have to wait?" Brand said to Mitch.

Mitch's answer, flatly, "Until they've done whatever it is they're doing."

Hours passed. The bare coolness of the converted room had evaporated, the air stiffling as the heat outside built up. The john ran until Brand had jiggled the handle at least a hundred times and Mitch lost at solitaire forty times in a row before discovering he wasn't playing with a full deck, before the door knob turned again.

The door opened with a current of cool air, and a figure stood at the threshold, bare arms bulging, tattoos rippling, bald head shiny with the heat.

"Hello, biker bitch," greeted Snake.

Chapter 25

Brand had been half-drowsy in front of the TV set, which had been able to receive only one channel all afternoon, one of the home shopping channels, which was better than nothing at all, when the door banged open and Kamryn gasped.

Cold shot through him. As he leaped to his feet, responding to the sound of Kamryn's voice, his glasses fell and he juggled them in midair.

But nothing could stop the Arctic blast he saw and felt, glasses or no glasses, not Mitch leaping to his feet and hurling himself across the garage floor toward Snake—he saw the black-and-yellow-diamond patterns of the inking on his skin rippling as if something reptilian blocked the doorway, something cloaked in a greater darkness.

It reached toward Kamryn, enveloping, stifling. It bore the KillJoy's touch. Brand screamed, "Kamryn!" His voice crackled and tore out of his throat. He jammed his glasses into his pocket and shot forward to protect her.

Mitch was already there. He lunged at Snake, who fended him off with a forearm, shoving Mitch back into the garage. Bodies behind Snake pushed forward eagerly. There seemed to be a small army.

Kamryn grabbed for him. "Mitch, don't. They want me!"

Mitch shook her off. He took a stride toward Snake, his hands curled, then swung about, bringing up his foot, his booted foot. The sole cracked into Snake's jaw, snapping his head back. Snake sagged into the arms behind him, still on his feet.

He shook his head and growled softly. "Mott."

A skinhead answered his call. Mitch blocked the first block, slid off the second, grabbed the kid, and slammed him head first into a wall.

Mitch balanced himself for the next one. "Brand, get Kamryn."

Brand took a step forward, forcing himself, afraid. He could feel the chill, the slimy chill, as it settled around her. Dead, she was dying and didn't know it, and he could do nothing! She pushed him back with her hand. She shoved something into his palm.

"Run," she said, looked upward swiftly.

Toward the cooling fan in the ceiling. They'd looked at it one or two more times during the day, then decided against it. She squared at the door.

He looked at the palm of his hand. The car keys. He dug them deep into the pocket of his jeans.

She took up a martial arts stance as Snake straightened, still shaking his head. Shark eyes fastened on Mitch.

"Let's finish it," Snake suggested.

Mitch flexed his shoulders and readied himself.

Brand started running, hit the lunch table, and then jumped onto the bathroom door. He hit and clambered up it, perched on top. He could hear the grunts and thuds behind him as he carefully stood and then his fingertips grasped the metal rafter that ran across the loft. He took a breath and jumped, launching himself high enough so that he could throw his arms about the beam. He caught it, and the bathroom door jerked out from under him, his legs waving.

A jostle of bodies underneath reached for him. Brand kicked up and wrapped his legs around the beam, breathing hard, his rib cage aching as if he'd been slammed into something. Below, he could see Mitch, fists flying, holding off Snake. Kamryn kicked once, and whirled. Her opponent staggered back and came on again. The inky smudge that threatened to swallow her stayed with her.

Brand gulped and pulled himself along the rafter as one of the skinheads began to climb up the bathroom door, taking his route upward.

He swung himself upward onto the wide beam as soon as a diagonal strut crossed it, giving him another handhold. He looked up. The fan was directly overhead. He looked into its silvery gleam, heard its blade swish-swish-swishing.

The diagonal strut carried him right to it. He shinnied up even as his pursuer got onto the main rafter, swung his feet up onto it and began to cautiously walk after him.

Mitch took a fall, rolled and got back up, dodging Snake. He took a hit in the flank from behind. Kamryn ducked, but could not avoid a capturing embrace.

Brand swallowed hard. It was up to him. He looked up at the flickering sky. The light hurt his eyes. His glasses bulged in his jeans pocket, along with the car keys.

He would have to try to kick the fan out of place. He steadied himself with a deep breath, then swung his hips out and kicked, feet up, as hard as he could. Expecting his feet to be sliced off at the ankles. Expecting pain. Expecting failure.

He did not expect to miss the fan entirely, but crashed into the housing where it had been welded into the ceiling. The welds popped and the dome fixture gapped open.

Brand grabbed himself up and slid out through that bulging gap, the fan still swoop-swooping a finger's length from the top of his head.

Brilliant light flooded him, painful light, flashes of white and silvery stabbings. Brand blinked and shielded his face, sliding down across the roof top. He found a rain gutter and skidded halfway down it before letting himself fall to the pavement. The Honda sat in front of him.

He got in. The car started immediately and he looked at the stick shift. He wasn't good in reverse, but he had no choice—he had to get a run on the corrugated garage door that stood between him and the others.

He pushed in the clutch and jammed the shifter into position. The transmission ground a little and then a hop, and he was in reverse, racing backward. Brand could see figures running around the corner of the building, headed his way from the front.

He jammed it into forward and put the accelerator to the floor.

The garage door crumbled on impact. It threw him forward, chin onto the steering wheel, his neck whipping and the car hopping to a stop, halfway through, sheet metal lying over it like a hood.

Kamryn came sliding under the door. She got to her feet, her lip bloodied, her hair flying. Brand leaned over and unlocked it. She threw herself in.

"Go, go, go!"

"Where's Mitch!"

"He's coming! You scattered everybody! Just put it in reverse and go!"

Flustered, he ground the gears but good. Protesting, the Honda backed up, tearing out of what had once been a warehouse-sized garage door. Paint scrapings and sparks flew everywhere. As the wreckage flopped, Mitch exploded through the jagged tears.

Kamryn had a back door open for him. He threw himself in, feet hanging out and she screamed again, "Go!"

Brand found first gear and forward. He saw a line of men running at him, and another car beginning to back out. He put the accelerator pedal to the floor. He shifted when Kamryn screamed at him to.

The Honda lurched forward as if it had been launched. Mitch slid on the back seat. Kamryn cried, "Hang on!"

Brand could not keep the car from careening across the parking lot. It seemed to have a mind of its own, the steering wheel alive in his sweating hands. He glanced off the moving car, sending it jolting into the front of the building. Figures scattered. He saw gun barrels everywhere. The car careened to the left. He oversteered back to the right, hit a parked pickup, saw a corner of the Honda's bumper go flying.

He took a turn veering. A small herd of motorcycles lay in his path. The Honda flew through them as if it were in a demolition derby. Classic bikes crunched and crashed in their wake.

Mitch got his door shut with a grunt. Kamryn shoved herself down in the passenger seat as Brand took the Honda speeding and bucking onto the main street.

"We've got pursuit." Mitch's voice, flat and amused, from the back.

"Brand's got 'em." Kamryn dabbed at her bleeding mouth with the back of her hand.

Brand didn't feel any such thing, as the Honda wove back and forth down the main street.

He looked at the speedometer. Eighty-eight miles an hour.

He found the highway on ramp and hit it, going south, at seventy, having slowed down to make the curve.

Kamryn said, "Next rest stop pull over and let me drive. In the meantime, step on it until you redline it."

"Redline."

She pointed a shaking hand at the dash tachometer. "Don't push it past that. Just drive it straight. Don't slow down unless we hit traffic." She took a deep breath. It sounded strained.

"You all right?"

"Yes. Just drive."

He wanted to look at her, didn't dare, had to know if the inky cloud had gone, saw her out of the corner of his eye as he sped down the highway.

The chill had faded. But he could still see a darkness crowning her brow, a veil across her beautiful, bruising face. But it receded slightly as he took his glance.

He hit ninety and kept it there.

"Remind me," said Mitch, "to give you some driving lessons."

They were all breathing hard. Kamryn disagreed. "I think he did fine. He even took evasive action when they started shooting at us."

Brand's mouth had gone dry. "Evasive action? I couldn't steer straight!"

Mitch started laughing. After a moment, Kamryn joined him.

Brand said, "I don't think that's funny." Kamryn laughed harder.

"Well, I don't."

"Oh, God." She wiped a tear from her eye. "Just drive, Brand. Just drive." She stretched both hands out, one toward Brand and the other toward the back seat. "My heroes."

Brand tried not to jump as she patted his thigh. He could feel the chill of her touch through his jeans. He brushed her hand off, stammering something about needing his glasses and pulled them out, feeling like a jerk.

The needle pricks of sunlight into his eyeballs subsided as he slipped the familiar shades on. He stared ahead at the road.

"Will they follow?"

Kamryn settled back into her seat. "We talked about Wyoming. Maybe we threw them off."

But Brand was shaking his head in answer to Mitch's idle question. He had felt the KillJoy. It had tasted Kamryn, and him. It wanted Kamryn. It wanted him. It would follow. There was no safety in taking the highway, no matter where it led.

If not the skinheads, then Rembrandt. If not Rembrandt, then chance.

Whatever form Death could take, it would.

He felt that more sincerely in his heart than he had ever felt anything.

But he could not voice it to them. Fear would not let him.

* * * *

Snake looked at the rippled and twisted fork of his motorcycle. A classic bike, gone, like that. It could be fixed, but it would take time and loving care. Time he didn't have.

That itch crawled around inside his skull. Snake put his hands up to his dome, dug his fingernails in until he drew blood, wanted to rake his nails through his naked skin until the pain drove out the itch. He wanted them, all three of them, and the urge filled his chest like a deep, angry shout until he lifted his chin to the burning Arizona sky and let it out a bellow.

Fleer dropped his handlebars, startled. The chrome piece hit with a dull *twang* and bounced into place next to the wreckage.

The force of his voice had squeezed his eyes nearly shut. Snake dropped his chin and opened his eyes wide, saw the others standing around the parking lot, staring at him.

He whirled. Viktor stood there, watching.

"Give me your keys!"

"They got my car, too."

"Not those keys. I want the keys to the SHO. I want that bitch, the boy, the other."

"I can send out a patrol," Viktor said slowly. "As soon as we know which direction they're headed."

Crawly feelings inside him turned him again, away from Viktor, south by southeast. "I know which way they're going," said Snake flatly. "Now give me the fucking keys!"

Viktor tossed them. They flew, sparkling through the air, like the American-built high-performance Ford they fit. Snake snatched them in mid flight.

Mott had his bike up, crippled but ridable. Snake knew where Viktor stored his prize vehicle. He swung aboard behind Mott.

"Move it!"

Mott kicked the gear shift, and the bike jumped away. Fleer ran alongside.

"What about me?"

"Kiss my ass," Snake screamed back over the roar of the engine, and swung, knocking Fleer right out of his baby blue eyes.

He wanted nothing but the road between him and his quarry.

* * * *

They ate blue corn tacos in Tucson while Mitch worried at the fender, pulling crumpled metal away from the tire. He kicked at the bumper until the Honda shuddered all over as he tried to straighten that out as well. He eyed the makeshift repair work critically in the restaurant parking lot lights before deciding he'd done as well as he could.

"It's a wonder it looks as good as it does." He took the last taco from the cardboard carrier, its purple-black soft shell oozing meat and lettuce.

"I don't think the patrol will be looking for us as a hit and run. Viktor doesn't like to attract attention."

Brand chugged down the last of his drink. The evening had begun to cool rapidly, a breeze rising off the arid countryside. Kamryn checked a map she'd bought at the last filling station. "I'll drive until we hit the summit at Dragoon. Then you can take it into Lordsberg."

Mitch nodded.

"When do I drive again?"

They looked at Brand. He put up a hand. "Do I have two heads or something?"

Kamryn folded up the map and threw it at him. "Navigate, smart-ass."

He caught it. "All right. But I have to ride shotgun to do it."

Mitch had driven the last several hours. "Fine with me." He rested his soft drink cup over a swollen right hand. "I'll ice my knuckles."

They loaded the car back up. Heading out of Tucson, Kamryn dropped the speed down to the state limit.

"Bor-ring."

"But legal. We don't want to attract any more attention."

Mitch pitched a piece of ice from the back seat. It clipped Brand in the ear. Brand batted it away. "Okay, okay. I'll shut up." He lay the map across his lap. "How about some music?"

"Be my guest."

He managed to find one station that wasn't golden oldies or country western, but as they headed out of Tucson and into the night, its broadcast grew weaker and more and more staticky. Soon there was nothing but two-lane highway and desert and darkness. An occasional glint of feral eyes from the side of the road as a coyote bolted past or a jackrabbit threw up its ears from cover were the only signs of life.

Brand felt himself going cross-eyed as the night grew older and older. The beams of the headlight seemed to weaken against the desolation of the countryside.

He was yawning when he saw it. The edge of the headlight beam barely caught it. Brand sat up straight and leaned forward.

A yellow dog, trotting along the rim of the road.

He choked down a breath. The animal reacted as if it heard the car motor—he had to be hallucinating, it couldn't be his dog—and it swung off the highway shoulder, onto the road.

It continued trotting as the Honda sped down upon it.

"Kamryn—" He flung out a hand to stop her.

The dog swerved into the full blast of the headlights and paused, wavering, blinded.

"The dog!"

"What dog?"

He shoved the steering wheel. The car flinched to the left, but there came a heavy thud and a yelp. Kamryn hit the brakes, and they skidded into the night.

"You hit him!" cried Brand.

Chapter 26

The Honda skewed to a halt, its rear tires off the road in the bordering ditch. Its headlights canted into the sky. Brand sat for a frozen moment. Kamryn pounded a hand on the steering wheel.

"Oh, my God."

Her voice thawed him. Mitch, tossed from the back-seat and wedged onto the floor, began to swear. "Son of a bitch—"

Brand clawed at his seat belt, freeing himself. As ditches go, it was minor, but enough to have the Honda in an awkward position. Tearing fingernails, Brand got the door open and levered himself out before Mitch finished turning the air blue in a way that would do a Marine drill instructor proud. He could smell the engine heat and burned rubber from the tires. The desert air smelled sharp and clear under it, and sounded terribly still. He pounded down the highway, following the skid marks, his heart drumming in his chest.

Either be dead or be alive. But don't be lying there shattered—I can't help! I can't put you back together! His heart throbbed in his mouth. Visions of a mangled dog filled him.

A golden dog. A retriever. Visions of the guide which had temporarily abandoned him in his dreams, but for

which he would do anything. Cross any bridge. Face
any darkness. Do anything he could, but please,
God, oh please, don't let there be blood and jagged
bones. Just let it be a little hurt. Just let it be dazed
and alive.

In the dark gray nothingness of the desert, something moved and groaned off the road. Brand angled
toward it, crying, "I'm coming! I'm coming!" as if his
voice could soothe the injured animal.

It rose out of the road dust and opposite ditch,
shoulders humped, emerging from the shadows and
into the dim reflection of the headlights though they
shone the other direction. It rose and rose and rose
until it stood taller than him, and shook all over.

The man said, "White men are bad drivers. White
women are worse." As Brand slid to a halt, he leaned
over, and dusted off his denims, jeans and jacket
vigorously, his long hair tied back from his shoulders,
his unmistakably Amerindian face weathered with
years.

"But I—I saw—"

The Indian grunted. He swiped a last time at his left
elbow. "You saw too late. Ran me off the road!"

He had seen a dog. He knew that. He *knew* it even
as he knew his name. Brand stammered. "B—but you—
but you—"

"Will be stiff in morning, but all right. No thanks to
white woman." The man narrowed his eyes and looked
closely at him. "Or were you driving?"

"No. I—I thought you were—"

"Hurt? No. I am old and wise, but I have good re-
flexes." The Indian straightened his shoulders, looking
past Brand, and he could hear the other two approaching.

Brand did not understand. "You can't be . . . I saw a dog . . . I saw—"

"I am Chiricahua. Apache." The Indian looked fiercely at him, at all three of them. "Are you afraid? You should be. Once, all white men in this part of the country feared the Apache."

"It depends on how much to drink they've had," Mitch answered dryly.

"Mitch!" Kamryn sounded shocked.

Mitch pointed his chin at the ditch. A damp and crumpled paper bag lay in the dirt, and a small wet patch was rapidly being absorbed by the dust.

"A beer," said the man. "For the road."

"Did I run you down—or did you fall down?" Kamryn got out, her voice still quavery.

"Ha!" The Apache laughed sharply and then laughed again. "Does it matter? No one is hurt." He put his hand out, fierce look fading. "I am of the Mescalero Apache tribe. Call me Yellow Dog."

Brand lost all feeling in his legs. His head swam. His vision narrowed to a single spot, filled by the other's face. He thought he got out a sound, a peep, before crashing.

"So the boy is all right?"

"Just tired. He's had a rough couple of days."

Brand could hear Mitch talking, sounding as though he were an underwater attraction at Sea World, his voice burbling through the nothingness which held Brand. If he held his breath, he could surface, he thought. He did. His ears popped. His cheeks bulged. Someone thumped him on the chest.

"Breathe, boy, breathe!"

He caught a whiff of sage and a faint smell of beer as he came up gasping. He lay in the car. A golden haze of light floated in the back seat, light that did not come from the interior dome in the roof. Brand blinked once or twice, as if he had just caught an October moon in the vehicle. Yellow Dog smiled back at him, even older looking than he had seemed standing in the night.

Kamryn asked, "Is he all right?"

"I think so," the Mescalero replied. "Are you?"

"What . . . what are you doing here?" Brand stared at the fourth passenger.

"Kamryn thought it polite to give me a ride home, since she ran me off the road."

The Honda bounced and jolted. Brand looked out the window. They had left the highway. Cactus and downed fences and shrub lined a dirt road. Clouds of fine dust drifted after them, motes shining like silver as he turned his head to the rear window. "We must be miles from 10."

"It would have been a long walk."

"What," Mitch put in, "were you doing out here?"

"Coyote scared my mule. He threw me. I walk home. Sooner or later, I'd get there. Maybe sleep in the ditch, let the mail truck pick me up." Yellow Dog watched Brand as he spoke. He wore a yellow-and-blue-plaid shirt that looked as if it had been pounded against many a stone in the river. His dark face was seamed with age, but fine-boned, and his hands moved as he spoke, small, wiry hands. His hair had a few pewter-gray strands in it, but otherwise were as black as they must have been in Yellow Dog's youth.

Brand observed, "Even a mule wouldn't take you too far."

"No. But I don't like to drive when I drink." Yellow Dog brushed another patch of grit from his denim jacket. He leaned forward between the two front seats. "There's my house now."

Two window patches gleamed in the night like opening eyes. Fencing surrounded it, except for the road's entrance, and a Ford Explorer and an Escort sat parked in the front yard. The compact had seen better years, but the Explorer looked fairly new. There was a patch of garden to the rear, and a stucco garage that sat alone. Also a corral and small shed. A mule stood outside the corral, his head resting on a fence pole, bareback, but wearing a bridle. There were shadows of other outbuildings not entirely visible from the front drive.

Yellow Dog swung his door open. "You come in," he said. "It is too late to drive much further. The boy is not well, and you—" he looked down at Mitch's hands. "Could use some ice."

"I don't think—" Kamryn stopped as Yellow Dog tilted his head, watching her.

"You are far from the road. No one will bother you here. I live alone now, except for the mule, but my house is big."

Brand could almost hear Mitch and Kamryn thinking. He had his hand in his pocket and could feel the amulet between the tips of his fingers. He blurted out, "I'd like to stay a while."

"Good." Yellow Dog nodded. "Boy and I have things to talk about." He paused, looked at the bashed-up fender of the car. "Maybe you'd drive better in the daylight."

Kamryn's ears turned faintly pink and she ducked her head as she followed after their host.

The house was cool, even after the stifling heat of the day, but as Brand passed through the threshold, he noticed the thickness of the walls. It was not adobe, but concrete block and stucco, stacked in double-thickness. The insulation against heat and cold must be incredible. Nothing inside was what he expected. The furniture was well-upholstered, green-and-blue plaid, with burnished pine arms and feet. There was an immense television in one corner.

"I have a dish," Yellow Dog remarked when he saw Brand staring at it. He took off his denim jacket and lay it over the back of the chair. "I would not live like this if I stayed on the reservation."

Mitch sat down in an upholstered rocker. "What do you do?"

"Construction foreman. Tucson and the area is growing. Big resort. People like hot, dry weather. I'm like a turtle. I stay in this shell if I get the chance. Winters aren't bad here, so it works out."

"Aren't you supposed to live up north?"

Yellow Dog looked at Kamryn as he solemnly fixed her a ginger ale and then handed it to her. "Four Corners?"

"Something like that."

"That is Navajo. I'm Apache."

"Oh. I . . . I'm sorry."

"Good." Swiftly, Yellow Dog fixed three more ginger ales and passed them around.

Brand didn't particularly like ginger ale. He wrinkled his nose as he took his drink. Yellow Dog said, "Drink it. Ginger is good for the digestion."

He sat down on the couch between Kamryn and Brand, ignoring the drink in front of him, and put his hands on the worn knees of his jeans. "Now tell me why you are driving in the middle of the night like there is a devil wind behind you."

"I don't think so." Mitch stared at him levelly.

"Then it is your loss. The Apache have been here for centuries. Think we care what you do? It won't bother me. I will still be here tomorrow, and the day after."

Kamryn rubbed her arms uneasily. "Not," she answered. "If the people I'm leaving behind have anything to say about it."

He took her slim wrist and pushed up the sleeve of her shirt, baring the faded but still legible tattoos. He looked for a moment then said, "You are not like them. They hate everyone."

She gently removed her arm from his hold. "If they come after us here, if they think you know something, they won't leave you alive after they find out what they know." Kamryn massaged an eyebrow. "And you have no idea what I'm like."

Yellow Dog tapped his cheekbone, under one coffee-colored eye. "I see. I know." He smiled, breaking his solemn words. "I am called Yellow Dog because I am cousin to the coyote—the coyote who is one of our gods. He is fast, quick, the trickster. The dog is almost as fast, but he is loyal. His motives are never in doubt. He is not a god, but he is good to have on one's side. We are fast and quick also. The ones who seek you will have a hard time finding me." Yellow Dog beckoned as if the outside world, the desert, would hide him.

Mitch drained his glass and set it down. "I think we'd better be going."

"You will not meet many friends along the road," Yellow Dog said to him. "I would not turn down one now."

"I don't know that you're a friend, and I don't know that, if you are a friend, I want to involve you in any of this."

"You are a soldier. You like to face problems," and

Yellow Dog suddenly smacked a fist into the palm of his hand. Kamryn jumped at the sound. "Head on." He dropped his hands back to his knees. "The sidewinder travels sideways across the sand. He is sometimes very difficult to see and avoid his attack."

"A sidewinder's a snake, right?" Brand asked.

"Yes."

"How did you know he's a soldier?"

Yellow Dog merely smiled widely while Mitch said, with irritation, "It's just a figure of speech. He's referring to how I attack situations."

"And your bruised knuckles," the Mescalero added.

Brand looked at Mitch. "I just want to stay the night. Just five or six hours of sleep. I don't want to run into any *snakes*."

"I have the room," Yellow Dog added.

Without looking at Mitch, Kamryn sighed. "It sounds all right to me."

"And me."

The lines along Mitch's jaws moved as if he ground his teeth. "Just till morning."

"Good. It is settled. I will go fix your rooms. You will sleep on the floor, but the blankets are very soft. They're Navajo," he added, with a huff of a laugh, and he got up and left.

Brand dreamed of Yellow Dog, for the first time in days, and the canine's feathery tail wagged in greeting, but he did not come close. Brand held out his hand, entreating, but the dog moved away through nebulous clouds of his imagination. Brand tried to coax him back and failed.

Then a calloused hand closed on his shoulder, waking him.

Yellow Dog the Apache looked down at him, moonlight barely touching his rugged face. "Come with me," he said, very quietly, not waking Mitch.

Brand got up from the sleeping pad and followed after the silent footsteps of the Indian, uncertain why he should follow, and uncertain why he should refuse.

In the living room, moonlight from the kitchen windows flooded the house with soft light. The stars hung like crystal in the desert sky. Brand stared at it a moment, drinking in the beauty.

"You don't see this in the city."

Yellow Dog held out a blanket, like a cloak and dropped it around his shoulder. "Come with me. You and I need to talk. Then sleep will come easier."

He opened a side door through the kitchen and stepped outside, barefoot, also wearing a blanket. Brand went after him, and their feet crunched on cold sand. Their breath fogged slightly on the air. Yellow Dog went to a small building and put his hand on the door.

"I get it! This is a sweat lodge, for medicine dreams and stuff."

Yellow Dog opened the door. "Actually, it's a portable sauna. But you're right, it's good for sweat and my arthritis." He stepped inside, the warmth enveloping him.

Feeling more than a little foolish, Brand stepped inside and sat on the opposite bench. Yellow Dog closed the door. There was a tiny light inside, with an amber hue, and a basket of artificial coals in an alcove on the floor glowed as they burned. Yellow Dog poured a dipper of water over them. An obliging hiss and cloud of steam arose.

Brand watched him. He snugged into the blanket, its colors grayed out. "What did you want to talk about?"

"What you saw on the road."

"How could I have seen what I saw?"

"And what was it you think you saw?"

"A dog. A big golden retriever, trotting by the side of the road. That *was* you, wasn't it?"

Yellow Dog did not answer directly. "Do you have a dog at home?"

"No."

"But you had great regard for this dog. When you thought it had been hit, you came to help. You cried for mercy for it. Would you do this for just any creature?"

"I thought I saw a dog on the road."

"It could have been a coyote."

"I know the difference." Brand looked at the basket of glowing coals. "There are a lot left in Orange County. You can see them trotting along the golf courses, or out by the trailer parks, or along the freeway. They almost look like dogs, but they're not. I know the difference."

"And this was not just any dog."

"No."

Yellow Dog dipped more water over the coals and then spread his hands to receive the steaming cloud. "Would you believe me if I said I was the dog you saw?"

He hesitated. "Yes."

Yellow Dog shook his head. "Your spirit answered before your mouth. I will not tell you if it was me or not. You must decide for yourself. But I will tell you of the meaning of your imaginary dog. A dog is loyal. He made his choice before the gods to be with man, to help him, to guide him, even if it meant his pride. The color yellow, in my world, is a color of the spirit, of the goodness of the spirit, and of guidance. If you believe in such an animal, only good can come of it."

"He helps me," Brand whispered, his throat suddenly tight. "I need to help him."

"The three of you were strangers not long ago." Yellow Dog suddenly changed subjects.

"Yes." Brand looked up. "How did you know?"

"Satellite television. Your face was on the news yesterday. A horrible picture. A skinhead was killed after he shot many people. She wears the skin of a skinhead." Yellow Dog grinned suddenly, as if enjoying the play on words.

"There's more."

"I thought there might be. I ask myself, why don't these three trust their white man police."

"I see things."

"This I also know." Yellow Dog moved his hand through the air, stirring up a rippling current of heat. "On the road."

"Everywhere. I think it's . . . I think it's Death. It's all over Kamryn. I can't let it take her. I can't!"

"Death is a dark god, but a natural one. He will come for all of us, boy. It does not help to fear him."

"Well, maybe it's not death. Maybe it's evil. I don't know, all I know is, I can see it . . . it knows my name . . . it wants me, it wants Kamryn and maybe even Mitch. And in my dreams, the dog took me to a woman, a black woman, in New Orleans, who told me she could help us."

"Help you what?"

"Get rid of the KillJoy."

Yellow Dog stopped moving. His eyes glittered in the slight illumination. "Is that its name?"

"It's what I call it."

"Then you must not. You have the truth of it, and you will bring it to you by naming it." Yellow Dog shifted on the redwood bench of the sauna. "Do you know the woman? Is she named?"

"She calls herself Mother. Mother Jubilation."

Yellow Dog poured a third dipper of water, and this time he dispersed the cloud with an eagle feather which he seemed to have produced from out of thin air. He looked into the steam. "Her way is not my way, but those who walk the spirit walk cross paths. I do not know her, but I know of the medicine she uses. Do you trust her?"

"Yellow Dog . . . ah . . . my imaginary dog led me to her."

"Then you must trust her also." Yellow Dog dug deep into the pockets of his jeans. He pulled out a faded blue bandanna. It was knotted in the middle. Laboriously, he undid the knot and opened it up. A wrinkled bit of root lay there, hardly bigger than the tip of Brand's little finger. "Do you know what this is?"

Brand shook his head.

"This is peyote. Mescal."

"Drugs."

"That is right. It only takes a very small piece, chewed." Yellow Dog knotted the peyote button back into the bandanna. Brand watched, faintly surprised, for he had thought Yellow Dog was going to use it.

He pressed the bandanna into Brand's hand. "Now you must listen and remember. The spirit walk for the living is dangerous if you do not have inner strength and peace. Before you take the peyote, you must be cleansed. You must be alone. Your mind must be calm. You must be like a lake in the desert, without wind, rain, or tide. You must not take more than a pinch, like so, of the button, or you will be horribly ill. Your body could die while your spirit walks."

"And above all, you must be ready to look into yourself and face whatever it is you see there. If you need to spirit walk, you must be ready to accept the truth, to fight the evil, to banish the darkness. All colors of the world are in the spirit world, even black. It is the absence of color, warmth, truth, love, hope, that is the enemy. You remember this."

Brand clutched the bandanna tightly, then he put it in his free pocket. "How did ... how did you know about us? I mean, really about us, not just what you saw on television."

"I felt a trembling many months ago when this spirit came upon the land. In my dreams, I called it the Devourer. Although I searched for it, it was not for me to see, only feel. Yet there was never any doubt in my mind that I would meet the warrior who would fight it, who would send it back to its own lands."

Yellow Dog had already called Mitch a warrior. Brand pulled his blanket tighter about him, chill tremors running through him despite the glow of the sauna cabinet. "We're trying to outrun it."

A vigorous shake of the head greeted his hope. "It must be faced and fought."

"But how?"

"I cannot tell you how the battle will be won. But you must know your enemy. That is the key. The spirit weakens ..."

"Then we won't have to fight it!"

"No. It weakens, then it must kill to be strong, and it will be strong until it does what it has been sent here to do. It will kill whoever and whatever it has to in order to remain strong."

"Like Curtis. Like the others."

"Whatever it must do, it will," repeated Yellow Dog firmly.

"What can I do?"

"It is tracking you."

Brand could not contain a shudder. "I think so."

"You must draw it near even as you must stay away until you are ready to fight it."

"How do I do that?"

Yellow Dog shrugged. "That, I cannot tell you. But you will do it, Brand the X. You will do it."

He thought of the amulet and brought it out. "Can this help?"

"This was made by a wise man. It carries symbols of power and medicine. It might be of some use." Yellow Dog rubbed a finger across it. "Couldn't hurt." He stood. "Enough steam for the night. You need to rest for the morning."

Brand found his eyelids incredibly heavy as he recrossed the yard, trailing Yellow Dog's footsteps. He stopped by the back door.

"But you didn't tell me," he murmured.

"Tell you what?"

"If you were a dog or not."

Yellow Dog laughed. He laughed and threw back his head, looking at the slip of a moon in the sky, and let out a howl. Brand jumped, and then from the wasteland around him, coyotes answered.

Yellow Dog let him in the house. "I'll never tell," he said, chuckling.

In the morning, Yellow Dog was gone and so was their battered Honda. Keys to the Explorer lay on the coffee table, along with its registration, and Kamryn's gun. Her baskets of clothes stood in the corner. An inviting scent led Brand to the kitchen where a huge platter of scrambled eggs and bacon waited for them in the oven, still fairly warm.

Brand opened the back door, just to check and see

if Yellow Dog had gone back out to the sauna to warm up his bones in the chill morning.

Nothing met his eyes but piles of rock and stone and brush.

Chapter 27

Delacroix stepped across the border at Aqua Prieto, mildly astonished at how easy it had been. Just beyond the walkway, a weakness struck him, made him stop and put his hand up, to catch his breath in the brisk morning air. The moment lingered, and he considered it, knew that the soul of the land itself was protesting him. He slipped a hand inside the pocket of his jacket, took out a packet, and scattered its contents upon the ground in a pattern which might have seemed random, but was not. The colored corn grains lay there until a mild wind diffused them further.

The weakness gripping him eased, bit by bit, until it faded, leaving a hollowness behind. That hollowness, he knew, came from the loa. He must urge it to feed again or else he and it would be too drained to do what they had come together for. He lifted his head. Stark and the other two stood impassively watching him, waiting.

"I am ready."

Stark had arranged for a van to transport him to El Paso. From there, he would rest and determine the flight of those he pursued. They were fleeing eastward, steadily, along a road marked as Highway 10. He had had Stark study the maps with him earlier, but in his heart, he felt he knew which way they would go.

Toward New Orleans. It could be no other place, for there lay his challenger who alone could stop him. She must sense him already. If not, she would before the end of the day. If she had sensed him, she would be calling for his prey to join her, for her strength lay in togetherness, in the bonds, and in the gathering.

His did not. He could attack them anywhere, but he would not. Not until that which was his was returned and to find it, to have it gathered up and presented back to him, he must look his enemy in the face.

The loa would herd them. He, Delacroix, would find out what was needed and obtain what he was owed.

Then they were the loa's. Whatever he would do with them, he would do. Then Delacroix would send him back.

Not before.

As if sensing his weakness, Stark took his arm and guided him to the waiting vehicle. Delacroix let him, then paused at the curb in the street. He put his hand on Stark's muscular forearm, and gripped, gripped tightly until the man's face paled beyond pale.

He would not have Stark think that his infirmity was physical.

He released his grip and stepped into the van. "Between here and New Orleans, a large city. All roads leading in from the west, going to the east. What would be the name of such a city?"

Stark looked at him. Thought a moment. Said flatly, "El Paso."

"Drive us there."

He nodded.

* * * *

NWS UPDATE HURRICANE YOLANDA 0900
EDT

HURRICANE YOLANDA IS NOW GRADED A
FORCE 2 STORM, WITH SUSTAINED WINDS OF
OVER 100 MPH, PROCEEDING NORTH, NORTH-
EASTERLY, HEADED TOWARD THE GULF
STATES. PROJECTED PASSAGE OF THE HURRI-
CANE INDICATES THE GULF OF MEXICO'S UN-
SEASONABLY WARM WATERS MAY CONTINUE
TO FEED ITS STRENGTH. AT ITS PRESENT RATE
OF SPEED, LANDFALL IS EXPECTED IN THREE
DAYS. WATCHES AND WARNINGS WILL BE IS-
SUED AS ITS DIRECTION STABILIZES. ALL RESI-
DENTS   FROM   GALVESTON,   TEXAS   TO
ALCONTE, FLORIDA ARE ADVISED TO BEGIN
EVACUATION PROCEDURES AND STAY TUNED
FOR FURTHER ADVISORIES.

Mother sat in her quiet room. The candy store was
dark and shut down. True to her promise, Geneva had
taken the girls and gone. Mother stared at the crystal
shards in the palm of her hand, rolled them carefully
back and forth, wary of their jagged edges, watching
them cast prism colors on the walls of the meditation
room. She had felt the intrusion of the mambo on
American soil, growing closer, ever closer.

He would come to her, in the wake of the others,
as much a force of nature as the storm that approached. They would all come together, she thought,
the natural and the supernatural. The mambo would
not expect that, perhaps, and she wondered if she
could somehow use that to her advantage.

New Orleans had begun to prepare for Yolanda. The
levees and canals were being sandbagged, and the
pumping stations were being manned with extra shifts.

The storm surge, which would come twenty-four hours before landfall of the actual hurricane, would be expected to be twelve to sixteen feet above those levees, if Yolanda came in directly. The wave would be devastating to a city already technically under sea level. The parishes below the city were being urged already to evacuate, for the 10 was their chief way up and out, through the bottleneck of New Orleans, and roads would be at a standstill if all parishes tried to leave at once.

Today evacuation was voluntary. Tomorrow, if Yolanda continued to forge a path toward them, it would not be. The emergency planners allowed for forty-eight hours to bring the population out. Already she could feel the sheer strength of the human will to hold the city together, to protect the lower parishes and bayous of the state, to shelter their fellow man. Race and religion would be forgotten in a few desperate hours to survive. All would be human, accepted, shared.

A quartz splinter slipped, slicing her palm, and blood welled up slowly. Mother dropped the other fragments and looked at her hand, pain forgotten. She drew a mirror to her and let the drops fall onto it and run into whatever pattern they would run before they thickened.

When the blood stopped dripping and not before, she looked into the hand mirror. She did not like what she saw.

"Hurry, boy. Hurry!"

* * * *

Midday, Lordsberg, New Mexico, they brought a loaf of bread and a pound of bologna and sat in the city park where Mitch showed them how to make fried bologna sandwiches, hot and juicy, on a small briquet barbecue. Kamryn wrinkled her nose and ate one before retreating to her nonfat yogurt. Brand ate half a loaf before shouting, "Who was that masked man?" for the seventh time that day and running off to catch a frisbee, snatching it from the jaws of a black and white border collie.

The boy and the dog's master exchanged friendly words. The plump-sided woman sat, gratefully, and let Brand run around with the dog. Mitch and Kamryn watched him from their end of the park.

"That boy needs a dog," Mitch commented.

"He's never had one."

"See?"

"That boy," Kamryn answered softly, "needs a lot of things. A decent family would help."

"And you're expert."

"No." She tossed her empty carton into a trash can. "Wish I was. Wish I knew what I was doing here."

"You're here because you can't go back."

Her head snapped around and she stared at Mitch for a quick heartbeat or two, then she visibly forced herself to relax.

"Back there? No. Not that I would want to anyway. Do you know what a relief it is?"

"What is?" Mitch finished the last sandwich and began to clean up wrappers.

"It's a relief to look someone in the face and not have a chant of ethnic slurs and labels run through my head. Not to have to peg them as to what I think of them and how I should treat them and what kind of payback I need to plan for them. Just to see *people*, ordinary people." She reached for a sweatshirt and tied it over her shoulders, loosely, despite the clear sunshine.

"You were brainwashed."

"I suppose. When it's something you grow up with, you don't know what other people do, how other people react, and then you're in school, high school maybe, and you realize that someone is twisted. Really twisted. Scum of the earth. Problem is—you don't know if it's you or them."

"You must have decided it was you."

"Eventually."

"You make it sound easy." Mitch perched on the corner of the weather-beaten picnic table.

"Easy?"

"Everyone should come to their senses that way."

She shook her head. "It's never easy. And it didn't just happen that way. There were ... other circumstances. No. Deciding to change my life was far from easy. What do radio psychologists call it? Leaving the comfort zone. Even beaten, abused wives will stay rather than leave the comfort zone when that's all they know."

"If it was a family thing, where is your family?"

"Around." Kamryn picked at the knot she had tied in the sweatshirt sleeves. "What about your family? Was being in the service a tradition?"

"Yes, more or less. I didn't do it right. I was supposed to go to college first, so I could be an officer."

"And you didn't."

"No." Mitch scratched his jaw. "I didn't like school. I tried to tell my dad he was lucky I hung in for my high school diploma. He didn't see it that way. I played professional soccer for about four years, until I discovered I wasn't really good enough, then I enlisted and went to see the world."

"And?"

"Dad was right. Being an officer is better. Or maybe not better, but easier. I know a lot of fine noncoms, most of whom wouldn't put up with the bullshit J.G.s try to give them."

"It was a career?"

"Maybe. It's hard to stay in now, with all the demobilization and downgrading. I was in for nine years. Now they would probably hang me if they could catch me."

Kamryn looked across the park, saw Brand still playing a lusty game of Frisbee catch with the border collie. She smiled in spite of the seriousness of their conversation.

"What made you leave?"

"Oh, no." He shook his head.

"After what we've been through, you won't tell me."

He stared into her eyes and said, "Damn straight."

"Don't give me that."

"All right. Then how about this . . . I'll show you mine if you show me yours."

She stood up by the edge of the table. "What do you mean?"

"I mean that there's a lot you haven't told me about yourself. I mean that there aren't too many ex-girlfriends of skinheads who could walk into an operation like that printshop and expect preferential treatment, and be shocked when they don't get it, and not shocked when one of their thug assassins comes after her."

"You know why Snake wants me."

"Yeah. That's true. What I don't know is why Viktor didn't whack him upside the head and tell him to forget it. Viktor didn't, so I'm figuring that whatever importance you had to them, all of a sudden it's just as important you're dead."

Kamryn sucked in her lower lip and chewed on it for a second. Then she answered, "What you don't know about me, doesn't affect what's happening here.

It's incidental. It doesn't have anything to do with Brand."

"It could get us all killed."

"It won't! I won't let it, if it comes to that. What about you? I don't buy the theory that Rembrandt will leave me and Brand alone if he decides we don't know anything. He tried to hang Brand to get some answers and I'm willing to bet that even if the kid had told him what he wanted to know, that noose would have stayed around his neck."

Mitch watched her face. Then he nodded. "All right. You're probably right on that one. I owe you this— when the time comes, I'll tell you what I can. But until I get some pieces of the puzzle together, you're better off not knowing. Fair enough?"

A breeze had picked up. It rattled through the bare branches of trees at the park's edge, and the evergreens swayed. It had a raw, dry edge to it. Kamryn resisted hugging herself against it. "Fair enough."

Brand came running up, cheeks blazing, his sunglasses a dark slash across his face. "I'm thirsty!"

"Let's buy some drinks and hit the road," Mitch suggested. "There's a mini-mart on the corner."

A Halloween cutout of Elvira and her gravity-defying cleavage dominated the store and an aisle-wide display of beer. Kamryn left Mitch and Brand to make fools of themselves over the vampire cult actress and her plunging neckline while she bought a six-pack of cold soda. A small TV set behind the counter was running local cable news as she waited her turn in a small line.

". . . from Tucson today comes the shocking story of a famed local tribesman who was severely beaten and left for dead on the construction site of the fabulous new Elysian resort grounds. Yellow Dog was unable to identify his assailants and this afternoon lies in critical condition—"

"Shit, no," Brand said breathlessly at her elbow. "No!"

She put her hand on his shoulder. "Quiet." She could feel his emotion tremble through him, wondering how he could bear it, hoping he would stay quiet so she could listen.

"Praised as a wise man as well as an astute and honest businessman, the Chiricahua Apache spear-headed many local drives for the destitute, regardless of their race. Authorities tonight have impounded a car he was reported to have been driving, though his employees say it was not his vehicle. Authorities are looking for a recreational vehicle he was said to drive. More later. Weather tonight, rain squalls coming in over the mountains, light to moderate, as the evening temperature drops, chance of snow flurries, not expected to hold—"

"That'll be three-fifty, ma'am."

Kamryn looked at the counterman. "Oh. Right." She counted out the change. She shoved the six-pack into Brand's hands, staring into a face numb of expression and said, as if she were talking to a child, "Get in the car."

Stricken behind the sunglasses, he finally nodded and shuffled away.

She followed.

The Honda.

Their fingerprints in the car. *Her* fingerprints in the car.

"What is it?"

"They got Yellow Dog." Emotion cracked Brand's voice. He stopped in the midst of another word, unable to speak at all.

"What?"

"It's on the news. They caught him and beat the crap out of him. He might live. He might not."

"Shit." Mitch started the Explorer's engine.

"My fault," Brand mumbled.

"It's nobody's fault! It was his, his—he took the freaking car. He should have left well enough alone. Should have left us alone." Her own voice sounded distraught to her ears.

Mitch wheeled down the street. "He knew what he was doing. If he hadn't done it, I was going to."

She looked at him. "Leaving us alone?"

"For a while. Until I caught up with Snake." Mitch's mouth pulled downward. "But Yellow Dog took off first." He cleared his throat. "What do we do now?"

"We have to make El Paso. If we have to drive all night." Across state lines. Sometimes highway patrol departments took a while to coordinate cooperation. Sometimes they didn't. She had decisions to make.

"No problem." Mitch scanned the skies. "Barring bad weather."

"Whatever it takes." She belted herself, and hugged her stomach tightly, feeling the money belt beneath her hands. Whatever it took.

*   *   *   *

"It's all here, sir." Purple bruises lingered under Trinh's eyes, testimony to his fatigue, but his expression was one of pride as he handed hard copy files to Rembrandt.

Rembrandt opened the first one, paged through, his reading speed quick, then slowing, as he became engrossed in the information. He looked up once. "You're certain it's the same boy."

"According to the databases. There's a printout of his photo ID for social services."

Rembrandt curled a corner of the report back, saw the photo, gray-scanned, but he recognized Brandon Dennis. "That's him." He continued reading. "This is remarkable, recruit." He looked up and steadied his gaze into Trinh's almond eyes. "This is to remain confidential."

"Yes, sir."

Rembrandt put aside the file, intending to read it more fully, his mind working rapidly. He picked up a file on the young woman.

Trinh had matched three possibilities, but he had circled one set of newsclippings in red. Rembrandt scanned them and he concurred with the match the recruit had made. He ran his finger under the headline. "My, my. I knew she was good with a gun, but who would have thought she'd pack an ax."

The lurid copy read: BROTHER, SISTER, WANTED IN HATE CRIME DEATH OF PARENTS, SIBLINGS, AND NEIGHBORING FAMILIES. Brother captured, but sister still free. Bodies hacked to pieces in frenzy, authorities say they have never seen anything like the carnage. . . .

"My, my," repeated Rembrandt. "What have we got here."

He looked up. "Dismissed, recruit, and excellent work. Would you mind telling Commander Meales that I'd like to have words with him as soon as is convenient?"

Trinh snapped off a salute. "Affirmative."

Josey came in after dinner. Rembrandt had already read the boy's file three times and the girl's file twice. He sat with the laptop in front of him, making plans.

"Nice of you to come," he said.

Josey flushed, difficult to do under his naturally olive coloring.

Rembrandt moved his chair around. "Please sit, Josey. I have something to discuss with you."

Meales pulled up a chair and did as requested, his spine ramrod stiff.

"We have a chance to save each other's butts."

The flush under Josey's late afternoon shadow grew deeper. "I'm not aware, sir, that there is a problem."

"I have a problem of which you are very much aware." Rembrandt tilted his chair back slightly. He balanced his chin on the palm of his hand, elbow on his desk, watching Meales. He could feel the ruined landscape of his complexion under his fingers.

"Christiansen."

"Bingo. He has been elusive, but I'm closing in on him. The services of recruit Trinh have been invaluable."

Meales returned, "You were speaking of our collective asses."

"Yes, I was. You were instrumental in picking this area for a camp and its location was based partially on your recommendation. But I don't recall that you've ever notified Bayliss that you're on the edge of a sweep. A regular, around-the-clock sweep."

"No, sir." Josey had gone white around the nostrils.

"We're in agreement, then."

"Yes, but—shit, Rembrandt. I didn't know myself until the place was half-built—"

"Better late than never."

Josey shifted uncomfortably. "The budget wouldn't have allowed relocation. Not yet."

"And you wanted your command."

Meales flinched, looked away. When he looked back, his eyes had lost some of their confidence.

"I think I can solve your problem, Josey, and I think you can help me solve mine."

"How?"

"Satellites have been known to fall out of the sky. I pride myself on the expertise I have gained. Do you know yet whether it's one of ours?"

"No. We haven't been able to crack it yet."

Rembrandt straightened in his chair. "Leave that to me, then. This is what I need you to do for me." He handed the commander a printout.

Josey scanned it. "Compile a video, build an isolation chamber, program a virtual reality presentation— This will take time."

"I want it ready yesterday. You have VR simulators for training. I don't need much time on a conversion, we're talking stripping in some videos from news footage. What you need to pay attention to is the speed of the animation frames on the virtual reality programs, inserting new frames at this synaptic speed. You have recruits out there who can do it. Use whatever manpower you have."

"Subliminal programming." Understanding dawned on Josey's face.

"Yes. And if my subject confirms what I think he will, Bayliss will be pleased. Very pleased. He won't need drugs to build an army. The late Dr. Susan Craig has already found a way."

Rembrandt slept lightly. He heard the soft knock on his door, was on his feet and at the entrance before the third soft rap.

"What is it?"

Recruit Trinh stood, swaying with tiredness, caught in half-yawn. He snapped his mouth shut. "Sir."

"Come in, son. You've been working hard."

"Yes, sir." A burst of a smile lit the taciturn Asian face. "But it was worth it, sir! I asked for permission to report to you."

Rembrandt settled himself in his desk chair and crossed his legs, pulling at the hem of his pajama bottoms. "It must be important to wake me."

"Yes, sir! I put flags out on your subjects in case any further inquiries were being made. I was woken up this evening by the graveyard shift with the news."

"Which is?" Rembrandt was aware his slight southern drawl made his tone sound more patient than it really was. It gave him an edge on occasions like this when his temper preceded his diplomacy.

"We have a fingerprint match inquiry on Kamryn Talent, lifted from the silver Honda accord registered to her, found as part of a crime scene investigation just outside Tucson."

"Bodies?"

"A local Indian spokesman, critical but improving, found beaten inside the vehicle. Our three are missing, and so is the Indian's fourwheeler."

Rembrandt drummed his fingers in thought. "That doesn't sound like our crew's M.O."

"No, sir. Tucson police reports, not released to the news media, suggests that skinhead and Neo-Nazi graffiti were also found on the site, suggesting a hate crime."

Rembrandt moved his head in denial. "No. No, that's not our girl. She's running. She doesn't have time to stop and fucking spray paint the place! No. Unless . . ."

"Sir?"

He met Trinh's tired eyes. "Nothing. Not yet, anyway. How soon did the flag come up?"

"Within the hour."

"Good. I want you to get into the system, if you can, and intercept any inquiry for fingerprint match from the FBI. I don't want anybody else to know our beauty's a fugitive. But I want you to request the Pennsylvanian prints and see if you can get a match on what Tucson's circulating. Can you do that?"

"Yes, sir, if the commander gives me time—"

"He'll give you the time. Do you have a description, license plate, VIN for the fourwheeler?"

"It's a 1994 Ford Explorer, forest green, Arizona plates—I've got it."

"Good. I want you to send that to Texas highway patrol, El Paso division. I want you to send it as an official request from the Bureau of ATF, that the girl is wanted on arms violations, is a suspected member of the Order." Rembrandt named a neo-Nazi militia group which had been somewhat dormant after a turbulent 1980s and which was now beginning to recover from the last siege of FBI and Department of Justice actions. The Texans were unlikely to question that. "And she may be on the run from California with an underage hostage and a companion. Ask that they be held, matter of national security, local bureaus to be kept out of the matter, I'll be jetting in from Albuquerque to pick them up when apprehended. They'll be traveling on the 10. They should be easy to ID and pick up. Can you do that?"

"I can try."

"Trying is not doing. I asked you if you can handle that, recruit. Because if you can't, I have to find somebody who can."

Trinh blinked rapidly two or three times. "I can do it, sir."

"Good. We'll let those good old boys be our hunting dogs, flush our quarry right into our line of fire. Now, go report to Commander Meales and carry a request for a chopper, immediate transportation to Albuquerque."

"You'll need the Lear."

"Yes, Trinh, I will. Please convey that also. And remind Meales that I intend to be bringing back prisoners."

Chapter 28

Rain pounded the windshield. The wipers of the Explorer made a slight tocking sound as they went back and forth monotonously. The headlights could barely pierce the curtain of night and bad weather. They had driven until midnight, when snow and ice had made the pass through Deming temporarily unpassable, the New Mexico highway patrol pulling traffic over until the roads could be scraped clear. A few cars had shot through, daring the bad conditions, but the patrol had managed to keep most of them back. They had sat in the Explorer, cold, even Mitch shivering, for three hours until finally waved on. Now he had little sense of where they could be.

Brand's ears felt the pressure of a steady grade through the rugged, barren mountains. He swallowed every few minutes trying to ease the pounding of his head. From his spot in the back seat, it looked as though Kamryn had gone to sleep, her head bent from her neck in an awkward angle, temple pressed to the side window. Brand couldn't sleep, his thoughts tumbling over and over.

Why hadn't he seen the darkness over Yellow Dog? Why couldn't he have warned him? Why hadn't his eyes, his damn eyes, *seen* the disaster coming? He could have done something. He could have saved the old man. It wouldn't have been all his fault.

But he hadn't seen it. Nothing. No smudges or patches or bolts of darkness anywhere about the wise man. And even if he had seen it, Brand thought, staring into the storm miserably, would Yellow Dog have believed him?

Why not? He had not asked questions about the other.

Brand was not used to being believed. He was, after all, Brand X, the stuff nobody wanted, the X-man.

It didn't matter! If he had only seen the peril, he could have saved Yellow Dog. His friend would not now be lying in a hospital somewhere, fighting for his life. If only.

He felt useless.

He should have done something.

Something flashed in the headlights. "Damn!" Mitch veered the car. Brand caught the barest glimpse of eyes—silvery, shining orbs, a leaping body through the beams, then nothing.

"Damn deer."

"Was that what it was?"

"Mule deer. Didn't you see its ears?"

"No." Brand leaned closer. "Wouldn't it be scared of the car?"

"Headlights blind 'em. They only know to run. It wouldn't be out in this weather, but it's rutting season."

Sex, thought Brand, sagging back into the bench seat. It drove everybody crazy. There were few deer in the Los Angeles basin. He couldn't remember having seen one in the wild before.

Mitch went back to his tuneless humming, which the windshield wipers nearly drowned out.

Had Yellow Dog leaped into the path of the skinheads, just like the deer, blinded for the moment, un-aware of the danger? He didn't think so. Yellow Dog had been around. He knew things that Brand could not figure out how he knew.

Mitch had intended to take the Honda as a decoy. Yellow Dog had done it instead. He knew what he might be facing, how dangerous they could be. But why the skinheads?

So Brand would be free to bring the KillJoy *after them.* Yellow Dog had told him he had to do it. He would do it, somehow. Lure the KillJoy to New Orleans.

And so Yellow Dog had taken the lesser danger, so he could take the greater. He'd decoyed the skinheads to give them time. To give Brand time. That was the only thing that made any sense.

Thoughts clicked into place. The pounding in his head disappeared as he made a half-yawn and his ears popped gently. The answer was worse than the questions.

Yellow Dog's sacrifice would be in vain if Brand did not do what he had been left free to do.

Mitch had spent most of his waiting time in Deming reading the road maps.

"Where are we now?"

"Just outside Las Cruces. Then, in this weather, a little less than an hour to El Paso."

Brand tried to imagine it as he looked through the car windows.

El Paso. *Come get me, KillJoy. I'm in El Paso. Looking for me? Come and get me if you dare.* He thought of how he'd first seen it at the mall, inky gusts of nothingness, black flames from the dead policeman's mouth and nostril. How it had come into the chapel over Curtis' body, a dripping, oozing blackness.

Something stirred. Brand turned his thoughts away quickly, shaken, for it had grabbed for him, striking cobra fast. Not thinking of it would be like not thinking of the word rhinoceros. Brand squeezed his eyes shut, and let Bauer distract him.

Kamryn woke with a jerk, breathing hard, her inner eye still filled with a vision and a voice. *Come on, Sis, I've got a surprise for you. . . .* She stared out the windshield, uncomprehending for a moment, then saw the sleet whirling down, white and gray against the headlines, the Explorer making slow but steady progress against it.

"Good thing we've got a 4x."

Mitch turned. The corner of his mouth went up. "You're awake."

"Just. I'd ask for a pit stop, but this doesn't look like a good time."

"We stop in this, we might not get started again easily."

"Tired of driving? I'll take over."

"I thought we agreed not to stop."

"I can make a change on the fly. I just scoot over, sit on your lap, take control, and you scoot out from under me."

"While I admit," Mitch said slowly, "the idea of your sitting on my lap has its merits, I don't think so."

"Has its merits? Oh, yes. I'm sure you'd appreciate that."

"Damn straight I would. It's been a long time since anybody offered to get close to me. You lose a lot when you're homeless. You lose yourself, your identity, your sexuality."

Kamryn found herself staring at him. "Do you?"

"It would be hard not to. Suddenly, you're not a man

anymore, not human. You're . . . homeless. Maybe a homeless man or a homeless woman, but not in a sensual way, just a gender label. No one would think of looking me in the eyes. What sex there is on the streets is generally rape."

"But you wouldn't—"

"No. Never. But that doesn't mean I didn't miss what I was missing."

"Of course not." Kamryn brushed her hair from her forehead.

"Is that what you saw in your boyfriend? Some kind of sexual identity?"

"I don't think I want to answer that."

"Sex or power?"

"Power," she said shortly. "The sex tends to be rather proprietary. Sometimes even violent. An aside. It's power." Feeling warm, she leaned forward and adjusted the defroster setting on the dash. "What about you? Did you leave a girl behind when you went AWOL?"

"No. When I enlisted. She waited for me. Then we were engaged for two years."

"Then . . ."

"She decided that a Marine staff sergeant wasn't what she wanted out of life. She married someone else."

"Who?"

"A banker."

"A banker does it with interest," Kamryn quoted.

"Oh, jeez." Brand rose out of the back seat. "Give me a break. Am I going to have to listen to this?"

She'd forgotten they weren't alone.

"Virgins have delicate ears," Mitch said, laughing.

"Who's a virgin!"

"You are," Mitch told him and reached back to thump him.

Aggrieved, Brand replied, "It's not my fault."

Kamryn put her hands up. "Okay, that's it. That's enough."

Brand looked at her seriously. "One can never have too much sex."

"I don't want to talk about it."

"You did, two minutes ago."

"That was then, this is now."

"How am I ever going to learn anything?"

Kamryn closed her mouth firmly, refusing to say another word.

*   *   *   *

The hotel was a huge structure, u-shaped and two-storied, occupying vaster grounds than even the Presidential palace, rainswept and new looking. Delacroix took the stairs to their rooms, and leaned across the railing.

"Nice place," he observed, his accented English dry with irony, as he faced the chain-link fencing topped with razor wire that encircled the hotel. To protect the guests and their vehicles, he'd been told. "This El Paso."

No one answered him. Stark opened a room door and held it for him. He entered, to a faint smell of disinfectant and lemon. The room was in cheerful colors, quilted spreads neatly arranged across the beds. Carpeting bent rose-beige fibers under his tread. Drapes matched the splendor of the quilted coverings. The bathroom porcelain was uncracked and as white as eggshell. This America, to take both crime and prosperity so casually.

He pulled up an upholstered chair to sit by the window. "Pull the drapes," he told Stark. "And leave me."

Stark hesitated, then did as he was told, going to join his fellows in the next room.

Delacroix bent his head over his hands.

Moments later, how long he could not be sure, it might even have been hours, tires squealed in the parking lot below. A door slammed, followed by another. Then the outdoor stairs trembled with the sounds of ascent.

He had left the door unlocked. Delacroix lifted his head. Footfalls rang the length of the hotel, then stopped outside his door.

It crashed open. A man stepped inside, blinking at the dimness of the room. He flexed, and his arms looked like two mighty constrictors at his side, skin rippling in inked tattoos.

"I've been waiting," Delacroix said.

Snake came to a halt, Mott on his heels, his head crawling and pounding until he thought it would explode, squeezing his eyeballs and brains out of his skull. He had walked, as he had driven for the last six hours, out of a kind of animal instinct, not thinking, not slowing even when snow had threatened the high desert roads. He had not eaten since leaving California, but it did not matter. His flesh crackled with fever. He could feel sweat running down his face like tears, and he could smell the rank smell of his body.

He had navigated by the thing curled up inside the bones of his head, by the itching and the crawling and the yearning. It did not stop until he stopped, here, inside this hotel room.

He wiped the sweat from his face, looking into the dim interior of the room and saw a nigger waiting for him.

A protest burst from his lips, shattering the silence.

The man, dressed in ivory linens, like a suit from the tropics, got to his feet. "You will not address me like that," he said, his voice heavily accented.

"And a frigging foreign nigger, too." Snake clenched his teeth. The cords in his neck bulged, as if bars in a cage for the words, but he got them out, anyway.

Mott shuffled his feet uncertainly. "He ain't the girl, Snake. Let's get out of here. Viktor's going to be pissed about the car."

"Come in and close the door," the black man ordered softly. "You are attracting attention."

"No fucking way," Mott began, but something hard poked him in the back of the rib cage, just shy of a kidney.

"Do what the man say."

Mott looked over his shoulder. Two more black faces stared back at him. A white man stood just behind him, and he carried the gun. Snake staggered forward as if obeying an unseen force, like a marionette pulled by strings, and Mott followed him into the room.

"Sit and tell me who you are chasing."

"I. Don't. Take. Orders. From. You." Snake forced each word out.

"Au contraire, mes ami. You do. I am Delacroix, and I am the master of the most important part of you."

Snake shrugged, fighting invisible chains, until his face glowed red with the effort.

Mott looked uneasily from side to side.

"I. Don't. Take. Orders. From. No. Nig—"

Delacroix waggled his fingers. "That is enough. Look in the mirror and tell me what you see."

Snake ground his heel into the carpet, turning in a slow movement, inch by inch, until he faced himself in the mirror over the bureau. He saw himself, shirt

rolled at the arms, baring his muscular limbs and tattoos. He saw his face, sweat-soaked and burning with
effort. His tattoos writhed and moved like something
alive. He clenched his fists.

Behind him, also visible in the mirror, Delacroix's
sharp, calm face. He began to chant softly.

That itchy thing began to claw at him from inside.

Snake tried to shake it off, but he couldn't. It was
inside him, inside. He ripped at his shirt, tearing it
open, felt it coil in his throat. He put his thick, knobby
hands at his throat, squeezing, squeezing, as if he could
smash it.

He drove himself to his knees in wheezing agony.
Then, as he looked back in the mirror, dizzied, defeated, he saw it.

An inky darkness began to pour out of him, out of
his hands, his throat, his ears, his eyes, his mouth, his
nostrils, streaming out of him, covering him, blanketing
him, a second skin.

Until the only thing he could see in the mirror was
himself, brown-hued, with black and yellow tattoos
upon his skin.

He opened his mouth to scream, but the other white
man was on him, muffling his horror with his forearm,
gagging him.

"See what you are," Delacroix said calmly, "and
know my orders. Release him, Stark."

Snake stood crouching on the floor. He raised his
hands in front of his eyes, staring at them, stared at
his mirror image.

"You are mine. What is done is done. Tell me who
the quarry is."

"Biker bitch. Kamryn. Some kid. Man. Homeless.
Scum."

Delacroix considered this, as if there had been a right and wrong to the answer, then nodded, pleased.

"Where are they now?"

"Coming." Snake gargled a word, then spit it out. "To El Paso."

Mott looked around the room in desperation, afraid.

Delacroix looked at him. "You must feed," he remarked to Snake. "Take him. This room has a lovely closet. Put the body in it."

Mott's mouth opened and shut like a fish on the hook. He took a step away from Snake.

He was not quick enough.

Chapter 29

"Take us through town and on into the airport." Kamryn put down the map, frowning. "Be careful. We don't want any tickets." They had gone from barren desert to a bustling commute through a major city. Cars jostled them from every side. The night had been long, and was finally gone.

"I am careful."

She followed the state trooper as he dropped off, then looked back. "Well, he was staring at something."

Mitch flexed his neck. "A ticket is a ticket. What are they going to do, throw us in jail?"

"Just remember: there's justice, and then there's Texas justice."

"What's that supposed to mean?"

"It means," Mitch answered Brand when Kamryn didn't, "that Texans have their own way of doing things."

"Well, duh. But what does it mean—" Brand stopped. "Are we flying out of El Paso?"

Kamryn, her tone short. "No."

"But then, why are we going to the airport?"

"We're going to park the Explorer in one of those long-term parking lots and then we're going to rent another fourwheeler."

"Because of what happened to Yellow Dog."

Mitch looked at Kamryn. "You think they might have a fix on the car?"

"Could. Why take chances?"

"Makes sense to me." Mitch eyed Brand in the rear view mirror. "Okay?"

"Sure." Brand had hoped for a moment that the other two had decided on a quicker route. The moment passed with an icy swiftness. He did not know if Yellow Dog had made it through the night. They had long since passed out of the range where his condition was featured on the local news, having put the entire state of New Mexico between them. The only thing he knew was that the KillJoy had drawn close.

Very close.

The orange-red of dawn bled out of the sky quickly, leaving it a dazzling blue. Brand let out a sigh and reached for his sunglasses. The lightning bolt etching had lengthened a bit, scratched across the face of the lens. The light did not seem to bother his eyes as much as it had, but as he watched Kamryn, he feared for her.

Darkness made an aura about her, a saturnine glow that was as far from an angelic halo as it could be. His pulse quickened at the recognition of what he saw. He was failing Kamryn, losing her, watching her slip away before his very eyes. He fingered the amulet in his pocket. Yellow Dog had not known if it would help.

But he had not thought it would hurt either.

Brand knotted his fingers in the black cord necklace, thinking to draw it out of his pocket and give it to her now, without delay.

Mitch informed them, "There's another trooper on my tail, approaching slowly."

Kamryn slid down in her seat. "Get down, Brand."

He ducked down. "What's happening?"

"Nothing. I'm not even sure if he's giving us a look over."

The heavy traffic sound of the major thruway traversing El Paso surrounded them. Mitch said nothing further, but the car moved in a smooth lane change.

"What's happening?" Kamryn's voice, squeezed, tense.

"Nothing. He's taking the off-ramp, leaving us. Probably wondering what doughnuts to have with his coffee."

Brand moved. Kamryn hissed, "Stay down!"

Mitch braked suddenly. The amulet, as he drew it out of his pocket, slid underneath the driver's seat. The charm was gone, as surely as if it had jumped from his hand. Brand patted around, looking for it, unable to find it. Then, the coolness of the metal answered his search.

He put it back in his pocket.

"What is it?"

"Gridlock," explained Mitch patiently. "Texas style." The Explorer moved in inches, until he veered sharply left and then began a moderate acceleration. "We should be at the airport in another ten minutes."

Kamryn got up and Brand followed suit. He could hear the overhead scream of jets as they circled the city outskirts. He'd never been on a plane. He watched their path with a certain envy. As they found the thruway exit to the airport, Brand saw another state trooper approach quietly from the right rear, then drop back. He opened his mouth to say something, then decided not to. Kamryn was about to jump out of her skin. Why worry her further? The trooper got no closer and then turned off approaching Airway Boulevard.

They hiked in from the parking lot rather than take

the shuttle. Kamryn threw the last of her belongings in a dumpster.

"We travel light," Mitch said ruefully.

"Clothes are replaceable." She wore a short jacket and stopped in the parking lot aisle long enough to tuck her revolver into her waistband at the small of her back. "Just give me the necessities." She did not meet Mitch's eyes when she looked up.

In a wing of the main terminal, they sat down to hot drinks and doughnuts. Brand had hot chocolate and three twists. Kamryn had picked hot cider and a plain glazed doughnut. Mitch took coffee, black, and a fist-sized apple fritter. They ate with sugary satisfaction. Kamryn stood.

"You guys wait here. I'll go rent the car."

Mitch got seconds on his coffee and Brand kicked back, listening to the sounds of a nearby passenger's CD player, Hootie and the Blowfish. Mitch blotted his coffee cup on the front page of the paper, Senator Haywood Bayliss celebrating the disarmament package defeat.

American Airlines announced that their 11:30 a.m. flight, connecting to Dallas/Ft. Worth and on to New Orleans would be their last flight of the day to that region because of the gulf states' hurricane watch. Brand found a quarter and wandered off to the arcade bordering the coffee shop and gift shop, the enveloping darkness and neon lit machines comforting.

Kamryn found him blazing a trail among the current high point holders on NOVA. She took him by the elbow and pulled him away.

"Where's Mitch?"

"He's gone to get the car. A red Cherokee. It's a hike, according to the rental counter, so he won't be back for about twenty minutes. I want you to watch for him."

"Sure. Where are you going to be?"

Kamryn looked at the flight departure monitor. She looked back at Brand. "I won't be here."

"Why?"

"I have to leave. The two of you will be fine without me." She had a small duffel in her hands, imprinted with the logo of the rental car agency. "Take this, give it to Mitch. He'll know what to do with it."

Brand stood shock-still, the bag pushed into his chest. "I don't get it."

"There's nothing to get. This is where we part ways. I can't—" She looked out the bank of windows toward the parking lot, and back again. "I can't do this any more." She let go of the bag, turned heel and started to walk away. Her footsteps clicked on the marble tiles.

Brand quick-stepped to catch up. "What do you mean, you can't do this any more?"

The two of them were walking against a tide of people coming out of the terminal arm where the gates were. He saw their direction.

"You bought a ticket. You're flying out."

"That's right."

"Leaving us."

"With a car. There's two hundred dollars in the bag and," she lowered her voice, "the gun."

"I don't want it."

People were beginning to stare at the two of them.

"I have to go. My plane's boarding. Brand—you can't bring that bag through with you."

"No. You're not going anywhere without me. You can't. You don't know what you're up against—I should have told Yellow Dog, and I didn't, and it's my fault they tried to kill him—"

She tried to outrun him. He kept pace. "You've got to listen. I'm not crazy. I'm not!"

"Brand!"

"Kamryn, don't go!" He grabbed for her arm. The duffel fell, spilled open, gun sliding and money flying, all under the belted x-ray counter. Airport security and the uniformed woman manning the x-ray machine looked down in total surprise.

"Shit!" Kamryn bent over, kicked the money and gun back in the duffel. She locked her arm with Brand's and stepped away from the X-ray threshold.

Security put his hand on his holster, and stepped with them.

Very quietly, Kamryn said, "It's time to run again."

"Not without you."

They turned and sprinted. A sharp whistle cut across the air behind them, echoing through the terminal. Kamryn angled into the crowds. Her arm tore loose from Brand's, but he could see her dark hair, among the passengers. She cut across a wave, headed toward a wing which was labeled: NO ACCESS. Maintenance only.

He followed.

He couldn't protect her if she left. Couldn't watch her cool beauty, couldn't laugh at her quirky sense of humor, couldn't be without her.

He cut across the flow of disembarking passengers and trailed across the forbidden wing. The corridor turned a sharp corner, but he could hear her rushing footfalls.

"Kamryn!"

She halted. Turned around slowly.

"Brand, I know you don't understand, and now I definitely don't have time to explain it to you. We're both in trouble here, now, and neither of us can afford to be caught. So you just go back that direction, and

I'll go this way. Find Mitch. Get to New Orleans. Do what you have to do." She backed carefully toward an emergency exit door off the corridor.

"Not without you."

Looking skyward, she said again, "I can't do this!" When she looked down, she froze.

"Please, Kamryn. Come with us."

"Now, son." A deep, pleasantly southern voice cut across Brand, from his rear, and the hair rose on the back of his neck.

"Son, I don't think you want to go anywhere with that woman. She's nothing but trouble. I have airport security with me. Put the bag down, turn around, and let's make this as pleasant as possible. Where's the other one?"

"Gone," Kamryn and Brand got out in unison. They looked at each other. Brand recognized the voice, saw the look on Kamryn's face.

The ruined man had caught up with him.

"Well, now. That matters a little, but it doesn't ruin my entire day." Rembrandt drew even with Brand. Impeccably suited as always, he wore a pleased expression. "If I have the two of you, I think it'll be possible to find him later. Don't you?"

Kamryn put her hand in the duffel. "I wouldn't count on that. Brand, step away from him and come with me."

Rembrandt raised an eyebrow as he guessed what Kamryn had in the duffel. "After all the trouble I went to to find you." He tilted his head slightly, still amiable. "You won't be walking out, little lady. The state troopers have been looking for the three of you and your car. They were most cooperative in letting me know you were here at the airport. Cooperative of you, too. I had just flown in about an hour ago. Put the bag down."

"No. Brand." Her eyes pleaded. "Come with me."

"This is a heck of a note, isn't it, son? First she doesn't want you, then she does."

Brand took a sideways step, uncertain. He knew Rembrandt wanted him. Kamryn was extraneous here. She had to get away, to find Mitch, to tell him—

"Kamryn, go on."

She moved back a fraction, stood with her back to the emergency exit door. She could feel it, she must! She stayed there, watching them.

Rembrandt smiled. "Maybe she'd respond better if you called her by her real name, son."

Kamryn grayed. The duffel shook in her hands. "Brand, don't listen to him."

"She didn't tell you, did she? Well, I've had occasion to do a little background check on this little lady. Her name isn't Kamryn Talent. In fact, she's no lady. She's an ax murderer wanted in the Commonwealth of Pennsylvania. She'd been on the run for about a year and a half now—"

Brand's words strangled in his throat.

"Isn't that so, Amelinda? Amelinda Terhuven. A nice old-fashioned name, Amelinda." Rembrandt reached for something in the pocket flap of his jacket.

"Nooo!" Brand screamed and lunged at Rembrandt. He knocked the black object out of his hand. It skidded along the tiles to Kamryn. She stooped and picked it up, throwing it in the duffel. Without standing, she backed out of the emergency exit door.

Alarms went off everywhere. Rembrandt shook Brand off, into the arms of a security officer and dashed out onto the tarmac.

A taxiing plane narrowly missed him. He looked, and could not see which way the young woman had gone.

"No sign of her, sir," confirmed security at his side.

"It doesn't matter," Rembrandt said grimly, looking down the runway, listening to the fury of departing jets. "I've got the boy."

Chapter 30

"Where's Brand?"

"Rembrandt's got him." Kamryn brushed her hair back. Tears streaked her face. She tried to wipe them, her eyes kept flowing. "Drive, damnit! Just drive before the troopers spot us."

He maneuvered away from the terminal, merging in with the traffic. "Then we were being watched."

"They caught up with us. They must have had the airport cordoned off the minute we pulled into the parking lot. This is my fault. I tried—I tried to leave."

"Leave?"

"It's an airport, for Christ's sake. I tried to take a flight out, leave you and Brand behind. I can't take a chance of being caught. You wouldn't understand."

His mouth thinned. "What I don't understand is how Rembrandt ended up with Brand."

"He did it! Trying to protect me again. Rembrandt thought he had us cornered. He threw me Rembrandt's gun and I took off."

"It's in the bag?"

"Along with mine. I tried to give it to Brand, told him to find you. He made a scene. We got caught at the x-ray gate. Shit! What a mess I keep making of things."

"Give me the gun."

"What?"

"I might need it. You've got yours. Let me see what Rembrandt was packing."

She picked up the duffel, reached in and rummaged around. She brought out the hard black object Brand had thrown her. "I don't—Mitch, it's a pager. Brand threw me a pager."

She held it out on her palm. He looked at it, reached out and took it, clipping it onto his waist band.

Kamryn tried to compose herself. She wiped her face dry again. "Mitch, God, who is he? How does he have the power to show up, and everybody toes the line? He had the state troopers looking for us. Airport security. Who does he tell these people he is?"

"I don't know who he is, but I do know what he wants. Ultimately." He made a turn back onto Airway Boulevard, leading back to the 10.

"Where are we going?" Kamryn could not stop shaking. She hugged herself tightly. Her teeth chattered.

"New Orleans. What he wants is in New Orleans, and that's where he's going to have to meet us if he wants it."

"What about the KillJoy?"

"That's another story. But it started in New Orleans, too. I have to go full circle." He took the on-ramp marked East and merged into thinning traffic.

"And leave Brand?"

"For now. If Rembrandt wants his goods, he's going to have to make a trade."

"But how's he—how's he going to know that? How are you going to get hold of him? How's he going to find us?"

"Easy. He's a smart man." Mitch tapped his belt. "He'll probably page us."

   *   *   *   *

Rembrandt sat in the President's Lounge. The plush surroundings nearly muffled the sound of the airport. He checked his watch. "She's no saint, son, or she would have come back for you."

Brand sat with his hands cuffed, resting on one knee. Loose shackles around his ankles kept him from running. A bump was rising on one cheekbone and his glasses were gone, irretrievably shattered. He kept his eyes narrowed against the glare of the fluorescent lighting, but the pain was not as it had been the past few days. He would rather have had the pain, and the glasses, all of it, instead of the darkness which patched in and out, like an incandescent bulb going out, like a TV screen fading into oblivion.

If Rembrandt thought he was Brand's worst nightmare, he had another think coming. The fact was obvious that if the agent were going to kill him, he would have. No, he was bait, and Brand knew it. He did not answer.

"I have to wait anyway," the ruined man continued pleasantly. "We need to refuel and file a new flight plan before we can get out of here. But I would say they're not coming to get you. No, it doesn't look like rescue is imminent. You're expendable."

Brand felt like a scab that Rembrandt enjoyed picking and probing. He turned to look fully at the man. "And you're a son of a bitch."

"Probably. Probably. But have I ever lied to you?"

"I don't know you well enough to know if you have. And that doesn't change anything. What good is the truth if all you talk about is evil."

"I suppose you prefer Lizzie Borden."

"Whatever it was, she didn't do it!"

"Son, I'm afraid she did. We've matched fingerprints from the crime scene in Pennsylvania with those out of the Honda which the Arizona state police were kind enough to put on-line for us. It's her all right."

"Then the truth lies." Brand kicked at the small teakwood table in front of him. There was an answering echo of a heavy thud.

Rembrandt's face went chill. He put up a hand, signaling for quiet. There were only the two of them sitting in the airport's executive lounge. Rembrandt put a hand out to the remote and muted the television set, although neither of them had really been watching the hockey game.

No other sound followed. It was, perhaps, too silent.

Brand felt a twinge of hope bloom in him. They'd been in the lounge for the last hour and a half, after security had escorted them there. Rembrandt had left twice to consult with his pilot, leaving one of the security force at the door, in case Brand had thought of shuffling to freedom. No one else even knew he was there, so it had been beyond hope to think Kamryn and Mitch could find him. He watched as Rembrandt rose smoothly to his feet, put his hand inside his coat pocket, and strode to the doorway.

"On the other hand," Rembrandt told him, "perhaps I was wrong."

He jerked the door open. The threshold stood empty. The security guard who had been placed there was gone, no sign of any occupant anywhere. Rembrandt backed in, shut the door, and locked it. He studied the interior of the lounge. No windows. No other entrances or exits. Brand followed his reconn.

Rembrandt came to him and hoisted him onto his feet. He bent down and undid the shackles. "I want you to stay with me, twinkle toes."

"Where are we going?"

"Somewhere a little more public. The Lear should just about be ready for us." Rembrandt pulled his automatic. Brand stared at its flat black surface. He wondered what it was he'd grabbed earlier and tossed at Kamryn, if it hadn't been a gun.

The ruined man linked elbows with him. He smiled down at Brand. "Now, son, I know you may feel this is your opportunity, but I wouldn't want to bet your life on it. You stay with me, and we'll get through this together. Understand?"

Brand pressed his lips together.

Rembrandt had been listening to the door again. Now he turned, and his eyes bored into Brand's.

"I could shoot you right here, right now, and put up with a hell of a lot less trouble."

"Then do it."

"No. You see, I don't want to. You and me, we're a lot alike. We're survivors. You might be expendable to Christiansen and the girl, but you're not to me. You have quality, son, a rare commodity."

Brand did not want to listen, but he could not look away from the other's compelling face. And then, behind Rembrandt's head, something peculiar began happening to the door.

White crystal had begun to form on its surface as the surface grew horribly cold. Brand could feel the drop in temperature down to his bones. Jackfrost formed before his stare, growing in streaks and flakes over the door. Brand clenched his jaws to keep his teeth from chattering and his breath hazed the air.

Rembrandt whipped around in amazement. Then, fog began to drift in through the minute cracks in the door jam.

A black fog.

Brand reared back.

Rembrandt had hold of him and braced himself. He clicked the safety off his pistol and raised it by his temple, in readiness to level and shoot.

The doorknob rattled.

The two of them stared at it.

Then the door burst open and the KillJoy walked in.

Brand forgot to breathe. He knew the man who strode in despite the cloak of darkness he wore, despite the fact that his skin now mirrored that cloak, despite the fact that he barely resembled a man at all. His sable and black skin rippled like snakehide, yellow diamonds brilliant scales upon the dark. He exuded the KillJoy; it issued through his every pore, and looking into his eyes was looking into black flame. Brand realized he wasn't breathing, couldn't breathe, and thought his heart might stop as well.

"Stop right there."

Snake hesitated in mid-stride, then came to a halt. He curled his lips back in greeting and inky clouds carried his voice.

"Your ass is mine."

Brand choked. The reflex started his lungs pumping again, his heartbeat skittering in his chest like a frightened, caged animal. This was the familiar, contemptible Snake as well as the KillJoy.

In the corridor behind, where white frost took on a blackish tint, he could see a man waiting, a black man in a tropical sand-colored suit, shirt open at the collar, a sharp-faced man with glass-hard eyes, a professorial type with the stare of an assassin. The corridor wall of windows looking out on the runways framed him. The sky looked a brilliant blue. Immense white planes rolled ponderously past. The black man stood with otherworldly stillness and took in the scene with keenness, then looked into Brand.

Into, and beyond. Brand saw the same kind of radiance about him as he had observed in Snake, but different. It did not overwhelm him, it was him, a negative aura that was like night to Mother Jubilation's day. He did not know why he thought of Mother as the balance to him, but it seemed natural. Like Yin and Yang. This man was not the KillJoy. . . . He was, quite probably, its master.

He wanted to shout at Rembrandt. *Kill him, and Snake will die,* but his throat stayed frozen. His lips trembled as he tried to force the words out. He could not turn away from the other's eyes. Impaled on them, like one of Vlad Dracula's victims. Why could he see the other that way? Why couldn't Rembrandt?

Two other men, young men, dark as their leader, stepped in to flank him, protective.

Light flooded the airport corridor as a plane moved past, letting the sunlight flood in, glittering, overwhelming.

Flare hit him. His eyes burst with the aura, white-blue, bedazzling. He jerked his head back with a muffled cry, seeing nothing but the painful flash.

It broke the other's hold on him. He craned his face toward Rembrandt, to his ear.

"Shoot him!"

Rembrandt jumped. Snake gave a snarl, no longer hesitant, and charged them.

Rembrandt let go. Brand dropped like a sack of wet cement. The ruined man had been holding him on his feet, and he hadn't even known it. His vision whited out, Brand crawled aside as the gun fired. Blurred vision overrode the flaring. Snake staggered and his chest blossomed red, but he shook and like an angry bull, dropped his head, and came on.

"No!" Brand cried. "The other one. Shoot the other one!"

The pistol spat. Brand saw bodies repel, hit the corridor floor, slide out of view. Tears welled up in his eyes, further blurring the images. Flare throbbed, then began to subside.

Rembrandt had no time. Snake hit him and the building seemed to shake. Rembrandt seemed to evaporate away from him, switched hands on the pistol, and came up swinging.

They grappled. Rembrandt wore an expression of slight surprise, as if Snake should no longer be on his feet. They sparred, Snake nailing Rembrandt with punches that drove grunts out of him. Brand thought he saw the KillJoy's master kneel down, examining the two bodies in the corridor.

Snake slipped in a trail of his own blood and crashed to the floor. He rose, rose on a cloud, his feet flailing, arms dangling, a broken marionette. He rose superhumanly and then rotated upright. He laughed.

Rembrandt brought up his gun. He emptied it into Snake.

Snake danced and quivered with each shot, dancing backward, staggering forward. Brand could smell the hot coppery blood flowering from him. He made a noise, a guttural growling deep in his throat, flexed his fists and came on again.

Rembrandt clipped off one last shot.

Snake's head exploded.

He dropped and did not move.

Brand felt sick. Rembrandt, breathing hard, blood trickling from his nose and mouth, reached down for him, yanked him onto his feet. "Let's go before that thing gets up one more time."

They reached the threshold of the lounge, the corridor empty except for slashes of blood. Rembrandt paused, looking side to side, calculating.

Brand looked back.

He wished he had not. The KillJoy geysered from Snake's body, spouts of darkness, coalescing, coming after them.

Coming after *him.*

Brand wanted to close his eyes, could not. Horror held him in fascination. The KillJoy spread out, batwinged, immense, enfolding.

It reached out for them.

He felt its icy touch graze him. His heart did a double-beat, then warmth flooded him. He opened his eyes. The KillJoy was gone.

Rembrandt ejected the empty clip. He slammed Brand up against the wall and held him there with an elbow while he put in a full clip. Brand could see one of the bodies slumped up against the other end of the corridor at the end of a blood smear.

He did not see the master.

Security flooded the corridor from both ends. Rembrandt put up his hand with the gun and then carefully slipped it back inside his suit coat.

"The perps are down."

Brand stayed against the wall as if glued to it. Security swarmed the body, then waved Rembrandt off.

"Your plane is ready, sir."

"Good. I'll fax you a statement. They tried to free my prisoner. One of your men is down, as well. Check the emergency stairwells." Rembrandt took Brand's elbow. "One step at a time, son."

The wind came up across the tarmac as they stepped

out. The Lear waited, door down, engines idling. Rembrandt hustled Brand across the open ground and up the stairs.

He sat Brand down, went up front to say a word or two to the pilot, came back and pulled the door shut and secured it, before returning to the plush bench seats in the main cabin. He unbuttoned his suit jacket and sat with a sigh.

"Well, son, looks like we made it." He smiled at Brand.

The KillJoy looked out of the black depths of his eyes.

Brand screamed, but no one else heard him over the jet engines.

Chapter 31

BULLETIN
HURRICANE YOLANDA LOCAL ACTION STATE-
MENT
NATIONAL WEATHER SERVICE NEW ORLEANS
LA
1200 PM CDT

YOLANDA A POWERFUL AND DANGEROUS
HURRICANE RATED FORCE 4 PACKING 150
MPH WINDS STRONGER THAN PAST HURRI-
CANES ELENA, FREDERIC AND ELOISE, RATED
WITH OPAL.

HURRICANE WARNINGS IN EFFECT FROM
THE MOUTH OF THE MISSISSIPPI RIVER TO IN-
CLUDE COASTAL MISSISSIPPI ... LOWER ST
BERNARD PARISH AND LOWER PLAQUEMINES
PARISH IN LOUISIANA, ALSO FROM MOUTH OF
THE MISSISSIPPI RIVER TO EAST OF MORGAN
CITY ... THIS INCLUDES THE METROPOLITAN
NEW ORLEANS AREA.

THIS BULLETIN APPLIES PRIMARILY TO THE
FOLLOWING PARISHES IN LOUISIANA ...

ASCENSION ... ASSUMPTION ... EAST
BATON ROUGE ... EAST FELICIANA ... IBER-
VILLE ... JEFFERSON ... LAFOURCHE ... LIV-

INGSTON ... ORLEANS ... ST HELENA ... ST
JAMES ... ST JOHN THE BAPTIST ... ST TAM-
MANY ... TANGIPAHOA ... TERREBONE ...
WASHINGTON ... WEST BATON ROUGE ...
WEST FELICIANA.

ALSO THE FOLLOWING COUNTIES IN
MISSISSIPPI

HANCOCK ... HARRISON ... JACKSON AND
PEARL RIVER

CRITICAL INFORMATION SUMMARY

LOCATION ... AT 1030 CDT HURRICANE YO-
LANDA WAS NEAR 28.1N AND 88.2W OR ABOUT
275 MILES SOUTH SOUTHWEST OF PEN-
SACOLA.

INTENSITY ... MAXIMUM SUSTAINED WINDS
ARE 150 MPH. YOLANDA IS A DANGEROUS SAF-
FIR SIMPSON CATEGORY 4 HURRICANE. SOME
FLUCTUATION IN STRENGTH MAY OCCUR BE-
FORE LANDFALL.

MOVEMENT ... YOLANDA IS MOVING NORTH
NORTHEAST AT 19 MILES PER HOUR, EX-
PECTED TO BRING THE CENTER OF YOLANDA
INLAND TOMORROW AFTERNOON OR EARLY
EVENING.

TIDES ... RUNNING 2 FEET ABOVE NORMAL
ALONG THE SOUTHEAST LOUISIANA AND MIS-
SISSIPPI COAST. TIDES COULD RISE 3 TO 5
FEET ABOVE NORMAL IN LAKES PONTCHAR-
TRAIN AND MAUREPAS, ALONG THE COASTAL
AREAS OF ORLEANS ... ST BERNARD AND
PLAQUEMINE PARISH. ALONG THE MISSISSIPPI
COAST, TIDES 6-7 FEET ABOVE NORMAL. AS
THE HURRICANE MOVES CLOSER, THESE
TIDES ARE EXPECTED TO BECOME MUCH

HIGHER, AS HIGH AS 12 TO 15 FEET ABOVE NORMAL.

EVACUATIONS ... EVACUATIONS HAVE BEEN CARRIED OUT IN THE COASTAL LOCATIONS OF SE LOUISIANA AND OUTSIDE THE HURRICANE PROTECTION LEVEES. MANDATORY EVACUATIONS HAVE BEEN ORDERED IN LOWER PARISHES. MISSISSIPPI EMERGENCY MANAGEMENT SHELTERS ARE OPEN, WITH EVACUATIONS REQUESTED. MOBILE HOME RESIDENTS ALONG THE MISSISSIPPI COAST ARE BEING URGED TO SEEK SHELTER IN SUBSTANTIAL BUILDINGS DUE TO GALE FORCE WINDS.

RAINFALL ... FLASH FLOOD WATCH IS IN EFFECT 3-5 INCHES EXPECTED IN THE EARLY MORNING HOURS AS YOLANDA PREPARES TO MOVE INLAND. FURTHER RAIN INTENSITY EXPECTED TO INCREASE. LISTEN TO YOUR EMERGENCY PREPAREDNESS CHANNELS FOR FURTHER UPDATES.

LOCAL ACTION STATEMENT WILL BE ISSUED AROUND 300 PM CDT.

The ticket agent nervously punched in the request, her hands shaking, trying not to look at the two men facing her over the counter.

"This is the last flight in."

"I understand that," the professor said, in his soft, lilting voice. "But it is most important that I gain a ticket for myself and my aide."

Perhaps not a professor, she thought. Perhaps she had guessed wrong about his demeanor. "Are you a doctor?"

He paused. "Yes," he admitted, almost reluctantly. "With the UN. I thought perhaps I could help. I am

used to . . . how would you say it? . . . working under
extreme conditions."

The man at his elbow shifted weight.

The ticket agent found two seats. She hurriedly re-
served them and cleared her system to print. "I'm so
sorry it's taking me so long. I'm really rattled. We had
some trouble here this morning."

"We understand," the doctor said soothingly.

"A shooting, can you imagine? The next terminal
over. Three dead. Not terrorists, though, thank God."

"Yes," murmured the passenger. "A tragedy."

The printer chucked out the tickets. Hands still
shaking, she separated them and put them in folders.
"Two tickets to New Orleans," she said, and handed
them over. "Mr. Delacroix, Mr. Stark. Have a safe
flight."

Delacroix smiled. "We hope to."

*   *   *   *

Mother Jubilation could hear a lonely saxophone. Its
player, like herself, had chosen to stay in the city despite the evacuations. The storm surge had begun to
rise, Yolanda already beginning to take a toll, despite
the fact landfall was a little more than twenty-four
hours away. New Orleans was a city that depended
on her canals and pumping systems against flooding.
Yolanda would overwhelm them. Even now the city had
begun to sink under the tremendous rising tide. Rainfall would worsen the situation. But she could not
leave. This was her destiny. She waited for the boy
and the white soldier and what troubled them. Mother
gathered up her stones and knucklebones, shook them
and played them out again.

They would tell her nothing. They had told her once, at dawn that morning, of a fearful danger. Now silence.

She cleared them from the table. She drew a pottery jar of cornmeal to her and dipped her hand into it. Letting it slide, grain by grain from her fist, she drew the sign of legba on the table, the supreme loa, the gatekeeper.

Open the signs for me, she prayed over the corn grain symbol. Open the signs for me.

All was still, except for the patter of rain which had fallen sporadically all morning. It would stop and start until tomorrow morning, then it would fall in torrential amounts, wind-driven, streets flooding, levees groaning. Jackson Square was empty of all its sidewalk chalk artists, its vendor wagons, its tourists, its lovers, its jazz musicians. Even the pigeons had gone and the great bronze statue of Jackson on horseback was curiously alone. The gracious white church which graced the west side of the square had its renovated doors sandbagged. The east side of the square facing the brewery/mall was bagged as well. The narrow and roguish streets leading down to Pirate's Alley and her small shop were all barricaded, waiting for the inevitable.

A well-worn deck of tarot cards sat by the rim of her table. Card by card, they began a gentle slide over the edge. No hand touched them. The tabletop had not moved, but the cards fell until every one of them landed on the floor.

Mother watched them.

She thought of standing to see how they fell, in what pattern, if any, which face up and face down, but before she could, they rose.

They gained the air in twos, like winged things, and began to fly about the room, high under the ceiling. They picked up speed with altitude and they made a

terrible rattling as they flapped, like cards pinched in
a bicycle spoke. Around and around they went, faster,
faster, until Mother's eyes hurt to see them.

Their orbit grew tighter, nearer. Noisier. They spun
about the table, eye height, faster, faster until they
could not maintain their course. One by one they exploded out of the circle, shooting across the room and
dashing to the floor until the last card, which fell into
her lap and lay wiggling, breathing like a spent animal,
until it quieted.

Mother reached down and picked up The Tower of
Destruction.

Her children were in danger, great danger, all of
them, all, even the ones she had sent away to what
she hoped would be safety. Mother rocked on her
chair, back and forth, and chanted her prayer of hope
and protection for them, whatever good it would do
any of them.

*   *   *   *

Brand could not see from where he sat on the floor
of the helicopter. He kept his face buried in his hands
where the pilot could not see his bloodshot eyes, could
not laugh at the fear he knew showed in them. He sat
in abject misery. He did not care that Rembrandt seemed
in control of the thing. He wasn't. Brand could hear it
in his voice from time to time. See it in a facial tic or
an off-color laugh.

It did not matter if Rembrandt stayed in charge or
if the KillJoy gained total control. Either way, he was
screwed.

The pilot began speaking and the chopper dipped
down, down. They were arriving, wherever they were.

Rembrandt pulled his feet in under him, preparatory to standing.

The chopper settled with a hard bump, and then the rotors began to slow. Rembrandt had him on his feet and out the door, ducking his head down to avoid the blades.

A uniformed man met them, a man not much taller than Brand who traded salutes with Rembrandt. He was compact, all muscle, and his olive complexion looked as though he shaved twice a day to keep the beard down. He appraised Brand as Rembrandt asked,

"Everything ready?"

"Yes, sir, it is. You have some messages waiting in your quarters, as well."

"Good." Rembrandt smiled at Brand. "First things first. Where are we putting him, Josey?"

"I've sealed off a compartment in the unfinished dorm, next to the com control. This way."

Brand had little time to take in the sight of what appeared to be a military base, complete with a patrol of joggers going past them, shouting in cadence. There was activity and noise, from the routine to the sound of planks being dropped in place and the whine of drills and air hammers.

He put his cuffed hands up, shading his face a little. Rembrandt pushed and prodded him in the right direction until they stood in a building which matched the officer's description. Rembrandt disappeared behind a narrow door, was gone a minute, then came back.

"Excellent job, Josey."

"Thank you, sir. Permission to withdraw, sir. I have other details to take care of."

"Did you get those Orleans P.D. uniforms I called for?"

"Yes, sir, we did. We're instructing a patrol now."

"Good." Rembrandt pulled out the handcuff key.

"What are you going to do with me?"

Something glittered in Rembrandt's eyes. "Whatever I have to. Right now, you're the key. You're the key that unlocks Christiansen and gives me what I want. Whatever it takes, it takes."

He guided Brand to the door and opened it for him. Inside, a pool of darkness. No light, anyplace, anywhere. Ceiling, floor and walls blended into total insulation. Brand's mouth went dry. The officer waiting to be dismissed stood stiffly, not looking into the chamber.

"What is this?"

"Your cell. You'll be alone in there, son, alone with your thoughts." Rembrandt put a finger to his mouth as if quieting himself. He tapped his lips twice. "Well, I told you I didn't lie to you. You won't be quite alone. You see, Brand, thanks to the wonders of technology, I didn't just dig up Amelinda's background. I found yours. I know all about Dr. Susan Craig and Georg Bauer and the excellent groundwork she must have done on your mind. So I'm not putting you into solitary alone. No. I've arranged a little refresher course for you."

"I'm not going in there!"

"You don't have any choice."

Brand dug in his heels. "Don't let him do this to me! You can't do this!" He tried to face the officer. "He's crazy. Look in his eyes. He's possessed. You can't do this to me!"

Rembrandt laughed, then stopped as the sound came out eerily cracked. He stopped so quickly his teeth clicked together and Josey stirred uneasily.

"Sir—"

"Commander, if there's any doubt at all who you

should listen to, I'll relieve you of duty, right here, right now. Susan Craig has created a cunning creature, a sociopath, who will say anything, do anything, manipulate anyone he can. Let's see if we can make a straight arrow out of him."

Brand dropped to the floor, dead weight, clawing at the frame of the door. Rembrandt let out a growl as he struggled to get him back on his feet, lifting him. "He tried to hang me once! Don't believe him—he's not who he says he is, he never is! Look in his eyes!"

"Sir—" Josey again, questioning.

"You can't make omelettes without breaking eggs." Rembrandt hauled Brand to his feet, held him limply. He shook, like a dog shedding water, and Brand could feel the KillJoy within him. They were fighting each other, fighting for control.

The KillJoy was still not in charge. Rembrandt was, but Brand realized he did not know which was worse.

Both would kill if they wanted to.

"Give me a hand, commander."

The officer hesitated, then took Brand's other arm. They shoved Brand inside and slammed the door.

For an eerie moment, he thought the world had left him. Then he collapsed, letting his legs fold under him. The concrete slab felt icy, as hostile as the darkness around him. But at least it was solid. He sat up and crossed his legs. His eyes strained, trying to adjust to the unrelenting shadow of the room.

Blinded, he dared not move. He did not know if Rembrandt still stood outside the room or if he still held the KillJoy in check. Brand could not see his hand in front of his face, would have no warning when death came.

Alone in the dark.

Old feelings began to crowd him, the panic, the closed-in fear. The walls would crush him, the ceiling fall. He panted in fear. Helpless, without control, there was no exit, no light, no protection.

He would die here, suffocated by his memories. Brand tried to regulate his breathing. Was there even air in here? He could not detect a current.

He'd been buried alive and alone. He would be sealed in and left to die. If anyone came to rescue him, it would be too late.

He shut his eyes as if he could lie to himself, but he knew the difference. The darkness was too complete, too overwhelming.

He was no good. He must be. He'd failed Yellow Dog, gotten him nearly killed. Kamryn, Curtis, Mitch, his father (wherever he'd disappeared to), his mother, the list went on and on. Not living up to his potential. Getting in everyone's way. Seeing things.

Crazy.

Psychotic.

Brand X, the stuff nobody wanted. Who could blame them? He'd let them all down. He had never been the boy who'd done the expected, what they wanted. He tried, he just didn't know how. Life seemed so absurd.

You're absurd, Jerkoid. Just *breathe*.

He concentrated on that. In, out. In, out. For how long? Minutes? Hours?

Seconds?

Colors pierced his eyelids. He opened them.

Soundlessly, a projection filled the space in front of him. It gave dimension to the wall. A fighter plane zoomed down on a landscape. The little illumination the projection gave bloomed with a spectacular display. Other planes winged close and out, some breaking away in flames. His hands itched for the trac ball controls of an arcade. It was a flight simulator, on a bombing run. Brand watched it curiously, taken in with the gamelike quality of it, then became aware of a crawling sensation behind his eyeballs, like an itch.

Or an assault.

He closed his eyes again, then opened them, watching the virtual reality program through a web of his fingers. Flash, flash, flash—the colored animation playing out before him moved with a strobelike effect. There was enough light in the program that he could see the dark that streaked it, the cloudy smears of his own vision overlaying it.

Death here. The evil touch of the KillJoy. He could *see* it. He thought for a moment he would welcome the final collapse of his sight. Then remembered it would leave him trapped forever in his mind, at Bauer's mercy.

A thing which had no mercy.

For a flash of a second, a bloody knife. A still photo of a face, a sullen man.

He was not even sure he'd seen it. Then he knew. He wasn't, because the images were being flashed too quickly for normal eyes to focus. But the brain caught the messages, saw them, retained them. Subliminal programming.

Rembrandt knew of Susan Craig. The imprinting. Bauer, the serial killer.

He was doing the same thing to Brand all over again. He must be. Hidden in those animated simulator frames had to be images of Bauer. The bloody knives and visegrips. The crime scenes. The victims. Had to be. Had to be. Feeding Bauer. Giving him the strength to overcome Brand finally.

Brand covered his face.

He cowered. He couldn't go through this again.

Alone.

Don't worry, kid. You still got me. Bauer laughed coarsely. He forced Brand's chin up, watched the project for another minutes or so. *That's old stuff. Boring. We don't like to be bored, do we, kid?*

Georg's cruel voice echoed inside the hollows of his mind.

"Get out!" Brand concentrated, and shoved. Bauer wouldn't budge. He stayed, firmly planted in Brand's thoughts. He couldn't stop thinking, couldn't stop hearing Georg, couldn't run without a guide through his dark place.

Yellow Dog!

He squeezed his eyes tight, calling the canine to him, imagining the golden retriever, his silky, wavy coat shining in the night. He fought to build the image the way he loved to see the creature.

Yellow, bright yellow, like molten gold. A spirit color. All spirits, all colors, like the rainbow, Yellow Dog the Mescalero had told him. The dog was more than yellow. He had a pink tongue that lolled in doggy laughter over sharp ivory teeth, coal black nose that he liked to put in the palm of Brand's hand, and eyes, warm, brown eyes.

Dog!

Brand had him, saw him. Yellow Dog tossed his head and whined uneasily. He barked once, low and demanding. *Follow.*

Brand could not move.

The dog came to him, whining, pressed against his leg, warm, real. He dug his fingers into the coat, sensuous, alive. He roughed him up, both hands, massaging and stroking the dog's flanks. Yellow Dog threw his head back and licked his face, hot, wet kisses. Tail thumping he moved around and through Brand's arms, wiggling with joy.

Then he stopped. Pricked an ear. Looked off into the nothingness. Let out an anxious whuff.

Brand looked, too. Could see nothing.

Hackles rose on the back of Yellow Dog's neck. Brand rubbed his hand along them. The dog turned his head, poked his nose at him, went back to alert. He whined.

Nice doggy, Bauer said. He was a presence, unseen but felt, a force, an invisible being who lurked in the recesses.

But the dog saw him. Yellow Dog backed up against his knees. Brand put a hand on the dog's head. He rubbed an ear. *Go away, Bauer.*

The dog jerked free from under his hand, dragged out, nails scuffling. Brand grabbed for him, heard the dog yelp as the unseen tore him away.

Dangled Yellow Dog in front of him.

We know what happens now, don't we, kid?

The sinking feeling in the pit of his stomach. Bauer liked to carve things up. Yellow Dog could not save him this time, could not take him away, could not show him the way out of his own mind. He coiled into himself, rolled up like a ball, shoved his hands in his pockets. He did not want to see or hear or feel ever again.

He touched the amulet. Touched the bandanna with the peyote knotted into it in the other. Grasped each with a hand.

Heard Kamryn's voice. *You're tougher than you think you are.* She knew the dark side. He didn't believe what Rembrandt said about her, but even if there had been a kernel of truth in it, he knew there had to be a story he hadn't heard. What she'd said at the airport . . .

could have been aimed at her as well as him. She knew the dark and bitter side of things.

Or not. Maybe he was Brand X, the stuff nobody wants.

Only I want me.

He wanted himself. He wanted to keep that spark burning. He had to be better than Bauer. He knew that! He might not be good, but he was better than that. He hadn't lost the colors of the spirit yet. He couldn't lose himself. He couldn't. There would be nothing left. He didn't want to explode and phzzt out like some arcade character.

That was the death that mattered, losing himself, his mind, to Susan Craig or Bauer or Rembrandt or the KillJoy. Or, like his mom and her dweebish husbands, to bills and mortgages and a relentless pursuit of some kind of mundane happiness.

He knew what mattered. Long hours in the psych ward had shown him the way as surely as Yellow Dog ever had. The schizophrenic, the catatonic, the psychotic, those locked behind the bars of Alzheimer's, the walking dead, those cut off from their minds as surely as the truly dead had shown him the truth.

Wherever Curtis had gone, he hadn't been there in that casket, KillJoy or no KillJoy. Not in that wooden box. Not among those satin pillows. Not trapped. Freed.

Not wrapped in a straight jacket, not kept in a rubber room, not tranquilized out of his mind. He was still here. Rembrandt himself had given him that recognition. He'd *survived*.

He had kept Bauer all these years, kept him at arm's length. He had done it and the realization of it filled him now. He *had* done it.

He was not Bauer. For all the imprinting and programming Susan Craig had fed him, he was not Bauer. Never would be, not unless he gave up.

Yellow Dog squirmed and yelped anxiously in midair, tossed in invisible, tormenting hands.

No! He screamed at Bauer. *Not again!*

The dog fell. He tucked tail and ran.

Brand alone with Bauer. He put up his hands, ready to defend himself, his self, all that he had in this world, all that he had been given, all that God seemed to have decreed he would be left with.

It's just you and me, sweet cheeks. Did I tell you how I like to do little boys?

They closed in the darkness.

Chapter 32

Rembrandt and Josey looked in on the boy. He slept, loose-limbed and slightly curled on his left side, his face smooth. The eyelid twitches signaling REM sleep were not visible. Nothing suggested that he was even still alive except for his light, rhythmic breathing.

"Damn."

"We've lost him."

"Probably." Rembrandt paced.

"It's not been twenty-four hours." If Meales had been restless the past night, Rembrandt had been relentless. The hollows of his face had sunken, the craters of his scarring sharp and savage, the eyes burning with a kind of manic fervor.

"Doesn't matter. Looks like he's completely disassociated. Classic brainwashing tells us to break them down, then build them up. He was a tough kid. He had an edge. It shouldn't have happened." Rembrandt took a deep breath, released it quickly, repeating, "Doesn't matter. I need bait, I still have it. As long as he's breathing, I can maneuver Christiansen into place. Get the Lear ready."

"Where?"

"New Orleans."

"Sir, there's no way I can get clearance for that! Yolanda is just off the coast. She'll be making landfall—" he checked his watch. "Less than eight hours after I get you in there."

"Just get me in there. Tell them I'm an advance member of FEMA. Set me down at Baton Rouge, if that's what it takes, and get me a vehicle. Do it now!" Rembrandt pressed, as Meales hesitated. "Do you want to be explaining to Bayliss?"

"No, sir."

"Then get me there. I'll find a way to do what I have to."

Meales saluted and left. Rembrandt watched him go, a hard glitter in his eyes.

Nothing would keep him and the boy from New Orleans.

Nothing.

It might even be easier if the boy were more dead than alive.

*   *   *   *

The rain in Louisiana was different from Texas, which was different from California, which was different from home. Kamryn sat at the slightly greasy window of the small hotel room and watched the waters pelting against it, knowing it was still hours before dawn. The room was cheesy by any comparison and the neon lights of Baton Rouge blinked on abandoned streets. She hugged her knees to her chin. She wondered where Brand was in the night, where Rembrandt had taken him, if he was even still alive. She wondered if she would feel it if he weren't, like some kind of surrogate mother, then decided that she probably would not, no matter what their connection. She had never known when her own parents had gone. So much for psychic bonds.

She had to believe there was hope for Brand, that Mitch had been right. Rembrandt had a use for him, therefore he would still be alive.

But what if Mitch were wrong?

She had come to rely on him, she realized, taciturn and unbending. Brand had been quicksilver, humor and dry wit, a teenage tumbleweed, moving here, prickling there. Mitch had always been there, silent, unmoving, unruffled. He had driven Texas in the face of a storm watch and never flinched. If she closed her eyes, she could almost see him, imagine him in his Marine dress blues, an icon. Semper fi. Had any motto ever fit a man better?

He was nearly the exact opposite of anyone she had ever known. She had left the bed they'd been sharing, together but apart, because the feeling of him next to her had unsettled her. She, who had told him truly that sex with Darby had never been a matter of loving and sharing, sensed that if she'd gone to him, laid her cheek on his chest, listened to the steady beat of his heart, she might have discovered something new and wonderful.

She did not have time for that. Both Brand and Mitch were asking things of her she could not give. Not now. Perhaps not ever. Her presence with them endangered them. She ought not to be here, except that she had failed in saying good-bye.

Kamryn laid her head on the windowpane, the better to hear the rain, to feel the drive of it against the glass, to lull her to sleep. Whatever the morrow brought, she had to try to be ready for it.

A roll of thunder. An attempt of the rain to break through sodden clouds, to break the leaden oppression of a coming spring rain. Levin bolt and crash and drum, but no rain yet. She'd come home early from her friend's house, leaving a planned overnight, unhappy with the attitude of the girls she'd grown up with, who'd been her schoolmates, who now looked at her askance. Their heads, and their lives, were empty lies. She left them behind for what would be the last time, she told herself, a life that she would not be going back to.

The house stood on its forty acres, white sideboards with dark green trim, the laurel bush shading its eastern corner, the curving driveway filled with dad's truck, mom's car, her brother's car and now hers. All older and serviceable except for dad's new truck, his pride and joy. The moon had risen, a young, full moon, casting shadows across the drive.

The house had been dark and she wondered if they'd lost power again. Passing the Vanderowen home, she remembered their property had been dark also.

A hazard of living in the country.

She approached the open door. Came to a stop, looking at it, like a mouth, waiting to swallow.

Mom would never leave the door open. She did not like insects in the house, and springtime the air was full of them, clouds of them, rising from new-plowed ground and freshly-bloomed flowers. Amelinda put a hand out. Touched the door framed in night.

Brought her hand away slick and sticky. She rubbed it dry on her hip.

"Sis!"

A flashlight beam caught her in the face, the light as powerful as a slap, and she took a step back. Beyond the circle of the beam's focus, she caught sight of Eric's face. He had tattooed himself anew, this time a swastika on the crown of his forehead, where the hairline, if he had left any, would meet it. He looked a little as if the inking had splattered, splotching him from head to toe.

"Sis! You're home early. Come down to the basement. I've got a surprise for you!"

He took her arm. He, the older, the stronger, the leader, the protector. He'd kept her safe from bullies on the playground, took her away when dad and mom screamed at each other about the bills, the lost pension when the unions had gone affirmative action; he who had first helped her realize why the world had gone bad, why they were angry, the lost majority. He who had gone in search of the truth, shared it with them all, eliciting Mom's silence and Father's grumbling agreement. He who had not been afraid to commit himself wholly to the movement.

Who stood there now, his iron grip on her arm, guiding her to the basement to show her—what?

She breathed hard in fear. He smelled of blood, oddly, and she could not understand why. Step by step, he took care to make sure she did not slip . . . *Why was the basement dark? Why were the steps treacherous, wet and slippery?*

"I have a surprise for you."

"A surprise."

"I did it.

"For you."

The last argument with her parents had sent her away for the night, but she'd come back early, finding the outside world even more condemning than home. They, at least, shared her burgeoning beliefs. They hated the way the world had gone wrong. They hated everything, even her, sometimes, but it was home.

Her feet touched the basement floor. Eric moved, and white light flooded the basement.

She blinked in amazement. There was no power outage. The moment dazzled her.

Then she looked. And saw.

Crimson, not black, splattered Eric. Splashed against the basement wall. Led into the room built below. Lying in a pool of red, a white arm, very white, very pale, from elbow to fingers.

A severed arm.

She caught her breath to scream. She knew that arm, those work-worn fingers, that ancient thin-banded gold watch.

Eric drew her close, kept her from breathing, from screaming.

"Sis. I have a surprise for you."

He put the flashlight on the shelf, exchanging it for the bloody ax laid there. Walked her across the basement, stepped over the severed arm as if it did not exist.

She knew then the only truth that would matter to her. *She was going to die.* Then and there, at her brother's hand, just as their mother had.

"Wh—where's Dad?"

He held her very close, just as he used to when he was twelve and she eight, and they were trick or treating, and he had been pledged to keep her safe from cars and the night and bigger kids. He spoke softly into her ear, tickling the faint buzz of hair she had kept.

"He got mad," Eric said. "He found out what I did last week, and he got mad." Forlornly, "He never really understood the movement."

"Last week? When you went to Tucson?"

His fingers tightened and she could feel the excitement in them. "We derailed the Sunset Express. We did it. For the Movement."

She had always understood that there would be

things which had to be done, domestic terrorism, institutions which could be changed only by violence just as they themselves existed in violence, but this? Attacking Amtrak for no particular reason except to do it?

"Eric—"

He recoiled from her. Had heard it in her voice, or seen it in her eyes. Unacceptance. Rejection.

"Amelinda," he answered sadly. He raised the ax.

She began to pray then. It would not help, but it did not matter. It was her final refuge. She alone had put out the manger scene for Christmas, had left the house and trudged across the snow and blackfrost to the Vanderowens to catch a ride to church, to sing, to see the wonders at Christmas and Easter and any Sunday she could manage. She alone in the house had ever seemed to care about the soul and of all the souls in that house ensnared by Eric's philosophies, she had been the last to fall.

She asked to live. She asked for the chance to undo all that she had done, for in the end, all Eric's manifesto had come to was simply death and bedamning.

He raised the ax high, higher, as if knowing he would need a tremendous swing to cleave her head from her neck. Above him the bloody ax head raised. Raised until it touched the wires which hung above.

She asked for forgiveness and promised to repay it somehow.

Eric took a deep breath and stabbed the ax head backward, at the pinnacle of his swing. It bit deep into the wires and into the beam which held them. His blue eyes bulged. His tongue fell forward out of his mouth and his hands fastened convulsively about the ax handle, and his booted feet danced frantically on the damp basement floor.

An aura flashed outward, yellow and white and pale

blue, flashed about her, separating her, keeping her from the electrocution. When it was over, Eric's hands slipped from the ax handle and he fell to the basement floor.

She groped across the workshop until she found the flashlight.

He breathed. He had not died, but she was free. She stumbled across his prostrate form, looked in the print shop which had been her father's pride and joy and saw the shambles there, the blood-washed walls and computers, copiers and printers, and what was left of her father in his coveralls.

She put her hand in her mouth to muffle her sobbing. She made her way to the laundry room where she saw the rest of her mother.

Eric groaned. She backed out of the laundry room and to the stairs. His body lay between her and the steps. He smelled burnt, singed hair and ozone, the bitter bit of a lightning-struck tree. The soles of his shoes were curled and smoking.

She stepped across him.

He put up a hand and caught her ankle.

Amelinda dropped the flashlight. It went bouncing down the steps. She fell on her stomach and tried to crawl up the steps, wet and sticky as they were, clawing at them, escaping.

He pulled her down a step. She kicked, heard her foot thud home, stood, and put her hands up. Felt along the beam, along the fried wiring, until she found the ax.

She ran her hands down its handle and prised it out of the beam.

Eric jerked her feet out from under her, his strength returning, fueled by pain and anger. He bellowed like a bull.

She remembered screaming, terrified and horrified. Raising the ax. Hitting him. Splitting open flesh and muscle and the arm which grabbed her went limp.

She screamed all the way upstairs and out into the yard. She screamed, thinly, the way a wounded deer in the sparse woods along the road screams when it's injured, frightened, but still alive. Her hands shook so she could barely get her car keys in the ignition. She drove out of control to the Vanderowens, the car sliding off the road and birm and into and out of the rainwater ditch, tires spinning.

She ran into their house, the front door thrown open, and stumbled to the wall, hands searching, blood-covered hands leaving prints searching frantically for the light switch.

Then she went from room to room, finding the family butchered there, including Claude Vanderowen, her brother's best friend, his skull freshly tattooed, now seeping a crimson pool into his mattress.

And she went to her car and sat, afraid. Looked at her clothes, splattered, and her shoes, and her car, and the tattoos upon her arms.

And, God forgive her, she ran screaming into the night to hide. When the rain finally came, it came heavy enough to wash her scent from the ground and groves, and flood out the small bridge leading to their road, and she was long gone.

But she was still screaming.

She woke, throat aching, her face wet. She put her hands to the cords of her neck and stroked them. They throbbed with a need that was almost sexual, the need to scream again, the need for release.

Kamryn uncurled. She crept across the room and

knelt by Mitch's side of the bed. She put her hands upon his face.

He woke instantly. He put his hand on hers, and then stroked her face, and felt the dampness there.

"I need to tell you my name," she said. "I need to tell you who I am, and I need you to hold me and tell me it's all right anyway."

The tears came again as he reached for her and lifted her into the bed, cradling her next to his warm body, raising the sheet and tucking her along his flesh, and then holding her close.

"Tell me," he said softly.

So she did, haltingly, and never felt him pull away. Instead, he held her closer, comforting her, stroking her hair and temple. When she'd finished talking, he put her head upon his chest, and plied his fingers upon the nape of her neck, gently massaging her.

"Don't tell me it doesn't matter," she said slowly.

"I won't."

They were silent for a while, maybe twenty minutes, then Kamryn said, "Tell me what to do."

"I can't."

"I should go back."

"From what you tell me, they'll free your brother if you don't show up as a witness. If the grand jury is still looking for you, it means the evidence isn't strong enough without your statement."

"They'll never believe me."

"You don't know until you try." He ran his hand down her arm, captured her wrist. "These were only skin deep. The rest of the truth goes all the way to the heart."

"I'm afraid."

He tilted her face until she could peer up at him. The edge of dawn had crept into the room, lightening it so that she could see him, the warmth in his eyes. "Brand is right. You are beautiful."

She became aware that a tension lay in his muscled body, that his rib cage rose and fell with a growing intensity, that an awareness of his closeness caught her breath. "No."

"Yes." He kissed her brow, brushing her hair back from her face. With both hands, he raised her so that she lay upon his chest, her face to his, and he kissed her eyebrows and then her eyelids when she closed them as he drew near. The feel of his fingers gently untangling her hair, combing through, sent a shiver down her spine.

"Let me make love to you."

She shook her head. "Not because of what we're going to face today. Not because of that."

"No." His voice thickened. "Because I need you tomorrow, and the day after tomorrow. And now."

The power of his voice opened her eyes. "I can't promise you anything—"

"I didn't ask. I'm tired of being alone. I'd like to be together, with you." He kissed her, roughly, closing her mouth against protests, tongue caressing, then probing her lips. He kissed her until they were both breathless. He slid his hands down her back, inside her panties, cupped her buttocks, drawing her close to him until she could feel his urgent need.

He took his lips from hers. "Will you?"

She took the last of his clothes off, then hers, and lay back down beside him. She ran her hand over his thighs, his legs taut, then cupped his testicles and carefully lowered her mouth over his hard penis. She took him in her mouth, tasting him, feeling him respond, his skin like velvet, his cock rigid. He did not move though she could feel him quiver.

She stroked her tongue over him one last time, then moved in the bed again, next to him. He reached for her breast, gently, strong hands with incredible feathery touches that made her tremble until he put his mouth to her nipples. He teased her with his lips and teeth. It made her throb and she wanted him then, hard and full and fast, but Mitch murmured, "No. Not yet."

He held her and stroked her, kissed the hollow of her throat down the fullness of her breasts to the tiny indent of her navel until she cried for him. When he entered her, and she rocked with him, moving to his movement, seeking pleasure with his seeking, it was like nothing she had ever felt before. It was not a crude thrusting until fulfillment, it was an embrace that touched all of her, intimately. He murmured loving words to her, even as he gasped when she came, and then he followed. They lay entwined in fragrant warmth, and when he left her, he got a towel and gently cleaned her, then took her in his arms, and held her until she dropped off to sleep, the light of the day on his face.

Then the beeper went off.

Chapter 33

The sky was gray, dark gray, and the rain pelted across the lake in wind-pounding sheets and gusts. Glimpses of its misty banks were revealed by breaks between trees, and bare-kneed cypresses, and brush. Driving against the beginning fury of the hurricane seemed to take forever. Kamryn checked her watch several times. "We told him two hours," she shouted over the howling of the wind and the drone of the engine. "We're never going to make it."

"He'll wait."

"How do you know? How did you even know he'd trade for Brand?"

Mitch steered as a limb trailing Spanish oak rolled off the highway. The Jeep's rear wheel caught part of it and bucked accordingly. "No secrets. Okay?"

"You won't do anything foolish."

"He doesn't want me. He wants something I've got. Giving it to him—that would be foolish. But he's got to think I'm going to give it to him."

The Jeep veered again. Mitch kept both hands firmly on the wheel. He downshifted.

"These winds are seventy miles an hour. They're going to double by the time Yolanda makes landfall, according to the radio."

He nodded. The road, except for whipping rain and

debris, was nearly empty. No one going their way, a few going out. The radio had been warning that anyone not in an evacuation center already had better be prepared to sit tight and wait it out, that travel was becoming too dangerous.

Kamryn wrapped her hands in her seat belt, trying to combat the constant jostling. "You know he's going to kill us. In this weather, he can make almost anything look like an accident."

"I know he's going to try." Mitch shifted. The car's transmission downgraded obediently. "How good a shot are you?"

"In this wind? There's no telling. It's going to affect the bullets. Accuracy is nearly impossible."

"He'll have the same problem unless he's using something with rapid fire—if he is, he's going to be spraying a target anyway. If he's not . . ." Mitch shrugged. "I'll take whatever chances we can get."

"We only have the one revolver."

"With any luck, we won't even need that." Mitch squinted through the frantic wipers, then hit the brakes, squealing across the road, and came to a halt.

Despite the seat belt, Kamryn practically stood on her toes. She stared aghast out the windshield at what Mitch had avoided. A gator, its thick tail lashing back and forth, half walking, half wind-driven, crossed the highway. It must have measured a good ten feet from snout to tail tip. It moved belly first into the rain-filled ditch and disappeared through high brush on the other side of the road.

The aluminum signpost that marked Metairie, Lake Pontchartrain Causeway swayed back and forth dramatically, then uprooted and tumbled down the banks after the reptile.

"We're nearly there. Now I want you to stay in the Jeep. No matter what happens. Understand?"

She nodded.

"If we get separated, what are you going to do?"

"Try and find that woman Brand talked about. Mother Jubilation. Pirate's Alley, near Jackson Square, in the French Quarter," she recited.

"It'll be flooding. It's only a few blocks from the Mississippi."

She looked at him. "I'll get through—but what makes you think she stayed? She'd be crazy. The radio said that area would be ten, twelve feet under the tide."

"She's waiting for us. She'll be there."

The highway swung in a long, low curve and the woodlands gave way to flatlands, dotted with houses, then neighborhoods, the skyline of New Orleans and the football stadium with its golden dome barely recognizable under the gray skies and heavy rain.

The New Orleans P.D. had the road barricaded, their emergency vehicles across the lanes, their lights flashing. They wore heavy yellow rain slickers, marked with N.O.P.D. and under it stenciled, Emergency Management.

They flagged Mitch down. Even with their slickers and their plastic hooded hats, they were drenched. They shone a flashlight into the Jeep.

"Sir, we're turning back all traffic. You are advised to turn around on 10 and head for evacuation centers as indicated by hurricane markers."

"We need to get in."

The policeman shook his head at Mitch. "Sorry, sir, but we can't allow that."

Kamryn leaned over. "My mother called. She's blind. She can't get out on her own!"

"I'm sorry, ma'am. Hopefully one of our workers or

one of her neighbors has stepped in to help. We're losing a levee and pumping station and it's only going to get worse. No one in. It's for your own safety." He had his hat tied on, but the wind caught the bill of it and it seemed for a moment that not even the tie would hold the hat on. He put up his hand.

"A work of art," said Mitch suddenly.

The policeman blinked. He shone the beam on first Mitch's face and then Kamryn's.

"All right, sir. You'll have to follow me in." He turned, said something to the three officers standing at the barricade, then went and got into one of the emergency vehicles blocking the roadway. He wheeled it out of formation and beckoned for them to follow.

"Son of a bitch." Mitch sucked on a tooth and aimed the Jeep after. "He's already got his men in place."

"How did he do it?"

"Who knows? With all the activity, it's possible they just stepped in and took over key positions. No one is going to have time to ask questions, check ID."

"How many do you suppose he has?"

"I couldn't guess. It's less ambitious, but more efficient if he only uses a handful or so. Harder to get caught. But he might have a whole damn army in here, patrolling the streets."

"Just for us?"

"Maybe. Maybe not. And maybe," Mitch watched the escort ahead closely, "he's planning something a little more."

"Like what?"

"He hasn't done anything, since the beginning, that I've expected. If he's with the government, he's with a part of the government that has its own agenda."

"CIA?"

"Something like that. Maybe even . . . private." They

drove past the HOME OF THE NEW ORLEANS
SAINTS, its parking lot bare, its golden dome dulled
by ceaseless wind and rain.

"Why you?"

"I was part of a patrol on a covert mission. We were
dropped in to Haiti. We were told that we were supposed to take in a money man, make contact with a
local dignitary, and make an exchange.

"Bribery?"

"A trade-off. Yes. We were supposed to be smoothing
the way for Aristide to stay in control. We brought in
someone, all right, an agent named Stark. He had to
have been Special Forces. The dignitary turned out to
be a local voodoo priest, someone very powerful—"

"Voodoo? You're kidding me."

"Not now." The Jeep fought him, water in the streets
spraying off its wheels, the escort in front of them
churning through and leaving a wake. The streets had
begun to hold water, their surfaces dark and slick, mir-
roring the buildings. "I didn't believe it either, then.
Stark was picking up some kind of drug the priest had
made, and he was dropping off test subjects—us—for
a project. Only, things went wrong. One of my men
had a bad feeling. We shot our way out. I lost several
of the patrol and Stark. We left the money behind. Got
the drugs."

"Heroine?"

"No. I don't know what it is. Brown—my corporal
who made it back and then committed suicide—he told
me it was zombie powder."

"What?"

"This stuff must be real. Men like Stark aren't sent
in on a whim. Chances are it's some sort of psychoactive drug that brainwashes extremely effectively. I
don't think it creates the undead, but it's possible it

does something equally terrible to the living. I saw that man's disciples. They were blind in their devotion to him."

"But why? Why would you want such a thing?"

"I don't know. I don't want to know. But you can bet Rembrandt and whoever pulls his strings have a truckload of plans. They've been on my heels since April."

"The others?"

The escort emergency vehicle signaled right. Mitch prepared to pull over behind it. They were the only ones in the Coach Royale parking lot. Canal Street ran straight down to the Mississippi where it was lost in the rain and tide.

"I'm the only one left. And they're right. I do have it. I'm going to trade it for Brand."

"And you have it stashed somewhere in New Orleans."

"Indeed I do. My corporal came from here. I brought his body back. And when I stood watch over his casket, I saw things I still don't believe. Some of them were supernatural, some of them initiated by Rembrandt. I couldn't tell you which scared me the most." He put the Jeep in park, left the engine idling.

She studied him, realization in her expression. "All this time, it's been you. You, not Brand."

"I don't know. I've never seen the KillJoy and I don't know why Mother called Brand. But I do know that you're right—it's my fight. That's why I came."

A man came to the glass lobby doors and looked out, nonchalant, one hand in pants pocket, suit impeccable, brilliantly-colored tie a slash that stood out against the gray, constant rain.

"There he is," Kamryn said. She undid her seat belt, ready to slide into the driver's seat.

"Across the street is the French Quarter. Her shop

has to be only blocks away. Drive it if you can. If you can't—"

"I'll do whatever it takes."

He nodded. Started to open the door, then hesitated. Kamryn smiled slightly, bent over, and brushed his cheek with her lips.

Mitch grinned then, and got out of the car.

If I, if we, get out of this alive, I'll go back. I swear, Kamryn thought. She'd go back and do whatever she could to put her brother away, even if it meant exposing her father's involvement in the intelligence network of the Brotherhood. Even if it meant she could not prove herself innocent, for she had been part of the family, and she had not been, totally. Eric had thought their father only shallowly linked to the organization, despite the small print shop in the basement, despite everything. Kamryn knew better. Newspaper reports about the murders had speculated that it was all Eric and her and when her parents had discovered it, they'd turned on them and murdered them.

Kamryn did not know why Eric had done what he'd done. Knowing now what she didn't know then, she suspected that the movement had attracted Eric not because of its philosophies but because of its violence. And that had led to a downward spiral for her brother. When she saw him again, face-to-face, if they let her, she would ask. *Why?* Maybe she would get an answer.

And if she did not? Kamryn stared through the downpour, watching Mitch slowly put up his hands, approaching the elegant French-styled hotel. Then, perhaps, there was always the future. That would have to be good enough. It was all any of them ever got, after all.

For now, her future was measured in minutes, per-

haps even less. She watched as Rembrandt came outside, shadowed by a N.O.P.D.-marked figure who
shaded him with a black umbrella. The umbrella immediately turned inside out and shredded as Rembrandt
stood. He had Brand with him, and motioned Mitch
to take the boy.

Something was wrong with Brand. Drunk or drugged,
he seemed limp as a rag doll. Rembrandt and Mitch
exchanged angry words. She had no hope of hearing
them through the wind, but she could see the look
on Mitch's face. Then, the four of them got into the
emergency vehicle, the N.O.P.D. officer driving.

She eased the Jeep forward to follow.

They crossed Canal Street and went into the French
Quarter, that famous section of New Orleans, narrow
streets, two-storied buildings with their balconies
wrapped by wrought iron. There were peep shows and
blues bars and art galleries and souvenir shops. Water
already flowed through the cobblestones and brick,
splashing over the curb and washing back. It would
not be long before the tide from the gulf and the river
would be licking at the sandbagged doorfronts.

The emergency vehicle took them through the
French Quarter and into streets less famous, less traveled, more dilapidated. They were traveling, she realized, back towards Metairie.

They stopped on a street with a church/mortuary and
churchyard, bordering an old cemetery. She could see
the whitewashed above-ground graves called ovens, and
the mausoleums, with their stone cherubs and angels
overlooking the burial sites. Spanish oaks buckled the
sidewalk, and magnolias shuddered in the wind. Whatever resistance might have been met at the locked
doors of the mortuary were overcome as the dark oak-
stained doors swung open. She got out of the Jeep, put

her gun in her waistband at the small of her back, and followed the four of them inside Shepherd's. The rain was, as it had been all day, in a deluge, warm heavy drops without end. The air felt hot and steamy.

Rembrandt noted Kamryn's arrival with a slight bow. "I wondered when the lady would join us."

Kamryn's attention riveted on Brand. The boy stood pale, listless, as if he could barely hold himself upright, his eyes blank and unfocused. "What have you done to him?"

"Nothing, dear girl. It's congenital, I fear. Events have conspired to collapse his mind. But I will still give him to you when I get what I want. Perhaps treatment will bring him out of it. Perhaps not. Nothing in life is certain." To the officer shadowing him, he added. "Watch her. She usually carries a gun. I have not had the occasion to watch her use it, but experience suggests that she can."

"Yes, sir." A young, stoic face watched her carefully.

Mitch had been helping to keep Brand upright. He set him down on a settee.

He faced Rembrandt. "I get what you want, and the three of us walk out of here."

"Correct." The ruined man smiled, the crags and pits on his face shifting with his expression. "You are free to go."

Without warning, Mitch swung on the N.O.P.D. officer. Three brutal chops of the hand, and the young man fell with a groan. Mitch shoved him under the settee with his foot.

Rembrandt had not moved, smile frozen in place.

"Just to even the odds a bit," Mitch said.

Rembrandt inclined his head.

Mitch looked at Kamryn. "It's in the chapel. I'll be right back."

She put a hand to her gun and drew it out carefully. Rembrandt waved both hands at her amiably. "You have nothing to fear from me."

She knew better.

The chapel's swinging doors swung back and Mitch emerged, carrying an urn, Uncle Godfrey inscribed on its side.

Rembrandt looked at him. "Show me," he said.

Mitch worked at the lid, pulled it off, reached in and extracted a string of packets, six in all, filled with ivory powder. He dropped them back in the urn and replaced the lid.

The various doors of the mortuary began to tremble in their thresholds, wood clattering. Startled, Mitch looked up and then around. The chapel doors started swinging to and fro under their own volition. The heavily polished floors started to creak. A chill permeated the building.

Rembrandt continued to smile, his expression expanding until it became grotesque. He reached for the urn, his back to the chapel.

Mitch grabbed Brand, hauling him onto his feet as if he were weightless. "Get out of here, Kamryn. *Now!*"

"What is it?"

"I don't know."

Rembrandt ducked over suddenly, reached into the downed officer's slicker and pulled out an automatic rifle, cocking it as he came up. He tilted his head, looking at Kamryn.

"Give me the urn and put the gun down."

Around them, the building moaned and wood creaked and walls swayed. Kamryn glanced to the side. Had the hurricane hit already?

"Do it!" Rembrandt snapped.

She looked at Mitch and Brand in dismay. The barrel of the rifle swung over to them, targeting them.

"Do it now."

He had his back squarely to the chapel. She saw a flash of motion through the tiny, stained-glass window. She gripped the gun tighter and said, "Let them get out of the building first."

"No!"

The doors burst open, catching Rembrandt in the spine. The rifle jerked upward, let out a burst of fire. Plaster rained on them and the building suddenly quieted. Mitch leaped and grabbed the rifle. He caught Rembrandt and clipped him in the jaw with the butt of the weapon. Rembrandt staggered back. Mitch slugged him again. The ruined man went down.

A black woman stood in the open chapel doors. She shook her head. "He does not learn, does he?"

"Was it you this time?" Mitch leaned over Rembrandt, patting him down for more weapons. He found a 9 mm in his inner coat pocket, emptied the clip, and dropped it. The N.O.P.D. officer groaned.

"Yes, it was I. But we must get out of here quickly before the hurricane does more than make an old building rattle." The woman leaned over Brand. She spread her hand and touched her fingers to his forehead. "Wake up, child. You are here. You have found me."

Mitch had taken Rembrandt's belt and was busy securing his ankles. "Kamryn, this is Mother. Mother, this is Kamryn."

She looked over her shoulder. "A pleasure, child." She wore a swirl of yellow and red and blue, a many-pocketed apron over her dress. She dipped her free hand into a pocket and pulled out a small, stoppered vial. She shook it, then pulled out the cork and waved it under Brand's nose.

The boy jerked and gasped. His eyes fluttered open. They batted once or twice before he coughed and a blush flooded his face.

"Get up," Mother coaxed. "We're not done yet!"

Brand saw Mitch taking in the last notch on the belt around Rembrandt. "Don't touch him!"

Mitch straightened.

"He's the KillJoy!" Brand stood, staggered a step as if his legs had gone to sleep, and reached out to hold onto Mother for safety. "Get away from him, Mitch! He's carrying the KillJoy!"

Mother said, "This way, and quickly." She did not wait. Half carrying Brand, she turned and went out through the chapel.

Mitch grabbed up the urn and Kamryn left with him as Rembrandt began to moan loudly, and his heels started thumping on the floor.

They ran past the churchyard. Gravemarkers began to shake in the ground. They started to topple. The ground churned. Over it all, Yolanda howled and poured.

"What's happening?" Mitch called to Mother Jubilation.

She shook her head, braids flying. "I don't know. We can't fight him here. We let him in, he can stand on this ground."

Beyond the cemetery wall, an oven burst open, its plaster crumbling. Kamryn caught a glimpse of something stirring inside, something rotten and determined to emerge. She screamed and ran after the others.

Mother opened the doors to a battered station wagon.

"What about the Jeep?"

"The front is watched."

"Rembrandt had us followed," Mitch said to Kamryn.

He climbed in, helped Mother slide Brand in. All doors slammed shut and she started the vehicle.

Kamryn turned for a last look. It smacked the glass at her face, half-flesh, half-skull, grinning in at her, as the car jolted into motion. She screamed. The corpse left a gory smear as it slipped down the window.

Mother pulled away with a screech of tires, as the wrought-iron fencing went down about the churchyard. Graves collapsed into the ground and rotting limbs bubbled up.

She took them through side streets, careening through a rising tide of water and debris, back into the French Quarter. They left the station wagon in a torrential gutter and waded toward a storefront where the storm surge had begun to batter the sandbags. She opened the candy store's door and helped Brand over the barricade. Mitch swung Kamryn over, handing her the urn.

They paused, clothes sodden and dripping, in the center of the candy store while Mother locked the door and barred it, moving a huge sheet of plywood into place over the glass.

"Somehow," Mitch said, "this isn't the way I imagined your shop."

Mother laughed, a warm, booming sound. "I practice my voodoo in the back," she said, and came up, patting Brand on the cheek.

Brand did not look comforted. "He's coming. I can feel him."

"It does not matter," Mother told him. "I'm ready for him, child." She crossed the shop, opened another door and held back beaded curtains. They crowded past her. The electricity flickered, then went out. Mother looked up as the howling wind grew louder.

A match flared. "Never mind it," the wielder said. "I will light candles."

They stopped and stared at the man sitting at the end of the room, his dark face shadowed by the candle-light, another man standing at his elbow.

Mitch lost all color as he stared at the second man who stood motionless as a statue.

"Stark." Mitch got out.

"And it is I, Delacroix."

Chapter 34

"You were left for dead."

"You should have made sure." Stark braced himself.

"If I'd known then what I know now, I'd have killed you myself." Mitch bit off his words angrily. "We're the only ones left, you and I."

"Soon it will be only me."

Mother's nostrils flared as she pushed her way to the fore of the group, bristling with outrage, the whites of her eyes gleaming. "How did you get in here?"

Delacroix inclined his head. He pointed a slender hand at Stark. "My man here has abilities in a great many things." His voice remained calm, lilting, but there was steel in it. He looked at Mitch and the urn. "I believe you have something that belongs to me."

Mitch hugged the urn tighter. "The world doesn't need a perfect soldier. It doesn't need a perfect war! I lost my patrol for this. My men, my *friends*, paid for it with their blood, and if you want it, you'll have to get it over my dead body."

Stark moved, peeling his lips away from his teeth in an uneven, fierce grin. Delacroix put a hand on his sleeve, staying him a moment. He narrowed his gaze on Mitch. "By Damballah and Aido Wido and other names which I shall not utter here, I made it. It is sacred to them."

Mother shook with the intensity of her retort. "The Bon Dieu holds nothing sacred that makes slaves of men!"

They looked into each other's faces, the woman and the man. Delacroix spoke softly.

"You have come a long way, woman. You have left many sacred ways behind. You are neither one nor the other—how can you think to stop me?"

Delacroix got to his feet. "The loa answers to me. He will take that which is mine, and my vengeance, whether you wish it or not. I cursed the Americans who came to my island and treated me with bad faith. I cursed those who gave the orders to do so. And, finally, I cursed the man who planned all of this. Give me the powder, and I will release him back to his place. He will bother you no more. Only I can do this."

Brand rubbed at his eyes and then put his chin up defiantly. "No way. You'll use it again. I can see it— it's written all over you. You don't have the KillJoy in you now, but it came from you. I can see it!"

Delacroix twitched a couple of fingers, as if flinging something into the air. Stark responded, lunging at Mitch from across the room. They fell on the table, crashing through it. They hit the floor and the whole building shook. An unearthly noise howled down and Mother looked up to the ceiling. Stark and Mitch thrashed, flesh thudding, while Kamryn let out cries of despair, but over it all, Mother heard the sound of something greater and more fearsome. She grabbed for Brand, anchoring him. The wood and bricks and beams of the building groaned, then screamed. Brand struggled a second in Mothers's arms, his ears filling with pressure, and then, with a BOOM!, the roof exploded from above, disintegrating into splinters and shingles

that flew into the hurricane. Kamryn shielded her face
and ducked away from the destruction.

Rain poured in, funneled off neighboring eaves. It
drenched Delacroix as Mitch threw Stark off him and
rose into a crouch, hands and feet ready. Delacroix
hissed something in French to Stark and pulled a long
knife from his sleeve.

Kamryn drew her gun and fired, three quick shots,
without thinking. Crimson splotched the ivory linen
suit. Delacroix staggered back to the wall, and sagged.
He coughed. Pink foam flew out, stained his lips, and
dribbled down the front of the suit. She stood in shock,
wind-blasted and rain-drenched. "God. What have I
done?"

Mitch held out his hand to her. "Kamryn. Give me
the gun."

"No." She looked back at Delacroix, his rich brown
face growing paler before her very eyes.

"What indeed?" he said weakly and wheezed, more
pink spattering his chin. "Now the loa has no master."
His eyelids flickered and his eyeballs rolled whitely
back into their sockets. The last breath gurgled out
of him.

Brand struggled in Mother's arms, gasping, choking.
"It's not true!"

The back door blew open. Kamryn jumped, startled,
the barrel of the gun wavering. Stark shoved Mitch
aside and leaped for it, disappearing into the storm.
Curtains of wind and rain hid him immediately.

"Let him go."

Mitch paused in the threshold. "My men—"

"Let him go. If he belonged to Delacroix, he is dead
already." Mother took a deep breath. "Now comes the
worse of it."

"Worse?" Kamryn stared at Delacroix's body. Her

hand shook. Mitch took the gun from her and put his arm around her.

"The loa," Mother said. "The KillJoy. We must destroy that which cannot be destroyed." She rummaged through the ruins of her shop, picking up items. She sifted through them with quick, brown fingers, filling her apron pockets. "Come with me. Hurry."

The streets ran with water like rivers around their knees. They held onto one another, forging step by step through the Quarter. Yolanda descended on them with all her fury. Signs swung on their iron holders and then twisted away, flung up into the gray and disappearing on the wind. Trees groaned, then slowly toppled, their roots jutting into the air, ripping up walkways and curbs. Lesser trees shattered into long, deadly spears.

She led them to Jackson Square, nearer the storm surge. Waves broke onto the park as if it were the shoreline, waves from the Mississippi, churned up destructively. Jackson, riding his bronze horse, looked as if he forded a raging river.

"There!" Mother pointed at the white beauty of a building, rising out of the flooded parkway and gray hurricane mists, St. Catherine's. Sandbags bulged against the water. Mother helped them climb onto the homemade levee braced against the wide double doors. She laid her palms on the locks and spoke a few words.

After a moment, the brightly polished lock plate and knobs moved and clicked open. Mitch handed Kamryn down into the cathedral's interior, Mother after her, and Brand last, then jumped down into the cathedral, his boots ringing on the floor. Together, they put shoulders to the door and sealed it behind them once again. The banshee wind shrieked in disappointment.

Kamryn shuddered. She pushed her wet hair from her eyes. She tried a smile at Brand.

He looked solemnly back. Then he reached into his pocket and withdrew something. She saw a silver and turquoise amulet on a black cord, nearly a twin to the one Mitch wore.

Brand held it out. "I got it for you. I want you to wear it."

"After all we've been through. After I lost you at the airport?"

He extended it further.

Touched, she took it from him and put it around her neck.

Mother clucked. "Children, we must hurry." She lifted her rain-cleansed brown face to the crucifix over the altar. "The choir loft. When the flood breaks in, we should still be above water."

Chairs had been removed from part of the loft. They sat on soft red carpeting. Mother spread out her many-colored skirts as she knelt and began to light thick, heavy based candles of white and red.

"It comes," she said. "And it must be fought, but we won't win by the flesh."

"What do you mean?"

She looked at Mitch. "The loa is a spirit. It influences the physical world, but its mortality lies in the world of souls. That is how we must face it."

Mitch shook his head. "Not good enough, Mother. Rembrandt will kill us first. You're not going to have time to go looking for some demon soul."

"There is more than one way to fight a war."

Mitch looked keenly at Mother. "I only know what I know. This is my fight. I want the rest of you out of here." He broke away, stood up.

Kamryn put up her hand. "You can't ask him to do that."

"I have not asked. He has volunteered."

Brand looked from Mother to Mitch and back again. "How will you do it?"

"I will send his soul on a journey. Even without fighting the loa, it will be treacherous." Mother reached into her apron and took out a small kit. She opened it. Inside lay a syringe and a packet.

"Heroin," said Mitch, looking at it.

"You use it?"

"No. But on the street . . ." his voice faltered.

"This is not a street drug. It has not been cut. It is pure."

"Jesus. You've been carrying that around in an apron?" He shook his head, disbelieving.

"White boy," she admonished. "Who would steal it from me?"

He did not answer, looked down, could not meet her eyes.

"I chose the cathedral. It should hold the flesh back while the loa hesitates to cross this threshold."

"But if it doesn't," Brand persisted. "What happens then? Mitch will be unconscious, right?"

"Mitch will be dying," Mother corrected. "On the verge between one world and the next."

"Who keeps Rembrandt away from us?"

"I do," Kamryn said grimly.

"Bullets won't stop him."

Brand went to the balcony wall and looked over. The great building groaned under the force of the wind. The noise seemed incredible. Water began to dribble in through the cathedral doors, along the flooring and the carpeting, a steady red-brown stream that looked almost as if the building bled.

Mother took a spoon from her pocket, and foil, and laid the syringe out. "Will you do it?" she asked, as she began to prepare the dosage. "They sometimes call it chasing the dragon. But you know the dragon is real."

Mitch swallowed tightly. "Do I have a choice?"

Brand could not watch. He could see the shining that was Mother, the darkness which fractured Mitch, and the dark clouds which surrounded Kamryn. He did not want to see more.

He did not remember how Rembrandt had brought him to New Orleans or how Kamryn, Mitch, and Mother had found him. He only knew he was here.

And so was the KillJoy.

Mother said to him, "What is it, child?"

He knew, as if he could see through the mahogany of the doors. "It's Rembrandt. He's trying to come in." The front doors boomed. A panel bulged, but held. A human yodeling howl pierced that of the wind. Rembrandt, screaming threats and venting his frustration.

"He'll find a way in," said Kamryn, her voice trembling.

"Sooner or later," Mother agreed. She rolled up Mitch's sleeve, and tied the arm with a band. Mitch looked at the needle as Brand stared at Mitch. "What if he doesn't find his guide? What if he doesn't win?"

Mother looked at him, her brown eyes mild and full of wisdom. "Then, child, we die here. And later, many others."

Brand closed his eyes tightly, shutting himself in with the darkness. And Bauer. And he could feel the edge of the Killjoy now, like a dagger, slicing into his mind. His thoughts. He shoved a hand into his jeans and withdrew the bandanna. He peeled it open. It was wet, but deep within its knots, the peyote button had stayed dry and knobby. He turned and looked at Mitch,

shining silver bright, with only a fractal of darkness
down him. He did not look at death—he looked at
souls. Mitch would not understand the darkness. He
would be lost. But Brand had a guide. The golden retriever waited for him.

The KillJoy waited for him.

"Mitch. Don't do it. It's me. I'm the one."

Mother looked at him. "Child," she responded softly,
needle in hand. Then she paused. Considering.

"It has to be me," he said pointedly to her.

Mitch looked him in the eyes. "You fight your way
and I'll fight mine."

"Exactly. But I have to be alone," he said, remembering Yellow Dog's voice and advice, the Apache wisdom
given him. "And I won't use that. Deal?"

Before Mitch could answer, the cathedral doors exploded. Smoke and ashes filled the air, and Rembrandt
vaulted in through them, and stood, water swirling
about his legs, his eyes glittering as he found the four
of them, illuminated by candlelight in the choir loft.
He held a searchlight in one hand.

"Well, now, sonny. Where have you led me?" He
picked out Brand's face. "Give me what I came for,
and we can all forget this happened. This is wild
weather. We can hide a lot of unfortunate incidents."

Mitch pushed the syringe away carefully and undid
the elastic band with a snap. "Kamryn, take Brand and
get him away from here." He took a candle and went
halfway down the loft staircase.

Kamryn pulled Brand close to her, her hands gripping his shoulders tightly. Mother stayed on her knees.
She began to take twists of herbs and branches out of
her pockets, muttering under her breath, laying out
patterns. "Take the boy," she said. "We'll hold him as
long as we can."

Rembrandt laughed, an eerie sound, that rose and fell like the hurricane's voice, piercing throughout the cathedral. "I have the area cordoned off. You can't get out of here unless I give the signal. I've planned too hard and too long to let this—" he stopped, shuddered, contorted, grimaced.

Brand watched, horrified, as black flame gouted from his streaming eyes, and Rembrandt hunched in desperation, fighting that other which drove him. He let out a roar which was more animal than human, and clawed at his jacket, his shirt, ripping them open as if the loa would burst forth.

Then, suddenly, silence. Rembrandt took a deep shuddering breath. He looked up. He had dropped the searchlight. It swirled away, bobbing up and down in the floodwaters seeping along the cathedral pews. The ruined man stared back into the loft where he knew his quarry stood, watching him.

"I've planned too long to let this slip away," he finished hoarsely. "Come to me, son, and bring me that powder."

Brand could feel himself aching to respond, those long hours closeted away, programmed, working inside him. He shuffled a foot forward, then dragged himself to a halt. "No."

"Now, boy. Just who do you trust here? Surely not him." Rembrandt looked scathingly at Mitch. "Who lied to you across country? Did he ever tell you just who he was? That he was responsible for leading an entire patrol into death?"

"You gave those orders," Mitch said.

Rembrandt laughed without humor. "And I'll give them again, if I get the chance. But I know what I'm fighting for. Do you? And what about that pretty girl at your back, Brandon? I told you about her before."

He turned his scarred and pitted face up toward the balcony, drawing closer.

"She took an ax and split her father's skull like a cord of wood. Imagine that. Then she turned around and did it to her mother, just like Lizzie Borden."

Brand could feel Kamryn's hand grow cold, could feel it right through his rain-soaked shirt. "Don't listen to him," she said, her voice quavering.

He found it hard to breathe. Harder to think.

"Women!" Rembrandt cried. "You can't trust any of them. Your mother. Is she looking for you? Seen any pictures of yourself on TV lately, Brandon? Think maybe she just gave a sigh of relief and hoped you killed yourself somewhere so that, finally, she wouldn't have to worry about you anymore. Could get on with her life? And what about the good doctor? Lies, liars, all. All of 'em, son. All liars but me. With me, you know what you're gonna get."

He held out his hand to the balcony.

"She didn't do it!" Words burst out of him, gusts of air, exhalations emptying him so that he could breathe in new air, fresh air.

Rembrandt withdrew his hand. "Trust her, do you? And what about her? Should she trust you? Does she know what goes on in your mind? Does she know what that psychologist buried in your boyish thoughts? The rapist and mutilator that looks out of your eyes? He like to watch you, girl?"

Kamryn made a muffled sound behind him. Brand could feel her shift away from him.

Mitch had descended another few steps closer. He pulled the string of packets out of his shirt, and held the candle close under them. The dampened packets took fire fitfully, hissed as they smoldered. "Forget them, Rembrandt. Your fight is with me." He threw the candles and packets onto the altar platform. The clothes draped over the benches caught with a yellow flame that filled the cathedral with light.

Rembrandt charged with a roar.

Mother turned on her heel, pushing at Kamryn and Brand. "Run! Now!"

Her touch seemed to break the bonds which had frozen Brand to the balcony. He sprinted across the loft to the door in the rear. A stumble or two behind, Kamryn followed.

He clawed at the knob. The door swung up, into darkness, and then Kamryn held up another of Mother's candles. Its light fell upon a hallway. "Go, go, go, go!" she cried softly.

He ran. He raced down a labyrinth of alcoves and rooms and then into a twisting corner where he narrowly missed a last niche. He forced himself past the door and Kamryn followed after. She held up the candle. Organ pipes filled the room. It was immense, and he thought of Christmas music, and the sound the cathedral must give out. She shut the door and locked it, and pulled chairs and equipment in front of it to brace it. She pulled her gun out of her waistband. The syringe rattled in her shirt pocket.

They looked at one another. Brand swallowed. "I'm not like that. Not really."

She set the candle stump on a speaker. Then she faced him, and rubbed her arms. "We're all like that, Brand. Sometimes. Filled with hate. But we have to try to be better." She touched the symbol at her throat, the charm he'd given her. "But you know that, don't you?"

He nodded.

"Do whatever you have to do. He has to get through Mitch first. Then Mother. Then me."

He nodded again and lay down. The storm raged over them. He could hear the building creak around them. Smell a faint scent of smoke and ash. They didn't have long.

He picked off a piece of the button, scraping and twisting it away with a broken fingernail, and put the rest back in the bandanna. He chewed it swiftly. There should be calm and quiet, but he could not help that.

Suddenly, the sky went quiet.

Brand blinked.

Then, he understood. The eye of the hurricane was passing. For a few moments, all was still. He closed his eyes.

To pass through, he had to know himself. He did. He knew himself, and he knew Bauer, who was part of himself, like it or not. He stepped onto a rainbow bridge and waited for the golden retriever.

The dog came, whining and unsure. Brand went to one knee and called him. He wrapped his arms around his ruff, and hugged the creature. As he did, he touched something. He looked closely. Yellow Dog wore a collar, though he never had before. A tag hung from it. "Cody," Brand read.

The dog looked up. Licked his fingers, pulling the tag away from him.

The dog had belonged to someone. Someone else had named him. "Cody," Brand repeated. Yellow Dog went down and rolled at his feet.

"Help me find the KillJoy."

Cody got up, shook, and pressed against his knees. Brand laid his hand on the dog's head. "Help me."

The dog stepped forward.

He did not know what to expect. A spirit walk, Yellow Dog had called it. You must know and expect to go in search of yourself.

An extension of what he'd already gone through at Rembrandt's hands.

Come here, sweet cheeks. I've been waiting for you.

No.

Are we going to kill someone? It's been a long time, too long.

No.

Killing the KillJoy is the only thing we can do.

No. It's the only thing you can do. I am not you. You are part of me, but I Am Not You.

It grew very cold.

Cody whined in distress and his doggish form became insubstantial. Brand held him a last time.

Go. I don't need you anymore. You're free. You have guided me to where I need to be.

The dog looked into his eyes. Brand smiled. There was nothing of darkness in those beautiful dog eyes. Absolutely nothing.

Go on, he urged, pushing Cody away. He turned his face and saw an opening in the darkness. It grew larger and larger. He pointed Cody toward it. Go on!

The dog bounded into the tunnel. He stopped, turned about, tail wagging hesitantly. He glowed as golden as the sun.

Go on! I can do this without you. I—I love you, old dog! Now go on!

Cody let out a joyous bark, and turned, racing down the tunnel. It swallowed him.

Darkness.

He stood alone.

It's just you and me, kid.

No. It's just me. You're only a part of me.

Brand took a step forward. The nebulous nothing about him swirled, grew colder. The KillJoy was very, very near.

You go for it, and I go for you, kid. You can't take us both on. Do it the easy way. Bring me in. Put me in charge.

No.

The darkness burst open with color, and in its midst, stood a thing which devoured, a black hole, waiting for him. It stood over a shining light which he knew must be Mitch.

Mitch who had tried his best, and was now about to be eaten.

"It's me you want," Brand said softly, stepping forward. "Really."

Rembrandt broke through the doors. He got to his feet with a growl that had nothing human in it and looked up, as if scenting them by their warmth and their blood. Kamryn stood, sighting down her revolver.

"Stop right there, Rembrandt."

The ruined man took a step forward. Kamryn fired. It knocked him down. He got up so fast, she had trouble targeting him again.

"Don't do it!"

His eyes flashed. The suit jacket flew open, and she could see the hole she'd put in him. He was battered and bruised and torn and rent . . . and she tried not to think of Mitch, of Mother . . of how he'd gotten this far. Not he. It.

Inky fog began to roll out of it.

"Dear God." And then Kamryn knew she was seeing the KillJoy.

She fired her remaining rounds. Rembrandt dropped.

Behind him, in the backstairs of the cathedral, she could smell smoke clearly. Kamryn shuddered. The gun fell from her hands. She grabbed Brand's shoulders and dragged him out of the pipe room, his heels scuffing across the floor, his body totally limp. Her shoulders ached as she kicked the door shut between them and . . . *it*. She took a deep breath. She had to do this. She kept pulling Brand down the hallway.

Something let out a gargling howl.

She hadn't killed it.

"Oh, God. Oh, God, oh, God. Hurry!"

She could hear it shambling after her in the shadows. Crawling, dragging.

A dense, dark mist began to roll up the corridor and coalesce by the stairwell. Kamryn kicked open the door behind her, finding renewed strength. She put her hand to her shirt pocket.

What was left of Rembrandt reared on its hind legs and charged after them. She struck with the hypodermic, plunging it into his neck, all that heroin. Pure, unadulterated.

She prayed.

Brand stared into the nothingness of the loa and knew it would consume him. It had no color. The colors of life, of the spirit, Yellow Dog had talked to him about. As if nothing of life and its colors were in themselves good or bad.

Only the nothingness, the evil, the spiritless.

He threw back his hands.

Come and get me. You can't do it. I won't give it to you, all the colors that make me up. The good and the bad. They're me. They're MINE. I won't die for you!

The loa took him.

*   *   *

Kamryn fell over Brand's still body, tumbled down hard. Her vision flooded with tears. She grasped him, twisted his limp form away from the lump of flesh that had been Rembrandt. His ruined face bled darkness.

Kamryn got him up, somehow. Half over her shoulder, half in a fireman's carry, she dragged Brand down the hallway. She fell through the choir loft door, choking, the air a smoldering gray. Rain from a roof giving way to the storm had put the fire out. Mother reached up to help her. Blood glistened on her battered face, but her expression shone.

The two women struggled to get Brand down into the balcony. The fog pursued them, rushed them, then, suddenly, vanished.

Mother smiled widely. "Oh, child. He's done it."

Mitch lay across the top of the stairs. Kamryn left Brand in Mother's arms and ran to him, swollen with what she felt and had never been able to say.

Mitch groaned. She knelt by him and helped him sit up. He held his head. She kissed his face, all over, until he asked her to stop.

"It hurts."

She kissed him again. "This hurts?"

"Yes." Mitch gave a crooked smile. "But it probably won't tomorrow. If we have a tomorrow."

Solemnly, Mother took Brand's still body in her arms. She began to sing to him.

Mitch absorbed that in silence.

Mother stopped singing. She let out a little sob from deep in her throat and shook her head.

Kamryn cried, "Brand!"

Mitch crawled to Brand's body and dropped his fist, like a hammer, onto the rib cage. "Come on, Brand!

You get to ride shotgun!" He leaned over and started pumping.

Kamryn knelt over Brand's face. She looked at Mitch, then leaned down and began resuscitation.

Curtis waited for him, with that slaphappy grin on his face, and a bright tunnel at his back. Yellow Dog let out a woof, beckoning Brand onward. He was half-way after Cody and his best friend when he heard the call. He turned slowly. He hesitated, and with that hesitation, he knew he would have to go back.

He didn't mind, he guessed. He looked down the tunnel one last time.

Curtis yelled, *Be seeing you later, X-man!*

Cody let out a farewell bark.

Brand nodded.

He went back.

His chest hurt. He blinked and groaned, then coughed and said. "I'm going to hurl."

"He's back."

Mitch sat back, breathing heavily.

Kamryn started to cry. Mother put her arm around her shoulders and said soothing things to her.

"I was dead?"

"Damn straight."

"Cool." He sat up. "Did you have to pound on me?"

"It worked."

Brand stared across the loft as if he could see the wreckage of Rembrandt's body beyond. Overhead, the wind began to cry again, thinly, weakly, as if the worst was over.

He shut his eyes. Inside, was nothing but silence. Bauer was gone.

He was alone.

He opened his eyes. He was not alone.

The stained glass windows of the cathedral flooded with sudden light. They struck every corner, even into the organ alcove. The moment shone briefly before Yolanda asserted herself again. Brand reached out as if he could touch the rainbow colors.

There was no darkness anywhere.

No matter where he looked.

He'd done it.

Epilogue

The chopper escort loomed low over New Orleans' International Airport. The President of the United States sat by the open door, looking out at the devastation. The Governor of Louisiana sat next to him, pointing out the various areas still flooded, the roofless homes, the massive loss of trees and utilities, their wires snagged and brought down by fallen limbs. Behind them, Secret Service choppers and the press followed. All touched down, the sky streaked with fading clouds and a sun trying its best to dry out the drenched city and parishes.

Senator Bayliss stood first, framed in the side of the chopper. Scorning the hands of aides and emergency workers, he jumped down to the tarmac, then turned to help out the governor and the president. Camera flashes and camcorder lights blazed on the trio as they walked to the waiting motorcade, which would take them to view the destruction wreaked by Hurricane Yolanda.

The press tumbled out of their choppers and flooded across the tarmac to catch the entourage, lenses focusing and film winding. Bayliss strode next to a frail-looking president. A remnant of the wind caught his leonine gray-blond mane and whipped it back from his broad, intelligent forehead. Bayliss appeared to ignore it as he gave an arm of support to the president. If he thought of the picture it represented, of the symbolism, the senator did not show it.

N.O.P.D. mingled with the suited Secret Service, jostling each other to protect the group. No one, it was said later, knew exactly where he came from. But he came out of the thick of the various protectors, still wearing a yellow rain slicker, dropped his hood and grabbed Bayliss, spinning him around on the tarmac.

Later, it would be said that his target was the president, and that Bayliss had tried to protect him, although video shows that to be inconclusive. All that is known is that he got to the senator first, bare-handed, and ripped his throat out. The attacker went down then, under an avalanche of gunfire and tackled by Secret Service men. He broke his neck hitting the airport tarmac, but others would say he already looked like a dead man, preternaturally pale and bloated, like a floater, a body that has been in water for a while.

The autopsy was inconclusive as to cause of death. Either the broken neck or the water in the lungs could have caused the demise. The attacker was identified as one Alexander Stark, a freelance mercenary, whose recent whereabouts could not be confirmed by the Secret Service or the CIA.

Bayliss bled to death in the ambulance speeding him to the only serviceable hospital in the area, in Baton Rouge.

*   *   *   *

"When were they born?"

Brand did not wait for an answer, but loped after the slim young woman who was showing him the way to an outside shed, redwood-sided, like the stone and

paneled home, and tucked up against it in a huge backyard. She wore a faded plaid shirt tucked into her
jeans, her malt brown hair swinging free to her shoulders. He watched her walking in front, then something
even more important than teenage beauty distracted
him. He could hear the soft grunts of pups under her
gentle voice.

"About the end of February. We don't expect them
to have their eyes open for a few days yet, but we're
already socializing them."

Amelinda brought up the rear. "Are they warm
enough out here?"

"Oh, yes. This has a sliding door attachment to our
den. They stay in the whelping box at night. We bring
them in. Later on, their mom will bring them in
through the dog door. They're just now getting their
legs. They scoot around on their stomachs." The young
woman came to a stop, calling. "Jennifer! I've got someone to see your babies."

The dog who came out of the shed, did so stepping
carefully about the wiggling bodies which surrounded
her. Her teats hung below her, full with milk, and her
golden hair had a faint auburn cast to it. She paid little
attention to the visitors, but thrust her muzzle into her
handler's palm. Her feathered tail glided back and forth
in welcome.

"Don't rush her or the pups," Karen guided, but
Brand had already gotten to his knees at the edge of
the papers and blankets which lined the shed floor.
She added in surprise, "Look! He's already got his
eyes open."

Brand let the sight of the nine young retrievers fill
his eyes, their fat-tummied bodies squirming around in
search of their mother and their littermates. They were
light yellow in color, and shorthaired, with no hint of

the wavy, silken hair which would grow in later, although their paws seemed twice as big as they needed to be. He looked at the pup with the open eyes. The creature seemed to be the most precocious one of the bunch. He already knew how to get his legs under his well-fed body and swim to where he wanted to be. Now, his littermates realized mom had left them, and although only a few steps away, were grunting and whining anxiously in search of her.

Only this one crept in search of Brand.

Jennifer shifted weight to swing her head around, sniffing at Amelinda, then carefully at Brand.

He held his hand out. She nosed his fingers thoroughly, then swiped a quick lick across them, and gave her attention back to Karen.

In the meantime, the pup was at his knees, worrying at the denim.

"Can I pick him up?"

"Carefully. Make sure you've both hands under him. If Jennifer frets, just show her the pup and put him back down gently."

"What color are his eyes?"

"Now, sort of a black-blue. As they get older, they turn a warm brown, just like they're supposed to." Karen smiled, her freckled face rippling. To Amelinda, she said, "This his first dog?"

"Pretty much."

"Goldens are great dogs for teens."

Brand carefully lifted the pup to his face, and looked, knowing he would not see anything more spectacular than a fuzzy-faced pup, barely two weeks old, scarcely used to looking at anything from his canine point of view.

Two vivid brown eyes looked back at him, knowing eyes, welcoming eyes, eyes full of life and all its intensity, full of love and loyalty and happiness. Brand sucked his breath in sharply.

"Brandon, what's wrong?"

The eyes faded to puppy newness, but the knowing in them remained. He pulled the pup close and tucked its warm body under his chin. "Nothing."

Amelinda watched him. She swung a wing of dark hair behind her ear. "Sure?"

"Positive."

She hesitated a moment, then asked, "Do you want him?"

"Do I!"

"You have your contract with us. Homework, chores . . . all that family stuff."

"I know." He did not look at her, afraid she would see the plea in his face, afraid she would deny him, his heart accelerating, even though they had had this discussion, he and Mitch and Amelinda, and this agreement. He'd been waiting months for this litter to be born, days until the dog breeders had said they would allow visitors.

Amelinda gave her hand to Karen. "I think you just sold a dog."

"That one? Are you sure? Don't you want to look at any of the others? Both mom and dad are champions."

"No," Brand answered tightly. His voice squeaked a little, in that way changing voices sometimes did. Or perhaps it was a voice full of emotion. He did not look up, his face pressed closely to the golden pup's flank, his fingers gently stroking an ear flap. As for the pup, he had contentedly gone to sleep at Brand's throat.

"Well," Karen remarked, shaking out a royal blue woven puppy collar. "That's what we're here for. You can visit him, after school, if you want. He won't be ready to go for another six weeks."

"Great."

"Got a name?"

"Yeah," answered Brand. "Dakota."

"Good choice." Karen slipped her fingers under Brand's chin to fasten the collar on the pup. "Named for anybody in particular?"

"I used to know a golden retriever," Brand said. "Cody. This is close, but different. A new life, a new name. That's the way it ought to be."

"Sounds good to me." Karen shook hands with Amelinda again. "Looks like our dog has got a boy."

Elizabeth Forrest

] **PHOENIX FIRE**   UE2515—$4.99
As the legendary Phoenix awoke, so too did an ancient Chinese
demon—and Los Angeles was destined to become the final
battleground in their millenia-old war.

] **DARK TIDE**   UE2560—$4.99
The survivor of an accident at an amusement pier is forced to
return to the town where it happened. And slowly, long burled
memories start to resurface, and all his nightmares begin to come
true . . .

] **DEATH WATCH**   UE2648—$5.99
McKenzie Smith has been targeted by a mastermind of evil who
can make virtual reality into the ultimate tool of destructive power.
Stalked in both the real and virtual worlds, can McKenzie defeat
an assassin who can strike out anywhere, at any time?

] **KILLJOY**   UE2695—$5.99
Given experimental VR treatments, Brand must fight a constant
battle against the persona of a serial killer now implanted in his
brain. But Brand would soon learn that there were even worse
things in the world—like the unstoppable force of evil and destruction called KillJoy.

Charles Ingrid

PATTERNS OF CHAOS
Only the Choyan could pilot faster-than-light starships—and the other Compact races would do anything to learn their secret!

THE MARKED MAN SERIES
In a devastated America, can the Lord Protector of a mutating human race find a way to preserve the future of the species?

THE SAND WARS
He was the last Dominion Knight and he would challenge a star empire to defeat the ancient enemies of man.

C.S. Friedman

Tanya Huff